WILBERFORCE

Wilberforce

H. S. CROSS

FARRAR, STRAUS AND GIROUX

NEW YORK

Farrar, Straus and Giroux
18 West 18th Street, New York 10011

Copyright © 2015 by H. S. Cross
All rights reserved
Printed in the United States of America
First edition, 2015

Library of Congress Cataloging-in-Publication Data
Cross, H. S., 1968–
    Wilberforce : a novel / H. S. Cross. — First edition.
        pages   cm
    ISBN 978-0-374-29010-8 (hardback) — ISBN 978-0-374-71342-3
(e-book)
    1. Boarding schools—England—Fiction.   2. Teenage boys—Fiction.
I. Title.

PS3603.R6739 W53 2015
813'.6—dc23
                                                      2015002964

Designed by Jonathan D. Lippincott

Farrar, Straus and Giroux books may be purchased for educational, business, or
promotional use. For information on bulk purchases, please contact the Macmillan
Corporate and Premium Sales Department at 1-800-221-7945, extension 5442,
or write to specialmarkets@macmillan.com.

www.fsgbooks.com
www.twitter.com/fsgbooks • www.facebook.com/fsgbooks

1   3   5   7   9   10   8   6   4   2

FOR CAMERON

PART ONE

PART ONE

Something was pressing the life out of him.
　　—He's moving, Matron!
Something searing—
　　—Step aside, boys.
Something dragging him down, lead on ankles—
—If you can hear me, open your eyes.
Something brighter than the sun, brighter than—
—That's it.
Blinding, aching, twiddling his brains.
—Can you tell me your name?
A pain that swallowed every breath.
—Wilberforce. Morgan . . . Morgan . . .
The light retreated. Into focus gradually, Matron's face:
—What day is it?
Tuesday?
—Wednesday?
—And the date?
—February . . .
Was it?
—I mean March.
It was.
—March . . . fifth.

3

Like dread in his ears.

—The Ides of March.

—What year is it?

He knew suddenly and wished he didn't. He had nothing against the year 1926, yet it seemed sinister, as if whatever had caused this pain had also granted him a kind of—

—The Battle of Thermopylae?

This he knew, and said. Light clicked off. Matron frowned:

—You'll survive, Morgan Wilberforce. Though I can't imagine you'll make the varsity if you keep smashing your skull about that way.

A throbbing, then, and a keen stabbing. Matron stepped aside, revealing Laurie in overcoat, Nathan muddy in rugby kit.

—You've gone mad, Nathan said.

—You were airborne! Laurie cried.

—Were you trying to kill him, or just yourself?

—Kill who? Morgan said.

—Spaulding, of course.

A wave of remembrance: the rugby pitch; Burton-Lee's fullback, a powerful boy in the Sixth called Spaulding; the sluggish, timid performance from his own side; Morgan's try blocked by Spaulding; then something in his mind clicking, like an electric plug seated into the mains, an animal sound from the pit of his stomach, and the charge across fifty yards of no-man's-land, Spaulding in his sights as if nothing else existed in the world.

—What happened to Spaulding?

—Not a scratch, Laurie said.

—And afterwards . . . ?

—They crucified us, Nathan reported.

—Hell.

Matron reappeared:

—That must have been quite a bump, Wilberforce. I'm sure you'd never use language like that in your right mind.

—Sorry, Matron.

—Sit up.

Sharp—shooting—arm-shoulder-spine—

—Ah!

—Is his arm broken? Laurie asked.

—No, Lydon.

—It went funny again, Laurie said. JP thought—

—I didn't, Nathan retorted.

—They said you'd gone and—

—Thank you, Lydon, Matron said. You and Pearl had best be getting to tea.

Nathan and Laurie moved towards the door.

—Lucky duck, Laurie said, you won't have to do the Plantagenet comp.

—I will eventually.

—He's right, Nathan said. Grieves never lets him off anything.

Grieves never had and never would, the brute. But that wasn't what was wrong. Was it? He looked to Matron, who was tying his arm in bandages.

—Can I go to tea, Matron?

—You'll stay here the night, she said.

—But I'm all right.

She knotted the fabric and fixed him with a glare:

—First, young man, I'm quite fed up putting that arm of yours back into its socket.

—It's the first time in forever, Matron.

—Twice in forever is twice too often.

He bit back protest.

—Second, the only way you'll be taking part in rugby for the remainder of term will be as a spectator.

—Matron! Please!

He struggled to sit up, but she held him against the mattress.

—I'm on the House XV, Matron! I—

—Furthermore, it is Friday the fifth of March, not Tuesday, not Wednesday, not the Ides.

—I know that now, Matron, I only—

—Last and finally, if you don't lie still, drink your tea, and behave yourself, I shall have to be firm with you.

He tried again to sit up but failed, prisoner to his injuries.

—Matron, I'm . . .

Mental arithmetic, sluggish subtraction . . .

—I'm seventeen years old. I'm not—

He dried up before her fierce and familiar gaze. Confident in victory, she left him alone in the empty sanatorium, alone in unyielding defeat. The ache returned then, not from his arm or his head or the bruises across

5

his person. This leaden ache had not been with him before. Before—an hour ago? Less?—he had been playing rugby football, feeling the air burn his lungs. Now in his mouth the aftertaste of blood, in his chest the dread of life turned ill, and in his bones the shock of impact—savage, fatal—with Spaulding.

 Matron told him to sleep, but something kept him awake. At first he thought it was the pain, but then he remembered that she had given him a draft to stop it.

His mother never made him drink foul things. She always put in honey so being ill didn't have to be worse than it was, she said. When he couldn't keep things down, she gave him boiled sweets and ice, hammered to shards in a tea towel. His father disapproved of indulgences, but his mother laughed when he came in to grumble, her rolling, catching bubble that always erupted when things got too serious to bear. When Morgan had fallen head over heels down the slope behind the shed, his mother had shaken with laughter as if it were slapstick, even as she went to comfort him. She would read him that book with the animal noises, and when they got to the page with all the birds—*tweet, feet, peet, fee-yoo*—she would repeat the one that made him laugh until he wheezed and begged her to stop; when he finally caught his breath, she would make to turn the page, but under her breath would escape *fee-yoo*.

He called, but she didn't answer. Then he remembered, and his pulse began to race.

Veronica used to tell him terrible stories that sent his thoughts racing, too, after dark, stories of spiders crawling up plugholes in search of human blood, stories of the Château d'If and its masked prisoner, whom she made him play in the cage beneath the laundry chute, stories of a boy who awoke one morning to find that Death had crept through his village, leaving only him alive.

He was not a little boy afraid of his sister's stories. He was not a Third Former afraid of the Academy's ghosts. Nor was he any longer fag to Silk, dreading the arrival of Accounting Saturday nights. He wasn't under sentence for anything now. No one existed who could hold him to account. No one could make his heart pound by saying to him, *Wilberforce, you troublesome boy, fall into line or suffer the consequences.*

Matron had drawn the curtain across the foot of his bed and wound down the crank to leave him flat for the night. Did something lurk nearby, beyond the curtain, something that exerted a fearfulness upon him even now in his seventeenth year? There had been no disaster of late. All that had happened was that he'd collided with Spaulding, banged up his shoulder, and lay now in the Tower. No one was dead. He would recover. Why the taste of iron? He'd sensed this wrongness before but had ignored it.

He'd felt it that day—the first time?—the day he arrived at the Academy. He'd almost forgotten to say goodbye to his mother with the excitement of his tuck box: licorice, potted meats, jams, boiled sweets—*every indulgence a schoolboy should have*, she said. When he and his father drove off in the Crossley, leaving his mother and sisters behind, he'd felt exhilaration, not fear. His father had taken him on every adventure he'd ever had, trekking through the Dales, the Cheviots, Dartmoor. At lunch in the pub, his father kept his advice brief: *Tell the truth, boyo. If you tell the truth, no matter what it is, you'll always find a way out of the muddle.*

When they'd pulled up to the Academy's gates, Morgan had felt a thrill seeing his new trunk and tuck box hoisted to the ground. The courtyard had been full of boys, and Morgan had seen Colin Frick, an older boy he'd known at prep school, waiting for him across the quad. His father shook his hand, and the wrongness struck. He'd stood frozen beside his father, unable to breathe with the fear that he might never see home again, or that if he did, it would be like Veronica's story, everyone dead. His father had squeezed Morgan's shoulder and said, *You'll survive. Write soon.* Morgan had broken away. Nothing was going to happen while he was at school. His mother and father, Veronica, Emily, and Flora, would be exactly as he left them, only better from the absence. His presence was not required to stop the world from falling to bits.

Colin had swept him inside to the houseroom, flooding him with chatter about the Academy, how things worked, what things were called, who was who and how they were to be addressed, so Morgan had forgotten about the wrongness. If only he could reach through time, seize the thirteen-year-old boy he'd been, and clip him round the ear: *Listen. Be careful. It's real.*

◆

He didn't have time to fear Silk Bradley. Not at first. The night of the fag test, after the Sixth Form had chosen their fags and Bradley had chosen him, Bradley took him to the study, produced a cane, and told him to touch his toes. Morgan had been too stunned to be afraid.

—You'll thank me, Bradley said. Gets it over with. Lets you know what to expect.

Four strokes later, Morgan did not feel like thanking him.

—See, Bradley said. Aren't you grateful?

Morgan thought it unwise to say no. Bradley handed him the cane and told him to put it away.

—What've you got in your tuck box?

Thrown off-balance by the question and by the incongruous sensation of holding the cane while still feeling its sting, Morgan told him.

—Bet the biscuits you're the first to get it, Bradley said.

Morgan didn't want to bet against his biscuits—ginger ones his mother had made—but he sensed he had no choice. Without saying so directly, Bradley made it clear that Morgan's tuck box was now his; Morgan might be allowed some of it, but for this he could thank Bradley's magnanimity and his willingness to overlook school practice. Bradley sent him back to the dorm feeling he was lucky to be the first tyro to get the cane, lucky to lose only his biscuits, lucky to belong to someone as sophisticated as Bradley. Bradley had a way of making him feel lucky, but there was nothing lucky about Bradley, unless it had been lucky to survive him.

Morgan called him Bradley, but to his friends he was Silk. It gave Bradley an aristocratic air, though there were no people of that kind at the Academy. Silk's things were no better than anyone else's, but he took care with them and ensured Morgan did the same. Unsatisfactorily blackened shoes were an early sore point.

Charismatic and popular among the boys, Silk treated masters with a smooth disdain. He was frequently accused of being a specimen of the current scornful generation. Bright without being swottish, he had a prodigious memory, especially for Morgan's failings.

—You're running up quite an account with me, Silk would say, and if you don't shape up, you'll have a very sore Accounting when it arrives.

Silk had pronounced *Accounting* with a capital A, and Morgan had not known whether he was speaking literally or not. The dread stole near, but Morgan told himself Silk was only trying to frighten him. He had to stop entertaining fears. The more one paid attention to them, the more powerful they grew.

He was not paying attention, and then the night came, the night he was startled from sleep by the door slamming against the dormitory wall. A chill as the blankets disappeared, then a hand on the back of his neck. No words, but a smell like the drawing room when his parents had dinner guests. His feet were on the floor, not pausing for slippers or dressing gown, and the hand yanked him by his hair out of the dorm, downstairs to Silk's study.

That night he found out about Accounting. He couldn't decide if knowing made it something to dread more, or the opposite. He still feared Silk, though not in the way he should have. As for the wrongness, he thought if he tried hard enough, he could banish the taste of it. He wasn't afraid of real things, he told himself. It was only cowardice.

Tell the truth, boyo, whatever it is. Whatever you do, don't lie to yourself.

✦

The day his Housemaster called him to the study, it had already happened, the terrible thing.

More than destruction, that day in 1922. He had never forgotten the date, and he would remember what it was in a moment. (Was he awake and trying to sleep or asleep and trying to wake?) That day in his Housemaster's study when he grasped, or was told (he'd only grasped it slowly and later, if indeed he'd ever grasped it), the new, savage life without his mother in it. The first time he'd understood that the dread was evidence of something real. A kind of taste, steely and ashen, testifying to the real presence of a thing he could not name.

That thing had laid waste to life, more suddenly and thoroughly than a grenade. She had been in the peak of health! He repeated this fact to himself every time he thought of her as if somehow repetition would expose the wrongness of it and reverse the fact.

Nothing reversed the fact. Her death was the first perfectly irreversible, perfectly hopeless fact he'd known. But the one good thing about death was that it left you nothing to fear. The worst had already happened. She couldn't die twice.

Why, now, the sour apprehension, as if the greatest wickedness lingered just beyond the curtain? Was he under attack, or about to be, now at his weakest, befogged by Matron's drafts?

9

He sometimes fell victim to a kind of high tide, wherein certain thoughts threatened to drown him, thoughts that belonged wholly to the past. But there were tactics that worked against the high tides, tactics to keep sane. Pints at the Cross Keys, number one. Vigorous exercise, number two. Number three . . . basically there were two. He kept wanking to once a day, and he made it a rule never to discuss with himself the things he thought about then.

He had to stop getting confused. He had not to imagine that the past was the present. When something had a name and date, it was history. The Glorious Revolution (1688), the Council of Nicaea (325), the Wreck of the *Medusa* (1816), the Gallowhill Ghastliness (1923), the Confirmation Catastrophe (1923). Now the Spaulding Smashup (1926). These events could be enclosed in parenthesis.

These events had no business assaulting him in the Tower, reminding him, for instance, of the way Mr. Grieves had looked at him after finding the skull. Trembling, he'd asked if Morgan had done it, stolen the skull and the photograph of Gallowhill; put one inside the other and buried them in the archaeology pit to be discovered during the dig; purposely desecrated the memory of Gordon Gallowhill, Grieves's predecessor, beloved history master and Old Boy.

—I ask you to tell me the truth, Grieves had whispered. I deserve that.

Mr. Grieves looked at him with a wide, wild stare. Unlike Silk, who seemed always to look through his skin to his most private parts, Mr. Grieves had looked through him entirely, to the other side, bypassing his essential self and everything Morgan wished him to see. Mr. Grieves had never believed his denials. He thought Morgan was responsible, thought—

The Gallowhill Ghastliness had nothing to do with the present. He had to put things back in their parentheses. There was no point in heaven or earth dwelling on Mr. Grieves or his mother or Silk, Silk in the changing room, Silk on the rugby pitch, Silk in the study—where were his parentheses? Silk Bradley (1922–23) full stop!

The thing beyond the curtain was drawing near. He could smell it, no longer metal, but sulfurous, like the bottle Matron had held under his nose after the Confirmation Catastrophe (May . . . *Parenthesis, parenthesis, wherefore art thou, parenthesis!* What had happened that day and why— none of it mattered because it couldn't happen again. Which was *why* it belonged in parenthesis! It was inhumane to lie paralyzed in the Tower, afflicted by the smell of that bottle, by the Headmaster's color-drained expression when Morgan announced his refusal to be confirmed. It was sinister in the extreme to hear again all the things S-K had hurled at him. Until that day, S-K had never paid him the slightest notice, but afterwards, Morgan knew every vile thing the Headmaster thought of him, some of them perhaps even—but S-K was not in the Tower! And the Confirmation Catastrophe had happened ages ago (May 1923). Take that, high tide!

✦

Spaulding was new this year, a form above Morgan and in another House. Morgan knew him only from rugby, and then only in the violent, unconversational society of the scrum. He was taller than Morgan, well built, with a smile that could stop trains. It had seemed like nothing to run at him, but now he'd gone and buggered his shoulder again, and whatever else he'd ruined in the process.

How many times did he need to repeat it to himself? When he let himself go, things got damaged. His elbow had never been the same since The Fall (1923). After months of painful stretching it more or less extended, but he could never lock the joint as he did with the other arm. And now, three years later, entirely of his own initiative and power, he had damaged something else; another part of his body would never work properly again, not in its original state. He hadn't thought of that when he'd charged at Spaulding, when he saw Spaulding looking at him, his expression melting curiosity-mirth-alarm, until the glorious impact, Spaulding's stomach giving way, Spaulding's arms catching him as the ground fell away, the knife of his teeth through his own tongue. Had he bit through his tongue the other time, too? Silk around him, wood paneling against his face, the high-pitched pang of his arm twisted back, then the skid down steps of stone, the bell-clanging blackness as his head hit ground . . .

After The Fall, Emily and Captain Cahill had come. (Hadn't they?) They came to the Tower and took him home. There was medicine that made him sleepy, and he spent the holidays with his arm wrapped like a mummy. He was in the Tower now, but his sisters didn't know of this disaster (did they?) and neither did his father. With luck, he would be better before the hols, and none of them would have to find out. He couldn't bear to spend another hols like the one after The Fall: his sisters talking constantly around him and about him, talking of his arm, his appetite, his sanity; his father impartial and consolatory, a man who no longer demanded the truth or detected its opposite.

✦

Morgan had never seen his father cry, but at the funeral there had been a moment of horror when "For All the Saints" began and his father's eyes filled. Morgan sent off a desperate prayer that his father would not succumb. The man's eyes briefly overflowed, but his father didn't weep, not then, not at the grave, not across the long day. But that night, when Morgan thought they were clear of the risk, when he was due to return to school, that night he had woken with hunger pangs. On his way to the kitchen, he'd passed his father's study and heard a sound that paralyzed him: his father's sobbing, fierce, animal-like, grotesque. Morgan had run back to his bedroom, hunger chased. In the morning, he had been unable to look his father in the eye.

Morgan had a reputation at school for not blubbing. He had not blubbed from homesickness, not after the Fourth Form's raids, not even from Accounting. Surviving his mother's death and funeral without tears had been the final test, and he had passed it.

Back at the Academy after the funeral, he could feel himself weakening. He'd always endured discomfort by thinking of his mother, how she'd cup his cheeks—*my brave one, a stór*—but now thought of her unmanned him. When he returned after three days away, he expected Silk to fault him for missing fagging duty, but Silk said nothing beyond grumbling that Fletcher had been forced to make the tea, and that it had been foul. For a moment Silk looked at Morgan with something like pity, a look that made Morgan afraid he'd offer condolences. But Silk turned to Fletcher and spoke as if Morgan weren't there:

—He's in a funk, Fletch. Not himself at all.

—He's getting lazy, that's what.

—Fletch. Have you no heart? Wilberforce has been through a terrible ordeal.

Fletcher spat into the fire.

—Have you ever suffered such a thing? Silk asked.

—I've suffered you.

—Don't be facetious, Fletch. 'Tain't Christian.

Morgan continued to prepare their tea, hoping Fletcher would divert Silk to other topics.

—What we need to do, Silk said, is take young Wilberforce's mind off his troubles. Don't we?

—If it'd get us toast without the char.

Silk made a show of thinking:

—I believe I know the perfect diversion!

—Touch your toes and count these out? Fletcher offered.

But Silk was hauling Morgan to his feet.

—Don't be hard, Fletch. He has a broken heart.

—I weep for him.

—Luckily, said Silk, I've got a remedy.

Silk lifted Morgan's pullover until it imprisoned his hands and head. Then Silk hauled him to the carpet, straddled him, and removed the pullover, pinning his hands at his side.

—A remedy, Silk crooned, guaranteed to cure complaints of the heart.

The thrill of captivity, the exquisite horror of being helpless to escape until the worst had passed. Morgan's blood pumped as it always did, dread transposed into an attractive and familiar key. Silk tightened the grip of his knees and applied a single finger to the center of Morgan's chest:

—*Pat-a-cake, pat-a-cake, baker's man, bake me a cake as fast as you can* . . .

So little pressure, but such pain—as if his chest would crack!

—Feeling better yet, young Wilberforce?

Then harder—

—See, Fletch, he's perking up already.

Morgan yelled and kicked, but Silk held him.

—*Then put it in the oven for Fletchy and me!*

Silk pressed down on Morgan's mouth until it hurt, too. Fletcher wedged a chair under the doorknob and removed Morgan's shoes and socks.

—Can't have you disturbing people, Silk said, thrusting a sock into Morgan's mouth.

Morgan breathed heavily through his nose. Sweat trickled down his neck.

—Silk—

—Shut up, Fletch. It's doing him the world of good. Color's come back to his cheeks. Besides which, I've never seen him blub.

—Yet, Fletcher said.

—Point taken.

Morgan steeled himself. If they thought they could make him cry, they were mistaken. He'd hadn't yet; he wouldn't now. And if a sudden fatigue swept across him, like despair but more exhausting, he ignored it. Silk would let him up in a minute, certainly sorer, but it would pass.

—Right, Silk said, the game is called Baker's Dozen.

A chill, despite sweat.

—That was number one.

What piercing . . . breathtaking . . . Could Bradley break his chest so easily, with a finger? He could no longer move, and the air—infrequent, searing—no longer mere pain delivered by Bradley's hand, but a heart-stopping agony, the hand of death on his very chest—he yelled through the sock and sucked air with his last . . . would he travel in a moment to the place where she was? A brief surrender was all it required. So small a sacrifice to feel her hand—

—*As fast as you can . . .*

To depart the world, to fall backwards into her arms . . .

—*Pat it . . .*

Never to see Longmere again. Never see Veronica, Emily, Flora. No Grindalythe Woods from the study window. Never again his father's embrace, bringing forgiveness. No more Accounting. Even the sting of the cane, no more. All this in exchange for release. His coin to her domain. She would want him. She would welcome him. Was that in fact the purpose of these tests, to draw him to her—

—*Roll it . . .* Hold still.

Come unto me all ye who travail and are heavy laden. Come to me, who made you, who waits to embrace you at the end of this last, long day.

—The game is Baker's Dozen, and that was number two.

Again racking—*come here*—roaring—*a stór*—blow—broken!—within his chest or his skull he never knew, but with this breaking, the flood. From every bone, every muscle, tears so long refused now rushed, and with them a love—a great and terrible love—for every good and wicked thing.

—That'll do.

Mouth unstopped. Air. Like oceans but sharper.

—What'd you do that for, Fletch?

—Let him up.

Pain, breath, attachment to this world; a furious grip that refused to let go, refused to depart when called—

—He's done, Silk.

—But I haven't even—

—He's blubbing. That's it.

Through tears, a swimming vision of his tormentors, Bradley and Fletcher, so wicked and so human.

—You're no fun at all.

Lightness now as if he would fly! Breath like a racing wave, and horror—

—Don't worry, Fletch, we'll improve him. He'll take the whole doz before long.

He had refused *her*. His own mother, alone in death, had held out her hand to him, and he refused. He was no longer the person he had been. Something alien, grotesque, this new self. Over her he had chosen the world and its wretchedness.

✦

Was he awake and trying to sleep, or asleep and trying to wake? If he could wrestle his way back, he could order his thoughts and do something . . . about whatever lurked beyond the curtain. His elbow might never straighten properly, S-K might never look at him with anything but scorn, Mr. Grieves might no longer trust him, Silk might never . . . but Silk was gone, not quite as she was gone, but gone from his ken. None of it could be put back, and who cared anymore? He was seventeen years old. He cared nothing for the opinions of his Headmaster, his history master, or his father. As for his mother, at least she would never have to know his father as he was now, a widower in London, drained of zest. Whatever skulked beyond the curtain could sod off, as far as he was concerned. He, Morgan Wilberforce, was seventeen years old—as previously discussed!—and subject to no one. He may have bashed himself about at rugby that afternoon or whenever it had been, but he was in control of himself now. He was not primed to dive down any staircases, to break any more bones or any more anything.

Whatever lurked in the shadows could perk up its ears and listen: The life of Morgan Wilberforce did not require breaking. It was buggered already. If the shadow wished amusement, it could sod off somewhere pristine, somewhere people still cared, somewhere worth busting. There was no amusement to be had at St. Stephen's Academy on this day in March 1926. The Academy was an entirely undiverting institution, languishing since the War, full of unremarkable people doing things of no import. He, Morgan Wilberforce, was no scholar, no wit, and no very remarkable athlete. He mattered nothing to anyone. He had outgrown preposterous notions of mattering. There was no fun, in short, to be had in their domain, so yon skulker-in-the-shadow could just take itself off where it had come from. St. Stephen's Academy and Morgan himself were too unexceptional for evil to bother with them.

 John Grieves disliked social occasions. There were benefits to being an undermaster with digs in Fridaythorpe rather than living within the walls of the Academy, such as the space, however brief, to think his thoughts undisturbed. In the minus column, his rooms were expensive to heat and required a quarter of an hour's bicycle ride twice a day in rain, sleet, snow, or occasionally sunshine. Also in the minus column, he had no private place at the Academy itself to confer with boys, except his classroom. The other masters thought him either put-upon or tragically acquiescent to the Headmaster's miserly ways, but he defended his arrangement to any who would, after seven years, listen: He would not have it another way. He cherished his autonomy in Fridaythorpe and his social horizons in the village. This last was not quite true, but it sounded plausible. But now, this Friday in March, for the satisfaction of a rugby wager, he was due to entertain Lockett-Egan.

John made it a rule not to socialize with his colleagues outside the gates of the Academy, but he made an exception for the Eagle, who had some years previous established a pattern of fortnightly fellowship at the Cross Keys, the only watering hole within fifteen miles of the Academy and John's refectory-cum-study in Fridaythorpe. They knew him there. He never had to place an order. When he walked in, tea would be brought to him, and food of some description. Over the years, they had learned the outline of his private life, but they did not intrude with conversation unless he initiated it. Masters from the Academy frequented the Keys Sunday afternoons; at these times, John confined himself to his rooms across the road. He justified his aloofness with the label teetotaler. In time, the explanation had become unquestioned fact, making sense of everything.

Tonight as the Eagle shouldered his way from the bar, John tried to look congenial, but all he could think of was the Eagle's alarming confession on the sidelines of the rugby pitch that afternoon.

—What's wrong? the Eagle asked him.

—Pocklington, John said. You can't take it.

—Finger off the trigger. I haven't even sat down.

The Eagle removed his overcoat, took a seat, and raised his glass; John raised his tea mug.

—How many more days in this godforsaken term? the Eagle asked.

—Fourteen.

—Any chance you'd abandon your Quaker ways and kill me now?

John grimaced.

—That's right, the Eagle replied, I forgot you're a saint. One who wouldn't have felt my entirely unchristian satisfaction hearing Clem's bookcases collapse this evening.

So that was the commotion during Prep. When Clement supervised the Third, little of the evening was devoted to preparation and much to mischief. John found Clement more aggravating than he wanted to. Clem was in his eighties, a gentle soul who didn't bully and didn't persecute, but his lessons and his House were disasters. John had no idea how the Eagle tolerated working under him. Of course he'd be tempted by offers from other schools.

—Any notion who was behind it? John asked.

—Too many notions.

—The Third are sowing their oats.

—The Third are feral beasts, as previously discussed.

They had discussed the Third Form ad nauseam, and there was no question—between the two of them or within the Senior Common Room as a whole—that this year's Third were a thoroughly bad crop. John often felt the school was on the verge of anarchy.

—We're all at the end of our tether, John said. But that's no reason to let Pocklington poach you.

The Eagle's neck colored:

—It's more that I submitted my credentials and they offered me a post.

—You—but—how could you? John exclaimed.

He realized at once this was the wrong thing to say.

—Just what sort of post is it?

—Housemaster.

John's heart sank. The Eagle had been waiting years to become a House-master at the Academy, laboring as undermaster in Clement's since before the War.

—I suppose congratulations are in order, John said.

It sounded grudging.

—So you see my dilemma, the Eagle said.

—What dilemma?

Now he was sounding bitter. It was no way to treat a friend.

—Burton.

—What business is it of his?

Of course Burton-Lee would interfere. He was loyal to the Head-master and had been at the Academy more than thirty years. John detested him on almost every ground, but if Burton could dissuade the Eagle from leaving . . .

—The thing is, Burton's had an offer himself, the Eagle said.

—What! From where?

—Some place in Dorset.

—What *place*?

—And he's thinking of taking it.

—But—but he can't! You can't! This simply makes no sense.

John's neck cramped. He could think of nothing to say, nothing to protest the monstrous notion of Burton and the Eagle both abandoning the Academy. The Eagle drank his pint in pained silence, and John real-ized the notion made every kind of sense. He collapsed into a sulk:

—Wilberforce wrecked his shoulder.

—Oh, yes?

—Partial dislocation, Matron said.

—Didn't he break his arm last year? the Eagle asked.

—Three years ago.

John remembered everything—curse of the historian—but, honestly, how could the Eagle have got to the point of confusing last year with three years ago? It required a perverse ignorance of time.

—And that was no accident, John told him.

—I thought he fell down some stairs.

—That's what everyone said, but obviously it wasn't true.

—It wasn't?

The Eagle sat forward, curiosity piqued.

—Of course not. Bradley was responsible.

—Bradley pushed Wilberforce down the stairs?

—Forget the stairs, John said impatiently. It happened in Bradley's study.

The Eagle goggled behind his thick spectacles:

—But you never told me this. Are you saying Bradley deliberately broke Wilberforce's arm and ribs and whatever else?

—Perhaps not deliberately, John admitted, but he did it. It was all to do with the digging debacle and—

—You mean your archaeology project?

—Yes—

—When they dug up Gallowhill's skull—

—It *wasn't* his skull.

—I know you always suspected Wilberforce, but was there ever proof?

—Bradley found proof, obviously.

The Eagle removed his spectacles and wiped them, as he always did when considering a thorny proposition:

—Back up, Grievous. Are you saying Bradley beat Wilberforce sense-less because he found proof of the Gallowhill business?

—It's the only explanation, John said. Number one, Wilberforce helped me dig the archaeology pit and so had opportunity to plant the skull. Number two, Gallowhill meant the world to Bradley. Number three, on the very same day that we're told Hazlehurst's JCR have dealt with the matter, we hear that Wilberforce is in the Tower, having fallen down a flight of stairs. So. I ask you.

The Eagle peered into his empty glass.

—That's a serious allegation. Did you discuss it with S-K?

—What do you think? John asked. But by that time Wilberforce had gone home, so S-K put it off until the next term, and then there was the blowup with Wilberforce refusing confirmation.

—That! I still can't believe he had the nerve to thwart S-K. I wouldn't.

—But isn't that precisely what you're doing with Pocklington? John argued.

The Eagle bristled:

—Refusing confirmation and resigning are entirely different matters.

—What makes you think the Head at Pocklington will be any less tyrannical?

—Nothing, the Eagle replied, but it will be a novel tyranny. And I'll have a House.

John felt desperate:

—With you and Burton gone, who'll help me stop the Third turning into . . . something that will make Bradley and Co. look like choirboys?

The Eagle sighed and then went to the bar for another round. He returned with a second mug of tea for John.

—Grieves, he said, you can't blame yourself for Bradley.

—I don't.

—If Bradley really did all that to Wilberforce, it wasn't your fault, no matter how incandescent you were about the skull business.

—I know it wasn't my fault.

—You don't know it. And you don't know that Wilberforce was behind the skull. Take some advice for once and let the grudge go.

—Grudge? John balked. Grudge against whom?

—Against Wilberforce, against Bradley, against yourself.

—You're a fine one to talk. You're bolting—

—Possibly, the Eagle said. But the point you're missing is Wilberforce.

—What about him?

—That tackle today was pointless and destructive. He's going off the rails, and you're the only person he respects.

—Me? Wilberforce doesn't respect—

—Of course it's possible I'm imagining the whole thing, the Eagle concluded. In which case there's nothing to worry about.

John's mouth soured. He set his tea aside.

—Do yourself a favor, the Eagle counseled. Cast a glance across Positions Vacant. You're young, clever, healthy, and decent. You could have a future of your own if you weren't so afraid of it.

The Eagle's remarks re Morgan Wilberforce were almost as disturbing as his news of impending defections from the SCR. He had foisted his Wilberforce theory on John without a sliver of evidence, but once John had regained the quiet of his little rooms, he was able to see that the Eagle's claims were ludicrous. Wilberforce was as slothful and indifferent in John's lessons as in any other. They had no outside rapport since the

Gallowhill business, and if the Eagle thought they did, it was only because his myopia (literal and figurative) caused him to conflate the years. The span between 1923 and 1926 might not seem to the Eagle the enormous era it was to boys growing into whiskers, but it was nevertheless a long time. It was long enough for boys to change unrecognizably, to stretch many inches, to come out in spots, to outgrow several pairs of trousers, to lose their voices and then regain them octaves lower, and to acquire the general narcolepsy of late adolescence. In short, the years between St. Stephen's Third and Fifth Forms were more revolutionary to the person than the Bolsheviks had been to Russia (stretching it perhaps, but never mind!); thus there was no reason for the Eagle to imagine that Morgan Wilberforce retained even a memory of whatever respect he once had for John, which was in any case questionable!

 Matron released him from the Tower Sunday evening after immobilizing his left arm in bandages and a sling. It was possible, she said, that he'd damaged more than his shoulder, but as the holidays would begin in less than a fortnight, he could wait and see his father's physician in Harley Street rather than inconvenience the surgeon. Morgan had little time for the medical profession, which tended to disagree in its opinions and restrict him in his activities. Indeed, Matron repeated her injunction against all Games, especially rugby, but she declared that nothing should prevent him completing his prep that night or any other. Morgan left the ward more vexed than he'd ever before felt upon escaping captivity.

He emerged from the Tower into the empty quad. The House windows glowed, laughter leaked from some raucous study, and puddles lurked in darkness, threatening to tip him arse over elbow onto the cobblestones. He felt feeble, and cold. Alone and half disarmed, he sensed in the quad something sinister, akin to the thing that had attended him in the Tower. But the Tower was already in the past. He was dressed and breathing ordinary air. He did not believe in ridiculous things.

Footsteps announced Colin slipping out of the gatehouse. Seeing Morgan, he flinched but recovered directly:

—Ah, young Wilberforce. Back from the grave?

—Reports of my death—

—Exaggerated, it would seem.

Colin crammed a bulky item into his jacket. It was an open secret that Colin and his studymate operated a distillery in their study, one allowed to prosper because they provided liberal samples to the prefects of the JCR.

—Supplies? Morgan asked.

—Nose out, Wilber. What'd you do to the wing anyhow?

—Nothing much. Should be back on form for the Fleas next week.

—Don't be funny.

—Matron isn't in charge of the XV, Morgan declared.

Colin exhaled derisively and headed toward the cloisters.

—What's that supposed to mean? Morgan said.

—Talk to Barlow.

—I will not talk to Barlow.

Their so-called Captain of Games was the most unworthy specimen to have held the post in the history of the school. Morgan spoke with him as little as possible, and when he did, most of his energy went to stopping himself saying inflammatory things.

—Spill it, Morgan said, before I get interested in your supplies.

Colin sighed:

—Barlow's put Darke in for you.

Darke was in the Fifth, a part of their circle but no friend of Morgan's. Morgan and Nathan were the only Fifth Formers on Hazlehurst's XV, and only just appointed. Of course, Darke would have been waiting to usurp Morgan's place.

—Barlow can bloody well take Darke out again. I'm playing.

—You might want to keep that to yourself, Colin told him. People are already saying you've gone off your dot.

—Does Spaulding say that?

—What's it to you what Spaulding says?

They turned into the cloisters, a ghost of a grin on Colin's mouth.

—Look, Morgan said, sod off.

The grin materialized:

—Here is me, sodding off. Off I sod. Enjoy your chat with Barlow.

With that, Colin exited to the classrooms, leaving Morgan alone beside the chapel. His heart pounded beneath the sling. He was supposed to be returning to ordinary life, not dealing with snags ninety seconds after escaping the Tower. People said all sorts of things about him, but normally they did not impugn his sanity. Presumably they questioned his tackle of

Spaulding, which might have been quixotic, depending on one's point of view. He'd own quixotic. He'd even own reckless. But off his dot? Luckily, such an attitude could be vanquished as soon as he played again; unluckily, that would involve shouting sense into Barlow, sod him.

And if Barlow's idiocy weren't snag enough, there was Colin, the central telephone exchange of the Academy. What he said, everyone said. The unwarranted smirk advertised Colin's doubt: that Morgan's tackle was perhaps not a failed act of heroism but rather a disordered attempt to throw himself at Spaulding. Throw himself literally and publicly at a boy from another House and year, a boy who possibly didn't even know Morgan's name before the tackle (though he did now!). This snag—unfair and untrue—needed unsnagging before it went any further. He swore and went after Colin.

In the lower corridor, Colin was ducking into the Fifth's empty form room. It hurt too much to jog—spite and malice—and by the time Morgan got there, Colin was disappearing into the cupboard. Morgan navigated the unlit room without falling over but found, upon reaching the cupboard, that it was empty, the object of some conjurer's trick. He felt along the shelves until a panel at the back gave way to his touch, admitting him to the chemistry lab.

—You, too? Colin complained.

Morgan peered into the dim classroom. Colin was gripping one of the tables as if preparing for mortal combat. Across from him stood Alex Pearl, Nathan's younger brother and the bane of Morgan's existence. How many snags could snag up in five short minutes?

—As you're here, Colin said to Morgan, you can remind this item where it belongs.

Alex, who belonged anywhere but the chemistry lab, turned to Morgan, wearing that smirk that always drove him—*one snag at a time*. Morgan crossed his free arm over the sling. It hurt.

—What brings you here? he demanded.

—Your resurrected body, Alex quipped.

One snag—three—however many—concentrate. The day before the Spaulding Smashup, Morgan, Nathan, and Laurie had discovered that Alex was experimenting with gunpowder. Even for the most-caned boy in the Third, this struck them as too much. The three of them had hauled Alex upstairs to a boxroom and set to work. After a string of lies, Alex had admitted stealing and dismantling a box of old shells and repackaging the powder in pellets. They'd had to draw blood before Alex revealed where he'd hidden them. Nathan had gone to dispose of the pellets while Morgan and Laurie had completed the course of moral suasion on his younger brother, at the end of which Alex had promised to reform. His presence in the chemistry lab made it clear that his vow had been empty. Morgan boxed him against the table:

—You belong in Prep.

—So do you, Alex retorted.

He looked Morgan directly in the eye as he'd done when they were dealing with him over the gunpowder. Laurie had held him down, and Morgan had applied a persuasion they'd once known. Alex had never dropped his gaze but had watched Morgan while he did it, letting Morgan see that he felt it, that he saw Morgan seeing him, that he knew Morgan knew himself how it felt, that he knew exactly what Morgan was doing, even as it hurt him, even as it brought him—steel-hearted Alex—to tears.

—Bugger off, Pearl, on the double! Colin barked.

Alex made to leave, but Morgan stepped across his path:

—Not so fast. Empty your pockets.

Alex sighed theatrically:

—Your titanic self-importance notwithstanding, Wilberforce—

—Got a vocabulary now? Do as you're told.

Alex twisted away, but not before Colin could seize him from behind. Morgan rifled his pockets, confiscated a packet of cigarettes, but found nothing explosive.

—Prep, Morgan commanded. And not another word if you want these back.

He held up the cigarettes. Alex eyed them longingly, but Colin booted the boy into the corridor. One snag, at least, could go to the back of the queue.

—I thought you were sorting that little beast out, Colin said.

Morgan rubbed his shoulder through the bandages, feeling cold again and hamstrung. Even Colin could see that Morgan was the only thing standing between Alex and chaos. Alex ran circles around his fagmaster, Kilby, their slow-witted, concrete-minded Prefect of Hall. Alex didn't even heed Nathan or Laurie anymore. He only heeded Morgan, and only when Morgan made him. How would he make him with one working arm? Just now, Alex had let him win—

Back of the queue. Everything would be handled in turn, and *next* in turn was people: what they were saying about him and why they were saying it.

—Has Spaulding said anything about the match? Morgan asked.

Colin closed the drawer where he had been rummaging and slipped something into his pocket.

—Not to me. Should he have?

—How do I know?

—Just what happened during that tackle? Colin asked.

—I knocked him down. That's all I remember. Brick wall of a brute thumped my lights out.

Morgan was a sportsman. He was not off his dot. Colin led him back through the cupboard.

—For no strategic purpose, Colin mused, you throw yourself at Spaulding. In the process you knock yourself out cold and bugger your arm so you can't play the rest of term.

—I can play—

—And now, Colin continued, minutes after escaping Matron's clutches, you come and cross-question me about Spaulding and what he thinks of you.

Colin snaked through the darkened form room; Morgan barked his shin on a desk.

—Whatever it is, Colin said, I'd put it out of mind. Spaulding's only got eyes for Rees.

—Rees! Morgan spluttered.

—I know, completely absurd as well as impossible, but I have it from a reliable source.

—Your source is having you on!

—Possible, Colin admitted, but given that it's Larkspur, unlikely.

The snags were overrunning any notion of a queue. If Spaulding fancied anyone, it could never be Rees. Rees wasn't even in the Sixth. He was in the Fifth, like Morgan. Furthermore, Rees was the most loathsome item in the form, if not the whole Upper School.

They were due to play Spaulding again next week. This time Spaulding would know who he was. Barlow could not drop him from the XV. End of story.

✦

Morgan kicked open the study door and found Nathan tinkering with their wireless.

—He lives!

—I've just come from Barlow, Morgan announced.

Nathan grinned:

—Uplifting?

At least Nathan was glad to see him, unlike Alex, whose every glance was a minefield. When Alex was younger, before his face had narrowed and lost most of its freckles, Morgan had thought the brothers looked nothing alike. He and Nathan used to pretend Alex was a foundling abandoned by gnomes. Now that Alex was almost fourteen, Morgan saw the same stab in each brother's glances, the same electricity in their grins. The only difference was that Nathan had no guile whereas Alex had nothing but.

Nathan cleared a space for him on the window seat and looked to him eagerly for news. Whatever snags might come, at least he still had this— this home in their study, Laurie and Nathan forever on his side, Nathan's smile, open and frank, never thinking him off his dot. Morgan slumped down and propped his arm on a pillow. Everything seemed suddenly to hurt.

—Not only is Barlow out of his tiny mind, Morgan complained, but he's dooming us to failure the rest of term.

Nathan commiserated: Their Captain of Games was a tyrant and a half-wit. Never had Games sunk to a more pitiful state. Indeed, without Morgan, Hazlehurst's XV would have little chance of beating even Clement's, let alone REN's or Burton-Lee's, but given Barlow's mental and strategic defects as well as his obstinacy, more tragic even than Creon's, Nathan concluded there was nothing to do but bow to cruel fate.

—What if the Head insisted?

—S-K won't take sides in House rugger, Nathan said.

—But if he leaned on Hazlehurst, he could take sides!

—You're funny. When's the last time Twiggy lifted a finger for anything besides his bottle?

Morgan's zeal leaked away. There was no point discussing it since he and Nathan agreed perfectly: Their Housemaster put himself out for nothing and nobody. He left every detail to the prefectorial discretion of the Junior Common Room, which could most generously be described as incompetent and slothful.

Nathan resumed the wireless and finally picked up a signal, admitting a scratchy drama to their study. Morgan's head began to throb along with his shoulder. Nathan had taken out his camera and was now squinting at him through the viewfinder. The first summer Morgan had spent with the Pearls, Nathan had scrambled along the Annaside waterline, snapping his Brownie with the restless energy he applied to everything; if forced to sit immobile on the window seat as Nathan darted up and down the study, Morgan felt he might indeed go off his dot. Matron had told him to return for a dose of aspirin before bed, but that wasn't for ages.

—If you won't do something about Barlow, I will, Morgan announced.

Nathan clicked the camera. Morgan hauled himself off the window seat and quit the study.

Why did the shadow linger even after he'd escaped the Tower? Surely whatever he'd imagined in the wake of injury was fantastical at best, delusional at worst, none of it relevant to ordinary life. In ordinary life, even the passionate contests of rugby football ended predictably, at least for his side. Why else would he have charged at Spaulding so suicidally except for boredom, sheer mortal boredom provoking a quixotic gesture one Friday afternoon in Lent?

He couldn't dwell on the unedifying. The fact was that he'd improved dramatically in two days, and with a good night's sleep he ought to be ready to play, or at least to run and pass with one hand. He needed only to get himself back on the XV before their next match against Burton-Lee's. Nathan was perhaps too sensible to think of a solution, but Laurie would be able to concoct one. If he could get back on the XV, he could take exercise, regain his equilibrium, and then when they played the Fleas again, he could show Spaulding what was what.

He found Laurie at the back of the library, cradling an oversize volume in his lap.

—Snails! Laurie cried. You don't have to sneak up on a chap.

—Guilty conscience?

—Always. You look heaps better. How's it feel?

Morgan sat down on the floor opposite his studymate:

—I need your mind a minute.

—Not sure you want it in its present state, but proceed.

Morgan explained the rugby dilemma. Laurie nodded as Morgan ran through all the arguments Barlow had rejected. When he finished, Laurie continued to nod:

—Why exactly do you have to play even though you nearly killed yourself two days ago?

—If I don't, we'll lose!

Laurie pondered this last remark, still nodding.

—Well? Morgan demanded.

—You won't like it.

Morgan kicked him.

—It's perfectly simple, Laurie said. Devote yourself to undermining the confidence of the other teams.

—How?

—Mental warfare.

—But what about our XV?

—You can forget that, Laurie said. You aren't playing, obviously.

—But, Morgan spluttered, I'm better, lots better.

Laurie looked at him, and the truth settled. His shoulder was aching steadily even now, and mental warfare, whatever that entailed, was the best he could hope for. He hated ordinary life. He hated ordinary everything.

Laurie glanced over Morgan's shoulder with something like impatience. The library was empty except for a couple of swots laughing at the other end of the room.

—Am I keeping you from something? Morgan asked.

Laurie's fingers tightened around the book.

—What've you got?

—Nothing, Laurie said.

His face was serene and bored. Too serene, too bored. Morgan snatched at the volume.

—Bugger off, Laurie said.

—I don't think I will.

—I'm warning you, Wilber, sod the hell off.

Normally Morgan would've had no trouble winning an object from Laurie, but now Laurie's twists sent a spear through him. He gasped.

—Sorry, but I warned you.

Laurie set the book behind him. Morgan breathed until the pain lessened. They didn't speak, but the conversation passed between them exploring the inevitable future, in which Laurie might refuse to tell Morgan his secret now, even tomorrow, but in which Morgan would persist until Laurie did tell him, at a time and place far less convenient than a deserted library at Prep.

—Oh, all right, Laurie said at last, but you can't tell JP. I'm serious.

They had an understanding about what to keep from Nathan, items ranging from the salacious to the irrational to the unjust, all guaranteed to send their studymate into a frenzy of indignation. Morgan couldn't imagine which Laurie would be cradling in the library, but he nodded in agreement and Laurie passed him the volume.

It was an atlas of the Orient, but Morgan saw upon opening it that the book was only a front for the pages folded inside. A periodical without photographs, dusty, with an uninspiring title.

—*The Pearl?* Morgan balked. Is that why you don't want JP to know?

But the title had nothing apparently to do with Nathan's surname.

—Is it some bit of Red rubbish?

Laurie bit his lip as he flicked to a page titled LADY POKINGHAM, OR THEY ALL DO IT; *Giving an Account of her Luxurious Adventures, both before and after her Marriage with Lord Crim-Con.*

He had never read anything quite so . . . *Pulling up her skirts, I threw Miss Arundel backwards on the sofa, and releasing my bursting weapon, threw myself between her yielding thighs, as I exclaimed, 'You have indeed relieved me of making an invidious selection, as I cannot restrain the heat of my passion!'*

—But where did you get it?

—Uncle Anton.

Laurie had any number of obscure relations, none of whom Morgan had met. The only member of the Lydon family he knew was Laurie's grandmother, who kept an odd, shamble-down place in Lincolnshire.

—Is there any more?

Frank Fane is to stay,
To be whipped in the hall,
To be whipped, till his whipping
Atones for you all.
Any boy that enjoys
A fine flogging to see,
I give leave to stay here,
With Frank Fane and me.

The Prep bell rang; everything throbbed; Laurie took back the book.

—God, Morgan groaned.

—Warned you.

They headed down to Sunday cocoa. Morgan was greeted enthusiastically by some and jostled by others, all of which helped subdue his physical distress.

—Ah, Wilberforce.

Mr. Grieves intercepted them as they approached the refectory arch.

—Sir.

—Glad to see you ambulating.

Morgan watched anxiously as boys flowed past them. He realized he was ravenous, and with each moment, the chances of getting an extra biscuit were draining away.

—Can I expect your Plantagenet composition tomorrow? Mr. Grieves continued.

—Matron's only just released him, sir, said Laurie.

—You ought to have some extra time at Games.

—Sir, Morgan protested, I'm playing.

Mr. Grieves snorted:

—Tiddlywinks, perhaps. I'll have a word with Barlow and expect your essay Tuesday at break.

—But, sir—

—Three sides, no less.

A fever upon him . . .

—Don't look at me like that, Mr. Grieves said.

—It isn't my fault I was in the Tower! Morgan protested. It isn't fair to make me—

—Get some rest, Wilberforce, and stop feeling sorry for yourself.

With a tap to Morgan's good arm, Mr. Grieves departed. Morgan looked to Laurie for some common outrage, but Laurie had joined the queue.

—And Wilberforce? Mr. Grieves called. You're welcome.

Laurie ushered him through the crowds, fetched his cocoa and biscuit, and relayed Mr. Grieves's tyranny to Nathan.

—What I can't stand, Morgan complained, is the sarcasm. If you're going to be a skunk, be one, but don't go all *you're welcome* at the end of it.

—He doesn't remember, Nathan told Laurie.

—Grieves was talking about the tackle, Laurie explained. He did his first-aid-in-the-trenches on you. He and Barlow carried you to the Tower.

Morgan had never heard a more unappealing report. An evening of snags and now this?

As they got up from the table, Laurie passed him a clipping: *Taking every possible advantage, he continued his motions with thrilling energy, till I could not help responding to his delicious thrusts, moving my bottom a little to meet each returning insertion of his exciting weapon (we were lying on our sides)—*

A crash across the corridor interrupted Mr. Grieves's lecture on Anne Boleyn. Morgan exchanged glances with Nathan, who reddened, and Laurie, who rolled his eyes. Mr. Grieves cleared his throat and continued.

The ruckus emanating from the Third's form room sounded like a collapsed desk, one of Alex's specialties, and Morgan felt perturbed all over again at his inability to keep the boy in check. When Alex had come to the Academy the previous autumn, the three of them had tried to contain him, but he'd quickly earned a reputation as Most Whacked (in the Third, but now the school). They'd hoped that Alex would settle down after Christmas, but Alex parried a scathing set of term reports with a wounded attitude: *Yes, we all know I'm not Saint Nathan. I'll never be good enough for you, sob!* After several performances of Misunderstood Alex, their mother took pity on him, their father took refuge in his writing shed, and Nathan took to wondering if he was too overbearing with his brother.

Alex had returned after Christmas emboldened. Each new escapade made the fags more arrogant and Alex more of a perisher. He'd never have got away with it under Silk. Silk would have put Alex in his place. Given free rein, Morgan would put Alex in his place. But he wasn't given free rein. He had no official authority over Alex and nowhere private to deal with him as required.

Morgan had been out of the Tower two days, yet the shadow lingered, casting a pall over everything. He reported to Matron every four hours for chalky aspirin, which made his shoulder hurt less but did nothing against the stiffness and general feebleness that made him feel at least fifty. He would not be playing any more rugby this term, he knew that now, so the Smashup had wrecked not only his shoulder but also his career on the XV. The embarrassing urgency with which he'd hectored Barlow he blamed on Matron's drafts. That explanation coupled with his scrupulously ordinary behavior had managed to scotch any rumors of off-his-dot-itude, but the solace of Uncle Anton's magazine had introduced new difficulties. Monday, he'd been forced to take Personal Exercise in the toilets during French rather than in bed at night, which had presented a dilemma come evening Prep: either he could break his unbreakable rule that limited PE to once a day, or he could lie awake in demented anguish. He knew too well the consequences of breaking the unbreakable PE rule, so he resorted to visiting the Cross Keys during Prep. That whole operation—from the agony of crawling through the tunnel and hacking through the woods to Fridaythorpe, to the awkwardness of lying to Nathan and Laurie about it—had testified to the shadow's contamination of the world since the Smashup.

Mr. Grieves squeezed addendum after addendum into the baroque diagram, which purported to elucidate the court politics of Henry VIII.

—Have you got that down? Mr. Grieves asked.

The Fifth murmured. Nathan peered darkly into the corridor.

—Don't think about it, Laurie whispered. Me and Wilber'll sort Alex out.

—With that wing? Nathan scoffed.

—I'm not an invalid, Morgan growled. I can manage your beastly brother.

—Like hell.

—What was that, Pearl?

Mr. Grieves turned from the blackboard. Nathan blinked cold eyes:

—I was asking Wilberforce what it said below George Boleyn, sir.

—It sounded like a bit more than that.

—No, sir.

Mr. Grieves and his chalk-covered gown returned to the diagram.

—Pearl has a point, he said tartly. So to ensure you've all managed to decipher this scrawl—

He scrutinized his handiwork:

—Which appears, I must say, to have been written by a ballet-dancing hippo with chalk in its toe . . .

No one chuckled.

—Please leave your exercise books behind. I shall review them. With care.

The room lapsed into sullen silence. Nathan's knee jittered as he listened for sounds across the corridor.

Morgan couldn't understand how Nathan and Alex could have grown up in the same household. Summers on the Irish Sea, Alex wore piratical costume; Nathan, short trousers and bare feet. Alex mooched around the house reading penny dreadfuls and the novels their father had written; Nathan strode down the sand, long-limbed, wiry, peering at tide pools through his camera. Alex disliked the water, but Nathan went with Morgan thrice daily into the sea. Thrashed side by side in the heavy, gritty surf, knocked back, upside down, sand and salt churning up their noses, they fought the undertow, until Nathan's hands closed around his arm and his hair, hauling him again into the air, onto the sand, leaning over him, flesh pink and lacerated by the sea, eyes bloodshot, lashes long, long enough to—

The bell dispersed their lethargy. Morgan tossed his empty book onto Grieves's desk and pressed through the crowd after Nathan and Laurie.

—What's the point? Nathan grumbled. No one's going to copy that tripe.

—Makes him feel better, Laurie said. He'll moan half the lesson tomorrow and then have it out of his system.

Across the cloisters, a cluster of juniors erupted into laughter.

—Oi! Nathan shouted.

The cluster laughed louder as Alex burst from it and dashed past the three of them with a taunting curse. Before Nathan could react, Morgan and Laurie pulled him into the dim, empty chapel.

—You can't let Alex needle you, Laurie said. If he wants to raise hell, on his arse be it.

—Mendacious little sod! I'm not stiff in my moral joints, and I'm not a fainting virgin, thank you very much.

—Perhaps not fainting, Laurie breathed.

—The point, Morgan said, is that Alex knows how to get you on the raw, and he loves to do it. Let me and Snail remediate him. If you try, it'll only give him more satisfaction.

—It's easy for you to take the high ground, Nathan said bitterly. You don't have a brother making a fool of you, busting things up right and left, driving your mother into the grave with worry, and—

Laurie kicked him. In a flush of embarrassment, Nathan stalked out of the chapel. Morgan followed, high tide of mothers—*you're grand, a stór*—He yanked his bad arm until the pain cleared his head.

—Speaking of rumors, he said, do you think it's true about Spaulding and Rees?

Except he wasn't supposed to be asking about Spaulding.

—It's rot, Laurie told him. Spaulding isn't even attainable.

—Larkspur says he is.

—But by Rees? Laurie protested. I mean, what a loathsome specimen.

—Larkspur says Rees's had half the House already.

—Larkspur told *you* this?

He'd found Larkspur in the toilets during Chemistry, and as a connoisseur of changing-room gossip, Larkspur surpassed even Colin.

—It came up, Morgan replied feebly.

—At least, Nathan grumbled, we can be grateful Alex hasn't gone in for that.

Such remarks were precisely why Nathan could never know about *The Pearl*, and why Morgan had not invited him or Laurie to the Keys last night, because that would involve an explanation of his PE difficulties, which would not only involve Uncle Anton's wretched magazine, but would also advertise that he, Morgan, had grown disordered in his personal habits and perhaps even in that regard gone off his dot. The reasons for lying to his friends last night were too complex to explain even to himself, but the point was that he wasn't planning on making a habit of it.

They strolled into French after the bell. As Hazlehurst had not yet arrived, they punted Rees's belongings around the room while Rees gave chase, complaining in his high, irritating voice. Once their Housemaster turned up and moaned at them to take their seats, Morgan's chest began to tighten, restricting breath, nothing to block the high tide rising by the second: Rees and Spaulding alone in the changing room; Alex in the study after dark, sitting on a striped backside, learning what his cock was for . . .

—*Le passé simple est simple*, Hazlehurst crooned.

—*Le passé simple est simple.*

It was essential that he think of something else: Tudors, Stewarts, Plantagenet intrigues, the cosine of 60, the meter of *Endymion*, the *passé simple* of *aller*.

—*Il allé?*

—*Alla. Alla*, idiot boy! *Le passé simple est simple!*

—Sorry, sir, but *Est-ce que je peux aller aux toilettes?*

Personal Exercise urgent. If he couldn't defeat the high tide, he'd have to resort to getting caned just to stop himself going mad.

That night at Prep, he excused himself from the study, again pleading pain too sharp to endure. With calculated gait he crossed the quad, but inside the Tower, rather than mounting the stairs to Matron's rooms, he used his penknife to spring the latch on the supply cupboard. Taking care not to disturb the mops and brooms, he let himself out the window to the grass beneath. A jagged dash across the playing fields, a stabbing squeeze through the poacher's tunnel, and a swift stalk through Grindalythe Woods brought him mercifully to the Cross Keys, where Polly, the landlord's daughter, brought him the usual.

—How're you keeping, pet? she asked. Still badly?

He allowed her to touch his hair while he mouthed flirtations. She was affectionate to him, but he didn't desire her. Laurie considered her plain, and Nathan declined her advances out of respect for Julia, a girl he claimed to have had during the holidays. Morgan classed Polly as a child.

He drank half the pint in one go. It calmed the back of his throat and sent an agreeable pulsing through his jaw and temples. He swallowed the rest and nodded for another.

He would drink the next more slowly, he told Polly. His shoulder would stop hurting halfway through the second pint, and by the third, the high tide would be well out to sea . . . if that's what happened to tides? The point was that the entire visit was medicinal, and anyone who said otherwise was a moralist.

Morality was something invented by old men who wished upon the young a life as desiccated as those they lived themselves, he told Polly. If he left the Academy to take a peaceable pint in lieu of Prep, he was merely making more of the evening than his fellows, who were in any case occupied consuming home brew, placing wagers, venting their frustrations on the younger generation, doing anything, in fact, but attending to the worthless tasks their masters had assigned them knowing full well they wouldn't even try.

—You have got a lem on, Polly declared tousling his hair.

She went to pull his second pint and winked as she placed it on the bar. Perhaps she wasn't such a child after all. As a matter of fact, she seemed to have recently . . . *Yesterday you were a child, Now a blooming blushing virgin; Female passions warm and wild—*

He dragged himself to the bar and exchanged his glass for the new one full of soft, thick, perfectly foamed bitter. Two gulps, three, cooling the gills, opening passages, oiling his joints as he turned back to the room—into the path of Mr. Grieves.

A mere six feet between them and the room changed color—warm yellow to a buzzing brown. Mr. Grieves wore a pullover, shirt open at the collar, fingertips at his trouser pocket as if he were about to remove a handkerchief.

—I think you'd better sit, Wilberforce, before you spill any more down the front of yourself.

Morgan righted his glass. Grieves produced the handkerchief, but Morgan pointedly used his own.

The brown moment continued, regardless of sense. Grieves fetched a mug of tea, which he placed on Morgan's table. He sat down. Morgan eyed him.

—What are you doing here, sir?

—I might ask the same of you.

He gestured to the stool Morgan had been occupying. Morgan dragged it to the opposite side of the table and sat.

—Last I checked, Grieves said, it wasn't out-of-bounds for an undermaster to take solace at the Cross Keys. Fifth Formers, however . . .

Morgan's heart beat in his throat with the buzzing fear, the hunger he used to know when there were men who could hold him to account, so painful and essential that he could hardly breathe.

But Grieves was not one of those men, not anymore. Grieves was an undermaster in a time when nothing mattered. Grieves, in fact, was nothing but a nuisance, taking it upon himself to interrupt the remedies Morgan had come all the way to Fridaythorpe to attain. Grieves needed taking down a peg.

—Are you going to tell S-K? Morgan asked flatly.

The man met his gaze, unthreatened and oddly unthreatening, as if capturing a pupil at the Cross Keys were an occasion for curiosity rather than indignation.

—I should, Grieves replied at last. I can't think how you've managed to skive off Prep, but please don't tell me.

—I wasn't going to, sir.

—What interests me, Grieves continued, is why you're here.

Morgan did not reply.

—The second night in a row, and without Pearl or Lydon.

Morgan took a slow swallow of his drink.

—Don't look so shocked, Grieves said mildly. You normally come together, don't you, Saturday evenings?

Morgan's head thumped, and he could feel his veins rushing blood to his heart, as if some agent were summoning it from the outposts of his body.

—I can see I've undermined your illusions, Grieves said.

—How long have you known, sir?

—September, if I recall.

Morgan took another drink.

—Of your Fourth Form year, wasn't it?

And choked.

—Careful.

Three years? He'd known for *three years*?

—Who else knows, sir?

—None that I'm aware.

Morgan drained his glass and signaled to Polly. Mr. Grieves nodded for another mug of tea.

—Drinking alone is never a good sign, you know.

—I suppose I'm turning bad, sir.

Mr. Grieves sighed and twisted his signet ring.

—How's that arm, by the way?

—It's the shoulder, sir. And it's fine.

—Not a shrewd tackle, I didn't think.

—No, sir.

—But it was brave.

Morgan glowered and looked around for Polly. She was working her way towards them, carrying a full tray.

—I thought masters only came here Sunday afternoons, Morgan said.

—Clearly.

Clearly? Clearly he thought that, or clearly it was true? Was it more offensive that Mr. Grieves had known about them for three years, or that he'd harbored such a secret and said nothing?

Polly set two steaming mugs before them.

—That isn't my order, Morgan said.

—All there is, luv.

—What do you mean, all there is?

—Don't snap at Polly, Mr. Grieves scolded. And don't look at me like that. You've been cut off.

—Sir!

—Two is more than enough for a growing boy.

Two wasn't enough, and he wasn't a boy!

—And you still haven't told me what brings you here.

—What makes you think I will?

—I think you should.

—Or you'll tell S-K?

Challenge. Dare. Ultimatum? Mr. Grieves tipped a spoonful of sugar into Morgan's mug.

They sat at the table as their tea cooled enough to drink. The brown moment persisted, but with it lingered something novel, something stirring and even welcome. He hadn't the first idea of Grieves's game, or why in the name of Hermes he had chosen this evening to intervene, having known about them for three years and having watched Morgan come to the pub on his own two nights in a row. Did Grieves imagine he might wrest tearful confessions from him (of what, even?) or that he might shine the light of his intellect upon Morgan's evasions?

—You're letting yourself get carried away, Grieves said at last.

If Grieves imagined it was his place to say such things, then he was going to have to be taught a lesson. Morgan was forced to endure a good many things, but he drew the line at being toyed with.

—That's me, sir. A regular tearaway.

—You know what I mean.

Morgan laughed; Mr. Grieves didn't.

—Heaven only knows what will have to happen before your . . . generation gets it into your heads—

—*To respect our elders and betters and be grateful to the dead*, Morgan said, supplying one of the Headmaster's favored phrases.

Mr. Grieves held his gaze:

—I would have said the other way around. Be grateful to your elders and respect the dead.

—What's there to respect about death? Morgan balked.

—I'd have thought you had a notion about that.

A cheap shot. Shabby and cheap. How dare Grieves speak of—though it was possible the man was not alluding to his mother but was instead resurrecting the ghastly Gallowhill Ghastliness?

Of course he was. The man was sitting there at Morgan's table accusing him *once again*—of tearing from a yearbook a photograph of Gordon Gallowhill (Old Boy 1884–90, history master, war hero, suicide), of placing it inside a human skull stolen from REN's lab, of burying it in the wretched archaeology pit for a prank. Except that he *hadn't*, and in any case the whole affair had happened *years ago*! This man had a memory like a steel trap, and he held grudges longer than a perverse elephant. If anyone was off his dot, it was Grieves. Morgan got up from the table.

—The Eagle's been offered a post, Grieves continued blithely. Housemaster at Pocklington.

A surge of alarm overtook Morgan:

—Will he take it, sir?

—Can't see why not. Burton-Lee's got an offer somewhere, too.

—*Burton?*

Morgan did not know what was more unsettling: the idea of losing Burton-Lee or the fact that Grieves was telling him unsolicited secrets from the Senior Common Room.

—But Burton's been here forever, sir. The Eagle almost forever. Why leave now?

Mr. Grieves gave him a look that made him feel culpable of any number of sins, venial and mortal:

—Why indeed, Wilberforce?

 The next morning, Grieves had the gall to take breakfast in the refectory without looking once in Morgan's direction. In chapel, the Headmaster droned about bounds-breaking, veering periodically into windy reminders about Prep: the Third, Fourth, and Remove were not to leave their form rooms without written permission; the Fifth ditto their studies; the Lower and Upper Sixth likewise belonged in their own studies, not loitering in the library . . . The SCR lounged just beyond S-K's line of sight, Clement dozing openly, Hazlehurst consulting a newspaper, Grieves resting his head against his hand, whether to soothe a headache or to conceal closed eyes, Morgan couldn't tell.

Morgan had woken that morning with a curious waft of hope, a hope that evaporated once he remembered the unsavory nature of his conversation with Grieves: not only had Grieves ruined his refuge at the Keys, but the Academy was on the verge of losing the Eagle and the Flea, who, with Grieves, were the only switched-on masters in the place.

The Headmaster dismissed them after a prolonged lecture, but with a scant ten minutes left to the first lesson, Burton-Lee declined to teach them, instead directing them to begin their prep while he attended to some correspondence. It took all of Morgan's restraint not to tell Nathan and Laurie everything of the night, up to and including the fact that the Flea's correspondence could only be with the horrible other school. Instead Morgan gossiped about sport and wandered restlessly to French.

There Hazlehurst set them to reading from *Le Figaro* and writing précis, a task Morgan ignored so he could concentrate on dreading History. What precisely he dreaded, he wasn't sure. If Grieves was going to peach on him, he'd have done it years ago. Besides which, to whom would he peach? Not to the JCR, who would turn teetotalers before they entertained complaints from undermasters. Not S-K, since revealing his knowledge to the Headmaster would expose Grieves to an inconvenient line of questioning, beginning with why he'd not spoken up three years earlier. And as for informing Morgan's Housemaster, why would anyone bother? Hazlehurst encountered worse offenses almost daily and avoided taking action on all of them.

At the Cross Keys, Mr. Grieves had revealed that he'd noticed Morgan, that he'd been noticing him for some time. And Mr. Grieves had revealed his own connection to the Keys, for he evidently possessed some signal with Polly—Morgan's Polly!—a signal with the authority to cancel Morgan's order. It dawned on Morgan that the Keys might be Mr. Grieves's personal haunt even more than it was theirs. Nathan and Laurie would have been scandalized if Morgan had been in a position to tell them.

✦

They poured into the quad for break and queued outside the tuckshop.

—Here come the Fleas, Nathan murmured.

A cluster of Burton-Lee's XV crossed the quad like a wolf pack. Their own XV did not go round together, but Burton-Lee's XV, perhaps as an expression of their dominance, traveled everywhere in groups.

—Ods bodkins, Laurie breathed, it's the King's bodyguards.

—Who's the king? Nathan muttered.

—Spaulding, Morgan said.

—Prob'ly can't even shit on his own.

The bodyguards arrived and cut into the queue.

—How's the wing? asked Buxhill.

Bux played wing forward, like Morgan.

—Mending, Morgan said.

—Fast, Nathan added.

—Not fast enough to save you from Clem's this afternoon, said Bux.

—Or REN's tomorrow, added Ledger.

Ledge was Burton-Lee's other wing forward, just as arrogant as Bux but less blatant about it.

—Not that it would've made a difference, said a voice from the pack.

Bux and Ledge stepped aside for the voice: Spaulding himself, towering, lean, powerful, with a mouth that seemed always amused. Nathan stepped closer, violating the buffer Spaulding's bodyguards had established:

—You've got a lot of nerve after what you did to Wilberforce.

—What exactly did I do? Spaulding asked.

Spaulding crossed his arms, supremely confident, his teeth miraculously straight. Unlike the bodyguards, Spaulding possessed intelligence, humor, and a magnetic presence. Nathan squared his shoulders but did not reply.

—He didn't do anything, Bux said, except stand there and be plowed down by yon minotaur.

Ledge addressed Morgan:

—Hear Matron's sidelined you the rest of term.

—That's a lie, Laurie snapped.

—It doesn't matter, Ledge told the pack. They wouldn't have come to anything even with their young wing.

—Now wingless.

—Hilarious, Laurie muttered.

Morgan drew himself to his full height and addressed Spaulding:

—Unfortunately for you, you'll never know.

—Know what?

Spaulding defiant, curious, tempted. Morgan held his gaze, heart thudding.

The pack reached the front of the queue, but Spaulding kept looking at him even after the others had turned away, sustaining a kind of silent conversation Morgan hadn't had since—

There could be no shred of truth in the rumor that Spaulding had been seduced by Rees. Spaulding was in the Sixth, Rees the Fifth; Spaulding excelled on every field, Rees on none; Spaulding was adored, Rees hated.

Indeed, Rees slumped into History well after the bell, daubing his nose ostentatiously with a handkerchief. Grieves squinted at him but said nothing. When it came to Rees, Grieves had no notion. Rees was a swot, though not half so clever as he imagined, and Grieves allowed him to show off. Despite having passed three and a half years at the Academy, Rees still failed to understand just how much showing off was reviled. Add to this his lugubrious manner, his laziness at Games, his inability to listen to what anyone was saying, and his spots, which he insisted on picking, and you had someone irredeemably obnoxious, someone they in the Fifth were forced to tolerate every single day of the year. If someone had bloodied his nose during break, it was the least he deserved.

—Well, then.

The form's attention drifted to Mr. Grieves, who leaned against the window, newspaper in hand. His habit was to begin lessons by reading them an article from *The Times*. Today's turgid offering concerned the new German cabinet: *Herr Luther's choice, a liberal policy*. Morgan deliberately looked away. If Grieves imagined that Morgan was going to start courting his approval, then he had another think coming. Morgan owed him nothing, and there was no way in Hades he was going to start swotting like beastly Rees. Grieves could drone until he was hoarse, but Morgan refused to show the least interest in Herr Luther's cabinet, his cupboards, his credenzas, his wardrobes, or his water closets.

—So.

Having concluded his reading, Grieves watched them until they began to fidget. His object apparently accomplished, he sauntered to the blackboard, pulled down the slate with the Tudor diagram, and announced that they could expect a composition during tomorrow's double lesson. A groan of protest filled the room, but Grieves ignored it.

—Any boy, he began—

They resented being called boys at their age.

—earning less than twelve out of twenty tomorrow will find himself in extra-tu Saturday.

They fell silent, not from fear but from grim recognition. Saturday afternoon was the match against Sedbergh School, their greatest rival. Having to miss it for extra tuition would be a severe penalty, but they knew Grieves well enough to realize he wasn't bluffing. Apparently the man still possessed the will and the wherewithal to make them work, if only for a day.

Grieves sat behind his desk and unfolded his newspaper, airily oblivious as they retrieved their exercise books and crowded the blackboard to decipher his notes.

Morgan copied the chalky schemata as well as he could. Under no circumstance was he willing to miss the Sedbergh match or to allow Grieves the satisfaction of giving him extra-tu. Obviously the man had decided to punish him (for bounds-breaking? For cheek? For . . . ?) by oppressing the whole form with a composition. Obviously, it was personal. Obviously, Morgan's only option was mental warfare: outclassing Grieves by actually swotting and then writing a composition clever enough to irk the man.

Copying complete, Morgan leafed back through his earlier notes and glimpsed something that hadn't been there before: Grieves's script at the bottom of the page, *To be continued.*

✦

That afternoon it rained with the force of punishment. Laurie and Morgan watched miserably from the sidelines as Clem's XV slaughtered their own. Nathan came away with a blackening eye, and Morgan with a chill that resisted the influence of hot tea before the study's grate.

Three long hours until tea, then Prep, bed, and ten more days— twenty-four hours apiece—until the holidays, which themselves promised nothing. He had squandered PE before lunch and was quickly feeling persuaded by the idea that twice a day wasn't really any different from once, provided he adhered strictly to a schedule. He felt himself on a precipice, unable to retreat and helpless to resist the plunge into grave error. He was powerless to stop the XV losing, powerless against whatever the shadow had planned, and powerless now to restore himself to sanity through physical exertion or stout porter. It was enough to drive a person to suicide, if a person were so inclined.

Morgan poked at their dismal excuse for a fire. The din of wireless dance music filled the study. Nathan took possession of the wing chair and began to browse last week's paper, tapping his feet in rhythm against the grate. Laurie lounged on the window seat behind a book of sonnets, which Morgan knew contained leaves of Uncle Anton's magazine. How he was meant to keep his head with Nathan's senseless racket and Laurie's blatant pursuit of Lady Pokingham, he had no idea.

—I'm off to the bogs, he announced.

Nathan and Laurie looked up listlessly but did not stir. His arm itched under its wrapping. His legs ached from lack of exercise. His stomach grumbled.

He avoided the lavatory (*was* twice a day any different from once?) and made for the cloisters. A din assaulted him even there, and in the lower corridor he discovered a full-on rugby match, attended by the Third and some of the Fourth. He could not remember having seen quite so much bedlam in a corridor, on a rainy half holiday or any day. He shoved his way through it to his own form room, only to find a knot of Third Formers, attending . . . Alex. Of course.

—What's the idea? Morgan demanded.

Alex looked up, surprised and annoyed:

—What are you doing here?

—It's our form room, Morgan said, not yours.

—Don't see anyone using it.

Morgan evaluated the group. There were eight of them, and while he would not normally have trouble thumping sense into eight fags, circumstances were subpar.

—Do you want something? Alex asked irritably.

Morgan opened his desk and removed a book to justify his presence:

—I was supposed to come and see Grieves.

—Grievous ain't here, Alex said, turning back to his friends.

Morgan seized Alex from behind, shoved him over a desk, and kicked him until he yelped.

—If you even think about messing the Fifth, Morgan barked, we'll send the lot of you to the Tower. Hear?

—Pardon? Alex quipped.

Morgan slammed Alex's head against the desk. He howled.

—Anyone else have trouble hearing?

The fags backed away. Morgan kicked Alex upright:

—Shut up before I give you something to bawl about.

He left more unnerved than he'd been. His good arm shook, his bad arm twanged, his trousers strained. He'd overdone it, obviously, but hopefully no one would find out. If word got back to Nathan and Laurie, he'd explain that he'd merely been trying to slam sense into Alex's skull. There hadn't been any blood, and anyway Alex was a virtuoso of crocodile tears.

Twice a day couldn't be a serious departure from once a day. What was important, surely, was that PE be contained within some bounds and not become a fixation. It was important not to be too rigid! Circumstances had changed since the Spaulding Smashup, so PE routines might change with them, for the time being, without unleashing madness. Twice a day; once per twelve-hour period. Done.

What he needed was privacy, a rare commodity on a rainy half hol. He tramped up to the boxrooms, but found them full of rival parties. What was the point of renegotiating PE if he couldn't get five minutes' privacy? Stomping down the back staircase, he cursed the Lower School, cursed the rain, and cursed the Academy. Someone was going to commit murder before the day was—

Out the rainy window, a figure crossed the playing fields, a figure out of uniform, a figure he knew: Spaulding, alone and clandestine, achieving the south-bounds hedgerow and disappearing through it.

◆

A bang startled Morgan awake. The study floor was hard, the light fading, his right side hot.

—You look like someone who let the kettle burn dry, Laurie announced, dumping books on the table and kicking the study door closed.

Morgan squinted. It wasn't night. It was day. He'd fallen asleep in front of the fire after PE, after . . . he jolted up—

—There's something—

Stood, unsteadily—

—Back in a tick.

And stumbled out the door.

Downstairs, around the kitchens, and up the passage to Burton-Lee's empty changing room. Twilight seeped in the half windows. It would be call-over soon. In his own House, call-over had sunk to the level of charade, but Burton-Lee ran a strict House, and his Head Boy, Spenser, possessed a legendary right arm. Still, Morgan doubted that someone of Spaulding's stature could have much respect for call-over.

As the changing room came into focus, he scanned the pegs for Spaulding's name. Spaulding's uniform hung there, empty of his body. Morgan sat down beneath it, his heart beating in his throat, the fabric of Spaulding's trousers brushing his cheek.

Rain battered the windows. Soon his dim sanctuary would become enemy territory as Burton-Lee's arrived to change for tea and Prep. Trespassing in another House was Not Done, and trespassing in another changing room was unmitigated taboo. If he was discovered there, he could expect . . . he wasn't sure what, but certainly the wrath of two JCRs and a month of awkward questions from—

A wedge of light, a door clicked shut. A ping, a lightbulb's glare—

—Bloody—

And a voice he'd know anywhere: Spaulding, hand on light switch, looking as though he'd just crawled out of a lake.

Morgan stood.

—What do you think you're playing at? Spaulding demanded.

Spaulding's mouth was no longer amused. Instead, a ruthless edge, and a note of moral outrage. Morgan suppressed the wild urge to laugh.

—Who else is here? Spaulding said.

—No one!

—Who was here, then?

—Nobody.

Hammering heart.

—I was waiting for you to turn up.

Spaulding gaped. Morgan sat back down. They breathed.

Something flickered in Spaulding's eye. He noted Morgan's position beside his own pegs. This would be the moment to grin, but Morgan didn't, couldn't. With a grim frustration, Spaulding peeled off his top and dropped it, heavy with water, into the basins. Ignoring Morgan, he stripped off the rest of his clothes and put them, minus his boots, also into the basins.

Then he turned on the shower tap and stood beneath it, cold water cascading down his shivering frame.

The muscles in his back stretched. Below, he was even more perfect than Morgan had gleaned through rugby shorts. The shower was brief, and when Spaulding turned around, Morgan saw the rest of what he'd come to see.

—Chuck us a towel, Spaulding said.

He spoke casually, as if Morgan belonged in that changing room, as if nothing out of the ordinary were occurring. Morgan pulled a towel from the basket and lobbed it at him. Spaulding rubbed himself down, draped the towel over his shoulder, collected his clothes and mud-soaked boots, and disappeared into the drying cupboard. An irregular drip from tap onto tiles, a pipe clanging to announce the hour of steam heat, but otherwise nothing, no one. Morgan strode past the basins, clutched the handle of the drying-room door, and pulled.

Inside, the pungent aroma of games kit. A small window gave the dimmest light, revealing rails of clothing, racks of boots, a wall of radiators, and, leaning against them, Spaulding.

—Push, or it won't stay closed, Spaulding said.

Morgan kicked the door. The radiators hissed and devoured the chill that had dogged him all the day. Spaulding took the towel from his shoulder and wrapped it around his waist with an ease that made Morgan's mouth dry.

—You like to flirt with death, Spaulding said to a row of boots.

—I like answers.

—Oh, yes?

Morgan sidled up to the radiators and pressed against them, letting them burn into his jacket and the back of his trousers.

—You're up to your balls in trouble, Spalding continued mildly. Don't imagine that wing'll let you off Spenser's wrist.

—Spenser can save it to wank himself, Morgan said.

A hoot from the changing room. Morgan flushed to his ears:

—What's through the south-bounds hedgerow?

He couldn't see Spaulding's face, but he heard a sharp intake of breath and then the clear shouting of boys on the other side of the door. Spaulding lurched toward him and wrenched open the window:

—Go on! Bunk!

A pounding energy propelled Morgan up the radiator and through the window. On the wet grass outside, he extracted feet from the casement. Spaulding reached for the latch.

—I asked the wrong question, Morgan said.

Spaulding hesitated. Morgan grinned:

—What's through the hedgerow isn't half so interesting as who.

Tea was excellent. Aspirin was excellent. The prospect of Prep, excellent. *To be continued?* To be finished! If Grieves thought he could cow Morgan Wilberforce, then he had fallen into error. Nothing appealed to Morgan more than loading his memory with historical minutiae to fire at Grieves with marksman-like precision.

But Nathan and Laurie refused to be quiet. They'd been complaining since tea, and now Nathan was damning Grieves to a sulfurous hell and Laurie was wondering aloud which circle their history master deserved.

—The ninth, declared Nathan. He's a traitor.

They showed no sign of sitting down, and no sign of shutting up so Morgan could pursue mental warfare.

—He's bolshie, Laurie said, but isn't traitor a trifle harsh?

—Not at all. Threatening the Upper School with a comp a week before the hols—

—Ten days.

—is a crime itself—

It was hard enough to decipher his own handwriting. How would he cram three pages of historical—

—but to interfere with the Sedbergh match and with such a vile essay betrays every rule in the book.

If he weren't allowed to concentrate, the excellence might evaporate, allowing the return of—

—Grievous might, Nathan continued, have been forgiven his bolshie white-feather rubbish if he'd repented of it, but his behavior towards the Fifth unmasks him for the traitor he is, and for that he deserves the worst hell has to offer. Would you allow him purgatory?

—Certainly not, Laurie said, but surely he belongs in the fifth circle.

—With the wrathful! Nathan brightened.

—With the sullen. This composition of his is one enormous sulk.

—About what?

About the fact that no one in Yorkshire could finish a thought without—

—About the fact that no one takes an interest in his beastly subject.

—No one takes interest in any subject.

—Ah, but you see Grievesy can't bear it, Laurie said. He's Sincere.

—I don't care what you call it. Making us swot under pain of Sedbergh is no way—

A thunderous clap silenced them, like a bolt from Zeus hurled into their realm. Like destruction from afar landed sharply upon them.

They threw open the window. Shouts and footsteps echoed below. Laurie dashed into the corridor. Morgan and Nathan followed, abandoning mental warfare for the rush of material destruction.

✦

The Third were behind the whole thing, someone said. They'd caused an explosion, Darke said; in the laboratory, Holland said. One of them was even now on his way to the Tower with burns, Larkspur said. The tale strained belief, but in the cloisters Burton-Lee's prefects had established a barrier. Smoke poured out of the laboratory windows, an acrid, sulfurous cloud that told of chemical mishaps. Masters and servants bustled about while the Lower School and Remove mustered in the center of the cloisters and the Upper School murmured on the fringes. Colin joined them under the refectory arch and delivered a preliminary report: Clem had been taking the Third for Prep when something had exploded in REN's laboratory. Clem had been too slow to prevent four boys rushing through the adjoining door, which was presumably how the one boy (Carter? Peel? Wentworth minor?) had managed to set himself on fire, at least such was the word on the perimeter of the cloisters. Morgan had seen no boy incinerated, though several looked as though they'd taken up with the chimney sweep.

Nathan scanned the cloisters for his brother, but Alex was nowhere in sight.

—What if he's the one who . . . ?

Before Nathan could enlarge on the idea, S-K emerged and ordered the Upper School back to its studies, promising six from his own arm to any who dared disobey him. Their own Prefect of Hall professed no sympathy for Nathan's anxiety and rejected their pleas that Nathan be allowed to check for his brother in the Tower. If Pearl minor had been injured, Kilby argued, Matron would have her hands full. Furthermore, Kilby told them, they could expect a JCR whacking in addition to S-K's six if they did not go to their study and stay there.

—I don't give a damn! Nathan snapped.

Morgan and Laurie dragged him inside before he punched Kilby.

There were no good men left in England. Any other JCR in history would have managed the crisis better. Even Silk would have done something to find out about Alex.

Laurie tried to calm Nathan by inviting Holland and Darke to their study to play Black Maria. Morgan let Nathan shoot the moon, but as Nathan recovered his equilibrium, Morgan's began to falter.

Was this explosion what the shadow had been preparing all along, awaiting only a trigger—head bashed into desk, changing room trespassed, third PE borrowed from tomorrow? He had damaged his own person by smashing into Spaulding last week. Had he now through his excess released destruction into the Academy at large? An actual explosion had torn through the school, and Alex—

Let him not be burned, Hermes, friend, let him not—

This was what happened when he let himself go. Finding Alex in the lab Sunday evening ought, after the gunpowder business, to have sounded every alarm. Had Morgan listened? Distracted by Spaulding and the XV, Morgan had dismissed Alex, the true threat to civilized existence. Alex had been taunting him that night, just as he had taunted Morgan in the form room this afternoon. Alex wanted sorting out, wanted Morgan to haul him back from his folly. He yearned for those times apart from the world, when they wrestled and Morgan won, and they both in their antagonism felt altogether alive.

Hermes, friend, let him—

If Alex was not burned, Morgan would never overdo it with him again. If the explosion itself would fade away as a minor accident, then he would never again trespass in another House. He would erase Spaulding from every list in his mind. If the shadow would now depart, Morgan would pull himself together. He would reduce PE to once a day. He would even submit to a PE fast on Sundays.

They drifted up to the dorms, where Colin had harvested fresh intelligence: the Third were officially being blamed for the Bang and had been threatened by the JCR with mass whacking. Unless the guilty parties owned up, the entire form would appear in games kit outside their respective houserooms at seven o'clock the following morning.

—God knows they deserve it, Laurie said, but first thing's a bit stiff.

Last and finally, Colin summoned one of the fags to repeat his testimony, that Alex was in the Tower and had been there since tea.

—Alibi? Laurie asked.

—Malingering, Nathan said.

Morgan felt a surge of elation, like a pint drained in one go.

—Matron's keeping him overnight so she can observe, the fag reported.

—Observe what? snapped Nathan. His being an idiot?

—The bark on the head he got at Games, the fag said looking darkly at Morgan.

✦

The next morning, Morgan saw signs that his bargain had succeeded. The JCR followed through on its threat, and the Third turned up to breakfast visibly subdued. No further word of burning reached them. Grieves had the spite to inflict his composition after all, but Laurie pointed out that the teeth would be in the marking. If Grieves depleted spectators for the Sedbergh match, the Headmaster would annihilate him; QED, Grievous was bluffing.

This was an optimistic hypothesis for an optimistic day. At Games, Morgan and Laurie watched from the sidelines as REN's XV made hash of their own, but this depressing outcome did not disrupt Morgan's sanity. He did not look for Spaulding. No one got injured. Disaster had been averted. The coast was clear, of high tides, low tides, hurricanes, and fog.

By the time Prep rolled around, he had to face the fact that the shadow had departed and that therefore he would have to keep his vows. He had already begun to forget Spaulding, Alex remained out of reach in the Tower, and the new PE regime would begin at bedtime (or possibly the following morning). In the meantime, he felt he ought to do everything possible to build up his equilibrium. He took Laurie's book of sonnets to the drying cupboard of their own changing room. *With a furious plunge, the dart of love shot true to its mark. The collision with her hymen was most destructive, and the virgin defenses gave way as, with an awful shriek of pain, she lost all consciousness. He completed the conquest and then lay soaking, trying to revive her sensibility by his lascivious throbbing inside of her, whilst we applied salts and restoratives to bring her round.*

Calm did not descend, which might have distressed him were he not inhabiting an optimistic age, but he *was* occupying an optimistic age, and in the optimistic age a second quick release could be permitted for the purposes of equilibrium. *The rod is delicious if skillfully applied after the delights of coition.* Or perhaps after a short reverie . . . *You're up to your balls in trouble* . . .

When he returned to the study with his usual excuse of the Tower, Laurie and Nathan fell upon him:

—What's the news? Who got burnt?

—How many were there?

They continued this inconvenient line of questioning until Morgan realized the awkwardness of his error. It might have been all right if he'd told the truth casually from the start, but now his omission had given PE a significance he'd never meant it to have. If he admitted it now, they'd think him thoroughly disordered, and Laurie might even get it into his head that Morgan had been in the changer with someone else.

—What did Alex say?

—Nothing. He . . .

—Quit diddling us around, Laurie said. Just tell the truth!

—What's the matter with you? Nathan demanded. You aren't yourself, and you haven't been for some time.

Morgan stood against the wall, breath caustic, as if gas had been re-leased in their room and only he lacked a mask. Here were his friends, his only allies anywhere on earth, denouncing him as a liar and a stranger. What were the countermeasures against gas, again? Hadn't Grieves said one was supposed to stand still, that those who tried to run made it worse? Those who stood on the parapets of the trenches fared best, Grieves had told him. Until someone shot them.

—I don't think you're being fair, Morgan said.

—Don't you? Nathan retaliated. Well, we don't think it's fair when you pretend you're on our side and then go conspire with Alex in the Tower.

—What!

Nathan turned to Laurie in fury:

—Told you he'd never listen.

—Are we your friends or aren't we? Laurie demanded.

—Of course!

—Then how are we supposed to defend you if you act this way?

How had things got to this ludicrous point? They suspected him of deceiving them and conniving with Alex to blow up the school? Did gas cause hallucination? He thought he remembered Grieves saying it took days to die from poison gas, and meantime one lay suffocating and burned in a field hospital. Was that chlorine or mustard gas he meant? Didn't the Germans give one of them up as ineffective?

—He's too bloody arrogant, Nathan hissed. This is pointless!

This wasn't the way things were supposed to be. He had heeded the warning of the explosion. He had opened and closed negotiations with the shadow. Danger had departed. He had reformed. But now his friends—allies since their first day at the Academy—were turning on him, pinning him literally to the wall, and letting him know they saw his lies. The shadow had left the Academy, but here in the cloister of their study, a sinister war had broken out, a war his friends had conspired to wage when Morgan's back had been turned.

—Can't you trust us? Laurie implored. After all this time?

A perilous weakness seized him—the yearning to confess to them everything he carried. *If you can trust anyone, you can trust them,* the weakness whispered. And what surrender it would be to trust somebody, to have somebody equal to the truth, someone who would demand it of him, all of it, and on hearing it would not flinch.

—I'll tell you the truth if you're so determined to know it.

Laurie crossed his arms. Nathan glared. Morgan opened his mouth, but the weakness turned to alarm. What exactly could he confess, to them or anyone? What words could convey the menace of the shadow, the allure of Spaulding, the mess of Alex—and was that even the extent of it? How dare they torment him by pretending they wanted the truth! The *truth?* Even his father could not wrest it from him anymore. How dare they behave as if the truth were explicable. Or endurable.

—If you must know, his voice said loftily, I was in the chapel.

—Right.

—Why? Laurie countered.

—If you must know, it's my mater's birthday.

They boggled at him. Good. He had more ammunition and was not afraid to use it. Oh, they were clever. They conspired to trap him? To resurrect that desperate longing. How dare they? How *dare*—

—She would have been forty-eight, his voice continued.

Their faces reddened. Sods. They deserved this and worse.

—They always talked about going back to Venice for it. Now of course, they aren't.

Their silence confirmed they took the lie as truth. When was his mother's birthday, actually? It was in March, but when again?

—If you were in the chapel, Nathan said ruthlessly, why didn't you tell us in the first place?

A rifle against his ribs; it was the eleventh of March—that was the date he'd written on Grieves's composition this morning, and that was in fact his mother's birthday. He caught his breath. This was not, absolutely *not* the moment to—he'd only said it to make them ashamed, and actually, since it was that day, not only could he have been in the chapel, but as far as the two traitors before him knew, he had been!

—If you must know, I was blubbing.

Let them eat that.

—If you've any more disagreeable questions to put to me, perhaps you'd be good enough to wait until I've returned from the bogs, unless you want to chaperone me while I go and be sick.

He detached himself from the wall. His good arm wrenched open the door, releasing him from that poisonous room. He stalked away without reply from his friends, without protest, without perception, without succor.

He needed to run around the playing fields, to sprint cross-country, to bang about in the scrum, to climb ropes in the gym, to bowl cricket balls, to swing bats, to do anything other than stand jittering in the washroom. Things were even more bashed up than he'd feared, but this destruction couldn't be blamed on anyone else. He was the basher. The Spaulding Smashup had been his fault, too, even though he hadn't meant to do it.

Had he?

The truth was he couldn't remember what he'd been thinking before he charged Spaulding. Had he been thinking at all? He remembered the slick of Spaulding's arm against him, blocking his try. He remembered the flash from Spaulding's eyes as he did it. He remembered . . .

What if this shadow had been with him all along, only of late growing dark enough to sense? What if he had plowed into Spaulding in some desperate bid to outrun it?

He tried to remember a time without it, but that time belonged to the other life, the life full of life, when they brought her breakfast in bed on her birthday, when his father kissed her in front of them, when her laughter overflowed everything, like the icing on the cake she made for herself and let him—but he couldn't think such things or he would shortly cease to breathe.

His father referred to the current age as some sort of sea journey. He would speak of being so many months out, as if he had boarded a sailing vessel and embarked on an odyssey of unknown length. Nine months out; two years out; forty-two months, one week, and three days out—the expression made Morgan want to punch someone's nose in. Was it the grave self-importance that enraged him, or the metaphor itself? If one was out, then presumably one could come back in. When would they turn the ship around?

 Two o'clock was surely the most hopeless hour of the night. Years after lights-out but ages before dawn, never had madness felt so close at hand. Rational thought had long ago departed—who knew how many months out it was now—abandoning Morgan to a body more agitated than he could endure.

That body was now in fact slipping from his bed and moving somnambulant from the dorm. He felt aches, stabs, drafts, but the body paid them no mind. He watched, almost curious, as the body repaired to the changing room, where it stripped off pajamas and donned mufti before continuing in stocking feet to the study. He observed, now quite curious, as the body gathered items from his drawer: money, wristwatch, and, most peculiar of all perhaps, the small, soft-bound volume Silk had given him that last night, the night they'd sat together in the study after weeks of not speaking; the night Silk had told him the secret of the poacher's tunnel; the night Silk had . . . not said goodbye, but failed to say it.

Morgan had never precisely understood why Silk had given him *Stalky & Co.* as his fag book. Silk had claimed that Gallowhill had given it to him, and in fact the penciled initials *G.G.* could be found inside, but why after everything would Silk have parted with it? And why, so long escaped from Silk, was Morgan now stuffing it into his pocket?

He followed as the body quit the study and made its way downstairs. There it turned in—peculiar—at the cloakroom, where it sought out his overcoat, scarf, and cap. It even—extraordinary—rifled through Holland's overcoat for Holland's gloves, the only ones known to exist in the House.

He had nothing better to do, nowhere to be, so he accompanied the body as it laced up his outdoor shoes, unlocked the garden door, and strolled across the moonlit playing fields to the poacher's tunnel, where it began the routines of gaining entrance to the woods.

Whatever could its purpose be? It couldn't be making for the Keys, as surely it knew that establishment was closed. It could only, Morgan realized with growing excitement, intend one thing. Finally, someone had recognized the bitter, bursting truth—that there was nothing left for him at that school, or anywhere in the east, west, or north of Yorkshire. Finally, someone had taken steps. Finally, someone was acting!

Until this moment he had classed running away with the histrionics favored by his sister Emily. One of his earliest memories was of Emily storming off to her bedroom after shrill confrontation with their mother, packing a bundle, and Running Away.

—Don't bother coming after me! she'd cried over their mother's protests.

This had been when they lived in the country, in the cottage at Longmere, and he had a mental picture of his father returning home shortly afterwards (on a horse?), consoling their mother, and then departing on the horse (with Morgan and Uncle Charles?) to search for Emily. They found her in a glade nearby, and Father had sent Uncle Charles back with the horses while he stayed to Reason with Emily. Morgan had a memory of riding his father's horse back to the cottage and announcing that Emily had been found! Safe and sound! Emily and Father returned, and their mother prepared a special tea with iced buns.

His legs were not striding through the woods in search of a special tea. His mother was no longer making buns of any description, his father no longer rode horses, and Emily had gone and married Captain Cahill. His legs were striding through the woods in pursuit of something altogether undemonstrative and compulsory. His legs were striding for one reason only: to shore up his sanity.

But how? The station lay in the opposite direction; what's more, his money would take him only a few junctions down the line. Surely the body did not propose to trek on foot to their destination? He may have traversed the Cheviots at the age of nine and survived Dartmoor blizzards before that, but how many hungry miles would it take to escape Yorkshire? Were they headed for London? Home, as his father called it? Decidedly not. If Yorkshire held nothing for him, London held less than nothing.

He hungered for somewhere distant, somewhere epic, somewhere full of valleys, mountain ponies, beacons, Brecons—Wales? Wales! Ancient Cambria, land of his father's mother's people! The body gave no acknowledgment, but Morgan knew he had discovered its secret. For Wales they were bound, though plainly they weren't going to walk the whole way, not with three shillings sixpence in their pocket. The path would lead them to Fridaythorpe, but there was nothing in that village beyond a public house, a church, and a post-office shop, all in the middle of precisely nowhere.

The post-office shop! He aha'ed to let the body know that he was onto it.

—So that's it, he said aloud. The post-office van!

They were to hitch a ride in the back of the post-office van, like some self-mailing parcel, posting themselves on to the next destination, Doncaster perhaps, and proceeding thusly to their terminus beyond England's western border. He smiled in triumph as they plunged deeper into Grindalythe Woods, later into the night, farther from the Academy and his friends, who had ejected him like so much rubbish from a life raft, farther from everything known—ten minutes out, a thousand paces out, half a mile out, out, out, and out.

✦

The clock on the church was stuck at half past seven. Beneath the dial, words mocked, *Time is short, eternity long.* They made him want to punch someone again.

The walk through the woods had warmed him, but it wouldn't last. He tried the front and back doors of the Keys and found them locked. This he considered unfair. What possible reason could there be to lock anything in Fridaythorpe? The post-office shop he found similarly inaccessible, though the mailbag languished on the stoop awaiting early collection. How utterly typical. The post office they locked, but the mail they left unattended in the night. People everywhere were idiots.

An unholy racket like the sound of a tin shed collapsing dispelled the quiet of the night. He ducked down a passage between the post office and the adjacent block of houses. Pressing his back against the damp wall, he rubbed his shoulder, now sore from being out of its wrappings. The noise grew louder, and he realized it was no collapsed shed but merely a cat fight amongst dustbins, loud enough to wake the dead.

He slid to the ground and held his arm against his chest as a part of his mind carried on jauntily with its caper: He must stay hidden down yonder snicket, in case the cats roused anyone. He mustn't be caught just as his adventure was beginning. He could watch for the van, and then, oh, what ripping yarns he'd have! He'd outgrown ripping yarns long ago, of course, but even Stalky grew up to stalk in India. If he was bound for Wales, it could only be because his full-grown courage demanded broad horizons. It was a shame the post bag wasn't big enough to fit inside of. That would have been the best plan; instead, he'd have to wait for the driver to load the bag and return to the cab before he slipped in the back. Oh, it would require timing, exquisite timing, and although it might hurt quite a bit given his tedious arm, he would prevail. He would, because that was the only turn his story could take!

As this corner of his mind prattled, he felt fatigued. A light flicked on above the post office, startling him to his feet and driving him farther down the snicket. He unlatched a gate and scarpered into the garden behind the houses. Presently, a woman in dressing gown emerged from the back of the post office and began to upbraid the cats. Other lights came on, in the house belonging to the garden and in the one next door. Morgan stayed hidden until the woman went back inside, but his mind continued painting a dashing picture of hitchhiking across the countryside, of food stolen from dustbins—unfortunately, the cats had got to Fridaythorpe's—of Huns thwarted, rescues achieved; even Stalky's attack on the Khye-Kheens would pale beside the campaigns that awaited him.

In the middle of the garden, there was a boulder surrounded by a patch of dirt. Morgan sat down on the rock and let his head rest upon his knees. He had no intention of falling asleep; he was merely huddling to conserve warmth and to rest his arm. His mind demanded he keep an ear for any approaching vehicle. Wearily, Morgan agreed.

When Emily ran away, it was daytime, and spring, and she left carrying a cloth as if for a picnic. She ran away demanding that no one follow her because she had perfect confidence that someone would. Not only someone, but the one person she wished to follow her, their father. She had probably performed the entire drama to force a crisis, a kind of closeness through confrontation with the person she trusted and loved and needed.

There was no one Morgan could expect to come after him. Even if the Academy could stir itself to realize he was missing, it would be midmorning at the earliest. He could not expect his father to come north looking for him. Even if someone filed a missing person report, how much interest could the constabulary take? He might be a schoolboy, but boys his age worked down the mines, in shipyards, in a hundred and one trades across the land. Soon he'd even be able to vote in elections, should they ever deign to occur. In all likelihood, the Academy would dispose him for bunking off.

But his father would worry, and so would his sisters, inconsolably. When they finally found him, Veronica would tear strips off him and then start all over again in the morning. She would make him feel wretched, as wretched as he deserved. Silly, vain, pathetic.

Though what should he do instead? Return to the Academy, haul himself back through the woods, back to the House, the dorm, and the two he had lied to? (And wasn't he the worst sort of liar, the kind everyone believed . . . ?)

Morgan raised his head and saw that all the lights had gone out, save the one in the house whose garden this was. The curtain lay askew as if someone had pulled it aside and not replaced it properly. He could see a wall and a bookcase, but nothing else—except for a garden door, which was opening and revealing a man, a man in dressing gown, a man who paused on the threshold and gazed into the darkened garden, a man who stepped off the stoop and padded across the wetted grass in slippers, towards him, a man he knew.

His body would not move.

Mr. Grieves stopped, stuffed his hands into the pockets of his dressing gown, and looked at him. Morgan looked back.

—Come on, Mr. Grieves said.

He beckoned as if nothing were amiss, as if there were nothing to refuse, nothing to resist, as if it were perfectly natural for him to fetch Morgan from his garden in the middle of the night.

The body did not ask permission but uncurled itself and stood. Mr. Grieves walked alongside, a silent companion across the swath of grass. At the door, Mr. Grieves gestured for Morgan to precede him. The body, rogue agent, stepped into the passageway and up a tilting flight of stairs to a door, which Mr. Grieves opened, admitting them to his rooms.

—Sit down.

The body did as Mr. Grieves bid it, collapsing into a wooden chair at a small table. Mr. Grieves retired to an alcove, where he lit a gas ring and put a kettle on to boil. He filled a toothglass from the tap and set it in front of Morgan. Morgan gazed at it and felt Mr. Grieves gazing at him, as if examining him for damage. It was cold in the flat, almost as cold as it had been in the garden. Morgan pulled the muffler over his mouth and ears, sleeves over fingers. The air from the room no longer touched him. Presently he would wake in his bed and ordinary life would resume, dry, heartless, but recognizable.

The kettle whined. Mr. Grieves assembled tea things: a pot wrapped with a flannel, unmatched cups, one chipped, which Mr. Grieves took for himself after wiping the other for Morgan, a tin of sugar, a nearly empty bottle of milk brought in from the windowsill.

—You drink that.

Mr. Grieves gestured to the toothglass and then rooted in the open shelving for another tin, water crackers, which he poured carelessly into the lid and set on the table. Dry crackers and water felt oddly appropriate, and under Mr. Grieves's gaze, Morgan drank and ate. His tongue seemed enlarged, its sensibility magnified, detecting the lead of the pipes, the lime and peat of the water, even the dust that must have lined the glass. As he emerged from the cocoon of scarf and coat, he began to sense the outlines of the place: cold, shabby, even more so than the studies back at the Academy. The floorboards here wore a rug, but it didn't look as though it had ever been beaten out, and it was unraveling along one side. Unlike the studies, Mr. Grieves's windows possessed drapes, but they, too, looked thirdhand and possibly moldy. The bed, which Morgan glimpsed through an arch, was larger than his own, but its mattress sagged in a way that made him think of a backache. Only the books on the shelves seemed cared for. Mr. Grieves's clothing hung out of sight somewhere, with the exception of a pair of socks, which dangled below the drapes, clipped in place by the window. Morgan could see no radiator, only a gas heater with a meter on it, like the one they'd had at that dreary hotel in Bournemouth last Christmastime. Beside the armchair languished a pile of exercise books.

Mr. Grieves's satchel bulged. A clock chimed the quarter hour, a clock that must have been ticking all the while.

Mr. Grieves unwrapped the pot, poured out the tea, stirred in milk and sugar, and plunked the cup before Morgan with a determined expression.

—Right, he said, I think you had better start talking.

There was a lump in his chest, and his blood had slowed to something hot and viscous. Irresistible, to sit there at Mr. Grieves's table, the man's eyes upon him. No one would disturb them. Mr. Grieves had nothing, apparently, to do besides cross his fingers around his teacup and let his thumb caress the chip.

—I didn't do it, sir.

Mr. Grieves's eyes widened.

—I didn't know about it either. I know who did, now, but I didn't then. I promise.

Mr. Grieves scrutinized him, his eyes deepest brown, impossible in the light even to distinguish from black. And as he stared, a chill crossed Morgan's scalp, announcing something uncanny. His mouth had spoken without his leave, but Mr. Grieves did not ask what he meant.

I didn't do it would most rationally refer to the explosion in the chemistry lab. It would be reasonable to say such a thing when caught out-of-bounds in the middle of the night. It would be reasonable to inform Mr. Grieves that he was not running away from punishment. But Mr. Grieves was not looking at him as though Morgan were speaking of the explosion. Mr. Grieves was looking at him as though they were speaking of the thing that had come between them three years ago and never quite departed. Mr. Grieves's expression was in fact a tell, one that confirmed Mr. Grieves still thought of that time and bore a grudge.

However freely Morgan might lie about any number of things, he was telling the truth about the Gallowhill business. He had not taken advantage of Mr. Grieves's friendship to ruin the dig. He had not insulted Gallowhill's memory by engineering the prank. He hadn't known who did it when Mr. Grieves questioned him that day.

—I believe you, Mr. Grieves said at last.

A weight, one Morgan didn't until that moment know he bore, seemed to slip from his shoulders, as he felt the pilfered gloves slip from his overcoat. He picked them up and set them on the table beside the cracker lid.

—I stole these, he said.

—From whom?

—Holland.

Mr. Grieves examined one of the gloves.

—Won't Holland miss them?

Morgan nodded. Mr. Grieves regarded him again.

—Why did you steal them?

—I needed them.

—Why?

The bald simplicity startled him, and he felt a pleasurably painful freezing like he used to feel before entering Silk's study for Accounting. Every other grown-up framed questions with commentary, sarcasm, rebuke, or with a clear indication of the answer they required. Mr. Grieves's query in its nakedness was at once more curious and more exacting than any Morgan could have expected.

—The cold, he said.

—And are you cold now?

Morgan dipped a fingertip into his tea and found it too hot.

—Drink that, Mr. Grieves said.

Morgan lifted the cup to his lips. Mr. Grieves, a human mirror, did the same.

—And? Mr. Grieves prompted.

Morgan held his cup closer.

—As we're in the confessional, you may as well out with it, Mr. Grieves said.

—Out with what?

—All of it.

And a wall rose up before him, like the waves Poseidon raised to crush Odysseus's ship, a wall of everything the question had summoned. Here they were, outside the Academy, somewhere in the free world, subject only to the softly ticking clock. They might stay here forever, that gaze forever upon him, forever ready to listen to the truth.

But he couldn't sit there eternally mute. Time did turn, and patience, even from Mr. Grieves, had a limit. If he continued to say nothing, Mr. Grieves would grow bored with him and decide his problems were better confessed to someone else.

—I don't know where to start, sir.

Mr. Grieves refilled his own cup:

—How about with what you were doing in my landlord's garden at three o'clock in the morning.

—Isn't three o'clock supposed to be the wickedest hour of the night, sir? The reverse of when Christ died on the cross?

—Don't evade.

So known to be cornered thus, the way Silk cornered him, but more clear-sighted. Silk had been able to see to his heart, but sometimes what Silk claimed to see there was only a reflection of Silk's own ideas, the ones from his idea shelf that he kept so proudly polished, regardless of their relation to reality. But Mr. Grieves was not a man to make guesses. Mr. Grieves relied on evidence. Now for instance, he had offered no hypothesis concerning Morgan's circumstances; he merely searched for facts. Already he could tell truth from evasion. Already in his understanding he had sensed the real Morgan Wilberforce, the one Nathan and Laurie missed, the one even Silk mistook, the one his father no longer sought.

—Morgan?

And now he was calling him by his Christian name, as he hadn't in years.

—I didn't know it was your garden, sir.

—Oh, no?

—No, sir. I swear it!

—I believe you.

A tightness in his chest noticed only in the loosening.

—Nevertheless? Mr. Grieves prompted.

—The cats were fighting, and I was . . . waiting for the mail.

Mr. Grieves turned those brown-and-black eyes on him again— believing, demanding, searching—until Morgan somehow, without the right words, without paragraphing, without thesis of any kind, unfolded the story: the trek through the woods, the post-office van, Wales . . .

—And yet, Mr. Grieves said, you didn't actually want to go to Wales, did you?

Morgan certainly did want to go to Wales. In fact he still wanted to go there. Wanted to and would!

—You made for Fridaythorpe, Mr. Grieves observed, not the station, which is closer to the Academy. You imagined a post-office van rather than a luggage car, which is bigger and easier for concealment. You chose a vague destination and lacked a compelling reason to go there. And you hid in my garden when you ought to have been pursuing transport.

It made him sound a duffer, fit for nothing but imprisonment in a run-down school amidst people who neither understood nor wanted him. He dug at the table with a fingernail.

—God knows I'm a complete waste of space, sir.

Mr. Grieves straightened:

—God knows nothing of the sort.

His skin tingled as though the air had grown heavier.

—You're focusing on the wrong thing, Mr. Grieves said.

—I suppose I ought to be focusing on how lucky I am to be at a school at all, to have food, clothing, friends, a family who love me . . .

He almost added *et cetera, et cetera.*

—That's undoubtedly true, said Mr. Grieves, but not just now very interesting.

—What in God's name is interesting, sir?

—Stop taking the Lord's name in vain, please. And stop wallowing.

Mr. Grieves's voice was mild though his words were not, as if he could take any amount of railing and respond unfazed.

—The question you ought to be asking is what.

—What?

—Yes, Morgan, what. What is it in that heart of yours strong enough to wake you in the night and take you from the only home you know to a vague and ill-considered destination you had no desire actually to reach?

The room didn't change color. There was no smashing that he could point to. It was more incremental, as if a heavy mantle had been laid upon his shoulders and was gradually revealing its weight. As he grew accustomed to its pressure, it grew heavier, yet it answered a longing so hidden it could only be known in satisfaction. To be held so always, to have his heart seen, known, and shown to him, to be reeled in from error so lightly, as if someone existed who truly knew right from wrong, someone capable of enforcing this distinction on him, someone for whom it was as natural as breath.

His father had been that kind of man once, but even then his father had never stood apart from the world as Mr. Grieves had done when he refused to take up arms in the War. Morgan couldn't fathom what would drive a man to such a stance, but whatever it was, it must have come from the clarity Mr. Grieves now possessed.

—Well?

—I don't know, sir.

—Of course you do. Try harder.

The mantle settled again, and a pressure in his throat that made his voice sound queer.

—I . . .

Was it possible that Mr. Grieves would not retreat? Was it possible that he would sit there telling Morgan to try harder until he provided an actual answer?

—I suppose I must have wanted to be found, sir.

So bald, and so inadequate.

—I thought as much.

Now the eyes! He *thought* as much? How could Mr. Grieves have thought *anything*?

—I didn't mean it like that, sir, I meant—

—Shh.

Then like a coal, Mr. Grieves's fingers touched his wrist, and Morgan saw in those eyes a softness he could scarcely endure.

—You've been lost?

Morgan cast his gaze to the tabletop, to the ridges in the wood where crumbs had collected, but it began to blur, and he retracted his wrist into his sleeve, his hands clasped together like a monk's. He needed a gesture that would make light of Mr. Grieves's words. He needed a rebuttal, but the mantle was so heavy, so protective in its burden, so desirable, so filling.

—You need a lot of looking after, don't you?

The warmth of that voice buckled the last support that remained, and Poseidon's wave struck, drowning his men, splintering his ship, and dragging him into that salty, breathless sea. Was it so easy to demolish his reserves, built with such effort all these years? The last time he'd been reduced to such blubbering had also involved a weight on his chest, a devastating pain there on Silk's study floor. How had Mr. Grieves accomplished as much barely touching him? He buried his head in his arms, helpless against the sea, until, like Ino's veil, a handkerchief appeared at his ear. He put it under his nose.

—I'm too old for that, sir.

—Are you?

Again his throat seized. Again he hid his face in his arms. Mr. Grieves went to put on more water.

—Let's review facts, Mr. Grieves said, running the tap. First, you were sufficiently motivated to abscond from the Academy tonight. Reason not yet established. Second, you left without supplies and you made for an illogical destination. Why? Because you wanted to be found. Third, you have confessed to glove theft, but your manner indicates a person far more compromised than such a crime would suggest.

Through salt water, Morgan's face burned again.

—Are you in some danger at the Academy?

—No, sir.

—Are you a danger to someone?

Was he?

—No, sir.

—Points off for hesitation. Have you done something wrong and fear being found out?

He'd done countless things wrong, all of them commonplace. He didn't fear punishment from any authority.

—I'm not afraid of being found out, sir.

—Then perhaps you're afraid of not being found out.

Morgan inhaled sharply, and in the moment that followed, he saw he'd given himself away. A grin colonized Mr. Grieves's face.

—Of course! Mr. Grieves said. In that case, young Morgan—

He wasn't young! He was seventeen years old!

—I think you had better make up your mind to tell me everything, and I mean everything. I'll grant you the seal of confession for the next . . .

He craned to see the clock.

—three-quarters of an hour.

—But you aren't a clergyman, sir. You aren't even a proper—

He stopped before he said *Christian*.

—Yes, yes, Mr. Grieves replied airily. We're all imperfect servants. But you're wasting time.

If anyone else had bid him make a full, vocal confession of every wrongdoing, he would have dismissed them as pious or naïve. Now, though, a hunger came over him for the particular form of discomfort Mr. Grieves had been inflicting since he entered the flat.

—I've lied, sir.

Mr. Grieves nodded, giving no indication whether he found Morgan's words surprising.

—I've been lying for a long time.

—To?

—My father. Pearl and Lydon. Everyone.

—To yourself?

He hesitated.

—Go on, Mr. Grieves prompted.

—That's all there is.

Mr. Grieves appraised him:

—You don't want people to know the truth.

—They wouldn't like the truth!

—And what is the truth?

Morgan felt there should be a falling sensation to accompany the dreadful precipice on which he stood. The truth, if he ever could explain it, would destroy everything.

Yet, wasn't everything worthwhile destroyed already?

—Love, sir.

—Yes?

—Yes.

—Loving people you oughtn't?

Morgan nodded.

—Go on.

—Love is perhaps a dramatic way of putting it.

—Perhaps.

How could he explain whom he had loved? Silk, Nathan, his mother, his sisters, that girl with the tennis serve, Mr. Grieves himself, and that was just off the top of his head, not counting those for whom he had only lusted. Was it right to love and wrong to lust? Wrong to love Silk Bradley, who had been so wicked and desolate, who had nobody perhaps to love him besides Morgan?

Silk had told him to pour a second cup of tea that day Fletcher had been in the Tower. Morgan had filled Fletcher's cup and set it beside the parcel wrapped in brown paper, which had appeared in the study that morning.

—If you tell anyone, you'll be sorry, Silk had said. Even Fletch.

Morgan had nodded, uncomprehending, and sat at Silk's command, like those other times, but not like those other times. Silk had sliced open the package, revealing Kendal Mint Cake and a letter he pocketed without reading. He broke the cake in two and set half before Morgan.

—Go on, he said, dipping his own into the tea.

Tentatively, Morgan took a bite. The mint was fresh, potent.

—Wiggie, Silk explained. Takes pity once a year.

—Lent?

—Birthday.

Morgan's head had spun wondering why Silk didn't have a hamper if it was his birthday, why no one knew, and why he wasn't sharing his godmother's present with his best friend.

—I can see what you're thinking, Silk had said, and it's a bore. Fletch thinks my birthday's in the hols. And the antecedents never send presents.

Morgan drank from Fletcher's cup, sharing Silk's only present, bound to secrecy in the gray light of day.

✦

Morgan Wilberforce sat at his table, eyes swollen and red. Outside, daylight crept implacably towards them. John had only seen him shed tears once before, in that odd encounter over the boy's birthday his first year. Wilberforce had waited all day for his birthday hamper and then heard Fardley declare the hamper wasn't coming, and what's more had never been ordered. It was shortly after the boy's mother had died, John recalled, the oversight surely due to the father's distracted grief; but it was custom at the school for parents to send birthday hampers, and when Fardley destroyed all hope, Wilberforce had buried his face in John's coat and wept, stirring in John a feeling both paternal and avuncular. John had killed that feeling after the Gallowhill business, but now—like divine reprieve after years of hopelessness—John could see that Wilberforce had been telling the truth after all. The night was wiping the slate clean of all dust, requiring neither contrition nor atonement. Like a simple misunderstanding, the past was being blown away, and John was sitting at a table with the same boy, albeit taller, inside the same cloister of rapport.

He wanted more than anything to sort this boy out, but his position at the Academy was ancillary at best. He had no authority outside his classroom and not much inside it. He had never done a dorm round, never communicated freely with a parent, never had a study to which he could invite boys for . . . what could it be called? Moral influence? For whatever it was men gave to boys. For the kind of thing the Bishop had given him before—but he made it a rule never to think of that time. He had never comforted (counseled? catechized?) any boy in the night. The closest he'd come was the odd night terror when his goddaughter was small. She would enter his room in the dead of night, take his hand, and begin conversing with him. It always took him longer than it ought to realize that she was failing to make sense and that she was not, in fact, awake. Morgan Wilberforce was most certainly awake. Would John be capable of such a sorting out, even if he possessed the means?

The boy had confessed to loving someone he oughtn't. Well, he wasn't the first boy, and he'd hardly be the last. John couldn't encourage him, but he didn't see the point in making a fuss over it.

—Has loving this person led you to do things you oughtn't?

Morgan Wilberforce went confused behind the eyes:

—Which . . . ?

He dried up.

—Which one? John supplied.

A blush. John was beginning to see the problem. Not an ardent public school friendship, but a whole raft of unsuitable attachments. He thought he knew something about both.

—Do you know what I think, sir? I think God's made a balls-up of this whole business.

—Oh, yes?

—Look at the world, sir. Look at the War.

John sighed.

There were so very many ways this boy needed sorting out, John felt nearly breathless contemplating them. He felt even more overwhelmed considering what the Headmaster would say about his hosting a late-night, out-of-bounds confabulation with a pupil. He needed to get this boy back where he belonged before a scandal ensued, or worse.

An idea came to him then, as they did when he wasn't trying, a memory of a book he'd been reading earlier. He fetched it from the windowsill and, flicking back in the pages, found the passage. He read it aloud standing under the lightbulb:

—*He said that it was not fair, when a man had made something for a purpose, to try to say it was not good before we know what his purpose with it was. I don't like, he said, even my wife to look at my verses before they're finished! God can't hide away his work till it is finished, as I do my verses, and we ought to take care what we say about it. God wants to do something better with people than people think.*

John could hear the question Morgan Wilberforce wanted to ask, and the boy's silence struck him as a kind of deep companionship, an acknowledgment that the question and its corollary—What did God want with Wilberforce? What did he want with either of them?—had no vocal answer. That Wilberforce appeared to know it said more about the boy than almost anything else that night.

A flurry of ideas began to come to John then, and he knew from hard-learned experience with ideas that the only thing to do was to obey without overthinking. He certainly ought not to ponder why he—dogged by insomnia and pacing his frigid rooms—should have investigated the carousing of tomcats at the same moment that a St. Stephen's boy had wandered into his garden, and not any St. Stephen's boy, but Morgan Wilberforce. The important thing was that ideas were continuing to arrive like a host of relatives. (Not that he had a host of relatives—but he made it a rule—never mind.) The ideas told him that whatever had driven Wilberforce from the Academy that night was neither single, concrete, nor precisely relevant; that the boy was compromised, but not in the way people might imagine; that the sorting out would take time and quite possibly require other hands; and that most essentially John needed to get this boy back to the Academy before his absence was discovered and circumstances became complicated by irrelevancies. John was certain as he could be that the answer to the opus called Morgan Wilberforce would not be found in his traipsing across Yorkshire, or Wales, but would grow somehow into itself after his return to ordinary life, arising this morning from the philistine dormitories of Hazlehurst's House, sleepwalking through lessons, and facing whatever else the day delivered. He had the idea that change was sweeping towards them. He didn't know what, but he could feel its breath cold on his neck.

Before any of this could transpire, however, Morgan Wilberforce needed conveying back to the Academy. A glance at the clock told him there wasn't enough time to send the boy on foot, and in any case, John didn't entirely trust him to return on his own.

He braced himself. It would have to be the bicycle. Lord, help them.

Mr. Grieves was out of his tiny mind. First, he fixed on the notion of cycling back to the Academy in the dark with Morgan perched on his handlebars. This quickly proved impossible, as Morgan had predicted. Undeterred, Mr. Grieves insisted Morgan balance on the book rack, which promptly broke, again as Morgan said it would. Mr. Grieves, ever resolute, instructed Morgan to sit on the bicycle seat whilst Mr. Grieves himself attempted to pedal standing up. Not until Morgan had fallen painfully onto the pavement did Mr. Grieves concede defeat.

By this time, Morgan knew, he could have been halfway home through Grindalythe Woods, but as he was not at liberty to explain his route, he could not dispute Mr. Grieves's view that Morgan had little chance of regaining his bed undetected even if he ran his best cross-country race of the term. Thwarted in his schemes, Mr. Grieves accepted the only logical solution.

—Right then, he said with the sternness of the classroom, you will take this bicycle and ride back to the Academy on your own.

When Morgan asked what transport that left Mr. Grieves, Mr. Grieves asserted, with stoical air, that he would walk. Morgan was to conceal the bicycle behind the disused shed some distance from the gates. Mr. Grieves would retrieve it and ride up at his usual hour. But first, Mr. Grieves enjoined Morgan to take a vow, solemnly looking him in the eye, promising that he would indeed return to St. Stephen's Academy, that he would brook no detour, that he would above all else extinguish any notions of running away—to Wales, to Westmoreland, yea even to Wetwang or Warte Wold.

The oath embarrassed Morgan. Whatever had taken him from the Academy had shrunk to mere fancy. He had no more intention of running away than he did of hanging himself from a rafter somewhere; that is to say, none at all. The sooner he was out of the place—hideous Friday-thorpe, Mr. Grieves's squalid digs, the whole uncolored night—the sooner he would feel right in his mind again.

—I promise, sir.

Mr. Grieves relinquished the handlebars; Morgan mounted the bicycle and pedaled down the Wetwang road.

The machine needed grease. The squeaking of the brakes and noise of the gears were enough to wake the neighborhood. As he swerved to avoid the dark potholes and pumped painfully up the slight incline, his earlier embarrassment ripened into mortification. How long had he spent cracking up, saying who knew what demented things, across Mr. Grieves's table? An ordinary person would never have behaved so. An ordinary person would be asleep in the frigid dorm, or perhaps, if awake, consoling himself with—no, an ordinary person did not console himself with such things. An ordinary person would be thinking of the coming rugby match. A person such as Spaulding, for instance, were he now awake, would be reviewing maneuvers, pondering his opponents' weaknesses, or retiring to the toilets to do press-ups.

It hurt quite astonishingly to pedal a bicycle with one squiff arm. Mr. Grieves had worried like a flapping sister over that as well, but Morgan had assured him that his arm was nearly better. Now, having spent the whole, torturous night out of its bandages, the arm was staging a fit of temper, extending its cramp across both shoulders and down his rib cage. He'd never noticed until just that moment how much one used one's arms to pedal a bicycle.

There remained the more nauseating task of facing Grieves in lessons. How would someone like Spaulding manage it? Spaulding would flash that grin of his, the one that drew everyone to him as magnets drew pins. Spaulding might even proceed to slack twice as hard in History and treat Grieves with as much coolness as he'd treated Morgan in the changing room. Spaulding would put the past behind him. He would permit no one—no undermaster, Housemaster, Headmaster, or friend— to perturb his calm. Whatever the circumstances, Spaulding would carry on—

Two figures moved in the darkness ahead. He clamped the brake and skidded to a halt; the figures froze, but after an exchange of whispers, they continued down the lane.

His hands shook. Both he and the figures were less than half a mile from the gates. Down this path, the figures could be headed nowhere else. He couldn't see any detail of their appearance except to notice that they were neither stooped nor juvenile. Morgan waited until their footsteps faded and then dismounted to push the bicycle the rest of the way.

He soon gained the disused shed where he was to store the thing. Thus unencumbered, he jogged as best as he could through the alley of trees. Darkness was fading, and he had no trouble seeing that the two figures had reduced to one. He had no trouble observing that single figure climbing through the Tower window, the window Morgan had used to escape, the one he required to return. And he had no trouble now recognizing that figure. Spaulding: ordinary, extraordinary.

A light appeared in Fardles's window. The gatekeeper was rising from sleep, preparing to extinguish the lamp and unlock the gates. As the Tower window closed behind Spaulding, Morgan dashed for it, confident that he could haul himself through before Fardles could stuff wrinkly legs into trousers. As he reached for the casement, though, he encountered firmness, a firmness hitherto unknown.

This window had never greeted him firmly. Ever since he had made its acquaintance in the Fourth Form, proud in his stewardship of the poacher's tunnel, it had treated him as friend and accomplice, permitting him to depart and return more evenings than he could count. But now, as Fardley stirred in his rooms, the window ignored the prying of his fingers. It stood latched in its frame, resolute against the likes of him—a boy who had shrunk off in cowardice, who had abandoned the Academy and all it had asked of him. Spaulding may have transgressed in the night, but Morgan had quit the field, and even though he was now returned, the Tower knew his traitorous heart. It knew what had caused him to charge Spaulding during that match. The Tower knew every dream he'd dreamt while lying unprotected within it. The Tower knew the covenant he had entered into with the Academy, whether or not he had realized it at the time, when Silk had passed to him the secret of the poacher's tunnel, making him its guardian, the heir of Hermes, that prankster Old Boy who had discovered the route. The Tower knew of wish slips in the Hermes Balcony; it knew of Mr. Grieves and the trenches they had dug that first year; it knew of every Old Boy to enter and depart, of Silk, of Gallowhill, of Hermes himself. And yet, the Tower refused him entrance, no longer caring for such a one, a boy who ran away.

✦

John got under the covers and closed his eyes. He thought he ought to sleep, or at least instruct his body to repose. He could feel weariness overcoming him just as it always did when there was no longer any chance for rest. His mind's eye saw Morgan Wilberforce at his table, red-eyed, drawn, pretense shattered. He felt the thrill of the boy's raw appeal, his eyes begging the relief he could not ask.

The timepiece at John's ear erupted. He slapped it silent and dragged himself into the dank, chill room. With cold water he shaved, cleaned his teeth, and bullied his hair into presentable form. He changed his shirt and socks, arranged his necktie, gave his suit a cursory brush. With an anxious yet excited glance at the mantel clock, he shouldered his bulging satchel and departed.

If he could understand somehow what burden Morgan Wilberforce needed to have carried, then perhaps he could find a way to pick it up for him. Perhaps John actually was needed, and perhaps the night was a sign writ large that he must not quit the field even if Burton and the Eagle did. Perhaps Morgan Wilberforce would abscond again during Prep tonight and meet him at the Keys. They might talk again. They might make a custom of it for the nights that remained to the term. They might—but he mustn't get ahead of himself. It was his unhelpful habit, he knew, to allow his mind to fly far in advance of facts, losing the plot altogether.

He had a composition to spring on the Remove that morning, and a lecture for the Third on Vikings. The Fourth would have to be flogged through a revision of their Charlemagne paragraphs, if such a thing was possible without actual anarchy, and as for the Sixth, he doubted he could stomach another day of their jaded complacency. He hadn't marked their compositions from four days ago, and he knew they would ask. The mere thought of the dog's dinner they would have made of the Reform Act, not to mention the English language, was enough to make him throw up his breakfast, if he'd eaten any.

But he could see the shed now where he expected his bicycle, and if Providence possessed a measure of mercy, Morgan Wilberforce would have kept his word and John would be permitted to cycle the last stretch and take the pressure off the blister that had formed vengefully in his left shoe. And in fact, there was the bicycle! He mounted it and filled with hope—that the blister would fade, that the highly irregular night would not lead to disaster, that despite his somewhat late arrival he would be able to cadge a bit of breakfast before prayers. He wheeled up to the gates, almost triumphant, and found them . . . locked.

Beyond them, in the middle of the quad, a heap of debris smoldered, filling the air with the scent of gunpowder.

John's heart began to race. He called out. No one answered. The Tower clock began to toll. As if in reply, Fardley burst into the quad from the cloisters arch.

—Hello! John shouted.

Fardley raised his hand as if silencing a nuisance of a child and disappeared into Burton-Lee's House. John called after him, annoyance rising. Whatever had transpired, Fardley ought to enlist John's help. He might be only an undermaster, but he'd been on a battlefield; it made no sense to leave him standing in the road like some kind of patent-medicine salesman.

Minutes passed. At last Fardley emerged from Burton-Lee's and waved his arms in the direction of the playing fields:

—Go round!

—Pardon?

—Go round! Fardley elaborated.

—Go round where?

—Thataway! Hazlehurst's study.

—What happened? John demanded. What's the matter with the gates?

—No time!

Fardley veered towards Clement's House, issuing over his shoulder another foghorn *Go round!*

John went round. Suppressing panic, he picked his way across the flooded playing fields, but his shoes broke the skin of ice, plunging his feet entirely into water. He cursed Fardley for his idiocy, cursed Hazlehurst for the location of his study, and cursed S-K for everything else.

✦

Morgan lay under the covers mentally retracing the madcap route he had been forced to take across the playing fields, through his Housemaster's French windows, ajar thanks to indolence or to the benevolence of some god, and up the back staircase to the changing room. The windows were glowing gray when he slipped back into the long, open dorm, but no one had been awake, and he'd regained his bed undetected. He was lying there, eyelids off duty, when Rabbet burst in to wake the dorm prefect at the other end. A fierce, hushed exchange, and Rabbet dashed away. The dorm prefect, after a moment of resentful hesitation, lunged from bed, snatched dressing gown, and followed their Head Boy.

Morgan realized he had been holding his breath. They were apparently not exercised about him, yet his mind raced: Had he left Hazlehurst's windows as he'd found them? Had he left anything amiss in the changing room? Had he been seen?

A pair of fags at the other end were whispering, and now it seemed they were out of bed, clattering about, receiving clattering visitors. Morgan could not, after a sleepless night, countenance fevered gossip. Whatever had roused the prefects would make itself known to everyone soon enough. Perhaps there had been a break in the recent mystery . . . what was it, again? Oh, how distant school business seemed! How could he drag himself, cotton headed, through the day?

Whatever was exciting the fags now stirred others from their beds. Morgan burrowed farther under the covers, his arm tingling and sore. He would get up in a moment, but now his limbs refused to budge, longing for the sleep they were owed, bewailing the failure of night to knit up their ragged sleeves, heavy, aggrieved, allergic to the day.

✦

It took John longer than he considered decent to decipher what was happening. Prefects, hastily dressed, dashed two steps at a time up and down staircases. Masters, half dressed, barked things after them and shouted orders to the servants, who moved more quickly than their sullen demeanors usually allowed. John sat at the masters' table for breakfast, joined only by Clement. A prefect said the grace, which seemed to disconcert everyone, as if the words were sacrilege if spoken by anyone but the Headmaster. Clement, in his typically serene manner, provided John a précis: Those with windows giving onto the quadrangle had been wakened that morning by a fizz and a crack and a whoosh, all announcing fire in the center of the courtyard. Various parties had rushed to extinguish it, but had been thwarted by doors whose locks were frozen with a substance thought to be wax. Two of Burton-Lee's prefects had climbed out windows, but by the time they reached the fire, it was waning. The collection of canes had burnt quickly, and the conflagration had not spread to the architecture, thank the Lord. In addition to the gates and the doors of the Houses, a good many of the school's other locks had been bunged-up, to use the language of the Third Form, and John was exceedingly fortunate that Hazlehurst's study possessed no lock, else he might even now be standing outside the gates, freezing like a tradesman. The fracas, Clement concluded, had been rousing.

Clem's serenity usually irked John, but this morning he found it refreshing, even comical. John wondered idly whether the form rooms would be opened in time for lessons, and if not, what S-K would do with the school. It struck him that obstinate normality was the only suitable response. If form rooms could not be opened, lessons must occur standing in the cloisters, seated on gravel in the quad, striding briskly across the playing fields, or in ranks in the refectory. S-K must on no account let himself be drawn by the business. He must not make precipitous announcements or idle threats. Prefects must not be authorized to take justice into their own hands. Investigations must occur quietly, and the school given the impression of solid, unruffled authority.

 S-K had gathered them into the chapel and was now letting loose with all the brimstone he possessed. Never in the history of the Academy had he witnessed such wanton destruction, such despicable anarchism, such utter disregard for one's fellow man. Where was their shame? Whither their pride? How long would they permit a perverse few to lay waste to the bonds that united them as Christians and as human beings? Surely the War had not been fought so that pert, amoral schoolboys could indulge themselves at the expense of an entire society. Thus was the way of wholesale dissipation, the way of cities whose doom had shortly come upon them, of Sodom, Gomorrah, of the idolatrous nations of Israel.

Coughing from the masters' pew interrupted the Headmaster's tirade long enough to recall him to his purpose. For they were not to imagine, vile wastrels, that he would spend another farthing of his outrage on them. (Morgan could feel the mental rejoicing within each boy, and likely master.) Nay! The Headmaster would leave them to rot in their own putrescence until the guilty parties came—or were brought— forward.

To that end, lessons were canceled. Games were canceled. Even meals were canceled. (A muted gasp, followed by tremors of grumbling.) S-K called for silence with the thunder of Yahweh, and got it. Until such time as this hideous misdeed vomited its perpetrators onto his study floor, until that time, the Lower School and Remove would be confined to the refectory. The Upper School would remain in its studies. Further, S-K boomed, pitching his voice even higher to drown out their protests, further! They were not to entertain illusions regarding the instruments of justice so crudely incinerated. The Headmaster had already ordered replacements, which his supplier had promised to dispatch posthaste. In the meantime, they had better know that the Headmaster's deputies were under direct instruction to spare nothing in the maintenance of order. To their chambers, therefore, would they go, and in their chambers would they remain until such time as the guilty stood before him, prepared to suffer his full and righteous wrath.

✦

A grim life, a hungry life, but one that miraculously provided opportunity to sleep. Morgan felt he had crossed into a new world. Whether the frontier had been passed when he'd crawled out the Tower window, or when Mr. Grieves had walked towards him in the garden, or when he had spied Spaulding on the road, he couldn't say, but the events that enraged the Headmaster failed to touch him. Who could care about pranks after such a night?

No study was to have coal, but they settled not unhappily into the unexpected free time. Morgan called bags on the window seat and stretched across it under a rug. The room had just begun to spin pleasantly when he heard steps. He opened his eyes to Nathan and Laurie looming above.

—What?

Nathan inhaled sharply. Laurie murmured:

—We'll hear it now instead of later, thanks.

He felt he ought to sit up. If they were going to haul him through last night again, he had no intention of taking it literally lying down.

—You were behind this whole mess, Nathan said evenly. Admit it.

Morgan relaxed:

—I wasn't.

—Then you helped.

—I don't know anything more than you do. That's the truth.

He shoved a cushion against the draft in the window and pulled the rug up to his chin.

Then—how did it happen?—Laurie had hurtled onto his chest, as he did to Alex when they set upon him. With iron knees, he pinned Morgan's arms to his sides, aided by the rug and Morgan's sling.

—What's the idea?

And someone had wrenched off his shoes and socks. A sick weight landed, heavier than Laurie's eight-odd stone. They were doing to him what they all did to Alex, the same technique to the letter.

Nathan elbowed back Morgan's head, pinched his nose, and stuffed the sock into his mouth. He struggled, helpless.

They said nothing. Silence was part of the technique. Nathan took hold of his hair and commenced the first interval. The technique never varied, and they had learned, both receiving in their youth and now giving, the chilling power of unvaried routine. You knew what was coming, which in ordinary circumstances would provide a measure of comfort; but you knew what was coming, so you could never entertain any doubts as to what would happen if you continued to resist.

He'd been sore before they began, and now he had reached the wall faster than Alex ever had. He yelled through the sock.

Nathan paused. There was no acknowledgment, as when Morgan did the same to Alex. No spark, no life at all. His friends not only had trapped him like a criminal, but were now regarding him as a vile object.

Laurie inched up his chest and tightened the vise. Nathan pulled the rug back—practiced, deliberate—and ran his knuckle across Morgan's chest until he found a place in Morgan's left shoulder.

The sock barely muffled his scream. Nathan let go of the place:

—We know you were part of it.

Crisp, civilized. They had learned from experts.

—We know you're lying, Laurie said.

He spoke not as they spoke to Alex, but colder. Nathan rested his knuckle against the place.

—But, Laurie continued, if that's the line you intend to take, then you've only yourself to blame.

Laurie's knees tightened. Nathan pressed.

It was essential to keep air flowing through his nose. Presently, they would take the sock out of his mouth, and he would be allowed to explain. But they hadn't believed him just now when he told the truth. They thought he could orchestrate an appalling prank and keep it from them. Nathan removed the sock, and Morgan gulped for air. The technique proceeded to the next stage, Laurie taking the lead:

—You look tired. Are you tired?

Morgan knew better than to answer vocally.

—You look as though you had a short night. Did you have a short night?

He nodded.

—When I looked, it seemed as though no one was in your bed.

His heart sank.

—Did it look that way to you, JP?

—It did look that way to me, Nathan said.

—It looked that way to JP, too. Was there anyone in your bed when JP and I looked into it?

Of course they thought he did it. How could they think anything else? Inside their hearts he was bled out and stiff.

—Perhaps there's a simple explanation, Laurie said to Nathan. Perhaps Wilberforce has a simple explanation.

—A simple explanation? Nathan repeated.

—A simple explanation for why he had a short night. A simple explanation for why there was no one in his bed when we looked into it. A simple explanation for why he saw and heard nothing of a pack of cads roaming the school, bunging up locks—

—Drugging Fardles and Matron.

—What? Morgan gasped.

The place. The place!

—Unless you turned invisible in the night, Nathan hissed, then we'll go on believing what our eyes told us, you lying sodding liar!

A punch. Tense and sickening silence.

—Ah, Morgan breathed at last, that.

Sock back in his mouth, technique stage three. He stopped struggling, stopped yelling except what he couldn't help, and reminded himself that the interval wouldn't last long. This was the encouragement. After the subject agreed to cooperate, he was given encouragement to continue.

When they removed the sock again, every part of him screamed. He caught his breath:

—I haven't exactly been going to the Tower during Prep.

—Obviously, Nathan retorted.

The place! Morgan howled.

—Did you think we wouldn't check? Laurie asked. With Alex in the Tower as well?

The room did not seem level.

—Are you planning to tell us where you have been going?

Would they believe him?

—The Keys. Obviously.

—And why's that?

—Needed some time to myself.

—That awful, are we?

—No!

—Who did you meet there? Nathan demanded.

No longer icy, Nathan's face flushed, too.

They misunderstood him so entirely! First they supposed he'd colluded with Alex, and now they thought he'd absconded from Prep with another boy, inducted this foreigner to the poacher's tunnel, brought him to the Cross Keys, and then returned home to lie about it. He opened his mouth to protest, but Nathan returned his knuckle to the place:

—Don't lie.

In fact he had met someone there, but Grieves was not what Nathan had in mind.

—It's . . .

His throat sore, tongue sticky.

—It's difficult to explain.

Knuckles.

—Ah!

The *place*.

—Stop! I'm not . . . Stop!

Laurie's knees slackened and he reached for Nathan:

—A word?

Miraculously, Nathan let go. Not only let go, but stormed out the study door.

—Don't move, Laurie commanded.

Vise slack, weight lifted, Laurie followed into the corridor. Morgan's shoulder pulsed, icy stabs.

Lessons were canceled. Games were canceled. Even meals were canceled. He had no desire to experience stage four of the technique, let alone stages five through ten. But where to start unraveling the truth?

A tendril of thought wrapped around his brain: It made little difference where he began. He might start by revealing that during Prep he had met Grieves at the Cross Keys, their heretofore private oasis. He might start with how he'd run away from the Academy without so much as a farewell note, or how he'd spent the early morning in Grieves's squalid rooms, blubbing like a girl. Perhaps he would like to tell his friends how Grieves had abetted his return to the Academy, or how he had observed Spaulding climbing in the Tower window? He might like to confess that he had lately invaded a foreign changing room to confront Spaulding, clothed and unclothed, on vague grounds, or that he harbored intent towards Spaulding, that he harbored memories of Silk that were not as black as he painted, that—

Laurie returned:

—JP's gone to the bogs.

Morgan sat up before Laurie could—

—Just tell me, Laurie said. I won't tell Nathan the blue bits.

Morgan stared.

—I have as well, Laurie continued. Obviously.

A cluster of freckles was coming up on Laurie's cheeks.

—You mean you've . . . ?

—Practically everyone has, except JP.

—You never told me.

—You never asked.

Morgan did not know what to say, at all.

—It doesn't mean anything, Laurie said.

Curiosity grew in him like hunger.

—It passes the time, Laurie concluded.

—But who? When?

Laurie shrugged.

—I'd rather not gossip. But, Thorne, presently.

Morgan stiffened even though he had never given Thorne a second glance.

—How'd you manage to . . . ?

Laurie examined the ceiling:

—I have a certain reputation.

—But!

—But indeed, Laurie said seizing control of the conversation. We aren't here to talk about me. We're here to listen to your confession so we can sort out what to say to JP and then sort out what to say when yon bunglers make it round to inquisition us all.

And through the mist of the day's breathtaking insanity, an idea occurred to Morgan—pristine, irrational, with all the clarity of perfection.

—There are things I can't explain, he said, but I'm telling the truth when I say I had nothing to do with the locks or the fire, and I don't know anything about them. Last night I . . . wasn't here.

—Why not?

No side.

—I had a mad idea of running away.

Laurie's eyes widened.

—But then I came back. Please don't ask any more. It's irrelevant.

—I don't call running away from us irrelevant!

—It's irrelevant to this business.

Laurie frowned into the middle distance, as he did when forestalling tears:

—The Fags' Rebellion, they're calling it.

—Who says the fags were behind it?

—The fags are behind everything.

The pristine idea began to shimmer.

—Two questions, Morgan said. What's this about drugging Fardley and Matron?

They'd have to, wouldn't they? Laurie said. Fardles hears everything, and what he doesn't hear, Matron does. Someone bunged things up right under their noses, and they didn't hear a thing.

—That doesn't mean they were drugged.

—Fardles was bleary this morning, even by his standards.

Pristine, shimmering, glowing like the dawn.

—Question two, Morgan said. How can I get to the Tower?

Laurie explained in a way that made Nathan agree to the plan.

—It's going to have to be real, Nathan warned. Are you sure?

—Yes, Morgan said.

Nathan bent down to pick up a cushion that had fallen and then, without warning, stood into a heavy uppercut to Morgan's chin. At the same moment, Laurie tore the shelf off the wall, sending photographs crashing to the floor.

Kilby was at the door in moments, frothy and demanding explanations. Nathan daubed Morgan's face ostentatiously.

—Wilberforce was trying to get a book down, and he fell.

—I don't know what you three think you're playing at, Kilby began.

—For heaven's sake, Nathan protested, waving the bloodied cloth, he's gushing something chronic.

—And his arm, Laurie said.

Morgan moaned from the floor.

—Matron will lose her stack if we don't get him to the Tower right now!

Kilby hesitated. Nathan smeared blood artfully across Morgan's jaw.

—Do you have another nose rag? he asked Kilby.

Kilby did not, at least not one he was willing to sacrifice to Morgan's gore, so, keen to escape either blood or Matron's wrath, he allowed them to go to the Tower.

—I've no idea what you've been up to, Matron declared, but if a bookshelf did this, I'm several Dutchmen.

Morgan hung his head.

—Right, Lydon, I'll take things from here. Back to your study, and tell Pearl to wash his knuckles with soap if they've split open.

Laurie left flabbergasted. Matron shook her head:

—Whatever it was, Wilberforce, I feel sure you deserved it.

In the end she decided his chin needed two stitches, which she said he could take and be grateful it wasn't worse. He breathed to keep the pain and his mind under control. He was there to observe her, not to feel sorry for himself, and certainly not to dwell on the dizzying transformations his friends had undergone in the last three-quarters of an—

—What do you make of this locks business, Matron?

—Don't try to draw me, Wilberforce. I don't gossip with schoolboys.

He felt the insult. She began to clean his face with antiseptic. It stung like a train whistle.

What had made him imagine he could cadge his way into the Tower, pump Matron for evidence of Laurie's wild drugging theory, cross-examine Alex (if he was still there), and by day's end solve the mystery of the so-called Fags' Rebellion?

—Hold still, wretched boy.

The fumes from the . . . iodine? carbolic something? were making him hot and sick. Matron gave his chin a final, searing daub:

—Back to your study, and no more nonsense.

Failure.

He'd got Nathan to break open his chin and bloody his nose for nothing. There would be no chance to do anything now besides languish in the study, claustrophobic with memory of the technique and of suspicions still not dispelled—nothing to do besides languish in a study *tedious* beyond description, while the JCR and other *drivelers* in authority failed to get to the bottom of anything!

He got down from the table, wavered, clutched the wall. His stomach brought up breakfast.

Matron put a bowl to his mouth and a chair to the back of his knees. He collapsed, his insides squeezing as if they would push out whatever was making things wrong. His eyes streamed. She took the bowl away but then brought it back as he retched again.

When it finally ceased, Matron led him to the ward and sat him on a bed. She gestured for him to undress, fetched him a nightgown, and helped him into bed like a feeble old man. She returned moments later with a glass of something. He gagged at the smell, but she made him swallow it. At last she left him to close his eyes, chin smarting, place aching, arm unfettered, unprotected, ungoverned, without its wrappings. A mummy disintegrating in the light of day.

 Inquisitions, as S-K labeled them, were proceeding apace. John imagined the Third subjected to the rack and felt a wistful sort of satisfaction. He had been deputized to keep order in the refectory. Housemasters were evidently too oppressed by the robes of their office to bother themselves with niceties such as how a hundred-odd boys were to be kept sedated in the same room for over two hours (thus far!) without breaks for air or water. Other masters drifted in and out, but none had a sense of what ought to be happening. S-K had mandated that absolute silence be maintained, but he had plainly not considered how this might be accomplished by the one man at the Academy whose beliefs precluded corporal punishment. John did his best: He sent the first five offenders directly to their Housemasters; their rapid and much subdued return calmed the waters. Next, he sent for supplies, dictated a passage from the newspaper, and commanded them to copy it twelve times. Finally, he instructed them to put their heads down on the tabletops while he read to them from the only semi-suitable volume in his satchel that day, Thucydides's account of the plague. He permitted them to visit the lavatory one at a time, exchanging the baton (written permission from him) wordlessly. By eleven o'clock, he wondered how much longer he could carry on with it all.

A pleasing vision crossed his mind, of corralling them into their changing rooms and then leading them on a vigorous cross-country run. In lieu of any better idea, and in half-desperate attempt to remind S-K of his existence, he dashed off a note to the Headmaster: *Dire straits here. Run?* He sent the missive with a bookish boy from the Remove and then concentrated on ignoring the low-grade murmuring that had grown since he'd left off, parched, with Thucydides.

Before very long, S-K materialized under the arches: harried, old, ex-majestic.

—Silence, he boomed.

The murmur died down, though not with the alacrity S-K typically commanded. Still, John thought, you had to give the man credit for gumption. S-K drew himself up with Victorian posture, swept into the chamber (such as he could with the tired gait that favored his left hip), and placed his hand on John's tabletop, as much to steady himself as to convey dominion. When the eyes of the room had fixed upon him, S-K removed from his inner pocket a piece of paper, expensive cotton rag, folded lengthwise. Perching his spectacles on the bridge of his nose, the Headmaster scanned the page.

—The following boys, he intoned, will attend my study.

He read out eight names (alphabetically, mixed Houses, all from the Third Form). A frisson rippled through the room. They did not dare whisper, but John could see them itching.

—The rest, S-K continued after a pause, will proceed to the changing rooms in silence, and I mean silence, and prepare themselves for a double dix with Mr. Grieves.

John could feel if not hear their astonishment and vague alarm. A dix was Academy code for the circuit of ten farms that served their steeplechases. A double dix was a training exercise reserved for the Upper School no more than twice a term. The Third would be hard-pressed by a single dix, never mind a double. After a night without sleep, John himself would be pressed to complete it.

Still, he reasoned, anything would be better than this imprisonment. Perhaps when they returned, showered, and changed, lunch would even be served?

S-K nodded his dismissal. John braced himself. They rose.

—Oh, yes, said S-K glancing back at his sheaf as if detecting a footnote, the following will attend Mr. Burton-Lee in his study.

He read out eight more Third Formers, again assorted, alphabetical.

—Mr. Hazlehurst has also requested the company of . . .

Another Third Form list, catholic in its character.

—Ah, and it appears that Mr. Clement would like the following to join him and Mr. Lockett-Egan in his study, immediately and without detour.

More names.

—And as we're about it, the rest of this list may cut along to Mr. Eton-Knowles for good measure.

That disposed of the Third. John relaxed slightly. He would only have to flog the Fourth; the Remove would be glad of the exercise, and if they weren't, they could suffer, as he himself would be suffering.

S-K made a final survey of his list, index finger ticking off names. Then, with a sovereign nod, he departed.

✦

Morgan squinted against the light. His mouth tasted foul. There was a rumble in the courtyard. He went to the window, which admitted an impossible scene: masses of boys jogging across the quad at the heels of Mr. Grieves. Like a mob of soldiers, they trooped unspeaking, cold in singlets, as the mist lowered into rain.

—What's the racket?

Morgan turned, and the curtain around one bed glided aside, revealing Alex. Not burned.

He wasn't ready, but he conjured the coolness of Spaulding:

—Cross-country. Fourth, Remove, and Grieves.

Alex looked askance, as if Morgan had reported pornography. The occupant of the other bed moaned for them to shut up. Alex scurried to

87

the door, checked for Matron, and scurried back to Morgan's bedside. A red-and-blue bruise swelled beneath the hair on his forehead.

—When did you turn up? Alex demanded. And what the hell happened to your chin?

Morgan touched his face reflexively and felt the tiny stitches. At close range he could see Alex's eye was swollen, too.

—Mind your tongue, Morgan said.

—I'd rather mind yours.

Morgan struggled for a riposte as Alex made himself comfortable on the bed, crossing his legs as if they were preparing for a game of Spite and Malice, minus the cards. This was not the interrogation Morgan had in mind. A wisp of fear rose inside him. He made to cross his arms, but his left didn't go that far.

—They say you missed the explosion at Prep, he began.

—They say right.

—They say someone got burnt.

Alex shrugged:

—Just Carter, little sod.

—I can hear you, came a voice across the ward.

Alex darted to the other bed and whisked back the curtain. A boy lay there, his hands mummified in white bandages.

—If you don't keep your mouth and your bloody ears shut, Alex began.

He leaned forward and murmured something. Morgan recognized the boy vaguely as a fag in their own House. Alex delivered a punch before closing the curtains on the boy.

—You are such a piece of work, Morgan said.

Alex shrugged again:

—Someone's got to keep an eye on things.

Morgan appraised him—*You need taking down a peg. You've got too big for*—then the boy's wrist was in his hand, and he was hauling Alex back onto the bed:

—That's what I wanted to talk to you about.

It was easy to haul him about. It would be easy to hurt him. Even with one arm.

—You are going to tell me everything, you little perisher. Explosion, locks, fire, all of it.

88

—Or what?

Or you'll have a very sore Accounting when it arrives.

—Or I'll make your life fifteen kinds of hell.

—Yes, *please.*

Not how things were supposed to go at all. Morgan dropped Alex's arm.

—I know you were behind it all. What I mean to know is how you drugged Matron and Fardles.

He had never cheeked Silk the way Alex was cheeking him, audacious, defiant.

—A neat trick, Morgan said, the way you dealt with the two of them.

A smile broke across Alex's face, and for the first time all morning Morgan felt a waft of hope. He was clearly too undaunting to force confessions from anyone, but now he saw that no force would be necessary. Alex was dying to confess and had in fact been exerting superhuman effort to keep from blurting it out from the start. Morgan felt idiotic not to have understood right away. Every prankster from Hermes to Laurie to Alex hungered desperately for acclaim. Alex had been confined in the Tower since the Bang, denied even a moment of applause. He was quite literally bursting.

—You've no idea, he said.

—Chemist, are we?

Alex leaned forward, his lips at Morgan's ear.

—There was a book in REN's room. It had things in it about drafts.

—Oh, yes?

—Nothing harmful, Alex said. Just something to help you sleep deeper.

—But how did you get Matron to take it?

Alex required no further prompting.

—I found one you can't taste. Then I got myself to the Tower and mixed it up, using things she already had in the dispensary! Slosh, teapot, good night, Matron.

Heat in his throat.

—You counterfeited your way into the Tower?

Alex grinned:

—I had help.

Morgan drew up his knees. Alex had gone to the Tower for the knock on his head, allegedly acquired at Games, but actually received in rapid confrontation with a desktop. Which meant that their encounter in the form room had not been accidental, or if it had been accidental, the outcome had not. He couldn't think of anything suitable to call Alex.

—So, Morgan said at last, you drugged them.

Alex beamed:

—It all worked out better than I hoped.

—But what about the explosion?

He could hardly bring himself to believe that Alex would engineer an explosion in the lab, burning yon Third Former so appallingly, simply as a cover for . . . what? Morgan felt mentally feeble in the face of it all.

—What's the idea anyhow?

—You wouldn't understand, Alex declared.

—Then make me.

Matron's voice cut across the ward:

—Alexander Pearl!

Alex froze.

—Yes, Matron?

Matron did not dignify the moment by asking obvious questions, such as what Alex imagined he was doing out of his own bed, much less sitting on Morgan's. Instead, she marched dramatically towards them, whisked the curtains fully open, and stood arms akimbo. Morgan quailed. Alex smiled wanly:

—Sorry, Matron. I was worried when I woke up and saw Wilberforce. His arm . . .

Alex allowed his voice to trail off in feigned concern. Morgan expected her to seize one or both of them by the ear, but she continued to glare in silence.

—I'm sorry for getting out of bed, Alex said. I didn't want to wake Carter.

Here Alex lowered his voice and indicated the bandaged fag.

—Please don't be angry, Matron. It's only . . .

Dramatic pause, artful swallow.

—everything's been so odd, and when I saw Wilberforce . . .

His voice trailed off again, and astoundingly tears pooled in his eyes. Matron pursed her lips, though not as severely as usual.

—Nevertheless, she said, this isn't where you belong, is it?

—No, Matron, said Alex, hanging his head.

He got up from Morgan's bed and came to stand beside Matron, prepared to submit to any punishment she might prescribe. He didn't go so far as to wipe his eyes, but he blinked as if to stop himself from succumbing to tears. Matron led Alex back to his bed, ushering him into it with a swat, but nothing more. She switched on his reading lamp and removed a thermometer from her apron. Alex opened his mouth and cleared his throat.

—Sorry, Matron, but please may I have some water when you've done? My throat's feeling all sandpapery again.

Matron felt his glands, placed the thermometer in his mouth, and told him to keep it under his tongue. Alex nodded in feeble compliance as Matron clomped over to Morgan, produced a second thermometer for his mouth, and then clomped away with Alex's glass. As soon as she passed through the door, Alex removed the thermometer from his mouth and held it to the bulb of the reading lamp. A tap turned on. A tap turned off. Alex, smooth and unruffled, put the thermometer back in his mouth. Matron returned with the water, found the thermometer's report of concern, and tucked Alex back into bed with the maternal brand of scolding she reserved for the unwell.

Morgan's thermometer did not impress her, and neither did his claims of lingering queasiness. She sentenced him to tea, dry toast, and magnesia, which she promised to deliver shortly. Morgan suddenly felt as queasy as he had just claimed. If Matron had been the kind of person to say *harrumph*, she would have said it. Instead, she pulled back the curtains around the mittened Third Former and, finding him asleep, departed the ward.

Not high tides, but something more sinister caged him, squeezing until there was not enough air. He had been spectacularly naïve. Had his pristine idea included a strategy to escape the Tower once he'd concluded his investigation? Had he thought through what he would do with the information he acquired? Had he made adequate preparations for what he might encounter in close quarters with Alex?

He had prepared for a more or less routine confession, but Alex's actual testimony struck him as grotesque. Not only had the boy turned his hand to criminal narcotics, but he had ensnared Morgan as unwitting accomplice in his scheme. Evidently, Morgan had gone overboard with Alex because Alex had meant for him to go overboard. He could hardly bear to think of the encounter, but hadn't Alex cheeked him brazenly, in front of seven fags? Just now, Alex had sat on Morgan's bed with the bruise on his head, wearing it proudly, like a brand, except there was no ownership between them, unless Alex was somehow gaining purchase—

He needed not to get confused. Alex had a habit of confusing him, but Morgan could tell lies from the truth, and the truth was Morgan had never encountered such a liar, so accomplished, so natural. Silk had lied reflexively to masters, but they knew perfectly well he was lying and simply couldn't be bothered to contradict him. Alex's performance with Matron had been so artless that Morgan almost believed it himself. If Alex could manage Matron so effortlessly—the Academy's most fearsome foe besides S-K, and even that was debatable—then what else had he done, or could he do?

Morgan had known Alex as Nathan's brother for three years; Alex had always possessed an attention-seeking strain, rebellious but manageable with the correct authority. Neither of Alex's parents possessed such authority, but Alex had always looked up to Morgan. And just now he had taken immense pleasure regaling Morgan with his exploits as criminal apothecary. Never had a boy more sorely needed sorting out.

Morgan wasn't a prefect. He had no study of his own, no private place beyond the curtain of his bed to deal with Alex. The only place he could possibly imagine was—out of the question. And even if the Hermes Balcony were *not* out of the question, the fact remained that he had not set foot in it for three years, since the wish slips and The Fall, which was confined to history and parenthesis and something he intended never to revisit, which was *why* the Hermes Balcony was out of the question. He had not even mounted the stairs since that day; he could hardly haul Alex up there in the present age. In the present age, he could only sit with Alex on a bed in the Tower, behind a curtain, close enough to smell his breath and see the pimple coming on his chin.

The squeaky wheels of Matron's trolley announced her arrival bearing something revolting she would force Morgan to ingest. But first she set to examining his arm and shoulder, testing range of motion, asking where it still felt tender, instructing him to press against her hands with what force he could. Seventeen years old, and he couldn't overpower her. She made him remove the nightgown and examined the places where there had been bruises and swelling, declaring him much improved. She handed him a glass of milky sludge. He gagged at the sight of it.

But then, like a perfectly timed wire from Hermes himself, came a knock and a voice calling out for Matron. Annoyed, she retreated to the corridor.

Her conversation with the messenger was plain to hear. The Headmaster demanded the presence of Pearl minor and Carter in his study. Matron informed the page that they would not be leaving the Tower today, for S-K or anyone. The messenger was evidently under orders not to return without the requested parties; he stood his ground with the confidence of S-K's authority, and dread of his wrath should the mission fail. Finally, it was agreed that Matron would accompany the messenger back to the Headmaster's study, where presumably she would set the man straight as only she could. Her shoes clicked down the steps, leaving Morgan naked behind the curtains. He set the glass on the bedside table and took a strip of toast from the trolley.

But Alex was up in a shot, diving onto Morgan's bed.

—What do you care why we did it?

Morgan, flustered, set down the toast and wrestled his body back into the nightgown. Any doubt that Alex was behind the scandals vanished. The Fags' Rebellion, Laurie had called it. If Alex unveiled his entire rationale, would it turn out to be Morgan's fault, at the root?

—I don't care why you do anything, Morgan said, but I'm amused you're too scared to tell me.

Something flashed across Alex's face—shame? anger?—that made Morgan feel cornered, alone with Alex where no one could see. It was always the three of them against the boy, or at least Morgan and Laurie. Even in the form room, Alex had been surrounded by friends. Morgan may have imagined dealing with him alone as Silk had once dealt with him, but it had never actually happened. Now that Alex had dived onto his bed, Morgan began to suspect that matters would never transpire as they had with Silk. That first Accounting, after Silk had cleared the ledger with the cane, after he'd made Morgan stand on the chair, made him strip, made him undergo that nerve-racking examination, that time Morgan had been too sore, too confused, too dizzyingly curious to exert any agency over the scene. But Alex would never quail before him, even when they sat with ten inches of blanket between them, Alex wearing the bruise Morgan had put on his head.

—If you must know, Alex said, I didn't touch a single lock last night.

—But you planned it. You supervised the whole thing.

Alex gave the abashed grin of one embarrassed by a compliment.

—It looks to have been a simple affair, Morgan said coolly.

—Like hell! It took weeks. You can't imagine what's involved getting platoons from every House to enlist for a thing like that. And not only enlist, but join the Covenant.

—Covenant?

—It was the only way. Otherwise someone would've spilt.

—You think S-K isn't getting anywhere downstairs?

—Of course he isn't, Alex said. Why d'you think he wants to see me and Carter?

—Because he has got somewhere, I'd have thought.

—In that case, he wouldn't have asked for Carter. Little weed had nothing to do with it.

Alex looked at Morgan with a defiance that made him stiff, challenging him as he had in the form room but without audience now. Would Alex drive him past reason, as he had driven Silk outside the Hermes Balcony? *Show me what's in there.* Refusing not once, not twice, such necessity, such folly. A change had come across Silk, revealing something Morgan had sensed before but never seen. Silk had not spoken, not in words. Arm twisted, face against panel, pressed as if for the technique, but then fumbling at buttons, furious, contaminating in a breath the other thing, the thing pursued in private, in concert, now here in wrath at the top of a public—Morgan had summoned this creature, compelled this alteration. When he twisted and broke free, it was only right that he fell, back, down, out.

A chasm opened now in the Tower, tempting him to hurdle reason and plunge into it. Only inches away, behind the fabric of a nightgown, Alex was naked.

Morgan pulled up the covers and leaned back with as much weariness as he could feign:

—Why go to so much trouble for a rag? What's the point?

—The point, Alex said, was to show them that we aren't going to take it lying down.

There were so very many things to take lying down.

—Take what?

—All of it! What fags have been taking since time immemorial.

If Alex had taken what Morgan had taken, would he have wished what Morgan wished in the Hermes Balcony that day, finding the wish slips and wishing three things?

—The serfs didn't take it, *le peuple* didn't take it, the Americans didn't take it, and we're not taking it. It's the Guy Fawkes of the Cad!

Alex actually raised a fist in triumph at the final, rehearsed declaration. He appeared to have paid attention to one minute in a thousand of Mr. Grieves's history lessons and combined what he had heard with the melodrama of his father's latest novel.

—Are you telling me that you and the entire Third planned for weeks to sneak through the Cad and pour soss into a lot of locks so everyone would know you don't plan on fagging anymore?

Alex looked angry and insulted:

—Not the entire Third, I told you. Everyone joined the Covenant, but only the cadre did it. And it wasn't *soss*. It was specially prepared, quick-setting wax.

—Presumably what was being brewed up in the lab when it exploded?

—We'd finished already, but some duffer failed to turn the gas off properly.

—You could have burned down the whole school!

Alex shrugged, seeming to think it a minor snag.

—You didn't mention the best part, Alex said. *La justice.*

—Where's the justice in bunging up locks?

—Keep up! Alex exhorted. The point wasn't the locks.

Morgan couldn't keep up at all.

—We bunged the locks so no one could douse the bonfire.

—In the quad?

—Every rod in the school consumed in flame!

Morgan felt cold as the logic of the campaign became obvious.

—That's what you call justice?

—We were planning to burn a few canes all along, but then the JCR went and whacked the entire Third yesterday—

—With reason—

—So we cindered them all. Gunpowder, treason, and plot!

The fist again. Morgan flushed.

—Gunpowder?

—You didn't think I gave up all of it, did you?

The chasm yawned, no place to stand.

—For a sure, quick fire, Alex said, you want gunpowder.

—But . . . there was no bang.

Alex grinned:

—Flour-water paste plus gunpowder, smear on canes, dry, fuse, instant inferno.

Morgan reeled.

—Don't you see?

The only thing he saw was a face that had never been shaved and a lip he'd quite enjoy splitting.

—What now? Morgan retorted. Presumably they'll pour hot water into all the locks and unbung them.

—Of course they could, Alex scoffed, but they'll stick from now on.

—That isn't funny. What if people get locked in places?

—If REN weren't such an idiot, he'd realize what we'd used and tell 'em what solvent to try. It wouldn't hurt the doors at all. As it is . . .

Alex chuckled in satisfaction.

—they're making a dog's breakfast of the whole thing, just like S-K is making a dog's breakfast of his giddy investigation.

Anarchy walked amongst them and had done for some time.

—What *exactly* are you hoping for? Morgan asked. And why bung the form rooms?

—Someone got enthusiastic.

—For God's sake!

Don't take the Lord's—quite an account you've rung up—concentrate.

—Let's see if I'm keeping up, Morgan said acidly. Doors get opened one way or another, S-K finds no culprits, yet somehow everyone knows the Third were behind it and so accept that the Revolution has begun, you're all let off fagging, the whack is abolished, everyone can do as he likes, and the Cad becomes some sort of daft modern girls' school where people run about naked, painting murals and dancing with scarves.

Alex fumed:

—I'd have thought that you, of all people, would understand.

—I don't understand? Morgan balked. Which part have I got wrong?

Alex looked him sharp in the eye:

—I wouldn't have expected the Heir of Hermes to take a line like that.

No one was supposed to know the Heir of Hermes, and if one did, one was never to speak of it. Alex kept looking at Morgan as if he had the means and the wherewithal to destroy everything that mattered. Morgan sensed he had fallen into a professional trap.

—How did you manage? he asked, rearranging his pillows. All those people traipsing through the school, stealing canes, pouring quick-setting wax, and the rest of it. You'd sent Matron and Fardles off to Neverland, but how is it no one else saw a single one of you out of bed?

—Interesting that, Alex replied. No one noticed anyone out of bed last night?

He was supposed to be interrogating Alex, not the other way round! Morgan always believed he'd escaped Silk in the end, but had he actually escaped him, now as he faced Alex, longing more than anything to tear the nightgown off him and show him—

—Did you drug the whole school?

—Drug? Alex protested. It's possible there was more than the usual bromide in the cocoa, but beyond that, I'm not deranged.

He needed to keep his mind on the chat at hand. He needed to isolate the past from the present, and in fact the previous night from the disordered stream of recent time. Alex's plan hadn't affected him because he hadn't gone for cocoa last night, because . . . because he'd been too agitated by Nathan and Laurie and their supreme unpleasantness. If they hadn't been so unpleasant, he would have gone for cocoa, in which case he wouldn't have woken in the night and done the preposterous things he'd done.

—I don't know where you get your scruples, Alex said. You do what you like, when you like. What's it to you if we break a few rules as conscience demands?

—What gets under my skin, Morgan said, are these tedious insinuations.

Alex again met his gaze.

—If you've something to say, Morgan continued, why not come out and say it?

—Cave! came the alarm across the room.

Alex thrust aside the curtain.

—Matron's coming, Carter hissed. And S-K!

Alex leaned in so Carter couldn't hear.

—You're a hypocrite, he whispered fiercely. You've got everything—XV, study, everyone likes you. You stalk who you want to stalk. You shag off through the poacher's tunnel, day or night. But you don't look, you don't see, you don't hear, and you don't understand.

With that, Alex slipped back to his own bed and pulled the covers over his head. Morgan's heart pounded.

Footsteps.

S-K appeared in the doorway, be-gowned and winded. He patted his face with a handkerchief. Matron was at his elbow, and seeing the curtains around Morgan's bed open, she shut them up again. S-K murmured something, and they moved to the corridor. Presently, she returned and rustled Alex along to her sitting room.

Morgan didn't see, didn't hear, didn't understand? What had he failed to grasp? He wasn't the kind of person who turned from the truth. His eyes and ears were wide-open!

After The Fall, when Emily and Captain Cahill had taken him home, drugged beyond sanity, he had waited in a stupor for his father to return. He had always imagined his father as a knight, in rough armor perhaps, but valiant. Despite involuntary memory of the plunge down stairs, despite fear, self-reproach, and the fog of medicine, he had clung to the certainty that his father would put things right. His father would come to his room, subject him to the burning light of judgment, and wrestle from him the truth of everything that had transpired at school. Even though life at home had changed unrecognizably, he knew that with enough time and will, his father could untangle him from what bound him: what he had done, suffered, courted, and allowed. When his father at last came to see him—arm, head, chest wrapped in bandages—the man seemed to have shrunk in size. He joked mirthlessly about the perils of rugby football, and when he asked if Morgan wanted to tell him anything, Morgan had said no. His father accepted his answer. His last hope for rescue, mauled.

S-K limited his interrogation of Alex to four minutes. Matron returned for Carter, as he evidently could manage nothing, not even a dressing gown, with bound hands. S-K kept Carter longer than Alex, but soon Matron ushered Carter back to bed and bade Morgan prepare for the Headmaster.

Numb, almost carefree, Morgan eased his arm into a dressing gown, crammed feet into too-small slippers, and followed her, observing his fate like a wisp above the sea, passionless, empty, on air.

✦

He was certainly getting old. He was already thirty, perhaps halfway through his life span. John's lungs and legs protested the double dix, protested mightily as he remembered them protesting his last steeplechase at Marlborough, the one he'd run after a highly inadvisable night imbibing with others in his year. They'd all been impaired, so he hadn't fared as badly in the finishes as he might, but John remembered regretting his excess. Now, in the Yorkshire March of his maturity, he could blame his ill condition on nothing besides age and insomnia. It seemed unfair to be punished for things over which he had no control. His windpipe and calves opposed every incline, his knees every downward slope. Most of the boys perked up after the doldrums of the three-mile mark, and John had deputized four members of the Remove to sweep up stragglers. He suppressed the urge to retch upon reaching the gates, though others did not. He waited there, skin steaming, until the last of the small fry had staggered inside. Shivering, he repaired to Burton-Lee's changing room.

It was not his choice to patronize Burton's House, but S-K had long ago assigned him that changing room, an atavistic reminder of his early efforts to make John assistant master there. Burton-Lee's House was physically the largest, and its changer well-appointed, which was to say the tiles adhered to the stalls of the shower, the showerheads pointed where aimed, pegs and benches withstood the weights allotted them, and most of the lightbulbs worked. It was, by the standards of the Academy, a palace of luxury.

John got under the showers. Most of Burton-Lee's had dressed and were claiming that a meal of some description could be found in the refectory. John allowed himself a moment's respite beneath the hot cascade, its needles melting the stiffness in his neck. He decided he would have a proper bath that evening no matter what it took. His landlady provided one Saturday evenings, but she had in the past taken pity on him and, for a price, drawn the tin tub outside of schedule.

Dolefully, he turned off the tap, buffed dry, and dressed. The changing room had emptied, leaving John alone amidst pensive drips. He rinsed his running togs in the sink and took them into the drying room, which was cold and ripe. His stomach writhed in a way he knew indicated hunger but which felt like cramp. He hoped the rumors of lunch were true. How could they not be? If S-K was going to send boys out running, he couldn't withhold food or he'd have a mutiny on his hands, from masters first of all. John chided himself for having taken the Headmaster seriously even for a moment. S-K hadn't carried out a full-fledged threat in years, although he had a nice line in the partially executed. That, combined with a thespian's power to entrance, had kept the hyenas at bay. Thus far.

John leaned against the thick door of the drying room as if it were an old friend he could sigh against and confess his weariness. It budged beneath his weight, admitting the murmur of voices without.

On instinct, he froze. The voices were locked in heated but hushed conversation just around the partition.

—Certainly not tonight, one voice insisted.

—But it's perfect, the second voice replied. No one will dare get up to anything now.

—We never should have gone before.

The first voice was baritone, familiar yet unrecognizable. It dawned on John how difficult it was to identify a voice without its face. Would he know any voice disembodied, even those most intimate to him?

—Don't say that, the second voice pleaded. You—

—Leave off, One snapped.

A bump, as someone knocking against a bench.

—You care too much what people think, Two said. This place is a wreck, full of the most—

—Will you stop talking, please?

—You're the only person who's ever made things worthwhile.

John recognized the second voice now, and the recognition brought a sensation like cold mud oozing down his back. It was Rees, the butt of every joke in the Fifth and possibly beyond. Rees had certainly put up with a lot during his time at the Academy, but he'd likely brought much of it on himself with his graceless personality.

—Look, the first voice said savagely, I'll think about it, but if you ever speak to me in public again—and I mean this—I will knock your front teeth in.

Rees sounded unfazed by the threat:

—If you don't want to be spoken to in public, then turn up where you've promised to turn up.

Another clatter, louder this time, as of a bench tipping over with someone on top of it. A grunt, and then one set of footsteps stomped away and out the door. John hesitated, realizing that he couldn't reveal himself now. He ought to have announced himself at the first moment, unmasked the two interlocutors, and demanded an explanation of their rendezvous. Since he'd failed to do this, he was prisoner to the drying room until the other footsteps departed.

He waited, shoulder trembling with the strain of holding the door, not daring to move lest it creak and give him away. At last, after an aggrieved sigh, came the sound of a bench being righted and a second set of footsteps trudging out of the changing room.

John slipped from the drying room and retrieved his jacket, shoes, and cuff links. When he'd finished dressing, he actually scuttled across the changer and peered into the corridor before emerging with performed nonchalance into Burton-Lee's House. He was annoyed to find himself unsteady, whether from the furtiveness imposed upon him or from the unexpected conversation, he couldn't say.

Evidently, Rees was carrying on with someone in the House. That someone possessed a fully changed voice and, despite Rees's peculiar air of command, struck John as Rees's social superior. Of course, most of the Academy were Rees's social superiors, but John had the distinct impression that Rees's interlocutor was older, someone in the Sixth. Not a prefect, as none of Burton-Lee's JCR (and John knew and disliked them well enough) would have permitted Rees to speak to him that way. Reviewing the roster of Burton-Lee's Upper School, John could not think of a single boy who fit the bill. Who would carry on with Rees?

To be perfectly fair, Rees wasn't bad looking if you ignored his personality—but who could do that? He was fit enough to aspire to success at Games but maladroit enough never to attain it. If he was lucky, he'd rise to the Second XV by his last year. If only he didn't care so much, something could be made of him, John thought. In the history classroom, a certain literalness and mental rigidity hampered his progress. He could memorize facts, but the point seemed always to elude him. Again, a lighter touch would have served Rees well, but as it was, the boy expended too much energy wrestling with the injustice, as he saw it, of exerting himself without reward. Since he couldn't grasp nuance, Rees found John's lessons difficult and irritating. He resented the irrationality of history, and John found his resentment tiresome.

John knew that Rees was the sort of boy he ought to try to win over, but really, if he took a hard look at his rosters, there were any number of boys more in need of winning over and more deserving of John's efforts, deserving because they . . . well, John couldn't with Quaker mind say why one boy ought to be more deserving than another, but he felt that some were. Morgan Wilberforce, for instance, could be colossally lazy, willfully resistant to a gift for perception, flippant, and disobedient, yet John found him worthwhile, more worthwhile perhaps than any other boy at the Academy. He could not say why. He did not think it was merely Wilberforce's good looks and talent at Games.

He reached the refectory and was cheered to find a meal in progress. The boys looked glum, however, and the meal proved to be only broth, bread, and water. Not even butter. He was famished, and surely the Fourth and Remove were as well after a double dix. He approached the servants to inquire about second helpings. Apparently the supply of broth was ample, but the Headmaster had decreed only once slice of bread per boy. When John inquired into the Headmaster's whereabouts, the kitchen staff declared such matters beyond their purview and frankly an unwelcome distraction to the onerous task that faced them of feeding two hundred boys after having spent an entire morning undoing the damage of vandals.

Eventually, John deduced that the Headmaster could likely be found in his study. He jogged across to the Headmaster's house, where S-K's housekeeper informed John that her master was not at home. When pressed, she admitted that he'd last been seen accompanying Matron to the Tower.

John, stifling the urge to slap someone, jogged across the cloisters, across the quad, and up the spiral stairs of the Tower. His legs dragged and his head spun as if he'd drunk too much rather than failed to eat enough. Matron was not at her desk, and the ward was empty save for two Third Formers asleep in their beds. John eyed the closed door of Matron's sitting room, and before catching his breath or losing his nerve, he knocked.

Matron cracked the door and looked at him askance.

—Is the Headmaster with you? he asked.

She assured him icily that the Headmaster was, and furthermore that he was not to be disturbed. John felt as indifferent to peril as Hercules. Perhaps it was the light-headedness, or his overboiled frustration at the day, or merely an urgent feeling of responsibility for the boys, but he swept past Matron into the room.

—Sorry to interrupt, he announced. It's the matter of lunch.

S-K drew himself up in horror at John's impertinence. And sitting on a straight-backed chair was Morgan Wilberforce, who leapt to his feet at John's arrival.

✦

Mr. Grieves showed not the slightest sign of intimidation before Matron or the Headmaster. With a bow of the head, he unfurled his demand: that the Fourth and Remove, having returned from a most grueling double dix, be given more to eat than one slice of bread and broth, unless Matron wanted masses of collapsed boys on her hands.

This elicited a flurry of conversation in which Matron visibly restrained herself from rebuking the Headmaster. Instead, she demanded that Morgan and Mr. Grieves leave the room and wait in the passageway. Never was Morgan more eager to obey her. They decamped, and the door closed behind them.

So commanding a moment ago, Mr. Grieves now seemed lost for words. Morgan adjusted his dressing gown. Mr. Grieves took in his appearance and squinted at his chin.

—Did my bicycle do that to you? he asked anxiously.

—Oh, no, sir. This was later.

Morgan hesitated, surprised at the urge to tell Mr. Grieves the truth.

—Did you have difficulty getting back?

—Oh, Morgan stammered, yes, I mean, no, that is . . .

What could he admit without mentioning Spaulding?

—That eye's coming up nicely.

Mr. Grieves tilted Morgan's head to examine his injuries.

—It's nothing, sir.

—A colorful nothing. Did anyone see you return this morning?

—No, sir.

—And did you see any of this business in progress?

—No, sir, Morgan answered confidently.

—Then why the interrogation?

Morgan's face prickled as it had in Mr. Grieves's rooms, his wretched heart displaying itself for any fool to read.

—S-K's talking to everyone, sir.

—A routine interview?

The remark dripped sarcasm.

—Not exactly, sir.

The voices behind Matron's door had died down. Mr. Grieves's mistrust stung, but then his expression changed:

103

—Can I give a hand at all?

Morgan was seized with the physical urge to fall upon his knees, to lay his arms and his head across Mr. Grieves's lap as he used to with his mother when the world threatened, and to feel Mr. Grieves's hands on his head showing him he would never abandon him.

Matron emerged and ordered Morgan back to bed. She told Mr. Grieves that the Headmaster would accompany him to the refectory and revise his instructions regarding the boys who had run with him that morning. Why in heaven's name had Mr. Grieves gone along with such a scheme in the first place? If he imagined for an instant that she would approve, then he was as bad as—

—Now, Wilberforce!

Morgan retreated to the ward, listening to Matron's clatter advertising to anyone within half a mile her overflowing displeasure at everything St. Stephen's Academy had that day begot.

✦

—You are an inordinately awkward young man, S-K complained as they strode across the quad.

—Please, sir, John said, I'm on your side, but I'm scrambling just at the moment to understand what that means.

—I don't need your criticism, thank you very much.

John had the sensation of handling a prickly Sixth Former. S-K was unhappy with him, but was it merely because John had disrupted his interview with Wilberforce? Or had the Headmaster discovered something compromising about John himself?

—Sir, have there been any confessions?

—None, S-K replied curtly.

It was important not to leap to conclusions. He ought not to imagine S-K's tone was anything to do with him.

—Any hints who was behind it?

Even if it could be.

—Or why?

—Nothing concrete, S-K replied. It's something to do with the Third, but they've put up a stone wall the likes of which I've never seen.

Apparently it wasn't anything to do with Wilberforce, then, or with his highly unorthodox sojourn in John's rooms. In the light of day, John couldn't imagine what he'd been thinking to take Wilberforce in and entertain him for hours. It had been ruinously unwise.

—Sir, what do you have in mind for this afternoon?

S-K stopped abruptly under the arcade and began to cough. John made a futile gesture of assistance as the Headmaster hacked into a handkerchief, eyes watering, looking even more frail than before. The man was not yet seventy-five, John knew, but he looked older. His hair was thinning to the point that he couldn't hide it, dark pockets hung beneath his eyes, the heel of his left shoe was worn down, likely a result of his bad hip. John knew S-K had been battling influenza all term. From the sound of his cough, John wondered if it had turned into something worse.

—Sir, are you sure I can't—

S-K waved him away and regained control of his breath. The form rooms had been opened, he informed John. They would resume lessons after lunch. Later, the Headmaster would make an address.

—I'll need you this evening, of course, S-K said.

John was not scheduled to supervise Prep, but he wasn't surprised to be drafted.

—Certainly, sir.

There went any chance for a bath. They were approaching the refectory, but something else was making John's nerves frantic. S-K appeared to have no complaints against John, thankfully, but if his expression in Matron's sitting room was any guide, Wilberforce had earned the Headmaster's gravest suspicions. Whatever the legality of their encounter in the night, John felt somehow that Wilberforce had become his project.

—Sir, John said, are you saying you don't believe the Upper School were involved?

—That is correct.

—Then why . . . ?

John hesitated. If Wilberforce had landed in hot water, would it help his cause or aggravate it to speak directly?

—It's obvious you are working yourself up to a monstrous bit of impertinence, young man, so you may as well out with it.

—I was only wondering why you seemed to be questioning Wilberforce so closely just now.

There. He'd said the boy's name.

—That boy! S-K exclaimed. I said I do not suspect the Upper School as a whole, but Wilberforce is a boy I maintain in the highest suspicion.

—Wilberforce, sir?

John's nerves went frantic again, but this time with a realization of his own naïveté. Wilberforce had run away on the same night as the Academy's most elaborate episode of vandalism; was he criminally gullible to have believed Wilberforce's denials?

—That boy, S-K continued, is a double-dealer, a liar, and an apostate.

John was entirely failing to follow.

—Apostate, sir?

—Morgan Wilberforce spits upon everything we hold sacred, S-K declared. We not including you, of course, though perhaps he would include you if given half a chance.

And as suddenly as the ideas had come to him in the night, John perceived the ghost within the conversation. He was a historian, so he ought to have noticed it sooner. The Head wasn't speaking of the present crisis; he was waging war in the past.

—Is this the confirmation business, sir? Wasn't that years ago?

They had reached the refectory. S-K drew himself up for oratory:

—I do not intend to banter with you, young man, upon matters you will never comprehend. Let it be known, however, that malevolent elements will never hide from me in my own school. I may not possess concrete evidence, but I am aware who moves for ill and who for good—and who for neither at all. Even at my advanced age, I can separate sheep from goats, and you may have every confidence that I shall do just that. Thy rod and thy staff comfort me!

Having worked himself up as in the pulpit, the Headmaster now made majestic entrance to the refectory. He strode directly to the nearest kitchen servant and held conference. He then gestured to a prefect to call the room to order. This accomplished, S-K addressed the school:

—Primus will commence at two o'clock, he said. After Quintus, tea will be served. You will then proceed to Prep. I have instructed your masters to ensure that you remain fully occupied in that interval.

He had instructed them in nothing of the sort, but John supposed the announcement was itself a form of memorandum.

—There will be no afternoon break. There will be no after-tea break. You will report to prayers at nine o'clock, directly from Prep. Any boy who trespasses today will be beaten. There are to be no warnings, no leniency whatsoever. Have I made myself clear?

A subdued *Yes, sir* from the room.

—In that case, luncheon is over. Proceed directly to lessons.

John looked to the Headmaster, wondering how to remind him of the runners.

—Stand for grace.

They stood. S-K pronounced it. As they moved to dismiss, he held up a hand:

—The Fourth Form and the Remove will stay as they are.

The guilty parties (or so they appeared) froze while the rest of the school exited sharply, but when S-K announced extra rations for the runners, their mood lifted as if they'd won any number of raffles. Several even thanked the Headmaster spontaneously. John wasn't sure whether to be impressed with S-K's legerdemain or unnerved by his volatility. It occurred to him that Burton and the Eagle might have sought other posts not from ambition, but to escape a mad captain's vessel. Burton in particular would never leave S-K's side, John realized, unless he considered the Headmaster beyond help and hope. That John had got away with the Wilberforce business on the night of the worst prank in the school's history did not inspire confidence in S-K's powers, and if the Academy were to labor under more days as unhinged as this one, John might actually have to consider other employment, not that anyone would entertain a pacifist such as him—but *one thing at a time.* For now, the Headmaster had, with only a few extra slices of bread and cheese, won this awkward segment of the school to his side. Give us this day . . .

And as it happened, the Fourth were due in John's history class for their first lesson of the day. They would repair there together, then, once they had finished eating, buoyed by nutrition, favor, and reprieve. Perhaps there would be a way to let them discover that John had petitioned for the extra rations. If they could realize this, it would go a way towards improving his relationship with this tiresome and lackluster group. It could go a way, perhaps, towards weakening their allegiance to the Third. Perhaps there would even be a way for John to suggest such a thing through historical parallel. If he could think of one, he could substitute it for the planned discussion of the Saracens and use the lesson covertly to assist the Headmaster's agenda. And if he could shift public opinion sufficiently from the tearaways, the vandals, and the anarchists, then he might be able to shore up S-K's government and persuade the Eagle and Burton—

He was becoming overexcited. Over the past twelve hours, not only had he provided clandestine midnight assistance to Morgan Wilberforce, diagnosed the Headmaster's ire towards same as classic distraction, rescued seventy-odd boys from starvation—not to mention discovering unseemly relations between two boys in Burton-Lee's House!—but presently he would command the attention of Fourth Formers, who could, if approached correctly, sway the balance of rebellion in the school. S-K had no notion, not an inkling, that an opportunity had presented itself. He was oblivious to the nymph of possibility undressing before him. But John saw things as they really were, and he could see his hour had come!

✦

—Matron, please, I'm not messing about, I promise, Morgan said. I feel fine now. It was only the smell of the what-do-you-call-it.

He tapped his chin.

—And the excitement of it all. Please, Matron?

He searched for another way to explain to her his urgent need to depart the Tower.

You don't look, you don't see, you don't hear, and you don't understand. What was he failing to see? That Alex had chosen him to smash his head into a desk, to haul him about, to admire his feats, to sit with him behind a curtain? When Morgan had discovered the Hermes Balcony, when he was Alex's age, he had found the wish slips and made a wish to be free of Silk. He'd always thought the wish answered, but was Alex asking him to . . . ?

—Now you listen to me, young man.

Morgan understood one thing clearly: he needed to be anywhere but the Tower, anywhere Alex wasn't.

—Get dressed.

A weight lifted as he realized Matron was discharging him. Even now she was opening a drawer for a piece of fresh fabric and tying it into a sling to replace the elaborate bandages. This would suffice, she told him, but he was on no account to contemplate football, fives, or any other sport besides light jogging for the remainder of term.

Morgan left elated with gratitude. He had learned something about the Fags' Rebellion without succumbing to the chasm; he had been reassured of Mr. Grieves's allegiance; he had escaped magnesia. He was free! And as he inhaled the clammy air, he realized he was hungry. He headed to the refectory, but even as his tongue began to water, thoughts of the meal summoned thoughts of the Headmaster, which summoned thoughts of their interview, harrowing in the extreme. That interview didn't bear recollection, and he certainly wasn't going to recount it to Nathan or Laurie, but he couldn't deny the sinister atmosphere that had accompanied a relatively unthreatening salvo:

—I'm bound to ask, Wilberforce, what you know of this dastardly business, but I feel sure you will tell me nothing.

Morgan had been relieved that he wasn't being forced to fabricate, but the Headmaster had quickly turned to a vague and unsettling line of interrogation touching upon Morgan's view of the Academy (more precisely, just what he imagined St. Stephen's was for), his self-opinion (just who he thought he was), his ambitions (just what he proposed to do with himself, now and in future), and his wherewithal (just how he imagined he could accomplish anything at all given the feeble moral and intellectual foundation he had built for himself in defiance of every effort from the Academy and indeed from S-K himself). Eventually Morgan had cottoned on to the thrust of the conversation. It was to be another harangue about his refusal—three years previous!—to go through with his confirmation. S-K had nearly expelled him at the time and would have, Morgan felt sure, if he could have justified expulsion on such grounds. However, Morgan's father had explained Morgan's decision as a matter of conscience, so S-K could only subject him to verbal pillory. Ever since that day, S-K had ignored him during theology lessons, which permitted Morgan to nap or daydream in the back of the room. During monthly celebrations of the Eucharist, Morgan remained in the pews with the unconfirmed juniors and stray Roman Catholics the Academy tolerated. His brushes with the law had been handled by prefects or masters, so Morgan had never come before the Head on disciplinary grounds. Today's interview was Morgan's first with the Headmaster since S-K's hour-long entreaty-cum-excoriation three years ago.

Why the Headmaster felt it necessary to raise the past at this exact juncture, Morgan could not fathom. Nor could he understand why such unwarranted harassment should have left him unnerved. He was entirely within his rights to have refused confirmation, and he was within his rights to persist in his refusal until the day he died. It didn't make Morgan an Insidious Moral Acid. It didn't have any bearing upon a group of arrogant fags rampaging through the school and taking a vow of silence stronger than the Headmaster's powers of intimidation. And it certainly didn't, as S-K claimed, tear up the roots of civilization, reaping irreparable damage, taking the Academy, a product of England's greatness (doubtful), and stomping it into the mud, like so many brilliant, eager, much-loved lives wasted—and for what?—in a tragedy Morgan and his generation would never comprehend no matter how long their shallow lives continued. The present ills, in short, were the inescapable consequence of profligacy in the young, and it was the Headmaster's well-considered opinion that Morgan was not merely an example of such degradation (*Was* twice a day any different from once?) but an actual magnet for the forces of dissolution. (He was no magnet, though he did seem to have attracted . . .)

People were streaming out of the refectory. He fought against the throng but quickly found himself in S-K's line of sight. The Headmaster threw him a murderous glare. He fled.

He let the crowd carry him to lessons and discovered his friends outside the Latin room. There was no time to address their barrage of questions before Burton-Lee swept down the passage, demanding silence and receiving it. Morgan whispered a bare-bones précis as they filed into the classroom: yes, Alex was in the Tower; no, he wasn't burnt; yes, he possessed valuable information—

—Wilberforce!

The Flea's voice froze them as a body.

—Sir?

—That doesn't sound like silence.

—Sorry, sir, I—

—Here.

The Flea pointed with a flourish to a spot beside his desk. Nathan and Laurie took their seats. From the chalk ledge Burton produced a stick, one Morgan had never seen, but plainly some species of cut switch.

—Sir, Morgan stammered, I—

—You heard the Headmaster. Needs must have. Here, please.

He gestured again. Morgan did not dare try to explain himself. He went where bid and bent over. Half a dozen fiery cuts followed. He gasped in surprise and pain but felt, as he stood up . . .

—Thank you, sir.

. . . that he had committed so many beatable offenses in the past forty-eight hours, he could hardly begrudge the Flea a quick sixer from an improvised weapon.

—Sit down, the Flea commanded. What is it, Pearl?

—Please, sir, Wilberforce wasn't there when the Head said what he said. He's only just got back from the Tower.

The Flea revealed no remorse. Morgan hovered by the desk, feeling light-headed. The Flea opened his mouth to scold but then ordered him into the corridor.

—Did Matron give you anything to eat? he asked, closing the door behind them.

Morgan shook his head.

—What were you doing in the Tower?

Morgan indicated the stitches on his chin.

—Accident, sir. And then I was queasy.

—Are you queasy now?

—No, sir.

—So that ashen complexion is an empty stomach?

—I—I suppose so, sir.

The Flea sighed and bustled back into the form room. He scribbled something on a piece of imposition paper and handed it to Morgan.

—Return to the refectory and give this to the Headmaster from me, please.

Crossing the cloisters, Morgan eyed the missive: *Give this boy lunch immediately. RBL.* Although he wished no further contact with S-K, he was almost beyond caring. His chin stung. The Flea's stick burned. Hunger-induced apathy had him in its clutches. He drifted into the refectory and by the hand of a loving god—Hermes, trickster, messenger, friend—encountered Mr. Grieves near the entrance and gave the note to him.

Grieves read it and then placed a bowl in front of him:

—Don't tell me you've been fainting at Horace.

—Ashen under the rod, sir.

Grieves frowned. He was wise about so many things; why couldn't he have a bit of humor about the stick? Morgan attacked the broth and bread.

—You, Mr. Grieves said sternly, are an ambulatory disaster.

—Sir?

—You get into trouble at least six times an hour.

—Only on a good day, sir.

Again, Grieves seemed incapable of humor. He left Morgan to eat, but just as Morgan had finished, he returned, removed the empty bowl, and took hold of Morgan's wrist as if he would wrench him to his feet.

—Listen here, Wilberforce. This is not a game. I have had quite enough tidying up after you these past twenty-four hours.

The remark hurt.

—Stop kicking up trouble.

—Sir, I—

—You're like an elephant in a crystal factory.

Morgan wanted to argue, but a string of blundered maneuvers paraded before him. Had he learned nothing in his seventeen years? Nothing from Silk, nothing from Laurie, nothing even from Alex?

Grieves continued to clutch Morgan's wrist harder than necessary. He felt like a child under rebuke.

—I don't mean it, sir.

—Precisely, Mr. Grieves said. You don't mean, you don't realize, you don't think.

He pulled harder.

—You must think, Wilberforce. You must.

Morgan felt feeble.

—I know, sir.

—Let me ask you something, in strictest confidence.

—Sir?

—What do you know of Rees?

Morgan blinked.

—Rees, sir?

Grieves let go of his wrist as if he'd just remembered he was holding it.

—Well?

—Nothing much, sir. Only that his pater is in the City.

—That isn't what I meant.

Morgan wondered at him. Mr. Grieves spoke as if in code:

—Who are his particular friends in his House?

—I don't think he has any friends, has he, sir?

—Do you trust him?

Morgan could not imagine where the conversation was heading.

—In what sense, sir?

—Do you think he is as he seems?

—I can't see him managing deception, sir.

Mr. Grieves grimaced:

—That is what I thought.

—Why do you ask, sir?

Mr. Grieves appeared to struggle with temptation and then give in to it.

—I've reason to believe . . . let's just say you were lucky last night not to encounter company on the road.

Morgan flushed.

—I'm afraid I don't follow, sir.

—Never mind. If you've finished there, cut along before you find yourself entangled in another interview with S-K.

Dazed by Mr. Grieves's bizarre about-face, Morgan decamped to the toilets. There he cupped water to his cheeks and waited for his heart to stop hurling itself around. What under Zeus's milky sky did Mr. Grieves mean? And what was he playing at? It was one thing to inquire discreetly about Morgan's exploits when encountering him in the Tower, but to initiate parley in an occupied refectory, and then to make unpalatable and astonishing suggestions about other boys—it was untoward. Masters always had favorites, and certain Housemasters had been known to conduct maneuvers hand in hand with trusted cadies, but Grieves had taken their alliance entirely overboard.

Morgan dried his face on his sleeve. Was the man actually unhinged? In retrospect, something about his rooms in Fridaythorpe was disconcertingly hermit-like. Why was he not living at the Academy proper? The other undermasters lived in the Houses. Lockett-Egan, for instance, served as attaché to Clement and essentially ran the House. Why did Grieves not occupy a similar position, in Morgan's own House, for instance? Hazlehurst certainly needed setting straight, or at least the energy to give a damn. Grieves, whatever one might say against him, gave a damn.

The edge had come off Morgan's hunger enough for him to think straight. What had Grieves actually said? The man harbored suspicions about Rees, suspicions that harmonized with the rumor Morgan had heard about Spaulding. It would be absurd for Grieves to approach Morgan over a rumor, so there was only one possible conclusion: Grieves knew that Rees had been abroad, too. It strained reason to imagine that Spaulding had trespassed with a third party while Rees trespassed independently with a fourth, all of them failing to encounter the marauding bands of Third Formers. There were limits to what circumstance could support. Which meant that Spaulding's companion had to be Rees.

Morgan longed for a cigarette. The idea of Spaulding with Rees was as distasteful as when Morgan first heard it, but now it possessed the weight of possibility. Rees and Spaulding were both in Burton-Lee's House and both enjoyed their Housemaster's good opinion. Spaulding's athleticism drew his Housemaster's loyalty, but Rees had attracted the Flea's sympathies for reasons beyond Morgan's grasp. Perhaps Burton knew Rees's people.

But even if Spaulding and Rees could be linked through rumor and circumstance, a liaison between them was impossible if one remembered Burton's particular vigilance against such things. How on earth could they have absconded together in the middle of the night?

Perhaps they had taken their leave for more wholesome purposes: drinking, for instance, cattle rustling, theft. Spaulding could have scouted the target in the afternoon—a nearby farm? the collection box of the church in Fridaythorpe?—and then conducted the burglary in the night, egged on by Revolting Rees.

A vision of Rees done for theft cheered Morgan considerably. How the mighty would fall, and how angry the Flea would be! S-K would have a coronary and dispose Rees in disgrace, perhaps after a public flogging. Such a sight would raise everyone's spirits. There just remained the problem of Spaulding. Surely such a sportsman could be spared the ultimate penalty? Watching Spaulding undergo a public licking might prove delicious, but expulsion, no.

Another idea came to him then, not shimmering as brightly as the morning's shimmering idea, but glowing like a bulb at the end of a corridor. It suggested a gentle course of action, and before any alarms could be raised, before the rest of his brain could resume its exhaustive and exhausting cogitation, Morgan's feet had decamped the washroom and were carrying him across the cloisters to the classrooms. Avoiding the Latin room, they carried him upstairs, along the upper passage, and down the far stairs to Lockett-Egan's English class, where reclined the Lower Sixth, dazed by torpor, kept just awake by their master's dynamic reading of . . .

—*Two vast and trunkless legs*—

—Pardon me, sir, Morgan said from the door.

Lockett-Egan paused as if hoping for reprieve.

—The Head to see Spaulding, please.

So many exorbitant things turned out to be breathtakingly simple once you did them.

 Spaulding was pale. Morgan led him through the cloisters, and at the turn to the Head's house, he took Spaulding's sleeve and pulled him through chapel doors, up stone steps, and along the darkened passage to the old chamber.

—What's the idea? Spaulding protested at last.

Morgan lit a match before the panel's keyhole. His hands at least had not forgotten the place. His knife sprang the lock, and the door to the Hermes Balcony opened.

Simple, breathtaking, once done. He stepped inside that aerie, its clutter of broken chairs undisturbed since his youth, its only light blue through stained glass, its view inside the chapel silent as ever, that secret perch where Morgan had sought refuge, where Hermes had stashed wishes, where—

—You'd better have a bloody good explanation.

Spaulding squeezed through the panel, blowing dust and every qualm away. New presence, new air. Two bodies side by side breathing in and out.

—No one comes here, Morgan said. Not even Pearl and Lydon.

Spaulding peered over the rail; a candle was glowing in a red glass far away.

—You're in danger, Morgan whispered, more than you think.

Spaulding caught his breath.

—They're onto Rees, Morgan said.

A flinch, like disbelief and fright.

—They don't know about you yet, Morgan said, but they will.

In a burst of motion, Spaulding kicked the railing, and the sound echoed through the chapel.

—It's finished anyhow, he said.

—Yesterday?

Spaulding nodded. Morgan longed to press his hand against Spaulding's chest and feel his heart pound.

—And last night?

Spaulding recoiled.

—You were on the road, Morgan said. You climbed in the—

—Was that you?

—You locked me out!

Spaulding froze, as if putting several things together.

—Sorry, he said.

—So the least you can do is give me an explanation.

Spaulding turned his gaze upon him. Morgan barely suppressed the urge to laugh.

—Was it burglary?

—What do you take me for?

—What then?

—You know what.

Morgan's heart beat in his cheeks. Here was admission: bald, impossible, true.

—But, *Rees* . . . ?

—I'm not going to explain, Spaulding said.

—Where did you go last night?

—Where did *you* go?

A tantalizing standoff. If only it could last . . .

—Ran away, Morgan said. Came back.

Spaulding scrutinized him.

—Quid pro quo, Morgan insisted.

He sat down on the floor and leaned against the paneling to illustrate resolve, and leisure. They could stay there all afternoon. No one would find them. Unaccounted time lapped about them, silence to be filled, air to breathe. Morgan licked his lips. Spaulding looked away:

—If you must know, we were at McKay's barn.

Morgan's arm twinged. Farmer McKay kept a ramshackle barn on the other side of Abbot's Common. Morgan had been there once with Laurie and Nathan, but Nathan thought the structure unsound, and Laurie objected to the smell. The place had a sad, reduced appearance that indicated sons lost to war, leaving an aging man with no one to care for his property and no hope for his future. The barn itself ought to have been torn down years before, Nathan had said, but evidently Farmer McKay could not be bothered demolishing it, allowing it instead to die the slow death of atrophy, planks slowly rotting, hay turning gradually to dust.

—Why go there? Morgan asked. It's grim.

Spaulding unbuttoned his jacket:

—Far enough not to be disturbed.

—And just what needed so much undisturbing?

Spaulding sat down and leaned against an old, broken chair.

—What do you think, Wilberforce?

His ears flushed. Spaulding had never before addressed him by name.

—Spaulding?

—What?

—What is it about Rees?

The question fell between them. Spaulding dropped his head onto his arms but did not answer. An idea came to Morgan, as logical as it was shocking:

—Don't tell me he's your first.

Head still on his arms, Spaulding did not protest. Morgan leaned forward and let his knee touch Spaulding's gray trousers.

—Is it true what people say about him?

Spaulding didn't move:

—Which part?

—The part that's hard to believe.

—If you mean Nell Gwynn, then yes.

Rees?

—In your House, or beyond?

—It's a nuisance outside the House, he says.

Preposterous!

—But how did he . . . ?

—Wilberforce, Spaulding said languidly, don't be prurient.

Morgan thought of Accounting, of the things Silk had taught him and the methods he had used. He leaned back as Spaulding was, allowing more of his leg to lie beside Spaulding's, setting his hand on the floorboards beside Spaulding's hands, not touching, not quite.

—How long?

Spaulding grunted:

—I can't begin to imagine where you get your nerve.

Morgan craved a cigarette but did not dare to light one above the chapel. Instead, he played idly with the matches from his pocket. As if in response, Spaulding produced a crushed packet and offered it to him.

If Spaulding proposed smoking, Morgan would smoke, whether overlooking chapel altar or S-K's very bedchamber.

They passed it between them. Morgan's fingers brushed Spaulding's.

His lips touched where Spaulding's had. They inhaled the same smoke through the same leaves and paper.

Spaulding was different up close. He seemed more human, though not entirely mortal. Spaulding possessed something ordinary people could never possess, and that something drew people to him. Here in the Hermes Balcony, distant outpost of Olympus, Morgan sat side by side with him and passed the dwindling cigarette back and forth as if such things were natural.

—Spaulding?

—Mmm?

As if they'd been friends for ages. As if sounds could replace words between them. Morgan allowed the sole of his shoe to rest against Spaulding's ankle.

—Did anyone see you, Morgan asked, coming or going last night?

—Only you.

—What about the fags?

—What about the brutes?

—Did you . . . ?

—See them wrecking doors and stealing canes? No, unfortunately. Wouldn't mind giving a few of them a good kick where it hurts.

—Are yours as bad as ours?

Spaulding grimaced:

—I don't think any are as bad as yours.

A bleakness amidst it all, that even Spaulding knew the anarchy of Alex and his cadre.

—Spaulding?

—That's what they call me.

—What else do they call you?

—I don't think it bears repeating.

—I'm Morgan.

—I know, Spaulding said. I'm Charles.

Charles. Morgan's uncle's name was Charles. Until this moment, Charles had been a round, traditional type of name. Now it emitted electricity like a poorly wired lamp.

—*How* do you know? Morgan asked.

Christian names were reserved for intimates; displaying interest in another boy's Christian name was not done.

—Do you imagine you're the only one? Spaulding said.

—*Only one?*

—The only one who likes to find things out.

Spaulding *liked to find things out?* Find things out about people, up to and including Morgan. Find things out up to and including his Christian name, which could mean a myriad of things, up to and including the desire to seduce him.

And here was Spaulding, pinching out the end of their shared cigarette, content to be kidnapped from lessons and to lounge in a balcony with Morgan, with whom he had previously exchanged but a few sentences.

—I suppose the others know, Morgan said.

—The others?

—Bux and Ledge and the rest. They never leave your side. You must have told them about Rees.

—Wrong, Spaulding said.

—Which part?

Spaulding turned to face him:

—No one knows, and I'd like to keep it that way.

—Then why tell me?

—For heaven's sake, Wilberforce, why do you think?

Spaulding licked the tip of the cigarette and placed it in the lining of his jacket. With equal deliberation he reached over with his free hand, felt for the buttons of Morgan's trousers, and began to work them open.

A flood of heat. His cock filled as it had beneath Silk's hand, but quicker, instant. Spaulding still reclined against the broken chairs, his left hand tucking away the cigarette packet, his right idly loosening Morgan's flies, his eyes gazing up at the ceiling, as if they were counting constellations together. Soon Spaulding's hand had gained admittance not only to his trousers, but to his pants, and with cold fingers was grasping him. Morgan inhaled, taken by the rough and chill, intent on not letting himself go.

Morgan unfastened his trousers the rest of the way and then reached over and unbuttoned Spaulding. It was happening. Everywhere, now, here. Spaulding was looking at him and touching him and breathing on him, and everything, everything—

A bell clanged. Spaulding leapt.

—Stay, Morgan whispered. They'll . . . we can . . .

—Don't be stupid, Wilberforce.

Spaulding pulled away, got up, buttoned himself.

—I assume S-K didn't really ask for me.

He spoke as if in the quad, not meeting Morgan's eye. Morgan still throbbed. Spaulding took his silence as reply. He dusted his clothing, pushed open the panel, and ducked into the passage.

—Charles?

Spaulding stopped but did not turn back.

—Do you fancy Rees? *Really?*

Spaulding's shoulders, so square a moment before, sagged.

—You can't make me rubbish him.

—I'm only trying to understand.

—No, you aren't, Spaulding said.

Morgan adjusted his clothing.

—Don't go back to that barn, he pleaded. It's ghastly.

—I have to.

—Why? You said it was finished. Is he blackmailing you?

—No one blackmails me.

Morgan stepped into the corridor and blocked Spaulding's path.

—If you say you have to, it means you don't want to. So why do it?

Spaulding moved Morgan's arm as if pushing aside a toll barrier.

—Perhaps I feel sorry for him.

He stepped past Morgan and down the passage.

—Don't you feel sorry for me? Morgan called.

—No.

Spaulding hurried down the stairs and disappeared into the crowd. Morgan followed, frustrated and unsteady. Spaulding had been seduced by Rees, the lowest of the low. Not only seduced, but turned. The incandescent Spaulding, who could have found eager welcome in any boxroom of the school, had lost sleep to trek out to McKay's barn, sordid, incommodious, foul. Spaulding had foundered even by his own admission. Exceedingly desired, exceedingly weak, Spaulding was almost too much to bear.

As if at gunpoint, Morgan forced himself to join the anonymous throng. How long could the day continue this-wise: formless, boundless, insanity-fueled? When he had arrived at the Academy—lifetimes ago?— he had felt imprisoned by the timetable, suffocated by the impossibility of a moment alone. The timetable hadn't altered since then, but its grip had grown weak, like failed elastic bands around the knee stockings he had worn when small. The Academy's edicts no longer bound him. If he chose to go somewhere besides lessons, he could. If he wished private audience with Rees, for instance, he could delay entrance to Chemistry and summon him as he had summoned Spaulding. If he wished to return to the Hermes Balcony alone, to sleep, to ponder, to exercise himself, for whatever purpose, he had only to go there now. In the confusion of this day, he could explain any absence. And if someone were to take exception, what recourse would they have? They could take the stick to him, but he knew, as every one of his masters knew, that such a maneuver would provide no deterrent, to Morgan or anyone, and would merely earn Morgan's exhausted scorn. As last resort, they could send him to S-K, but S-K could do no more than deliver a stale, years-old harangue, as he had already done that morning. Morgan was free to do as he pleased, more free than pupils of the scarf-dancing girls' school he had conjured to insult Alex's revolutionary ambitions. The airy-fairy girls would be bound at least by a fear of offending one another, or by a desire to please their bride-of-Lenin mistresses. No such concerns bound him.

Lacking a more original idea, Morgan trudged to REN's classroom. He sank down between Laurie and Nathan, uninterested in their glances. REN swept into the room and fiddled with the pole, moving slabs of blackboard up and down until he achieved a pleasing arrangement. Muttering to himself, he leafed through some decrepit tome and then shouted at them to begin taking notes. With a desultory movement they scrounged exercise books—their own or others, it scarcely mattered—and began sketching in vague correspondence with REN's remarks, which he recited loudly, only occasionally raising his eyes to ensure mayhem had not taken hold of the room.

Morgan lowered his head, suddenly dizzy with fatigue. The fabric of his jacket cushioned his cheek like the firm, outsize pillows they'd once had at Longmere. A busy corner of his mind attempted to record the various hours since he had last slept properly, where he had been during those hours, what had occurred between the tollings of clocks, and what he had learned about the matters of the age, about the fags and their rebellion, about the War, about Silk and Gallowhill, and then his mother was clutching him between her knees to towel his head dry, and back in the dorm, just as they were rising in the dark of morning, one of the fags, the youngest and smallest, like Laurie when they had first come, this boy stood in the niche by the washroom, stood there in nightgown and bare feet, bursting into tears, plaintive and forceful, and Morgan went to him to find out what was so very much the matter, and the boy cried out, *Mr. Grieves!* This boy had seen Mr. Grieves's dreams and he knew the awful secrets that tormented his heart. *Poor Mr. Grieves!* This boy mourned for him, and suddenly Morgan did, too, his heart straining for Mr. Grieves, whose sorrows were known only by this boy and by Morgan, who had known them already, who had in fact been watching out for Mr. Grieves, who even now longed to take from Mr. Grieves those things that seared him—the whole slew of unsalvageable humanity—to relieve him of these sorrows he didn't deserve, poor Mr. Grieves, secret Mr.—

—Oi.

Something poked his ribs and cut his shin. His eyes flashed open to see Nathan and Laurie staring at him, appalled. His lungs heaved. He was sobbing out of his dream, though the reason for it had evaporated. He swallowed, and scraped face against sleeve, subduing his renegade eyes.

 No learning would occur that day. In cynical mode, John might argue that learning scarcely occurred any day, but he reined himself in. Gallows humor was one thing, nihilism another.

Powerless before the lunacy that ruled the East Riding of Yorkshire, John rallied to carry on. He would continue, just as he continued in that gray Saffron Walden Meeting House to wait on the light, season upon season, year upon year. The light might fail to shine upon him or within him. God might decline to speak to him or through him. The Holy Spirit might conceal its influence from his eyes. Yet despite everything, everything before and everything yet to come, he resisted the sin of despair. His heart might long to despair, but his will refused it satisfaction. Others had suffered as he never would, and still they maintained their zeal. They worshipped in the catacombs of Macedonia, in Japan while outwardly denying it, under lash, under fire, they praised their maker and redeemer. Under the circumstances—these or any—John knew no justification for abandoning hope.

The Fifth dragged their feet into his classroom and drooped into their seats as if their slumbers had merely been interrupted by the bell. John had planned on reading to them, but as he greeted them, he had to admit that his throat was parched after reading to the abominable Third. That group's smug composure had all but proven their responsibility for the night's chaos, and now they had departed to oppress someone else, leaving him with the more intractable Fifth, bored beyond repair with everything His Majesty's realm could offer.

—Please take a sheet of impot paper and tear it neatly in two, he heard himself say.

Some errant lobe of his brain had taken command and was instructing the form to write the name of a historical figure on one half, and on the other half a personal secret.

—You mean a secret that person had, sir?

—How are we to know anything like that?

—Don't be so literal, he scolded. Write a name on one side, and some secret, related or not, on the other. Don't share with your neighbor. Yes, of course you should fold it up. Don't be a nitwit.

John produced two tins from his desk and dumped their contents unceremoniously into the drawers. He passed tins down rows, directing the Fifth to place names in the blue tin and secrets in the red.

—What's this got to do with history, sir?

—Are you going to make us write something?

—We couldn't possibly write anything, sir, after the lunch we had.

—What if someone finds out our secret? Then what, sir?

—Don't put a real one, idiot! Holland's secret's real!

John refused to let verbal disorder rile him. They were awake now, and although he would surely have cause to regret it, the errant lobe declined anxiety. It sailed forth in the lee of its brilliant idea.

—Right! John said pitching his voice to the back of the room. The game is called Chairs.

Groans.

—Sir!

—Can't we have independent reading, sir?

—Chairs, John repeated. Last to bring his papers to me—

This as he strode down the aisle and retrieved the tins.

—will be It.

A pause in which they translated his command, then they rushed his desk, elbowing one another to get their papers in the correct tins. Rees was still cogitating in his usual constipated manner. He would easily be the last. And now, having resumed their seats, they were indeed waiting for him.

—Never mind now, Rees, John said. You're first in the Chair.

Cries of mock horror accompanied Rees's march to the front, in which he affected martyrdom but accomplished only a priggish gait. Capitalizing on the sense of drama, John swept his desk chair forward and gestured gallantly for Rees to sit. With a look of supreme disgust, Rees sat. Applause broke out. John raised a hand and made it cease. With the elegance of a court butler, John offered Rees first the blue tin, then the red. Rees opened one slip from each as if expecting scorpions.

—Read silently, John instructed. Say nothing.

Rees read them and passed them to John. Without satisfying his own curiosity, John tucked the papers into his waistcoat.

—The Chair is now occupied by a historical figure. He—or she as the case may be—in addition to possessing an eminent biography, also possesses a personal secret, which may well be unknown to this very day. Your task is to unmask both. Right! Roundheads—

He gestured to the right-hand row of desks.

—and Cavaliers.

He gestured to the left. The Fifth sniggered. John was perfectly aware of the anatomical usages of the terms, but he pretended ignorance.

—Each side will take turns asking a question of the Chair. The answer may not exceed one sentence, so ask with care. The Chair must answer truthfully but may not mention his or her identity or secret directly. If, upon hearing your question answered, your side wishes to essay a guess as to the Chair's identity or the Chair's secret, you may. Incorrect guesses will forfeit a turn. Correct guesses will earn the side five bonus points in the next examination.

John had played this game, or something like it, at student parties in Cambridge. They did it with historical and literary figures, but the addition of the secret—where had that come from? The game was challenging enough, he recalled, merely guessing the Chair's identity if the Chair played along, which he doubted Rees could; but to introduce an alien element, a secret that likely had nothing to do with the actual figure in question, wouldn't that muddy already murky waters to the point of nonsense?

Sense was overrated. Forty minutes remained to his enforced society with these creatures, and the lobe had determined they would spend it guessing Rees's secrets—fiction or fact, who actually cared? *Alea iacta est!*

—Are you a man or a woman? a representative from the Roundheads asked.

Rees curled his lip into a sneer:

—A man, you impertinent scoundrel.

Oohs rolled through the room. The Cavaliers' first questioner stood:

—When were you born?

Rees consulted the ceiling:

—As the Great Regent was assassinated. Cruelly, I might add.

This was just the type of arcana Rees was wont to latch onto without having the slightest notion of its implications. It was also the type of showing off that went such a long way towards alienating his peers. John could see none of them followed. A few faces cottoned on to the general period, but even John had to think before working out the year to which Rees referred, and even longer before it struck him who had been born then. By this time, several more questions had passed, establishing that the Chair had died a painful death; that he had escaped at least part of the death to which he'd been sentenced; that he had fought as a soldier; and that he had been born in England.

Despite his irritation at Rees's ornate display of historical minutiae as well as his artificial acting style, John could not deny that Rees had thrown himself into the role. And once John had worked out who it was, he had to admit that Rees's performance was canny. He strung them along, growing more irate with each turn, taking on more and more the resentful psychology of a misunderstood martyr. Yes, he had endured torture. What of it, worms? No, he had not been burned at the stake, not precisely. A brilliant red herring, John realized. He was in fact—and the Chair assured them this was not merely his own vast opinion of himself—among the renowned of history.

And on it went, until the Roundheads put it together and named him: Guy Fawkes, in the flesh. Rees managed a disdainful nod but remained in character, for there was still the secret to guess, and John had garnered no clues during the first part of the examination as to what the secret could possibly be. He tried to predict the imagination of the class. Would it be violent? Whimsical? Depraved? John felt sure their imaginations ranged across every spectrum, but what would they dare write upon anonymous papers on such a day as this?

The sides closed in with rapid questioning. Was his secret generally known? It wasn't. Was it a sin? Fawkes confessed that it was. Did it involve a woman? It did not. Did it involve murder? It did not. Theft? Blasphemy? False witness? None of the above. John watched the class grow bolder as they suggested crimes of increasing vulgarity: fornication? lying with a beast? Greek love? Rees grew incensed in his denials, his face turning red, his voice rising in strident disavowal, to the point that John began to wonder how many of the denied crimes Rees had ever perpetrated, or at least contemplated.

—Where did you commit this crime?

John thanked God for Morgan Wilberforce, who had the self-command to haul the conversation out of the gutter and ask a pertinent question.

—Under torture, Rees/Fawkes replied after a ghastly pause.

Furious whispered conference amongst the Roundheads, and then Wilberforce raised a hand to indicate a guess from his side.

—Did you apostatize? Wilberforce asked.

Rees dropped his head in shame, resigned before his executioner. Like Iago, he said no more, holding his posture dramatically until it dawned on them that Wilberforce's guess had been correct, and the Roundheads had won both points. Rejoicing broke out across the form. John allowed them some celebration and then offered his hand to Rees, still frozen in tableau.

—Well done, Rees.

Rees held his pose a moment too long before raising his head, still cloaked in the aura of Fawkes.

—Thank you, sir.

John felt the remark as reproach. Rees was looking as if he saw into John's errant lobe. Rees set his jaw as if to say, *You think you can take me for granted as everyone else does. You think you can orchestrate clever games and cast me in the role of despised and that I will not notice. But I do notice. If you cut me, do I not bleed? I expect their scorn, but yours, sir?*

Rees looked away, and John realized that the form had, in his reverie, begun chanting rhymes about the fifth of November, demanding a penny for the Guy and suggesting Rees's immolation.

John had done this. He had introduced into his classroom a game whose object was to put Rees on the spot and see what he did. He hadn't chosen Guy Fawkes or apostasy, but as with all wicked deeds, fate had intervened to help it along. What would S-K do if he found out—not only that John had been playing games in lessons on such a day, but that—Lord, help him—he had permitted a mob mentality to gather momentum and make mockery of the Gunpowder Plot, mockery that turned even now to riotous celebration of the morning's bonfire in the . . . *What had he been thinking?*

—That will do!

John raised his voice. His heart raced.

—I've no idea, he projected carefully, what on *earth* you imagine you are about. Sit down.

His scathing tone worked. They shut up and sat. He turned to someone he could reliably bully:

—Lydon!

—Sir?

—Perhaps you can recall for us what the Headmaster said very clearly at lunch about his expectations for your conduct this afternoon?

Lydon shuffled and looked at the floor.

—Well?

Lydon summarized S-K's threat.

—In that case, whatever possessed the lot of you to behave as you just have? Most especially when I had gone out of my way to offer a lesson that diverged from the ordinary, knowing the weight under which you have all labored today?

They did not answer him. John's voice developed a lofty, offended tone as he made it clear that taking advantage of his generous nature was the type of thing he would have expected only from selfish wretches, or beasts. What's more, he was quite beside himself to discover that they would make light of the repugnant vandalism that had been perpetrated only hours before. The Fifth mumbled but appeared too depleted to do more under rebuke.

—You may well mutter now, John persisted allowing his reproof full range, but it's all a bit late, isn't it? How do you imagine it felt for Rees, having gamely played his role, forced to sit there listening to the lot of you carrying vindictively on?

Morgan Wilberforce raised his hand:

—Please, sir. We were wrong, but it was only in fun.

John would not, he told them, dignify such an excuse by bothering to tear it to shreds as it deserved. In fact, he would waste no further words upon them. For the remaining minutes of the lesson they could begin their prep—

—But, sir, we've already got prep in Latin and Chemistry!

Their prep, which would be an essay of no less than two hundred fifty words outlining precisely what evidence existed to support or to refute the notion that Guy Fawkes could have renounced his faith. Due tomorrow, no exceptions.

The form looked daggers at him, but he did not care. He told Rees as gently as possible to return to his seat. Maddeningly, Rees seemed bent upon maintaining his role and moved with a steely arrogance that made John want to strike him quite firmly across the face. How they would, any of them, finish this execrable day without finishing one another off, he had no idea.

◆

The aspirin had worn off. Lunch had worn off. Yet another lesson remained in the day, the one at which Nathan and Laurie would expect a full report on Alex. But what he was at liberty to say about Alex would fill one side of a postcard, and the person he had been while interrogating Alex had—he realized—expired.

Now he was a person Spaulding considered worth notice. Earlier in the balcony he had not realized the fundamental conversion under way, and when Spaulding had said he did not feel sorry for him, Morgan had flushed with disappointment. But if Spaulding did not feel sorry for him, why had he unbuttoned his clothing? He could only have done it by express intent, a free and full will. Spaulding wanted Morgan not out of pity but out of desire for what Morgan was. He wanted him for himself, because of himself. Spaulding reached for him—Spaulding who was everything and had everything. If Spaulding could desire him, who knew what kind of person he might secretly be, or become?

They arrived at French, where Hazlehurst began to interview them in various tenses on various topics. Soon he would instruct them to interview one another, and Morgan would have to deliver his account to Nathan and Laurie. He had no desire to revisit a single moment of the Tower, and he had every desire to revisit the Hermes Balcony, its blueness, the ghost of incense, and the ticklish, utterly—

—What on earth's the story with Alex? Nathan demanded.

Morgan reported the bare facts from the Tower, not facts about the bare, of course, but facts stripped of unnecessary detail, not that he ought to be thinking about stripping while speaking sotto voce with his friends—he had to concentrate with every muscle or he would—Hazlehurst drifted near, forcing them into the conditional tense. If they traveled to Monte Carlo, Laurie would hire a motorcar and traverse the Alps. Nathan would relax himself by the seaside, encounter some young ladies, and dine at a restaurant. Morgan would make the games, play at cards, and win many francs to construct his castle in Alsace-Lorraine.

Quickly he finished his report: Covenant, bromide, wax, gunpowder, revolution. Nathan looked ill. Hazlehurst passed by again. Laurie would perhaps mount a sailboat and travel with some friends to Italy, where they would speak Italian. Morgan would promenade the countryside, discover a daughter at a farm, and buy her milk. Nathan would kill animals.

These two had no inkling of the revolution that had occurred within him! They spoke as if he were the same person they had always known, a person concerned with explosions, locks, the residents of the Tower. Laurie claimed to know the bandaged fag, at least by name:

—Carter. He did that sonnet about snow, in the poetry competition last term.

Morgan and Nathan regarded him, dumbfounded.

—Little weed can hurl a couplet like a lethal weapon.

Morgan couldn't spare an inch of his mind for poetry, for bandaged fags, for Alex, or for the things that excited his friends. He needed aspirin. He needed food. He needed to see Spaulding, meet his eye, and know— that Spaulding saw him, wanted him, and knew him, for his secret true self.

After a tea that scratched at their hunger, they repaired to the study for Prep.

—First business, Laurie announced, the fags.

Nathan excavated the last of their biscuits and some tinned pilchards that proved inedible once exposed to light and air. Laurie installed himself on the window seat and called for bright ideas. What were they three to do about Alex, about the Fags' Rebellion, and about the Headmaster's resolve to get to the bottom of it?

—What do you imagine there is to do? Morgan protested. They've got their wretched Covenant, and Alex can look after himself.

Laurie could not accept such logic. If this was Morgan's position, then he was blinded by exhaustion and lack of exercise. Morgan lay on the floor and stretched his shoulder while Nathan and Laurie examined the matter. They discussed stealing here, dashing there, conferring with this one and with that; they considered emergencies, contingencies, tendencies, every *cies* under the sun except the pertinent point—that it was not their concern. After much heated verbiage, it dawned on Morgan that the problem for Laurie was that the Fags' Rebellion actually wasn't his affair. He knew the truth of it, but he had not abetted the crime. He was not even under suspicion. The most sensational caper in Academy history had been pulled off without Laurence F. Lydon, victor of the Great Prank War (1923). As for Nathan, he seemed torn between a desire to shield his brother from harm and a desire to see him get the lambasting he deserved. Barring expulsion, Nathan hoped Alex would be made to suffer in a way he'd remember a very long time, or at least the remaining ten days of term.

They debated like a useless parliament. Morgan wondered if other studies were similarly wittering or were confining themselves to complaint and gossip, freed from the ambition of Doing Something.

—Alex should own up, Laurie argued, not only for our sakes, but for his own.

—S-K'll crucify him, Nathan said.

—He won't dispose him, Laurie replied. S-K never disposes anyone. Can't afford to.

—Still.

—Your brother won't be able to sit down for a week after S-K has finished with him, but he'll earn people's respect.

—The fags'll idolize him even more than they already do, Morgan broke in. How will that help?

With this, Nathan grasped what Morgan had known from the start:

—There'll be no living with him!

—It's a good reason to own up, Laurie reasoned. Think of it, hero and martyr.

He sighed wistfully. Morgan got up from the floor. The debate had got out of hand. If he didn't haul Laurie down to earth, they'd careen into even more trouble than the day had already brought. He pulled up a chair and prepared to kill Laurie's illusions:

—The trouble with you is you're jealous.

—Jealous?

—That you never did anything half as good.

—I did the skull! Laurie protested. I even had you two going.

—If you start on that, Nathan said, I'll swear I'll break your nose.

Morgan recaptured Laurie's attention:

—Face it, Lydon, the only reason you're exercised is you wish you were in Alex's place. You'd love nothing more than to march into S-K's study and confess the whole thing.

—He could still do that, Nathan observed.

Laurie brightened.

—Don't encourage him!

—I could do it! Laurie declared. I could tell S-K everything, the lab, the wax, the gunpowder—

—And get yourself a public licking!

—It'd be worth it, though.

—No, Morgan said, it wouldn't! Have you completely lost your mind?

—No more than you have lately, Nathan muttered.

Morgan kicked him and turned an icy gaze on Laurie:

—I've had quite enough bollixing from S-K today. I don't need you confessing to the worst crime in the history of the Cad.

—It is the worst, isn't it?

Laurie was growing more envious by the moment.

—Look, Morgan exhorted him, just think this through! You confess to S-K. He whacks you from here to Christmas, in front of the whole school.

—Maybe you'd get the birch! Nathan added.

Morgan kicked him again.

—Then you're the one who can't sit down for a week, *and* all three of us will be under suspicion, so we won't be able to go anywhere or do anything!

Laurie's face had acquired a dreamy expression:

—And once it blew over—

—Don't—be—moronic! The Third will know you didn't do it. Alex will know you didn't do it. They'll tell everyone, and you'll be left looking like . . . like . . .

The association that sprang to mind was too prurient to voice in front of Nathan.

—Like someone who thought quicker than they did, Laurie said.

Morgan resorted to kicking Laurie:

—You'll look like Frank bloody Fane.

Laurie blushed.

—Who? Nathan asked.

—The point, Morgan continued, is everyone will know you're a fake. They'll think you're deranged or pathetic, and they'll think the same of us.

—You'll be a pariah, Nathan concluded, at last catching on.

—And so will we!

Laurie sat down slowly, as crestfallen as a child informed that Christmas was canceled.

—Right, Nathan said firmly. You're not going to S-K. At least not to confess.

—None of us are going to S-K for bloody anything! Morgan cried. Because—it is absolutely—nothing—to—do—with—us!

—Shh, Nathan scolded. You'll have yon bunglers in here.

—If it's nothing to do with us, Laurie retorted, then why did you have JP thump your face open and tear down our photo bracket?

Nathan and Laurie were glaring at him, united again. They had no right to cross-question him; the point was—a combativeness seized him. They were both mentally defective, he told them, and so were S-K and his entire apparatus. Any sane person could in five minutes concoct a way to sort out Alex and the fags. Why not publically ignore the whole thing? Deny the Third their hour of persecution. More important, he continued, deny them the chance to invoke their ridiculous Covenant. Have the locks cleaned. Then, after a brief interval, oppress the Lower School in ways small enough to evade protest but persistent enough to chafe. Occupy their time with extra Games. Send them on long daily runs, ostensibly to build their fitness, but actually to drain their energy. Expand the list of fagging duties. Summon them for pastoral chats in Housemasters' studies on half holidays. Schedule extra confirmation lessons. Seat them together at meals under the supervision of prefects to reform their table manners. Do anything, in short, to keep them busy and exhausted but to avoid the impression of deliberate persecution. Keep the atmosphere benign, but take their leash and shorten it until they hadn't an inch.

And that was only one idea.

Laurie shook the crumbs from their biscuit tin into his mouth. Nathan slipped their flask from the bookshelf and took a pull.

—Do you think, Laurie asked Nathan, that our panjandrum will offer his insights to the Reverend Headmaster?

—Can't think how S-K's got on without him.

—If you ask me, Laurie continued, our resident percher will flit straight over prefect and join the SCR, next term.

Nathan gasped theatrically and hid the flask from Morgan's sight. Laurie fell to his knees:

—*Before thy throne, O God, we kneel: give us a conscience quick to feel*—

—Shut up.

—*A ready mind to understand the meaning of thy chastening hand.*

Nathan joined Laurie belting out the hymn S-K made them sing at least once a month:

—*Wean us and train us with thy rod*—

—Very funny—

—*Teach us to know our faults, O God!*

Morgan shoved past them to the far side of the table and slammed open an exercise book.

—*For love of pleasure*—

—Just what do you think you're doing? Nathan barked at him.

—Prep.

Laurie stopped singing:

—What *prep?*

—History.

Laurie reached for his exercise book and threw it across the room:

—No one is doing that.

—I am.

They sniped at him with further recitals of the hymn, but he fetched his exercise book and compelled his mind to return to the relative simplicity of the history classroom, where Rees had so thoroughly violated Code by submerging himself without reserve into something that wasn't Games. Such a performance, if delivered by someone like Spaulding, would have had the opposite effect, of course. It would have amused and inspired them. Spaulding undergoing their interrogation would have composed himself in Grieves's chair, tossing off answers and admissions of torture as the ashes of a cigarette, which he would have smoked with an insouciance that bordered the erotic.

But the erotic had no place in prep. The subject at hand was Fawkes, not Spaulding (though he wouldn't mind Spaulding's hand at—), *Fawkes,* in re gunpowder, torture, apostasy, and so forth. From the moment of his capture, Fawkes was doomed to execution. His inquisitors employed torture to uncover conspirators, not to force him to renounce his faith. His Catholicism, in fact, was a valuable point for the Crown. If he were to disavow his faith, it would undermine the object lesson the Crown wished to present, namely that Catholics were depraved in every way and would, if not suppressed, destroy parliamentary government. If Fawkes had wished merely to assassinate the King, he might have found more support, but to threaten the British Parliament with explosion by gunpowder was to launch an attack on the Magna Carta and on the birthright of every man, woman, and child in the land. This was the reason Fawkes had become the most reviled man in British history and why they burned his effigy each November. Guy Fawkes would never have apostatized because he would never have been asked to apostatize. It simply did not happen.

The bell released them from hostile tedium, but even as they groaned their relief, it summoned them to prayers. In the crowds, shoving had an edge. Prefects cuffed indiscriminately. They filed into the chapel and collapsed into House pews, fractious and exhausted. Laurie polled the area for gossip. Morgan closed his eyes.

Whyever had Grieves given such a lesson? And what hand moved behind Rees's chance selection of Fawkes and apostasy? If the Gunpowder Plot represented narrowly averted chaos of the worst sort, were the Fates attempting to draw a parallel with Alex's conspiracy? Certainly by casting the horrible Rees as Guy Fawkes, the Fates had rallied everyone's antipathy. But what about the selection of apostasy just after S-K had renewed his accusation towards Morgan of the same? Perhaps he'd misunderstood what the word meant, after all. He'd always had the idea that apostasy meant denying one's faith out of expediency, but when he had refused confirmation, there had been nothing expedient about it. S-K had pressed him about what he didn't believe, but Morgan had been unable to explain. Haltingly, he had confessed that he couldn't pronounce the vows. When asked which words troubled him, he declared that they all did.

He no longer remembered what the vows were, other than some proclamation about renouncing evil. Did he not wish to renounce evil? Put like that, of course he did, but as he recalled, it had not been put like that. Then as now, the Headmaster treated his refusal as a grave falsehood, a perverse rejection of a thing Morgan purportedly knew in his heart to be true. He might not be sure, then or now, what was true, but he certainly wasn't going to abandon his position after all this time. Besides, S-K's harangue that morning had not been designed to convert, but to broadcast the Headmaster's dedicated mistrust of him. Guy Fawkes had not been invited to apostatize and neither had he!

A rustle at the back announced the arrival of the Common Room, which processed down the aisle followed majestically by S-K. Clement shuffled to the piano, adjusted reading glasses, and announced in his wavering voice the hymn, the same one Laurie and Nathan had just wielded against Morgan. *Of course*, the Headmaster would deploy it on such a night when he wished to make a moral point. They hauled themselves to their feet and prepared for reproach.

Before thy throne, O God, we kneel.
Give us a conscience quick to feel.

His conscience was sentient, thank you very much, and it didn't take a change of posture to spot the shadow, at hand, sowing doubts about the vile confirmation affair and injecting him with a fully out-of-the-question urge to sort out the entire Lower School. But the shadow could sod off—

Bring us, O Father, nearer thee.

And take with it obnoxious sentiments such as this one, which were in any case below the belt. He may have craved such drawing near to his own father one time, but that era was as dead as the War; such pangs did not belong in his chest today. And as for drawing near to Spaulding, let him not deceive himself. Spaulding had gone along with a bit of miking off lessons, but he had not followed it up with glances across refectory or chapel. He was surely not thinking of Morgan now. By no stretch of the imagination could he be considered passport to another—

For sins of heedless word and deed,

The last thing Morgan was going to do was to start feeling remorse for mocking people like bloody Rees. Only some tragic George Arthur type would regret knocking Rees off his pompous perch. Morgan wasn't sorry for starting the penny-for-the-guy rag, and he wasn't sorry for a single punch or kick he'd ever given the beast. S-K adored a Tom Brown morality. He probably learned it from Arnold himself somewhere in the depths of the last century. Even the name of this tune was out of date: St. Petersburg? Ha. The Tsar's palace lay beneath the tanks of Leningrad.

For lives bereft of purpose high
Forgive, forgive, O Lord, we cry.

The Academy had called him once to great things, but that had been the ambition of a little boy who knew nothing of the world, nothing of himself, and nothing of the bites life could and would dispense. The present was no place for old-fashioned longings, to do good, act good, love as he had been made to love, loving them all with all their failings, in dusty balconies or the dead of night with nothing to offer besides biscuit crumbs, tea, and a squeaky bicycle.

Consume the ill, purge out the shame
O God, be with us in the flame
A newborn people may we rise
More pure, more true, more nobly wise.

They sat in disgust, cramming hymnbooks back into the pews. If they indeed required forgiveness for anything, it was for lives of low purpose, or none. There was no essential purpose in the Fags' Rebellion, in the intrigues of House and Games, no purpose to his father's toil at the firm, nor to the hideous babies his sisters were sprouting or the hysteria over radio towers, Germany, the weather—none of it mattered in the slightest degree.

S-K moved to the pulpit. Morgan braced himself.

—I do not intend to waste precious words on this damnable business, S-K announced. Yes, *damnable*. That is the word this business merits.

If only fire would consume all this.

—Over the past fifteen hours you have made it abundantly clear— and I include each and every boy in that pronoun—*abundantly* clear that you hold with disdain everything I have devoted my life to offer you. My *life*. Night and day, my life.

The Headmaster looked small inside the pulpit. He was not wearing his gown, merely suit and school tie.

—Others, too, have devoted their lives to your service.

He gestured to the SCR.

—And are continuing this devotion in the face of callousness. In the face of indifference. In the face of hearts grown cold.

Cold, hot, shadow, fire, his head couldn't hold all of this.

—I am perfectly aware of what you think—all of you, each of you. You regard this business as a prank. And I am perfectly aware that the target of a prank ought not to exercise himself, but to take it in good humor. Having registered my disapproval and having encountered your wall of silence, I ought to bow to convention and exit the pitch. Ought I not?

He let his question hang, apparently unironic, for their consideration. They didn't dare murmur, but Morgan could feel tremors coursing through the pews, eager to shout back *Yes!* and *Yes!* Yet even as they suppressed their cries, uneasiness stole upon them like mustard gas. Their Headmaster had just violated a profound point of etiquette. He had made visible a code that had never been spoken directly, because the light of day exposed it as hollow, cynical, cold.

—It will come as no surprise, S-K continued, that I am no disciple of convention. If I were, I would not have devoted the last forty-six years, perhaps my final years, to founding and building up this academy, here in the far reaches of Yorkshire, apart from city, university, cathedral, apart from the men whose society might have given me—the personal me, Andrew Saltford-Kent—pleasure and satisfaction. If I adhered to convention, I would have passed these years elsewhere, doing work that might have brought me acclaim, or at least personal comfort.

Grieves was gazing into the middle distance. Burton-Lee regarded the Headmaster intently. The Eagle looked pent-up.

—I am a man, as you repeat scornfully to one another, from another age. *Of* another age. An age that permitted things to matter. An age where a word such as *purpose* meant something. *Noble* meant something. *Conscience* meant something. Those boys cut down in their finest hour, boys I loved, we all loved, those boys gave their lives because they believed we had made something in this land, something worth defending to the death.

Bodies rustled in pews, full of impatience and vexation.

—I know what you are thinking. You are thinking that those boys died because the things they believed in were an illusion. There is something I must tell you. It is essential. Are you listening?

He looked down the rows, catching eye after eye.

—Those boys we loved died because of woeful leadership, because of failures, because of disease and wickedness and apocalyptic advances in the machinery of destruction. That, boys, is why they died. They died because there is evil in the world.

Morgan shivered. Here was their Headmaster, a man finished in every sense of the word, clutching the corners of his pulpit as if this were his last chance of saving them, and what did he tell them? *They died because there was evil in the world.*

—Their convictions, the convictions of this Academy, were part of the force laboring to keep evil in check. They were not a candyfloss dream for which those boys died. They were the reason those boys lived.

From lives devoid of—

—Boys . . .

His voice soft, paternal, full of regret almost tender.

—Whatever you believe, try to make sure that it's true.

As if he loved them so deeply, so secretly, as much as he had loved those other boys.

—By their fruits you shall know them. Evil mocks. Evil scorns. Evil lies. Evil destroys. Please, boys, please . . .

He spoke as if there were tears in his eyes, as if they, not he, were about to be cut down.

—Try to do the other thing. Speak truth, build up. Do as that one man did. Do as we are bid: with all your heart, with all your soul, with all your mind, with all your strength, love.

His voice a whisper:

—Love.

 John was dreaming of summer at the Bishop's house in the years when he used to go there, before everything in the middle chapter went wrong. The first chapter, he explained to himself in the dream, covered the time before his mother departed. The middle chapter stretched from that mangling hour until the day he met Meg at Cambridge. It encompassed the time he called his youth, the time he made it a rule never to review. Why, he asked himself, had his imagination trespassed into the middle chapter? He might be dreaming, but he had not entirely relinquished reason, else how could he so discourse with himself?

The air in the Bishop's garden swarmed with pollen. The Bishop's son, his former friend, played noisily just out of view. His own father lounged on the patio, his collar unfastened in the heat—but it wasn't right, he insisted, his father was dead, and he had never unfastened his collar where anyone could see.

John was roaming the kitchen, and Mrs. Hallows was giving him a plum. The Bishop wanted to see him, she said. John, nervous but somehow eager, drifted up the paneled staircase to the Bishop's study.

Inside, the Bishop bade him stand before the desk, as he always did when chastising John and Jamie. Only now John was alone, the Bishop's son still playing loudly in the garden. The Bishop remonstrated with him about his decision to forgo confirmation. Didn't he realize the error into which he was slipping? John tried to explain: it was a matter of conscience.

—Conscience my right foot! the Bishop protested. No conscience would instruct you in such a maneuver. That inkling is not the call of conscience, young man!

John tried again to explain: He couldn't join the War because he couldn't kill another person. To do so was murder. But he had helped as he could, he told the Bishop, who was growing bored with him and opening the window to call Jamie.

—Come here, boy! the Bishop barked at his son. I want a word with you.

Jamie jogged in from the garden wearing cricket flannels and a pajama top. He met John's eye, and then, rather than coming into the study as he had been bid, he dashed away down the staircase.

John tried again: he couldn't be confirmed because the light of God was in every person, and he couldn't kill it, but he had driven ambulances, he had felt death in his hands, his very arms.

But the Bishop was standing in the downstairs hallway, addressing an assembly of John's father, Jamie's sisters, and the servants:

—I have given my life. My life. And cowards like this one—

He waved in John's direction.

—break down what I have spent a life building up. By their fruits shall ye know them. They destroy. They mock.

John tried to protest, but his mouth made no sound. The Bishop pointed at him:

—This one is a double-dealer, a liar, and an apostate.

Everyone turned to look at him except his father. His father, as he had that terrible Christmas, turned his gaze away, turned his chest away, turned his entire self away and walked out the door, where the summer swallowed him up.

John ran after, but the air was filled with fireflies, dazzling him and pounding like the guns had, night after night. A trench was at his feet, and at the bottom lay Jamie, bloodied, groaning, gangrenous. John scrambled down to help him, and Jamie turned to him in agony and regret, his body now lifeless, wet with blood, heavy as mud. The body was still warm, but John knew he could not revive it. He knew the absoluteness of death, its sudden arrival and its silent, eternally silent, face—

✦

Morgan turned over. His shoulder ached. He wanted to wake up. He needed to wake up. Something urgent was happening, something irretrievable that he needed to attend. *Wake up.* Even this tendril of thought spun like spirochete, spirit-chete, spirillum, Spitalfields, where Jack the Ripper cut those women, cut them up, cut them out of the fabric of life, the living coat of colors.

—Do you renounce Satan and all his works?

He had to wake up, or he would get it wrong, the things the bishop chap had asked him in S-K's study that day.

—My godparents did promise three things in my name.

The bishop chap had come to the Academy so they wouldn't have to go to York for the laying on of hands. He couldn't go to York, for hands or anything. They didn't live there anymore, and no hands lived in that minster, minister, sinister—

—How many commandments are there?

—There are ten.

—And can you say them?

One, one God; two, idolatry; three, blasphemy; four, Sabbath; five? Like the fingers on his hand, which he used to grasp himself, what was the fifth?

The bishop chap wore frock coat and gaiters like in picture books. They had to say the creeds, all of them, with the right words in the right order, but his throat was closing and he was swallowing to keep it open.

—Do you believe in the Holy Ghost?

If there was a Holy Ghost, it would open his throat and fill his lungs with wind. S-K said the Hebrew word meant spirit and also wind, but Morgan's throat refused both. Something pumped blood through him, but his throat let nothing by, as if a fist had him, fit to strangle.

—Do you renounce—

Gasping . . .

—Do you—

Gasp . . .

—Wilber—

Gasping gas more foul than the sulfurs of hell. But he wasn't in hell. He was on the bench outside S-K's study as he had woken that day, Matron looming as she had. Like then, he was choking back to life, coughing dinosaur ooze, retching from the smell.

That day, he'd refused to go back into the room and face the bishop again. But now, this time, he could say a different thing. Spaulding stood in the window, the sun fell warm on his back, and Spaulding watched him learn to breathe again and waited to hear what he would say. Spaulding had come specially, not because he pitied him but because he believed in him. Spaulding knew what was true, and he was telling S-K he needed to see Morgan, it was a matter of life and death, and he was taking Morgan to the balcony where Hermes had gone as a boy, when he'd learned the secrets of the Academy and winepressed them into wish slips; Spaulding was opening the door, and there was nothing more to pretend, nothing more to resist, and he was wanted and wanting and reaching and reached for—

✦

John inhaled and sat up in his bed. Dawn was breaking. He was exhausted from dreaming, and for what? It was all nonsense. The Bishop had taken him to task countless times—him and Jamie both for their adventures and misadventures, the tree, the pond, the canal after dark, what they'd seen in Flora's bedroom, what they'd done to Lucy's dolls, everything Jamie had lured him to and inducted him in—but never had John resisted confirmation; indeed, he'd been eager for the Bishop to prepare him. Later, the Bishop had not examined him over his pacifism as

John was no longer visiting the Rectory. And Jamie Sebastian, so far as John knew, had not died in the War. John had neither seen nor heard from any of them in twelve years. Twelve years was nearly half his life. It ought not to feel like no time.

There were reasons—unassailable reasons!—why he made it a rule not to dwell on the middle chapter. To be assaulted by it in sleep, and in such a vexing time, was tremendously unjust.

He hurled himself from bed, stumbled into his other room, lit the burner, and singed himself. He was not the person from the middle chapter. He was the person from the current and final chapter, the Convinced Quaker, the man Meg had drawn into her family, when his own had— this time was not that time, and the last thing he needed was to wake drained of energy and morale by absurd dreams. Morgan Wilberforce was the confirmation refuser, not he. S-K accepted John's pacifism and had from the beginning. No one was dead today, no one would be dead tomorrow, and in any case he lacked the time to discuss it with himself since he needed to get to the Academy as soon as possible on this already hectic Saturday in March. His dreaming mind could just consider what he said—mark, learn, and inwardly digest. That was all!

S-K absented himself from morning prayers, which should have felt like a bigger relief. The Flea read announcements as if the previous day had never happened: Laundry for REN's House would not be ready until teatime. Games would commence half an hour early and would consist of two steeplechases, junior and senior. A murmur of protest from the Fourth and Remove went unremarked by the Flea, who dismissed them with the air he adopted when he was too fed up to bother.

In History, Grieves made them read a dense chapter on the Hundred Years' War and write out the answers to questions from the blackboard, as if they were Third Formers. The Flea oppressed them with an unseen, and so the morning progressed, punishing them with work and silence. At break, Colin approached with the latest rumors, but Morgan scanned the crowd for Spaulding . . . there amongst friends, sovereign with loyal retainers. Standing in the tuckshop queue, Morgan watched him, but Spaulding never once looked his way. When his turn came, Morgan bought a kill-me-quick and ate it without tasting. Across the quad, Spaulding laughed in a way that made Morgan want to go and—

—Get your skates on, Laurie said.

The bell was ringing, but rather than ignore it, Nathan crammed two kill-me-quicks into his pocket.

—What's the idea? Morgan protested.

Nathan took his arm and broke into a jog.

—Keep up, Wilber. Didn't you hear?

Morgan hadn't heard a word, and he couldn't bring himself to care. At the toilets, he broke away:

—Meet you.

—REN! Laurie called after him. Lines!

The concerns of aliens. He inhabited a different world, one in theirs but not of it.

Was it too much to jape Spaulding a second day? If he tried and Spaulding refused, yesterday's world would disintegrate, leaving him prisoner in a flat and lethal land. The heaviness of nightmare pressed on his shoulder, which throbbed from being slept on wrong. He splashed water on his face. One didn't make a try every time one had the ball. To do so guaranteed defeat.

The cloisters had cleared as if the entire school had spontaneously acquired the habit of punctuality. It granted sixty seconds' peace and quiet, anyhow. He ambled down Long Passage, but just as he reached the classrooms, someone appeared on the center grass, exclusive preserve of prefects and masters. He couldn't endure bollixing from the JCR, but it was too late; he'd been seen. He braced himself for censure.

Except it wasn't a prefect. It was Alex. Morgan groaned.

—Released or evicted?

—What's it to you? Alex retorted.

—You're an impertinent little sod.

—Such is my aspiration.

Alex hopped off the grass and stood before him, a taunt. Morgan seized him by the collar and pulled him into the alcove beneath the library:

—Don't suppose you heard about S-K last night.

—You suppose wrong, Alex said. Old Howitzer's gone off his dot. I'm certainly not impressed.

—If you'd heard S-K, you wouldn't talk that way.

—I suppose you're going to set me straight.

—You suppose right.

Alex relaxed against him:

—Get on with it.

—I think, Morgan said, twisting Alex's arm behind his back, you had better start by telling me what you're going to do about this whole mess.

—Nothing, Alex said serenely.

—Someone has to own up or we'll never get any peace.

—Hurrah.

Morgan kicked him.

—What if someone else confesses to S-K?

—If they do, they'll be killed by the Covenant.

—Someone outside your Covenant.

Alex wriggled away:

—You?

Morgan scowled.

—You'd best look after your own skin, Alex said, straightening his jacket. You can start by keeping your nose out of other people's affairs and your arse out of other people's changing rooms.

—Pardon? Morgan responded with his best imitation of Grieves in a strop.

Alex did not flinch:

—And remember what happens to people who interfere with the Revolution.

A smirk:

—They find their necks under the falling blade of the guillotine.

✦

—Wilberforce! REN bellowed as Morgan let himself into the classroom.

—Good morning, sir.

—Don't you give me cheek, young man. Just what do you have to say for yourself?

—Only what a pleasure it is to see you, sir.

—Sit down, reprobate. I suppose you've an elaborate excuse for your tardiness?

—Not at all, sir.

—Then you may do me the honor of three hundred lines, by Primus tomorrow, if you please!

—It will be an honor, indeed, sir.

Morgan sat.

—And another fifty for your impudence!

Morgan nodded, as to the victor in a fencing bout. The Fifth chortled. REN relieved his frustration with several minutes of invective, but Morgan calculated he had come out ahead. His cheek had amused the form, and his sangfroid in the face of three hundred and fifty lines had drawn grins from Nathan and Laurie, so presumably it was a reasonable facsimile of the Morgan Wilberforce they expected.

The lines themselves were an inconvenience. He loathed lines on every ground and had not actually done any the entire term. He could not abide being chained to a desk writing useless words when he ought to be out doing something, though of course lines were intended to produce just such irritated discomfort, to waste one's time, and to force a sort of manual obedience. They lacked the Sturm und Drang of corporal punishment and deprived one of the praise that came with courageously enduring the cane. One had to complete them alone, excluded from general attention and interest, and then, when one submitted them, the master or prefect typically tore them up before one's eyes, emphasizing the futile nature of one's labors. This, the gesture said, was for nothing. You suffered for nothing. You sacrificed time and effort, and you have absolutely nothing to show for it. The mental suffering of watching one's labors destroyed, however meaningless one considered them whilst doing them, always struck Morgan more deeply than he expected. The first time it had happened to him, in prep school, he had actually burst into tears, to his mortification. He hadn't blubbed over lines at the Academy, but he had felt several times that he could.

—Amaurotic ambitions of amoeba, REN spat.

Morgan was fed up to the back teeth with talk of the Fags' Rebellion. He would have liked to spend Prep in the Hermes Balcony with Spaulding or, failing that, in Fridaythorpe talking with Mr. Grieves. But Spaulding was refusing to know him, and Grieves had that morning treated him as coldly as he treated anyone else.

—Rampant as rhizobium, REN continued.

Morgan needed to rein himself in. Grieves was his history master, not his Housemaster, not his father, and certainly not his friend. The sooner

Morgan's mind grasped that fact and adjusted his behavior accordingly, the better he would be, all of him—heart, mind, body, even soul if he possessed one. As for Spaulding, Morgan had better not deceive himself. He might lie to other people, and increasingly it was of the utmost necessity to lie to an increasing number of people, but he could hear his father now: *You can lie to other people, boyo, but not to yourself.* Actually, Morgan retorted, you could very easily lie to yourself. Most people did. *You know what I mean,* his father's voice replied. *Don't be contrary.*

It was the height of absurdity to speak obstreperously to oneself in one's head, even if one imagined one side as one's father. And at any rate, he agreed with his father. He didn't want to lie to himself. He wanted to know the truth, and the truth was he had yesterday endowed a chance encounter with inflated significance. Spaulding had paid him attention for less than half an hour, and he had leapt to exaggerated conclusions about his exaggerated self, his exaggerated purpose, and his exaggerated place in the vacuous world. He had permitted a bit of changing-room-style muck-about to raise in him the most callow of hopes. He had lapsed into the naïve. Such was the bald truth. The sooner he detached himself from Spaulding—memory of him, sight of him, thought of him—the sooner he could recover his sanity. Lines that evening would therefore prove a boon. An irritation certainly, but perhaps after all a salutary irritation.

A knock interrupted REN's diatribe. The laboratory door had no glass; they heard rather than saw the intruder.

—Pardon, sir. The Head to see Wilberforce.

REN perked up at the ominous announcement.

—Off you go, Wilberforce.

Morgan's stomach sank.

—Put your things away, REN told him cheerfully. I shouldn't think you'll be back.

A low chortle from the form, this time not with him, but against him. He closed his exercise book and deposited it on the shelf.

—Lines at Primus, REN chirped. Wouldn't want to have to double them, would we?

Morgan ignored the gibe and with iron dread departed REN's chlorine-scented realm. He shuffled down the corridor, through heavy doors, and—

Spaulding.

146

Fire.

Spaulding.

Spaulding gestured to the chapel and disappeared up the stairs.

It was real.

He wasn't naïve.

Everything good was real.

He dashed up the stairs and found Spaulding beside the panel that guarded the Hermes Balcony.

—Wasn't sure how you'd jimmied it, Spaulding said.

Morgan sprang the lock. They ducked inside. Spaulding sat down. Morgan sat down, fought for breath.

Then Spaulding was pushing him against the railings and opening his trouser flies. Morgan reached for him, but Spaulding pushed him onto his back. He lay there, heart racing, cock hard—immediately, immediately—thrill at being overpowered, at allowing himself to be overpowered. Spaulding pinned Morgan's free hand, his other imprisoned in the sling. Thus bound, Morgan surrendered himself to Spaulding and whatever he wanted to do.

Time cut loose. For a spell, he felt nothing besides Spaulding's knee in the palm of his hand, Spaulding's green eyes upon him, and Spaulding's fingers doing what they were doing. He thought of nothing besides the one thing his brain could think: *I want it.*

—Don't, Spaulding warned. Not until I say.

Spaulding held him still, warm, strong, smelling of something Morgan knew but couldn't name. Just as the torment began to ease, Spaulding touched him again:

—I'll tell you when.

He spoke sharply, but the kaleidoscope of his eyes darted in and out, green rings flecked with brown, an amber fire warming that most human miracle. Morgan wanted wholly to please him, to honor him with obedience, to encourage him in this and everything by playing entirely along.

—When? Morgan groaned.

—Hold still.

Warm, wet, flicking the spot that pushed him with the force of every temptation onto the edge. Straining, hungry for the next stroke. Then the warmth withdrew.

—I said I'll tell you when.

Spaulding grinned, looming over him.

—Please? Morgan begged.

Spaulding was enjoying this, perhaps even more than he was. Morgan reached again, but Spaulding took his hand and held it down.

Nothing had ever been this good, not even in his imagination. *I couldn't have dreamed you up,* Morgan wanted to say. Who could have guessed a person would exist to conquer him so? This wasn't Silk. This was free and joyful surrender, to something more thrilling than the world had ever before shown him. Nothing had the power to kill it now that he knew it, and nothing he could do, nothing he could say—

—Now.

Now. A thousand, rushing—*now!*

Lungs, air, in, out, green-and-brown still trained upon him. Even now, when no eyes should look, they looked on him. They looked on him because they desired him, even as he lay conquered and drained. The ruins of the Hermes Balcony lay around them, relic of another age. This green-and-brown lion had crashed through every wall, not to savage, but to sit as he did now, with the one he had wanted all along. Shadows, trenches—all swept aside by this new and real life.

Green-and-brown still held him in its ray, even as Spaulding took a handkerchief and did what one used to do to oneself, in the age when one didn't look. A wave of sleepiness brushed across him, but he clung to the green-and-brown, which burned on him now with a homecoming he had craved as long as he knew.

Spaulding did up Morgan's flies and buttoned his jacket, those hands straightening his tie, those fingers brushing against the stitches in his chin, a minuscule kind of pity.

Time, having nearly perished in the deep, regained its stay. From the steeple above, it tolled, a terrible pulse that wrenched them back to the morning hour, to the school, to the damp and dreary March of their year.

Spaulding looked up, no longer as he'd been, and as he slid off Morgan's knees, an abysmal sorrow stabbed. This harbor did not belong to him. Spaulding was preparing to depart, to cast the green-and-brown on another, on that most loathsome creature the earth had ever belched up.

—What about Rees?

Spaulding's face darkened. Morgan wished he could take back the question and the sour voice that asked it. Spaulding looked away, pulled away, leaving Morgan unweighted and cold.

—He says he'll . . .

—What?

Spaulding moved to the corner of the balcony and peered over the rail, his whole self consumed with Rees.

—Who cares what the brute says? Morgan protested. He'll say anything under the sun, and none of it true. You should've seen him doing Guy Fawkes in class. It was enough to make you sick.

Spaulding looked back at him, pity, sorrow, disappointment:

—He says he'll hang himself.

Morgan caught his breath, at Rees's nerve, at Spaulding for believing him and for looking at Morgan as though—

—Has he got any rope?

Spaulding drew back. The crass weight of material fact had apparently not occurred to him.

—Just what is it he wants you to do? Morgan asked.

Spaulding blushed:

—I don't fancy trekking back to the barn just now, with everything.

—Good.

—But if I don't go, he says . . . that's where we . . .

Morgan's tongue soured. The vileness that followed pleasure now pounced, clamping him in its jaws all the harder for having been delayed. Spaulding and Rees were We, and they went to lengths far greater than the Hermes Balcony to achieve it. The balcony was cold, drab, and scruffy, the green-and-brown a figment of his imagination.

Morgan got up and dusted his clothes.

—You're clever, Spaulding said. What would you do?

—I would never have messed about with Rees in the first place.

Spaulding winced:

—I know.

It didn't sound like affirmation. It sounded as though he knew Morgan lacked some essential human capacity.

—Still? Spaulding said.

Spaulding stood between the broken chairs, a gray-suited schoolboy, mostly grown yet unprepared for what stalked him. His humility and his need melted everything, until Morgan was weak again before him.

—I don't know what I'd do, Morgan said at last. But if you give in to him today, he'll only carry on with it tomorrow and the next day, as long as he likes.

Spaulding's shoulders tightened:

—I know.

✦

The morning was interminable, but at least it had spared them yesterday's trials. John's classes behaved themselves. S-K had not yet made an appearance, and John wondered, not for the first time, what would happen if the man became seriously indisposed. Burton-Lee normally stood in when the Headmaster was obliged to be elsewhere; he would surely serve as Deputy Head if S-K fell ill for an extended period, a notion, once conceived, that stirred John's unease. While it was true that Burton shared John's ambition to elevate the intellectual attainment of their pupils, rather than the usual public-school aim to churn out good sports with good manners, John suspected that Burton unleashed would make life unpleasant for everyone, most especially for him. Burton's vision for the Academy would certainly be filled with athletic and disciplinary excess, a vision unmoored in its enthusiasms from the Academy S-K was trying to conserve. Not that John approved of the Academy as it operated presently, but when he had first come, a mere seven years previous, S-K's Academy had still lived and breathed, a world of loyalty and faith, one that would accept a pacifist into its midst not because it in any way approved of his pacifism, but because it respected his having withstood attacks on the basis of conscience.

The Lower Sixth were writing a short essay. A knock at the door revealed Rees, looking flushed and worse for wear.

—Head to see Spaulding, sir.

His voice was raspy, as confessing a secret in stage whisper. John gritted his teeth at the manufactured melodrama of it all. He had no notion why S-K should want to speak with Spaulding—John would have interviewed several others in the Lower Sixth first—but apparently Rees had himself been confronted. John regretted ever having made Rees the center of attention. It had only egged him on, and now he was attempting to drag Spaulding into his misfortunes. Hopefully S-K had rattled Rees, if not on the grounds he deserved. John bade Spaulding go and waved Rees back to wherever he belonged.

John was inordinately hungry. Had he remembered to eat breakfast before departing his digs this morning? There had not been anything, he remembered now. He had returned much later than planned, the shops had been closed, and—he simply couldn't keep track of housekeeping details in the face of midnight visitors, improvised bonfires, unexpected duty hours, complex bicycle arrangements, not to mention the ever-shifting developments each day seemed poised to inflict.

The lesson was almost over. Shortly luncheon would bring relief, provided S-K hadn't again mandated a meal more Spartan than inmates could expect in York Castle Prison. He ought to mark at least two more exercise books in the eight minutes that remained. Why did he set so much written work? Here before him was the mere tip of the iceberg, the Fifth's prep from last night, their surely unsound arguments on the evidence for Guy Fawkes and his apostasy (short answer: fat chance). He couldn't do it. Not just now. Tonight he would do it. He was off duty tonight. He would return to his digs in time for tea. He would purchase biscuits. He would even, he decided, treat himself to shepherd's pie and parkin at the Keys. Then—post steeplechase, post shower, post parkin, nursing a pot of tea in the warmth of the Keys—then he would storm through the abysmal pile of compositions. He would work like the motor of a Halford Special. He would dust through the Fifth and consign memory of the entire Guy Fawkes lesson to the bin; then he would devour the tepid study questions of the lower forms and the tangled paragraphs of the Sixth. In fact, he vowed he would not turn out the light until his satchel was fully addressed, and tomorrow night he would cycle home unladen! He could hear his Magdalene supervisor now: He ought to make a start on the pile in the last moments remaining to the morning. To refuse would be to encourage the demon sloth. Even if he only skimmed the contents, it would be easier to face them later. His supervisor had been correct in everything (save his disapproval of pacifism), but still, John felt the urge to sulk in the face of this man summoned by mere thought. John sighed aloud and opened the top book in the pile. It belonged to Lydon. John flipped through it but did not find the assigned composition. Joy blended equally with outrage. He tossed the book aside and addressed the next: a mere five sentences! He would savage it later. The next four revealed equally paltry efforts. In the final minutes of lesson, he surveyed the entire pile from the Fifth and discovered only five that required marking, the remainder having declined to complete the assignment. Among the five he was pleased—disproportionately pleased—to find Wilberforce, who usually numbered himself amongst the idle. For Wilberforce to have done the prep last night indicated genuine effort, especially as Pearl and Lydon had returned blank books. Wilberforce's composition (and on quick glance it appeared worthwhile; at least it stretched to two sides) felt to John a vote of confidence. Wilberforce was saying to him, in the only language available, *The things you teach us matter, sir. I understand you.*

✦

Morgan was starving. He had by stroke of genius deflected Nathan's and Laurie's horrified interest in his summons to the Headmaster. It was, he told them, another of the Academy's howlers. S-K hadn't sent for him; Matron had sent for him, to administer one draft in advance of the other directly before lunch. Who could make sense of it? He wasn't supposed to be lying to them anymore, but he couldn't get into Spaulding, especially not with the glance Alex was throwing him across the queue (*keep your arse out of other people's changing rooms*), threatening to puncture his composure and leave him spewing the truth (*I couldn't have dreamed you up!*). But then S-K materialized, led silent procession into the refectory, and pronounced grace with record coldness. Morgan glimpsed Spaulding three tables away: flushed, distrait, and blasting him with the green-and-brown.

How was he meant to survive this cloak-and-dagger of glances? Noise exploded through the hall, harsh and nauseating. It didn't help that the soup was greasy, that Laurie made lavatorial jokes about what was floating in it, or that an aroma of onions pervaded the air. Morgan scanned the hall for Rees; he'd been absent from the last lesson and was absent now. Morgan hadn't seen him in the Tower when he'd gone for his aspirin just before the meal. He choked down the soup and pulled himself together. Only in the pages of a penny dreadful would Rees go and hang himself. Obviously he was sulking somewhere.

Madness could not reign unchecked forever. Even the Jews got out of Babylon eventually. The trick to an impossible mess, his mother taught him, was to begin in one place and refuse to be discouraged by the enormity of the thing. He couldn't repel a whole army of evils, but he could, if he chose, take Rees down a peg and curb his infernal nerve. He could do it easily. Rees would collapse like a matchstick tower in the face of the technique. Given quarter of an hour and some privacy, Morgan could put an end to Rees's infuriating threats and beat back the column of insanity.

The problem was getting Rees alone. He was too old to be forcibly abducted and too hostile to come willingly. What's more, Morgan felt he had exhausted the Head-to-see ruse. He could explain to his friends only so many aberrations.

And now in the middle of the meal, S-K was descending from the masters' table and extinguishing conversation as he swept between the benches and came to a halt before REN's junior table. There he spoke to three boys, who turned red as though seized by fever. Then S-K returned to the masters' table, noise resumed, and the objects of S-K's address were devoured by the surrounding boys; Morgan half expected to find their bones after the meal, cleaned dry and spread across the benches. As the table fags cleared, Burton-Lee called for silence and announced new arrangements for the afternoon's steeplechases, none of which mattered to Morgan since Matron had confirmed that he was forbidden to run. He was to spend the afternoon in his study, she said, or he might if he wished take light exercise in the—

Some ideas shimmered, but others blasted through darkness like the Eddystone Light. Matron had ordered him to forgo the steeplechase. She had restricted him to the Academy while the rest of the school took to Abbot's Common. He was at liberty for almost two hours, free to track Rees to his bunker, be it study, dormitory, even changing room (*Alex!*). The Eddystone Light overflowed the gloom: he would uncover Rees this very day, and once he had him alone, he would roll up his sleeves and set the stockfish straight. Technique, and more technique. Rees thought he'd blackmail Spaulding? Morgan would sort the sprat out before the first runners hit Nut Wood, and then—then! There was a gully just beyond the last turn on the course, a gully he could achieve in some few minutes at a light jog—Eddystone, Holyhead, all paled beside this! If, after dismantling Rees, he could achieve the gully, and if Spaulding could achieve it with him, what a quarter of an hour they might spend! Spaulding would have to give his lieutenants the slip, but certainly Spaulding possessed the necessary cunning. Morgan had only to tell him of the plan. In a minute luncheon would end, and they would drift en masse to the final lesson of the day, after which they would repair to changing rooms for the run. What he had to do was to slip Spaulding a note, now before lessons resumed. He had to jumble against Spaulding as if by accident and in that one jarring moment, he had to tuck the note into Spaulding's pocket, slipping his fingers into the fabric of his—

A voice within him bellowed in despair. Morgan, filing out of the refectory with his friends, wondered just what demanded such vexation. The tide was turning, dangling before him a glorious opportunity to do for Spaulding what Spaulding could do not for himself in the life-giving radiance of Eddystone—the voice exhorted him to untangle his metaphor and reattach his brain. He proposed passing Spaulding a note? A *note*? Notes could be found. Notes could be read. Notes were off the agenda.

Morgan deflated as the crowd swept him into the washroom. There Laurie clambered onto the basins to address the mob about what he'd learned in the refectory:

—Someone has gone to S-K and confessed.

Shock and consternation from the assembly.

—S-K told three of REN's fags to come to him after lunch.

—Which ones?

Laurie reeled off two names but couldn't swear to the last.

—So the fags *were* behind it! someone cried.

—Do you think so? Laurie retorted.

Nathan glowered in the doorway. Morgan knew what he was thinking: Someone had confessed to S-K, but Alex had not been summoned?

—I'd hate to be the one who peached, someone else said.

The assembly murmured and began jointly to imagine an array of punishments inflicted by the Headmaster on the guilty, and by the guilty on their betrayers.

Had Alex sold his comrades? Morgan couldn't believe it. What would he gain?

The bell rang, and Morgan was propelled out of the washroom to French. He had not worked out how to tell Spaulding about the gully, but at least the fever that had gripped the school would shortly break. More confessions would ensue, tears, recriminations, punishments, perhaps even expulsions, but then S-K would stop holding grudges against the rest of them.

Term would end in a few days, and they could depart for Easter cleansed. Come summer, everything could return to usual—as long as someone put Rees in his place and foiled his extravagant plot against Spaulding.

A knock at the classroom door once again disturbed their lesson. One of the fags from lunch entered, eyes bloodshot; he handed Hazlehurst a note and fled. Hazlehurst opened it with relish.

—Ah! It appears that our esteemed Headmaster wishes to speak with Wilberforce.

—Again? Laurie hissed.

A current coursed through the room. Nathan turned to him, astonished and betrayed.

This was the true summons, one direct from the Head's study given the messenger, one that could testify only to involvement, complicit or direct, in the abysmal matters that beset their world. This was the destruction he had been sensing, waiting to take him when he was weak and unsuspecting.

He floated out the classroom door and along the corridor towards the Headmaster's house. One of the fags must have seen him going out or coming in and had peached to curry favor with the Headmaster. He made a decision: whatever S-K knew or demanded, Morgan would not implicate Grieves. He had gone to Fridaythorpe and changed his mind. That was all. And he would not implicate Spaulding or Rees, since it was a damnable fact that he could not expose the latter without the former. The important thing was to hurry the interview along so S-K would release him (to what end he didn't care) before the lesson finished. Once dismissed, if only temporarily—O Eddystone Light!—he could position himself in the cloisters to collide with Spaulding after the lesson and deliver the note he would now have time to craft with perfect clarity and anonymity: *Fern Farm Gully, solo.* Surely Spaulding would catch the drift of that!

At the turn by the chapel, something seized him from behind, a hand over his mouth. He knew its scent, its texture. He surrendered to abduction.

Spaulding dragged him up the stairs as if hauling him off for a thrashing. Who knew salvation would arrive with such force? He'd always thought of good things as benign, almost anodyne, but now he understood that the really good things—things capable of remaking a life—tore into existence with power and might, with pain even, but rather than destroying, they turned their teeth against every cord that bound them. Spaulding wrenched his shoulder at the top of the stairs, and he understood that the best things would hurt, in the best possible way.

Bypassing the Hermes Balcony, Spaulding dragged him to the light at the end of the corridor. There he produced a piece of paper and held it, trembling.

It was starting, it had already begun, the life more thrilling than any he'd imagined, a life full of goodness no shadow could ever take. Morgan took the paper and unfolded it.

A wild script scrawled in pencil. Its author could no longer endure. Its author was not made of the stuff of giants. Its author had a heart that bled when stabbed. If Spaulding had been able to remove himself even briefly from his great, great height to condescend to the poorest of the poor, the author's life would have taken a different course. The author had reached his limit, and the time had come, the time had long come—Spaulding handed Morgan a second sheet, where the missive continued—long, long, longtime come for the author to Go into Night. Death would not be proud but would have Pity, he hoped, upon him, upon his soul, and upon the soul of Spaulding. The author hoped that Spaulding would find peace once the author had gone from his realm, no longer a cankerous sore on his gleaming future and dazzling present. The author wanted Spaulding to know, whatever life might bring in distant years, that he, the author—a third sheet—had loved Spaulding, truly and rightly and in the best manner known to man. His sentiment would not waver. It would continue into always. That was the last word of his earthly testament. Spaulding must not think of trying to stop him. He would have accomplished his dark work long before Spaulding read this, and Spaulding must on no account distress himself. Spaulding must only remember that he had been loved once perfectly. Spurred, Love departed this world for a better one. He would see Spaulding on the other side.

Morgan's chest seared. He burst out laughing.

—This is priceless!

Spaulding tensed as though he'd been punched:

—It isn't funny.

A wave of shame, which had the inconvenient effect of making him laugh more.

—I know.

—Then stop laughing!

Morgan rallied rational thought: Spaulding had abducted him from lessons to show him Rees's maudlin suicide note. To be brutally honest, they would all be better off without Rees. The world would be one soul deprived, and who knew what Rees might contribute to society once he'd grown out of the worst of his appalling tediousness, but really. If Rees succeeded in killing himself (a mighty *if* in Morgan's opinion), the school would be shocked, Spaulding would feel awful, even Morgan would feel awful. There would be a tremendous furor, which would drain attention from the wretched Fags' Rebellion, to Alex's everlasting fury. Ha! Two tasks accomplished at once: an end to the suppurating splinter that was Rees, and the terrific, unanswerable thwarting of Alex!

Such thoughts were awful, of course, simply inhuman. He couldn't quite abandon them, but at least he knew they were wrong.

Spaulding was still shaking as he took back the pages.

—I've got to try and stop him, Spaulding said. I was with him just before lunch. He can't have got far.

He was with Rees just before . . . ? Rational thought. *Rational thought.*

—You say he threatened to hang himself?

Spaulding dug in another pocket and produced a stub of rope a couple of inches long.

—Don't tell me that was with the note?

Spaulding nodded, looking greener by the moment. Morgan groaned in exasperation. Despite his colossal ineptness, Rees had managed to create a crisis. He'd thrown Spaulding—*Spaulding*—into a panic. He'd even raised dread in Morgan. Rees—damn him!—had made himself the center of their attention, he'd made them rush after him, he'd made Spaulding care.

—Where's he going to do it?

Spaulding appeared to be struggling not to retch. His eyes watered.

—Not McKay's barn! Morgan protested.

Spaulding nodded.

—Bloody Christ!

Spaulding looked shocked, at Morgan's anger or his blasphemy, he couldn't tell.

—I was thinking, Spaulding quavered, if I could get away during the run . . .

—Don't be daft. If he's going to do it, he's doing it now. How long does it take to get to the barn?

Spaulding thought Rees couldn't get there in less than an hour.

—He'll be there any minute now, Morgan said. Reckon quarter of an hour to sort out his rope work, at least the same again to think about it. We might just make it.

Morgan couldn't remember Spaulding looking so baffled, or so child-like. Morgan took him by the wrist as if he were an actual child and without explanation led him down to Morgan's House, where they barged through the green baize door and into his Housemaster's study.

—He doesn't keep it locked? Spaulding asked, astonished.

Morgan released that wrist—so warm, so wide—and preceded him out the French windows, across the garden and the playing fields, and up to the ruined walls of the lodge.

—Wait, Spaulding said. Explain.

—You can have an explanation, or you can get there before Rees tops himself.

—But the barn's in the other—

—Raise your right hand, Morgan commanded.

Spaulding was too surprised to argue.

—Repeat after me.

Morgan pronounced the vow the Keeper of the poacher's tunnel was bound to impose on all who accompanied him through it. Spaulding repeated it.

—Right, Morgan said hauling up the paving stone, mind your head.

He dove into the tunnel, wriggled through damp and mildew, and surfaced, not into a flea-ridden trench but into the bosom of Grindalythe Woods. Spaulding emerged muddy, detritus in his hair.

They ran up the path. Morgan's school shoes slipped in the mud, and he fell hard on his hip, but Spaulding was there, pulling him to his feet. Changing their shoes would have involved detours to two changing rooms. As it was, their shoes would be wrecked, but at least term finished soon.

Morgan had no idea how they would explain their absence, but whatever Rees had in mind, they would stop him. There would probably be an interlude of argument, but eventually the three of them would trek back to the Academy. Morgan wanted urgently not to have to take Rees back through the poacher's tunnel. Even if Rees could keep his mouth shut about it (a bigger *if* than his ability to hang himself—and how exactly had the horrible Rees found himself an actual length of rope and learned to tie it?), even if the suicide manqué kept mum about the tunnel, a bond would thenceforth exist between them, and Morgan wanted no bond with Rees. Of course, by the time they reached the barn and talked Rees down from his perch, the steeplechase would have begun, so there would be no rush to return and they could take the road. If they got back before the end of the run, they would only have to answer to their Games Captains. A brief, painful encounter, and the matter would be closed. No House-masters, no S-K, no histrionics of any sort. Morgan would rather not have a JCR thrashing if he could avoid it, but in this case, he would probably not be able to avoid it.

At least he would be taking it for Spaulding. Spaulding would get worse since Burton's JCR were savage, but Morgan would suffer alongside Spaulding, not literally alongside, but Morgan would suffer *for* Spaulding. Spaulding would know it, and Spaulding would remember.

A worse outcome would be finding the barn empty. Or finding Rees there but in no danger of suicide. Could he literally mean to kill himself? Rees was squeamish under the cane. He shied away from the scrum. He protested loudly when abused by his form-mates. In short, he was a big girl's blouse. How could such a specimen monkey up the rafters of McKay's barn, tie knots properly, and strangle himself willingly to death?

The whole thing was bunk, and Spaulding was running and slipping through the woods straight into it. Worse, by coming when pulled, he was showing Rees that he cared, that this was the knob to turn whenever Rees wished to control him. It was a disaster.

They arrived winded at the bit of wall that overlooked the barn. The building stood deserted, ramshackle, almost fragile at the bottom of the slope. Spaulding leaned against the wall, catching his breath, his cheeks and lips red, forehead perspiring, tie disarranged, breath fogging before his mouth, the mouth Morgan wanted to feel, doing what it had done before and rescuing the day from destruction.

—I'll go, Morgan said.

—No.

—If he sees you, he might . . .

Morgan pulled his arm out of the sling to hoist himself over the wall, but Spaulding cupped hands beneath Morgan's foot, those fingers gripping his shoe, fingers so able and knowing, fingers he hoped would touch more than his shoe, perhaps shortly, perhaps very shortly indeed! Spaulding lifted, and Morgan was over the wall, skidding down the slope.

At the barn, silence. A door hung uncertainly on its hinge. Morgan slipped inside.

Dim, mildew, decaying air. Then a rustling.

—Don't come any farther, warned that unmistakable voice. I'll jump.

Morgan craned to see into the rafters. Rees sat astride a beam, a flimsy rope connecting it with his neck.

—Rees, Morgan said, don't be an idiot.

—Who is that? Rees demanded.

—It's Wilberforce. Come down before you hurt yourself.

Rees shifted. The rafter creaked.

—I'll jump.

Morgan tried to keep his voice calm:

—What do you want to jump for?

—You wouldn't understand!

—That rafter's only just got your weight, Morgan said. It certainly won't hold if you jump.

—It will.

Clearly a logical approach wouldn't work with someone like Rees, someone divorced at least from the laws of mechanics.

—If you're going to hang yourself, Morgan said, you want to make a clean snap of it.

—I shall.

Rees squirmed as if to stand on the rafter.

—Hold still! Morgan shouted. If that breaks, you'll fall but you won't die. You'll wind up paralyzed.

—I don't care.

Morgan had never faced a more infuriating opponent. A buoyant stubbornness rose within him:

—Do you think you could wait just a minute?

The rafter swayed. Rees froze.

—If this is really it, Morgan continued calmly, what shall I tell people?

—I've put it all in a letter, Rees declared. Someone important is going to find it. He'll tell everyone.

—If you mean Spaulding, he already found it and showed me. Why d'you think I'm here?

Rees teetered but caught himself:

—Where is he?

The voice urgent, plaintive.

—Not here, Morgan said. I came instead.

—But . . . ?

He was enraged to feel a sliver of pity for Rees. Rees did love Spaulding, in his pathetic, unreciprocated way.

—Do you think a sorry old letter would get Spaulding to hack all the way out here?

Morgan knew what it was to love without reason. He steeled himself to kill in Rees the shoot that that lived in him.

—Spaulding thought it was hilarious, absolutely sidesplitting.

—He didn't.

—You should've seen him. We cut lessons and— What? You didn't think you were the only one?

—I don't believe you.

He could hear in Rees's voice that he did believe, and he could feel the blade slicing into that heart, perhaps not perfect surgery, but with enough heat to cauterize the incision once done.

—It was a bit much, don't you think? Morgan continued relentlessly. *Farewell, adieu, auf Wiedersehen?*

Rees had stopped fidgeting.

—He wanted to take it to your Housemaster and S-K, Morgan said. I convinced him not to.

—They'll see it when I'm dead.

His voice did not carry the power it had.

—I made him burn it.

—You what?

The beam shuddered. Morgan pressed on brutally:

—If you jump now, you'll die for nothing. Spaulding isn't here. No one will see your letter. People will think you were wet.

—I'm the only person in this place who has the courage to end things on his own terms.

—You think suicide is courageous? Morgan balked.

—It's better than living like dirt on everyone's shoes.

—Is it? I thought it was a sin.

—You're such a hypocrite, Wilberforce.

The second person in twenty-four hours to call him a hypocrite.

—I'm not saying I care about sin, but I certainly don't think killing

161

yourself is ending things on your own terms. It's ending things on death's terms.

—Wilberforce?

—What?

—I don't care what you think.

With that, Rees swung his leg over the creaking beam, and his body slipped, falling in a breath.

Morgan shouted. He kept shouting. He lunged beneath the beam to catch Rees. Except the rope held. The beam sagged. The rope shifted around Rees's neck, wrenching it back, biting into his throat and the underside of his chin, holding him above the floor just out of Morgan's reach.

Then Spaulding was there, and Spaulding was shouting at Rees to pull himself up. Rees was kicking and scratching wildly at the rope to relieve the pressure around his throat. But the rope was accomplishing its work. Regardless of second thoughts, regardless of the worth of suicide, the rope did the thing it had been made to do: hold its fibers together and bear its weight, the weight of Rees, of his error, of his ill-conceived affection.

Morgan reached for Rees's feet. Spaulding dragged a piece of wood for him to stand on.

—Stop kicking, damn it!

Every instinct in Rees's body told him to kick, to protest this slow strangulation, but the sound of Spaulding's voice and its far-reaching power made him permit the rope its grasp just long enough for Morgan to press upwards on the soles of his shoes and begin to relieve the pressure.

—For God's sake, Morgan cried, hold still!

And Spaulding was climbing up to the rafters, crawling along the beam that was aiding the gradual asphyxiation of Rees. It shuddered and swayed.

—Don't! Morgan called. It won't hold you both.

—Just a second, Spaulding said.

He wriggled forward, reaching for the rope. Rees writhed.

—Hold still! Spaulding cried.

Morgan's shoulder protested, but he pushed with all his strength, as if he would hold all of Rees's weight in the palms of his hands.

Let him get the rope. Let Rees not die. Let this thing not come to pass. Please.

Nothing intervened. Except that Spaulding touched the fringes of the rope. Spaulding tugged at the knot. Spaulding opened his penknife and dug at the fibers, until they frayed, loosing their weight, which swayed beneath them, pulling tighter the loop around Rees's throat, concentrating blood in his face, eyes bulging, hands grasping desperately to finish the divorce Spaulding's knife had begun, until enough entropy ensued, and the beam itself—neglected in their suit—let loose its joints and sent its load crashing, in obedience to gravity, bringing Rees down on top of Morgan, knocking the wind from his lungs and kicking them both free of the rafter, which crashed to the ground with a mighty, unanswerable destruction.

✦

Silence where it shouldn't be.

Eyes open, so he thought. Brown. Dust. Something rolling off him.

—Rees?

A moan.

—Spaulding?

The iron present.

—Spaulding!

Morgan tried to sit up. His shoulder screamed, stabbing pain through—

—What happened? a voice croaked.

Rees, altered.

The pain seized all thought, until Rees wrenched him to his feet. Squinting through the dust, they took in the barn—changed, catastrophically.

Spaulding lay twisted beneath the rafter, mouth open, eyes closed. Morgan climbed through debris to reach for him.

The hand was warm. The arm was warm. The neck and the chest were warm.

But the chest no longer moved. The blood no longer pumped, except to seep out the back of his head. The color had drained from his face, leaving it a sallow, sickly white. Spaulding's face looked now as lifeless as Morgan's mother's had looked when he had peered into her coffin. Hers, too, had looked as though it were sleeping, but her skin had been hard and cold, not like skin at all. Spaulding's was still warm, still soft, like the skin of the living, like the skin of one who had risked himself for another. Except he wasn't living, Morgan knew. He knew this wrongness.

The hurt returned—from his arm now dangling uselessly, from his head, from the bruises ripening across him, and most loudly from the interior, the marrow—bringing with it the taste of blood, and the euphoric horror of a life forever wrecked.

The main pack in the junior steeplechase had rounded the first bend, turning west and striking out across Abbot's Common. John's limbs protested after the previous day's abuse, but he was grateful to S-K for allowing him to set pace for the juniors rather than the Upper School, as was his custom. The Fourth were already suffering, so he was keeping the pace in check. If necessary, he would cut the whole thing short, S-K be damned.

It would help if the rain held off another three-quarters of an hour, but it had been misting, and now, as they slogged up the slope, it began to fall sincerely. The clouds had lowered, concealing the extent of the Common, exactly the type of day that boys went missing on the moors; John kept a close eye on the snake of runners, mindful that none diverged in ignorance from the course.

In fact there were two figures ahead, across the Common, emerging from the mist. He didn't think they could be his party; they might have come from the Upper School pack though its course ran nowhere near. John hoped he wasn't about to encounter an absconding pair, some boys from the Upper School who'd cut away to pursue . . . whatever nefarious activities they could concoct. If possible, he would pretend to believe whatever excuse they offered.

The figures slipped down the slope, falling to the ground several times. He now saw they were not wearing running kit, but something else, full uniform. Like wounded soldiers, the figures helped each other across the field. The figures, he realized with dismay, belonged to boys he knew well.

The next hour blended with the hours that followed. Sometimes when John thought back on it, he recalled every detail with a horrible excitement. He could recall Rees's senseless keening at the sight of him. Morgan Wilberforce's steely demeanor. His own fascinated alarm seeing Wilberforce's dislocated arm. The thrill of speaking sharply to Rees and demanding he pull himself together. How unhesitating and sharp his judgment had been, dispatching the fastest runner back to the Academy for help, halting the run, turning it around, sending it back from whence it had come. Then running as fast as he could up the brutal, slippery slope.

John was familiar with death. He was accustomed, or had once been, to shifting the corpses of young men. He was not accustomed to fashioning a makeshift stretcher to transport the body of a Sixth Former in school uniform, or to carrying the body of a pupil in tandem with Fardley across a squelching field and loading it into the back of Fardley's lorry. He knew what it was to ride in the back of rough vehicles with bodies that shifted at ruts in the road, bodies that moaned constantly, intermittently, or not at all. He knew the sticky feeling of human blood outside the body. He had many times permitted it to soak his clothing, not, however, the bare skin of his legs in running shorts and not his clammy singlet. John had suffered cold, wet, mud, and snow in the line of duty, but all stood apart from this interval fighting chill in the back of the school lorry as his blood returned to its usual temperature, unlike the blood in the other body, which was turning fortysome degrees Fahrenheit, though as he recalled, it took several hours for heat to depart entirely.

Rees and Wilberforce he had ordered back to the school. Wilberforce had resisted, wanting to help recover the body. Of the two, Wilberforce looked a just-walking casualty of battle. John had snapped Wilberforce's arm back into place there on Abbot's Common before it did any more damage hanging crazily at his side. He had not yelped at the procedure or revealed any discomfort even when John bundled the arm roughly back into the discarded sling. He appeared not to feel the blood coursing down his cheek, which had split open, or from his mouth, an injury John ascertained as nothing more than a bitten tongue, though it looked as though he'd had his throat slit. Rees appeared essentially uninjured apart from some grazing at his collar, but he continued to wail almost hysterically, so John sent him back to the Academy under the escort of two boys from Rees's own House. Wilberforce, having endured John's setting his arm, insisted on leading John back up the slope, to the scene of the disaster.

John examined the body. Wilberforce, in the grip of a strange euphoria, insisted that John feel for a pulse, at the throat, at the wrist, anywhere possible. John assured him Spaulding was dead, but Wilberforce drew him back to the body several times, insisting he'd seen the chest move, or that he'd felt a pulse. Spaulding was still warm, Wilberforce kept repeating. Surely John could revive him.

John had been reduced to dragging Wilberforce physically from the scene, taking him outside, and speaking to him in the most brutal terms. Wilberforce was by this time beginning to shiver, his skin pale against the blood smeared across it. Something seemed to have shaken loose inside his brain, John thought at the time, though later he recalled many men from the trenches speaking the same way, as if every restraint upon conversation had been destroyed.

—It's my fault, Wilberforce had said. I made him try to stop Rees.

—It was an accident.

—I should have let him go to S-K, but I wanted to be part of it.

—Wilberforce—

—I wanted Rees to die. I didn't want to kill him, but I thought it would be easier if he was dead.

—You didn't make it happen.

—I did try to help . . . I held him up while Spaulding—

John had been forced to disrupt the conversation by seizing Wilberforce's bad arm and dragging him, through dint of physical pain, away from the barn and back to the Academy.

Wilberforce babbled the entire way back, spilling every kind of confession. John hoped he wouldn't remember the things the boy had said. He hoped he could shortly forget the details of Wilberforce's assignations with Spaulding, of the utterly corrosive menace that was Pearl minor and his schemes, of the appalling literature Lydon had been importing to the Academy, and of the treatment Wilberforce had endured in his youth under "Silk" Bradley, a thoroughly poisonous creature if ever there had been one. John did not shock easily, but he had to work to conceal his shock now. The state of the Academy was acutely worse than any of them imagined. It was like the body of a soldier revealed, upon cutting away clothing, to be rotted through with gangrene. At any rate, it had all blown up now. There would be no putting anything back the way it had been, the way they had imagined it to be. He felt the irrational exhilaration he'd once known in the face of destruction, the same exhilaration that was surely now coursing through Wilberforce, prompting him to divulge transgressions of the worst sort.

John wished ardently that he had a study, a room, anything, where he could lock Wilberforce until his senses returned. He would have settled for passing the boy into the custody of his studymates, but in the chaos of the quad he had to abandon Wilberforce at the gates and go immediately with Fardley to recover the body from the barn.

John hoped he would be able to agree with himself, in the future, not to think of that day. He decided, rattling back to the Academy in Fardley's lorry, that he would indeed scour the paper for advertisements. He would box his things before the holidays, and once he had installed himself in Saffron Walden with Meg and Owain and his goddaughter, he would not leave that refuge until some other establishment had accepted his services. Perhaps he could teach urchins. Perhaps the maiden aunts could be persuaded to furnish him a few hundred pounds to establish himself in some impoverished parish. At any rate, he would not return to the East Riding of Yorkshire after Easter; whether or not the Academy continued in its existence mattered not to him.

His presence was demanded at nearly every confabulation over the following forty-eight hours. Burton-Lee resented this, and John did not begrudge him the ill feeling. Rees was sent away the first evening. In his distress, he confessed everything to his Housemaster, and Burton arranged his removal before the Headmaster could involve himself.

S-K, deprived of the chance to unleash fear, grief, and fury upon Rees, vented them instead upon Morgan Wilberforce. John tried to insert himself as a kind of counsel for the defense, but the Headmaster only turned his wrath upon John, repeating to him in florid, Old Testament rhetoric a sampling of Wilberforce's unfiltered confessions. Pearl minor was summoned and interrogated, but he denied all charges as the ravings of a distraught witness.

Wilberforce would be made an example, S-K announced to the SCR, Wilberforce, without whom no tragedy would have come to pass! Even Burton-Lee in his impaired state protested. Wilberforce was certainly compromised, Burton conceded, but his chief crime, besides an unprecedented lack of common sense, was inserting himself into business that wasn't his own. S-K changed his mind at least eight times on the day following the accident, informing poor Wilberforce each time of his newest fate. He would be flogged publically! (S-K had Fardley dig up some ancient birching block and arrange it prominently in the chapel.) He would be expelled in the night! He would be flogged every day that remained in the term but permitted to stay! He would be flogged daily and then disposed! Finally Wilberforce's father arrived from the London night train. John did not catch sight of the man, but he learned that Wilberforce had been taken away. Disposed or not, reports varied.

On the afternoon of Wilberforce's departure, S-K fell into a fever and was consigned by Matron to his bed. Only two more days remained to the term. They carried on with lessons because they had nothing else to do. Lockett-Egan accepted the post at Pocklington, and when John asked if they needed anyone else, the Eagle actually wrote his new employer to inquire, but returned the news that all posts had been filled. John was invited to send along his particulars in case something should open up.

He boxed his things—a motley collection of clothing, books, and mismatched crockery, fitting into three suitcases, his trunk, and a crate his landlady supplied—and arranged for them to be posted on to Saffron Walden. He drafted the simplest of resignations, copied it in a fair hand, and placed it in his pocket, intending to give it to S-K's housekeeper as he left for the station with his bicycle and rucksack.

The final morning of term he arrived at the gates with the last of his worldly possessions only to discover an atmosphere of renewed sensationalism. He made for the SCR, where the commotion was half outrage, half thrill. The *Daily Mail* had got hold of the story and plastered the Academy's woes across the bottom of its front page. *Public School Boy Dead. Tragic accident or lovers' tryst gone awry?* A photograph of the interior of the barn (still standing, rafter fallen) accompanied the article, which aired every prurient rumor and unfortunately mentioned all the real details of the case, including the school's poor discipline, one boy's attempted suicide after having been spurned—John could not stomach a black-and-white recital of the sinking ship that was St. Stephen's Academy.

During breakfast, three gentlemen arrived at the gates, not fathers, but apparently representatives of the Board, which in all of John's time had maintained a policy of complete nonappearance. These men convened the Housemasters and, after nearly an hour's conference, emerged only to disappear again into the Headmaster's house. The boys departed for the holidays, leaving the halls empty and unnatural.

That afternoon John was cross-examined by the Board. They seemed almost as anxious to determine who had informed the press as they were to decide S-K's ability to carry on as Headmaster. John did not care. He could not care. He told them what he knew, left his resignation on the Headmaster's desk, and got into the cab he had called to transport him to York.

The car bumped along the Wetwang road, his bicycle wedged into the boot. Through Fridaythorpe they jumbled, past the rooms where he had spent the last years cloistered from the world, occupied, he'd thought, in something worthwhile. Behind them now the Cross Keys, where he had spent so many evenings poring over schoolboy compositions, observing their gradual improvement. Gone now the two evenings he spent with

Morgan Wilberforce, who had confided, amidst the things John hoped to forget, that he wished ardently for John to be his Housemaster, that he wished to come to him of an evening and talk things over, that there were things, so many things, he longed to discuss.

The cab rattled away from St. Stephen's, John's home of six and a half years. He had left another school after six years and had never—would never return. His childhood and youth had passed away, along with both parents and the person he had been. The Bishop had passed away, if not literally then for all practical purposes. Jamie had passed away. Now Morgan Wilberforce was passing away. What the future held, John could not fathom beyond the dark road, the swaying cab, and the lights on the walls of York, glowing in the distance, a beacon in the meanwhile.

PART TWO

18 The trouble with life was that it would go on. Especially when it oughtn't. Ruthlessly it continued until, more ruthlessly, it ceased. There was no way as with a gramophone to lift the arm, remove the needle from the disc, and grant respite from the din.

Morgan tried to sleep, but his body had the uncooperative habit of awakening. It was indecent to wake in his father's house after evacuation from the Academy and find that the world had not ceased. Vehicles were braking outside the windows. Someone downstairs was baking bread. Throngs of people were at that moment going about their daily affairs with no notion, no notion at all, of what had occurred. Even his father had gone in to the firm, or so Morgan learned when hunger forced him from the bedroom. Betty informed him that his father would not return until tea-time. She offered food but no further instructions for what he ought to do with himself.

The day carried on carrying on. Then, after the night, another day broke and persisted. His father, disturbed by what Morgan had witnessed yet exasperated by what he saw as Morgan's propensity to involve himself in other people's melodramas, looked into schools for him; none were satisfactory, for reasons Morgan never bothered to discover. His father contacted the man who had educated him in his own youth. The man, though ancient, had come to dinner, made Morgan's acquaintance, and apparently agreed to tutor Morgan pro tem. Easter came and went. Morgan refused to go to church, and his father, lacking the will he once possessed, did not insist. A perplexing series of letters arrived: from his Housemaster, announcing Morgan's expulsion from the Academy; from Burton-Lee, retracting the expulsion; from Nathan, enclosing a newspaper clipping about the disaster, which Morgan burned upon seeing the photograph; from Laurie, chattering frantically about inconsequential items; from his Housemaster again, informing them of Morgan's possible reinstatement; from his Housemaster, advising the probable lack of reinstatement; and finally from Burton-Lee, declaring officially that the Academy welcomed Morgan back should he be well enough to return at the end of the holidays.

Morgan's father looked to him for direction. Should he return to the Academy? Should he be educated at home by the decrepit tutor? Should he enroll at a frankly questionable crammer somewhere in Berkshire? Should he leave school directly and apprentice at the firm?

As protest against life's obscene continuance, Morgan essayed no opinion. His father denounced him as indolent, spoilt, and obstreperous. His sisters arrived in serial to berate and cajole him into taking some decision. He refused. And still the days relentlessly continued to break, meals continued to appear, baths continued to be drawn, and newspapers continued to arrive full of apparently essential matters. His father's physician spitefully declared Morgan's shoulder much improved and ordered him to remove the wrappings and follow a course of stretching and strengthening thrice daily. This tedious item from Harley Street also commanded him to take fresh air for a minimum of two hours each day, to attend at least five social gatherings in the fortnight remaining to the holidays, and on no account to shirk proper school.

Morgan loathed the man. What's more, this verdict had the outrageous effect of galvanizing his father, who summoned Morgan to his study, not the study Morgan associated with the man, but the alien chamber in the newfangled London house. As paterfamilias, he announced that he had taken a decision: Morgan would return to St. Stephen's Friday next. He would hear no more of the matter. Not only did he expect Morgan to follow his physician's advice to the letter—something he would confirm daily—but he also expected Morgan to pull himself together in short order, to apply himself to his studies, to play his cricket manfully, and forthwith to keep his nose disentangled from matters that did not concern him. That was the paternal word. He had had more than enough of Morgan's self-indulgence. He had put up with it out of consideration for Morgan's difficulties losing his mother and growing so very many inches so quickly, but he informed Morgan that his indulgence was at an end. He advised Morgan not to test him. It was time for Morgan to stand up and be who he was. That was all.

 There was something humiliating about boarding the train for the journey north, back to the Academy, or what remained of it. Had he not four weeks previous resigned and cleared out his possessions to Saffron Walden? Had he not after a suitable period of recovery launched himself into the search for a new position? Was he so weak-willed that he could not execute one plan?

Before resigning, John recalled having seen *The Times* brimming with positions vacant. He had the impression that young, physically capable men were hotly sought. Vacant posts, however, proved less suitable than he'd anticipated. He had been unable to secure a reference from S-K not, he explained, because the Headmaster of St. Stephen's refused to endorse him, but because the gentleman was incapacitated by a health crisis. Lacking this document, only the shadiest of characters were inclined to entertain his application. John had visited two families to interview as tutor, and found them . . . off-putting? Vulgar? *Unsatisfactory* was the fairest term. One charity school in East London would have been happy to have him but was unable to offer a living wage, though it did offer dingy tenement accommodation (infested, to be accurate). John was prepared for discomfort, but his prospective pupils, when he examined them, were so dull, so incurious, so . . . foreign sounding, that he felt he'd wandered into a prison camp for Gypsies. They showed no interest in him or in any topic of history, literature, philosophy, or current affairs. He wondered if they'd been drugged. All this combined to dampen his missionary zeal and make him long for the relative stimulation of a third-rate public school.

But that was not why he had boarded the train north. That move had been a last resort, and the inevitable result of his failure to think things through. Having fled the dispiriting interview in Stepney, he arrived home not to the balm of sympathetic family, but to his former colleague Lockett-Egan perched on the drawing-room settee. He was being given tea by Meg, who failed to interrupt her duties to soothe John. Worse, Lockett-Egan had entirely charmed Meg and turned her to his scheme, which he proceeded to unfold. On the one hand, his unsurprising goal was to persuade John to return to the Academy; on the other, John professed himself bewildered since, he explained for Meg's benefit, the Eagle had himself left the Academy for a college superior in every way. But the Eagle, it transpired, had been persuaded to return to the Academy as a Housemaster—persuaded by members of the Board, by Burton-Lee, now Headmaster pro tem, and by Clement, who had offered to relinquish command of his House to Lockett-Egan. John's former colleague and friend put extensive pressure on him to come to the aid of the school, but John, though depressed by the disastrous visit to Stepney, had refused, citing a higher calling to educate the poor. The Eagle had left gravely disappointed.

That might have been the end of it, except that two days later John returned damp and exhausted from a run to find Burton-Lee installed on the same settee, balancing the selfsame teacup. This John found desperate and distasteful, but also oddly thrilling. A discussion ensued in which Burton employed all of his persuasive and coercive skill to convince John that he was indispensable, selfish to refuse, not to mention a key element in the soon-to-be-determined new regime. John's will had not fared as well this time; he had agreed to ponder the matter.

Pondering proved a monumental error; it cast unforgiving light on John's urchin-teaching scheme (naïve) and his circumstances (untenable). As he lay in his narrow bed against the wall that abutted Meg and Owain's, John felt almost dizzy. How could he face the Academy again? Yet, how many mornings could he sit beside Meg without putting his mouth on hers? It was one thing to pass the holidays with them, treating Meg as his friend and Owain as something better than a scoundrel; it was quite another thing to install himself indefinitely in their household.

His goddaughter commenced a heartrending campaign to convince him to stay in Saffron Walden, climbing into his lap and assailing him with every reason her seven-year-old mind could think of or invent. Meg, too, urged him to find employment nearby, though John suspected (when out of her presence and thinking clearly) that she wished him to go north, as she had before when S-K engaged him, even in his state, providing work for his hands, stimulation for his mind, and for everything else, the solace of routine.

The coup de grâce in his present dilemma was delivered by Meg's husband. If it hadn't been for Owain's loud opposition to the Academy and his imperious presentation—suddenly—of a position for John in his own firm, John might have told St. Stephen's no forever. As it was, threatened with Owain's employ and facing a future of chaste good-night kisses that would not cease at the end of the holidays, John went for a run in the rain where he spoke to himself in unvarnished terms: his own wife was seven years dead, Meg's husband was not; unless he wanted to ravage this life as he'd ravaged the life before it, his only option was to pack for Yorkshire, where he had vowed never to return.

✦

He wondered if he'd survive the train journey. Having spent two ghastly intervals in the toilets, Morgan was beginning to hope he would expire, or at least be carried off to hospital at the next stop. Disobligingly, his body recovered, enough to drink black tea between Peterborough and Grantham.

He had never been one for suicide, but as the train hauled him towards the unspeakable place, the word clamored at his mind, inviting into his ill-defended fortress the memory he hoped would one day seem as fiction. He believed the things he had said about the act on that unspeakable day, but he had to stop thinking of that—rope—beam—blood— it was the worst hour of his life. He hoped there would be no worse. For so long, he'd believed that the worst hour had been that one in Hazlehurst's study, when he realized about his mother. (Had he been stupid, or had Hazlehurst been vague? He could never remember quite well enough to judge.) But that alteration, catastrophic though it was, had long been absorbed into the water table; the unspeakable day still flooded the downs. He wasn't the type to convince himself that facts were not facts, but he needed to stop living intolerable spans again. Surely it was enough to have lived them once.

✦

John found the Academy in a frantic state. The opposition had formed a minority government, and somehow Burton-Lee had passed every sort of legislation. Metaphors weren't perfect, but it did have the air of a lifelong backbencher catapulted by bizarre circumstance into Downing Street—although the metaphor collapsed there since Burton hadn't moved into S-K's house. That edifice remained unoccupied save by S-K's housekeeper, the Headmaster having been removed to a convalescent wing of Scarborough Hospital, from whence it was feared he might never return. Beginnings of term were always hectic, the return to the yoke and resumption of a thousand details, but normally the disorder was the result of an old-fashioned attitude towards organization. Now the atmosphere shuddered under the weight of Burton's elaborate diktats. There was no time to unpack, Fardley informed John at the station, for the Headmaster pro tem had requested his presence post-posthaste.

Burton had thought of everything, even things that in John's opinion did not require consideration (for instance, a timetable dictating when each Housemaster would write to each parent and inform them personally of the new regime and its roaring success). S-K had always limited beginning-of-term functions to one staff meeting, followed by a generous tea in his house. Burton demanded their attendance at multiple summits. John had been careful to bring a packet of headache tablets (procured by Owain somewhere foreign), and he made liberal use of them. They reduced the pressure inside his skull but did nothing to relieve the tedium of professional gatherings or the barely suppressed current of fear.

Speaking only glancingly of S-K's pneumonia, of Spaulding, of the *Mail* disaster and the locks-and-bonfire mess, Burton did everything in his power to convince them that the school was returning to normal, or better. The Board had taken vigorous measures to calm parents (and, John suspected, to convince them not to withdraw their sons). They would find their rolls nearly full and their charges anxious to put last term behind them. This, Burton stressed, must be their first priority. To this end, he proposed a two-front attack on the decadence he claimed had led to the school's woes: increased physical discipline and increased physical exercise. No discussion was needed of the former, at least for John's colleagues. As for the latter, John wasn't averse in theory, but in practice he and the rest of the SCR objected to Burton's new rota for supervising drastically expanded Games. It was bad enough, they argued, to receive pitiful wages, to be expected to teach six lessons in a day (involving up to six preparations), to have to supervise Prep four days out of six, to have ordinary Games duty and a hundred other undefined responsibilities; but on top of all that for Burton to propose a further four hours per week, each, supervising cricket, fives, and cross-country—Burton softened his request by assuring them that the current workload was temporary, as indeed was his headmastership (though it went without saying that he hoped to become more than Headmaster pro tem once the Board had finished flirting with the notion that a more glamorous man existed who would take the helm of a foundering school). Once the Academy had been stabilized, the Board promised to organize funds to hire additional staff, but in the meanwhile, needs must have. After a third conference running over seventy minutes, they grew too fatigued to argue.

Back in his disarranged rooms that first night, John realized that Burton had given no sign of what he expected of John personally. Had the man gone to all that trouble to retain him merely to fill the duty roster? It was possible. Probable. Only a dolt could have believed Burton's flattery.

But the anxiety growing even as he cleaned his teeth had nothing to do with his gullibility. It rooted in Burton's plans for the school, specifically in his emphasis on physical discipline. S-K, having registered disapproval of John's pacifist methods, had tolerated them from beginning to end (Was it really the end?), but Burton had given no such assurance. If they came to blows over it (figuratively speaking!), would Burton undermine him before the boys or even sack him? It had been absurd to imagine he could find suitable employment elsewhere, but he couldn't live in Saffron Walden, and neither could he bow to Burton's wishes and revert—he'd abandoned those errors when he abandoned that self. He was a Quaker and a pacifist, Meg and Cordelia were his family, these boys his vocation. That was the truth and nothing else.

At least Burton had succeeded at one thing: he had distracted them from the grotesque reality of the school without S-K, and the world after Spaulding.

✦

Piling out of Fardley's car and into the quad was like staggering into some clearing station just back from the front. Nathan and Laurie pounced with forced bonhomie. They peppered him with questions about his shoulder and behaved as though he had merely been rusticated for injury. Still, it

179

was preferable to the way they had treated him after his mother, with that infuriating delicacy that had forced him to bloody Nathan's nose.

All the talk was of S-K, where he was, what was wrong, when and whether he would return, and how the Academy would proceed without him. Morgan refused to care. Instead he recounted with pulverizing detail the objectionable parties he'd been forced to attend in London, the pompous opinions he'd been forced to endure, the tedious exercises he'd been forced to undertake, and the tyrannical decrees he'd been forced to accept under pain of paternal wrath.

✦

As John was not a Housemaster, Burton conscripted him for a stack of administrative tasks he would normally have undertaken himself: preparing notice boards, drawing up rosters and timetables, coordinating supplies. By the time John made it down to the quad, most of the boys had arrived, but rather than dispersing to their Houses, they were milling about in the courtyard. Masters, too, lingered outside, greeting boys and mumbling with one another. Soon Burton appeared, surrounded by prefects, and announced that tea could be found in the refectory. John was impressed, and relieved. S-K had never offered such refreshments. The prospect would lift the general mood.

The Eagle drifted over and stood beside him:

—Once more unto the breach.

—Sinews stiffened?

—Teeth set, the Eagle said.

John saw him then, strolling towards them, flanked by his friends. John's brain stopped working for a moment, and his heart.

—Hands out of pockets, please, Wilberforce, the Eagle said.

Wilberforce scowled and, in slow motion, complied. Catching sight of John, he shoved Pearl and Lydon and exploded with the two of them into raucous laughter.

—Gods preserve us, the Eagle muttered.

—But, I thought S-K disposed him. What's he . . . ?

The Eagle adopted the philosophical air he turned against all Academy follies:

—Board rescinded. They don't like disposing.

—But—

—Neither does Burton.

John didn't know where to start—what Burton had done, when, whether, how—but they were being swept into the refectory where tea and food awaited them, and before John could disappear down the foxhole of his rage—that they could stand aside as he single-handedly managed Wilberforce and the barn that day, that they could allow him to resign and then strong-arm him into returning without once mentioning the *essential* detail of Wilberforce's reinstatement (he'd almost refused!) and then, without having the decency to tell him what the rest of the SCR plainly knew, to leave him flat-footed discovering Wilberforce in the quad—before his temper could run away with him, a rush of sugar from the cake combined with a rush of something else, something radically humane and incongruous, yet—he realized in an instant—familiar. It was like that afternoon at Cambridge when he'd first cast eyes upon Meg; how she'd huddled with him against the mantelpiece (no witness from before), how the molding supported his neck (Jamie left behind) like a hard pillow, her voice, dense and melodic like Elgar, her eyes, as if she forgave him without even knowing why, how when she told him of the Peace Testimony, his longing for the Front was evicted by a longing for—how she kissed him on the cheek and called him her friend, how in an hour he was rescued—mercifully, miraculously—into the person she saw and loved. That person now stood along the wall of St. Stephen's refectory. That person was being given tea and a second chance, a chance with this boy to show just a portion of that grace. All right, he wasn't the boy's Housemaster, but Wilberforce had not passed away from him after all. And even if Wilberforce was fixing him across the room with a hostile expression, warning him in no uncertain terms to keep his distance, John's pulse raced with eagerness and gratitude. He could wait for the boy to approach him. There was world enough and time.

✦

He was just about averting Bedlam, and then the bell fag came through to wake them Sunday morning. They'd endured the beginning-of-term service the day before, its relentless optimism enough to drive a chap to drink, if a chap didn't drink already, and now they were due for the Eucharist, normally the second Sunday of the month, but also at the start of term and on other tedious occasions that littered the season after Easter. Morgan cared nothing for the service itself, but when the vicar came, it all lasted long enough to kill a chap with boredom.

His nerve decamped when they got to Christ Church Militant; luckily they were kneeling. He pinched the skin between his thumb and forefinger as the vicar went down the list: King, bishops and curates, this congregation here present, all in trouble, sorrow, need, sickness—

—especially our Headmaster, Andrew Saltford-Kent.

And any other adversity . . . Fingernail pressed—

—For all thy servants departed this life—

Knife—

—in thy faith and fear—

Ice—

—beseeching thee to give us grace so to follow their good examples . . .

Wait.

—Partakers of thy heavenly kingdom . . .

Wait . . . had they not . . . ?

—Our only mediator and advocate.

Wait, wait, *wait* . . . but they were on to the next, bewailing sins and wickedness.

—Burden of them is intolerable . . .

They hadn't said it, the name that began with S.

—Forgive us all that is past . . .

They were supposed to—

—Newness of life . . .

Had they said it before, last term when he wasn't there?

—Through Jesus Christ—

He was a fool. Of course they had said it, as the names of all Old Boys were said when they—when it was the place to say them. He needed to wake up absolutely. They'd said it in the past and the past was done. Thank Hermes, thank Zeus, thank all of Olympus.

It was thanks to them, surely, that no one else said the name either. No one asked him to recount the day. No one afflicted him with nauseating concern. Whether anyone thought of it Morgan didn't care, so long as they didn't speak. The only shade of the past was gossip, slight, of Rees. Reports winged in of Rees installed at a school dubbed *wet as Bedales but third-rate*, so it was known that Rees had gone on to plague other people, people who at third-rate-wet-as-Bedales probably deserved it.

The other absence was—just—he couldn't—

Burton summoned John by note during the first week of lessons. A tyro delivered the missive folded in Burton's trademark style, and as John opened it, he could feel the tension spreading through his Fourth Form lesson. The tyro lingered, expecting a reply. Having finally dismantled the origami, John scanned the note, which rather than announcing an unpleasant interview for one of the Fourth, instead requested his presence in Burton-Lee's study during the break. He looked up; the tyro was still waiting.

—I'll be there, John said curtly.

Mirth erupted.

—Oh, sir, what've you done?

—You're for it, sir!

John shut them up with ill humor and set them copying from the blackboard. He realized as they wrote that he'd mishandled the moment. His testiness made him look guilty, like a trespassing boy himself. Which he wasn't! It was offensive for Burton to summon him like that rather than simply speaking to him in the SCR as a normal human being. The only explanation was that Burton proposed to haul him onto the carpet for the indiscipline of his classes. John doubted his were worse than any others, but he wasn't prepared for that contest today, and what's more, he had planned to use the break actually to bolster discipline by polishing up his lesson for the Fifth. They had returned from the holidays not merely dull, but openly contemptuous, and as for Wilberforce, the boy hadn't spoken once. In saner times, they would feel a modicum of concern about their promotions to the next form, but since S-K had allowed summer examinations to atrophy into mere formalities, a none-too-subtle sneer came over his pupils' faces whenever John mentioned exams. His only hope was to disarm them with ingenious lessons that could slip a poniard under the mail of their boredom and rouse some curiosity, however fleeting, in their jaded, naïve hearts.

He had to wait outside Burton's study nearly six minutes. Break lasted only twenty. He could have been concocting something—anything—for Wilberforce and the horrible Fifth. At least S-K had left them alone to get on with things!

—Ah, Grieves, forgive me.

Burton swept across the corridor and in one fluid movement unlocked the study door and breezed inside, depositing books on a table and striding to the windows to haul them open.

—It's the cricket, Burton began.

John hovered near the door. Burton had not invited him to sit and had not taken a seat himself. Having opened the windows, Burton pitched around the study rifling drawers and shelves.

—What about the cricket? John replied.

And what kind of an opening was that anyhow? *It's the cricket.* Had he missed the entire introduction?

—It's disgraceful, Burton declared.

John continued his attitude of confusion, but he knew what Burton was talking about. The expanded timetable called for every boy to have practice daily and matches thrice weekly; thus far the cricket had been slovenly, soulless, soporific.

—I'm putting you in charge, Burton said.

—I beg your pardon?

—Of the cricket. Sort it out.

—In charge how? How on earth am I meant to—

—That's your affair.

John was caught feeling half-flattered, half-used.

—I'm not sure what you mean by *sort out,* John replied, but you can't expect me to reform the cricket games of two-hundred-odd apathetic, ill-disciplined little troglodytes.

Burton blinked. John blinked.

—Concentrate on the Fifth, Burton told him, and the Lower Sixth.

Wilberforce's form, Spaulding's form. Second chance? More like Augean stables.

—Just what sort of authority are you giving me?

—Unofficial authority.

John exhaled in vexation; unofficial authority meant full responsibility and no power.

—The trouble isn't the cricket, John told him. The trouble is Spaulding.

Burton inhaled sharply as if John had uttered an obscenity.

—Why wasn't he mentioned Sunday?

—That is entirely—

—We do it whenever an Old Boy dies, John persisted. We even kept Year's Mind for Gallowhill, two years running—

—Will you kindly hold your tongue! Burton barked.

John held his breath. Burton lowered his voice:

—The time to have done it was then. Bringing it all up now—dragging us through it—would be calamitous. Not to mention cruel.

—I disagree.

Burton looked suddenly old.

—November perhaps, but not now. The Board concur. That's an end of it.

John felt desperate.

—In that case, he said, I don't see how you expect me to get anywhere with that lot. Seriously, *cricket*?

Burton sighed:

—Tend to the strong plants. Prune, fertilize, don't overwater. Make them send their roots down for food. When they've established themselves, they'll compete with the weeds.

—Are we still talking about cricket?

Burton snatched a book from his desk and lurched out of the study:

—Start with Wilberforce.

John flushed.

—But—he's got no time for me.

—He trusted you enough to spill a rangy confession, didn't he?

—That wasn't my fault.

Burton paused at the quad door, slamming John with his gaze:

—Morgan Wilberforce is disobedient, headstrong, reckless, sexually immoral, a hard drinker and smoker, and nowhere near as clever as he imagines.

—That's terrifically unfair!

Burton opened the door:

—Prove me wrong.

✦

Morgan, Nathan, and Laurie disappeared from batting practice once their Deputy Captain had ticked them off the list. They'd stashed a change of clothes in the old lodge, and divested of cricket flannels, they crawled through the tunnel and traversed the woods to Fridaythorpe. At the Keys, Morgan paid for the first round and flirted, as they always did, with Polly.

Plump without being rotund, Polly wore her chestnut hair loose, pulled back in a kerchief. Her face was clear and rosy, and the color of her frock made Morgan notice that her eyes were a robin's-egg blue. She laughed at his flirtations but did not reciprocate as she had in the past. Somehow she had become shy in a way that made Morgan feel he couldn't touch her.

Not that he'd ever touched her, at least not in ways his father would construe as touching. He'd tickled her, kissed her cheek, squeezed her hand, but none of this, he felt, could be considered touching, per se.

The ale worked its way into his bloodstream, and Morgan began to feel as if he'd emerged from battle, though five days of an indifferent term could scarcely be considered battle. Still, as he gazed across the wobbly table, he saw Nathan and Laurie doing the same. He was exhausted. He'd been exhausted the entire hols, which according to his father's physician was because his shoulder required extra sleep yet prevented him from sleeping properly. That was Morgan's excuse and he was sticking to it, but he couldn't see what Nathan and Laurie had to look so shattered about.

Nathan drained his glass and nodded for the second even though Morgan and Laurie were only halfway through theirs. When Polly brought the round, she caught Morgan's eye and then looked away. He noticed a sprinkling of freckles across her nose. When she turned back to the bar, he saw that her frock clung to her figure and that her apron nipped it in at the waist. The seam in her stockings was crooked. Morgan was seized with the idea of straightening it using only his teeth.

He drank his pint.

—Is it Alex? Laurie asked apropos of nothing.

Nathan lowered his head.

—I've resolved something, he announced.

Morgan and Laurie looked up.

—I'm not going to discuss my brother, Nathan declared. At all.

Morgan did not know what to say, but Laurie had no such qualms:

—That's a load of tosh. Why on earth won't you discuss your brother with us?

—Because!

Nathan lowered his voice:

—If I start discussing him, I don't know where I'll stop, and there are things it isn't right to say about family, no matter what.

—Is that your father talking? Morgan quipped.

Nathan's jaw tightened and he took another long drink.

—It's only because of your letter that I'm here at all, he told Morgan.

Morgan winced at mention of the unguarded drivel he'd written Nathan over the holidays.

—The medicine they shoved down my throat—

—Hang on, Laurie said. Are you saying you weren't going to come back, JP?

—That's right, Nathan said.

—But why?

Nathan exhaled heavily:

—My father wasn't exactly thrilled about last term, was he?

—Which part of it?

—All of it. And once the *Mail* ran that piece, well, he wasn't keen for us to come back.

—My grandmother was the same, Laurie said, but once the letter came explaining that S-K was ill and the Board were sorting things out and the fees would be reduced this term, she came round.

—They've cut the fees? Morgan said.

—Keep up, Wilber.

Nathan's jaw stayed tight. He looked wistfully from his second empty glass to Morgan's and Laurie's nearly full. Laurie moved them out of Nathan's reach and resumed his inquiry:

—Not to put too fine a point on it, JP, but your pater's stretched finding two sets of fees. Why wouldn't he send you back once they reduced them?

—You are out of line, Lydon.

Laurie persisted:

—Was it Alex who didn't want to come back?

—Please, Nathan scoffed. He was dying to, the little . . .

—Sod?

—Jackdaw.

—Well, Laurie reasoned, of course he'd want to come back. He just pulled off the biggest rag in the history of the Cad and got away with it.

Nathan sighed heavily.

—What did your mater say? Laurie continued.

—She was with Alex, as usual!

—You mean *you* didn't want to come back?

Nathan signaled to Polly for the third round.

—Take it easy, Morgan said.

—Shut up! Nathan snapped. And quit nosing into my affairs. I'm here. What more do you want?

He left the table. Morgan felt he'd been slapped.

—That's a *yes* then, Laurie murmured.

—But . . . why?

What had Alex told Nathan about him, in the sanctuary of home, never expecting to see Morgan again?

—When you left last term, Laurie confided, Nate was angry, an absolute black temper.

—Over what?

—Over what S-K did to you! Blaming you, messing you about, *disposing* you.

—Oh . . .

Laurie wedged a beer mat under the table leg:

—It's possible someone did a bit of *service-propagande* on how you found yourself at that barn.

Morgan flushed to the roots of his hair.

—But the point, Laurie said, steadying the table, is JP. He went simply *firebrand* against S-K. Never seen him in more of a bate. He was writing his father twice a day about it. I only just stopped him writing his MP.

Morgan's mind spun. Nathan returned to the table with the third round, which he drank aggressively even though Morgan and Laurie were still on their second. He avoided Morgan's gaze as he did whenever he was furious.

Morgan addressed his pint to defeat the rising tide of revelations. Laurie began to babble about moving pictures, and Nathan knocked rhythmically on the tabletop, as if applying the technique to furniture. No one interrupted Laurie's monologue, but somewhere at the bottom of the second pint Morgan sensed a new and more welcome twinge—the thrill of realizing that things did not stack up.

—One question, Morgan said quietly. Were there newspapermen hanging about the Cad?

—No, Laurie said.

—And did either of you go to out to the barn?

—Don't be macabre! Laurie retorted.

Not stacking up, not even a bit.

—JP?

—I thought you said one question, Nathan growled.

—Right, Morgan said, here it is. How did the *Mail* get a photograph of McKay's barn with its rafter fallen down?

Nathan helped himself to Laurie's third pint. Laurie looked from one to the other.

—Hang on, Wilber, are you suggesting . . . ?

Morgan narrowed his eyes:

—Oh, I'm not suggesting, I'm knowing. You—

—Shut up, Nathan warned.

—*You* are a regular double agent. How *could* you go there?

—It wasn't difficult.

—Wait, Laurie said, just wait—

—Who else knows? Morgan demanded.

—No one.

—Besides your pater, of course.

Nathan and Laurie both gaped at him.

—Keep up! Morgan exhorted Laurie. This one hacked out to the barn, took the wretched photograph, developed it, and sent it to his pater. Who sent it to the *Mail*.

Laurie laughed in astonishment:

— You can't be serious!

—S-K deserved it! Nathan cried. Alex was getting away with his rubbish, S-K was treating Morgan like a beast, Spaulding was *dead*, and nobody was asking what a sewer this place had become. It was unforgivable!

His ferocity silenced them. Morgan passed Nathan his third pint as the news sank in. Upright Nathan, logical Nathan: in protest against injustice and out of loyalty to Morgan, he had leaked the story and photograph to the *Mail*, betraying the Academy and bringing down S-K.

—What were you planning if you didn't come back? Laurie asked at last.

Nathan glowered.

—They were quarreling over it. Father knew someone at Giggleswick, but she said we couldn't afford it.

Morgan's father had never discussed money with him or before him. The subject was unsavory.

—Colossal bore, her on about fees and him about cesspools. But then your letter came.

—It changed his mind? Morgan asked.

—No, Nathan said. But he telephoned your pater, and when he put the phone down, he came in and told us we were going back. So here we are.

Laurie had a thousand questions, but as far as Nathan was concerned, the conversation was finished. They settled the bill and trudged back to the woods. Nathan was dragging, having polished off five pints to their two, but they pressed on to make call-over. At the fallen tree near the tunnel entrance, they stopped to catch their breath.

—There's only one part you haven't told us, Morgan said through stitches, and that is what Alex has to do with anything.

Nathan tried to be sick, but failed.

—He got what he wanted, Morgan continued. You both came back. So what's this resolution not to speak of him?

Nathan spat heavily. A chill cut through the spring afternoon.

—Tell me it isn't true, Morgan begged.

Nathan bent over, hands on knees.

—Oh, sodding hell! Morgan complained.

—What? Laurie demanded.

—Alex knows, doesn't he? He knows about the *Mail* and he knows about the photograph. Little beast has JP right under his thumb.

—Hell's bells, Laurie said as the full enormity dawned on him.

Morgan felt the strength leave his limbs. Laurie cursed with every word in his vocabulary. Nathan finally achieved his ambition and vomited.

✦

—Wilberforce, a word?

Mr. Grieves assaulted him on the way out of tea. Morgan cast about for rescue, but Nathan and Laurie had gone ahead. He had so far avoided direct encounter with the man and hoped he might pass the entire term without speaking to him. If Grieves said anything—one single word—about last term, Morgan would abandon him where he stood. And if he intended to set upon him with pity, Morgan would cut him to the bone. *I don't intend to discuss it, sir, at this time or any other.* That he would deliver frostily. Why the devil had he ever—ever!—said to the man the things he suspected he had said? Never mind! If he prevented Grieves from speaking of it, if he firmly blocked any vulgar stabs at intimacy, if he presented Grieves the face of cynical youth, then he would never have to mind.

—You weren't at batting practice this afternoon, Grieves declared. Why?

A brief but tactically disastrous moment passed while Morgan absorbed the salvo.

—I certainly was, Morgan retorted. Ask our DC.

—Oh, I did, Grieves replied. Unfortunately, his clipboard didn't bear any resemblance to what I saw on the upper pitch.

—I wasn't on the upper pitch, obviously.

—No, and you weren't on the other pitches either.

—You seem to have had quite a bit of free time, Morgan said acidly.

—As a matter of fact, I had no end of free time.

Morgan scowled. Rather than lose his temper, Grieves lounged against the arch.

—Have it your own way. The point is you weren't batting when you should have been, so you can bring me this—

He fished a newspaper cutting from his breast pocket.

—copied over six times by break tomorrow morning.

—What? Morgan balked.

—You heard me.

—But—you're not—it's none of your—

—Let's take that as read, shall we? Grieves said coolly. Like it or not, I've taken an interest in your cricket, and unless you pull yourself together, you'll find yourself victim to these little injustices on a regular basis.

—But—

—If you've any complaints, take them to the Headmaster pro tem. Otherwise, lines, my desk, break.

Grieves folded the cutting into Morgan's jacket pocket and gave his good arm a clap.

—And you can mind your tongue. Masters in this school are still addressed as sir, whether you like what they have to say or not.

Morgan's ears burned.

—Good night, Wilberforce.

And the man left him there, alone in the pointless archway, outmaneuvered—trounced.

✦

—What the hell is that? Laurie demanded at Prep.

Morgan had sparred with a punching bag in the gym rather than complain to his friends about Grieves's monstrous injustice. He couldn't face Nathan's outrage or Laurie's scrutiny. Now he had no choice.

—The most putrid pool of putridness ever published.

Laurie read over his shoulder:

—*Everything, small and great, from Summer Time to the aseptic method of surgery, has been fiercely opposed and ridiculed in the period of its innovation.* Why are you copying this swill?

—The spite of Grievous, J.

—What, lines?

—I'm not discussing it.

Miraculously, they accepted his word. Laurie retreated to the window seat with a book. Nathan occupied himself repairing their wireless aerial. Morgan sat at the table and began to copy the protracted article. *Within recent memory, lawn tennis has been thought effeminate and selfish.* He'd never thought it any such thing. He'd thoroughly enjoyed it at Longmere every summer. As a matter of fact, lawn tennis had been the occasion for his first seduction of a girl. At least, Nathan had said that it counted as seduction even though he had only kissed her and touched the front of her dress. He was getting hard at the thought of it even though the Rosemary Romance was years ago, an Easter in many respects like the one he'd just passed: handicapped, imprisoned, agitated beyond measure.

The passage moved from lawn tennis to the game of cricket, declaring it *the source of that spirit of unselfish team-work which has undoubtedly made England what it is.* Did Grieves believe this excrement? The clipping went on to recount cricket's humble beginnings as *a coarse and dangerous pastime which men of breeding ought at all costs to avoid*; to describe a number of spectacular injuries sustained by players over the years; and to extol the puke-worthy *refiner's fire* that was an afternoon of overs spent in defense of wickets and pursuit of runs. It took him nearly a quarter of an hour to copy the thing out once. His hand was sore.

A knock at the study door interrupted their labors. Alex let himself in without waiting for permission.

—Bugger off, Laurie commanded.

—That, Alex said.

—What? Nathan replied.

—I need it.

Nathan lurched to his feet, snatched a book from the shelf, and bundled his brother into the corridor, closing the door behind them.

Laurie, slack-jawed, turned to Morgan:

—Tell me that isn't what it looks like.

—How much d'you think he's giving him?

Before they could say any more, Nathan returned, replaced the book, and resumed the wireless:

—I'm not discussing it.

Morgan flushed with outrage:

—If he's blackmailing you, you ought to tell your pater. It isn't right.

—I said I'm not discussing it!

Laurie fled behind his book. Morgan exhaled aggravation and embarked on the second copy of Grieves's abominable clipping.

✦

Morgan Wilberforce delivered his imposition, though with such naked contempt that John felt he'd miscalculated. He accepted the lines, and as Wilberforce waited, John opened a fresh exercise book he had taken care to procure that morning. Uncapping his fountain pen, he wrote the date at the top of the first page and extended the book to Wilberforce:

—Sign.

Wilberforce was too shocked to comment. He took John's pen as if it might bite him and wrote his name below the date. John capped the pen, blotted the page, smoothed out the clipping, and unscrewed a pot of paste. He wasn't handy and had never kept a photo album, but he took his time and behaved, as the minutes of break ticked by, as if nothing could be more soothing or satisfactory than applying adhesive to the back of a clipping and pressing said newsprint into an exercise book beneath Wilberforce's sloppy signature. Despite a deliberate iciness, Wilberforce fidgeted, absorbed and horrified by John's actions.

By the grace of God, John managed to affix the article and to close the paste pot without spilling anything, tearing anything, or getting anything unpleasant on his clothing. He placed the exercise book in the drawer of his desk conspicuously beside the attendance ledger. This accomplished, he tore up Wilberforce's unexamined lines and deposited them in the wastepaper basket.

—That will do, John said with forced cheer, off you go.

He could not recall a more murderous expression. His hands were still shaking when he poured his coffee in the SCR. None of his colleagues had mentioned the business, so presumably word had not got round. Not that it was significant! It was a workaday episode of school discipline. There was no reason for anyone to think about it for a single second.

Had he won the encounter, or had he gone overboard as he seemed to do so much of the time? Wilberforce would probably deign to appear at batting practice that afternoon, but would he tolerate John's talking to him? And what if he didn't turn up? Would John be able to enforce such a penalty twice? He'd hoped that the theatrics with the exercise book— signifying who knew what?—might impress his will on the boy in some intangible fashion. He knew what Burton-Lee would say: *Never threaten what you aren't prepared to deliver. Make sure every gesture is crystal clear. If ever you allow ambiguity to stand, ensure that serves your aims. Never engage in slovenly discipline; it's worse than no discipline at all.* But Burton wasn't there, not mentally and not, John noticed as he scanned the SCR, physically. He had no intention of discussing Wilberforce with Burton, but unfortunately he did need to discuss something else with the Headmaster as soon as possible: his lodgings, and the awkward fact that his landlady had raised the rent on his rooms in his absence. He'd procrastinated for a fortnight, and now the rent was due. Managing Wilberforce seemed like a float down the river compared to confronting his nemesis-cum-employer on a matter of finance. Still, what can't be helped . . . He sidled up to the Eagle, who was locked in tense dialogue with REN.

—Either of you know where I might find our esteemed Headmaster pro tem?

A severe expression seized the Eagle's face. John cursed himself for his graceless style of interruption.

—He's occupied, REN announced flintily.

John left them before the Eagle decided never to speak to him again. The coffee was watery, the conversation in the room hushed. It occurred to him to wonder whether something unpleasant was afoot. Finding Clement asleep on the chesterfield, John took the coffeepot to Hazlehurst and refilled the man's cup, his best stab at an overture.

—Good chap, Hazlehurst murmured, clutching his forehead.

John forcefully ignored the condescension, which was no different from usual, and sat down beside his colleague.

—Bit of a morning?

—Infernal hay fever, Hazlehurst moaned.

—I meant Burton.

Hazlehurst moaned again.

—That. It's not cricket, is it?

—Isn't it?

Hazlehurst feebly sipped his coffee.

—Board sending those swine in with their accountancy flunkies, harassing us when the term's not a fortnight old.

John felt he had to feign understanding to get a full report:

—It's a bit much.

—And how was Burton supposed to know? If S-K's records didn't mention it, precisely how was he to guess we owed Stoakes . . . what was it?

—Four hundred, the Eagle said.

—Four thousand, REN corrected.

—I'm sure it wasn't as much as that.

John still wasn't following, but he was fairly sure Stoakes was the name of the Academy's coal supplier. And if S-K owed Stoakes money, whom else might he have owed?

John felt a wave of pity for Burton, followed by a crest of joy that he himself had not been saddled with any serious responsibility within the school.

—It's absolutely none of their affair, Hazlehurst declared. And I'll tell you one thing!

—Yes?

—If a single one of those *trade* unionists tries to poke his red snout into *my* House, I'll make sure he feels the jaws of the crocodile!

John murmured appreciatively, dizzied by his colleague's array of metaphor. He had never been fond of accountancy, and he felt thankful yet again that his responsibilities as undermaster included no such drudgery. The only numbers he needed to keep straight were the balance between his wages and his expenditures, which comprised the limited food items purchased outside the school, coins for his gas meter, any hot baths beyond once a week; stamps, stationery, books; birthday and Christmas gifts for the aunts and for Meg, Cordelia, and Owain; repairs as necessary to his bicycle; train fare to Saffron Walden and to the aunts as well for Christmas; that was about it. The tin in his rooms served perfectly well for collecting his funds and distributing them as needed. If he couldn't escape the unpleasantness of money, what perks remained to his profession?

The bell summoned them back to lessons, and although the skies promised fine cricket, the fact that he had not confronted Burton at break meant that he'd have to pursue the man after lunch. And given the intrusion of the Board's accountants, or whoever they were, Burton was even less likely to take John's raised rent in good humor. His stomach soured.

He was supposed to be past this! He had not returned to the Academy to be oppressed by dread or to suffer chaos under different leadership. He greeted the Fifth tersely and then inflicted their first composition of the term. As they floundered before the question of geographical factors in the Industrial Revolution (hint, coal seams), John shored up his defenses against the unsavory developments in the SCR. Whatever was happening, surely Burton had the vigor and the bloody-mindedness to resolve it satisfactorily. Burton was not S-K.

Incredibly, whispers persisted in the room despite the composition. He swept down the aisles and confiscated four scraps of paper, which he hurled unread into the wastepaper basket. The atmosphere quieted, but not entirely.

He knew it was a mistake to dwell on the things Wilberforce had confessed to him, particularly in this new era and with the new Wilberforce sulking at the back of the room, but he couldn't help it. Would the noxious weeds of last term really disappear because Burton declared them past? What about the present atmosphere? The Third were behaving too well to be trusted, and the Upper School were tense, resentful, withdrawn.

There were times, and this was one, when John ardently wished he could unplug his cortex from the mains. Thinking was all very well, but not cogitation towards no end. It was a new era, days were getting longer, and the Academy was on the cusp of an entirely new existence. In the meantime, he was going to have to slog through thirty-two essays on coal. Why had he set this wretched composition, except to shield himself from having to interact meaningfully with Wilberforce and his cadre? Where, God, was the cord to his brain, and how could he pull it, if only for a spell?

 John's eyes were aching in the bright afternoon. He ought to have worn a hat. He made sure that Wilberforce caught sight of him, and then he set himself to observing the practice of Hazlehurst's Upper School. Batting was not an exact science, and for the most part, if asked, John would have told them to carry on. The most essential factor in learning to do a thing well, he struggled to convince his pupils, was practicing the thing repeatedly over a long period. Youth was impatient and hungry for gratification, but if they weren't prepared to hit fifty thousand balls, they would never get anywhere with a bat. Ditto with bowling and fielding.

But batting practice at the Academy was an unserious affair, something they did amidst banal adolescent chatter. John watched from a distance and evaluated each boy's stroke. A few attracted his attention for their obvious flaws. He took out a snub pencil and notebook and listed the boys whose batting needed adjustment sharpish; there were four in addition to Wilberforce. Beginning with the easiest, he sidled up to Colin Frick, who regarded him warily but appeared faintly intrigued by John's suggestions. When Wilberforce finished, John cornered him out of earshot of the others.

—Does your left shoulder still hurt?

Wilberforce frowned:

—It's all right. Sir.

—There's a hiccup in your stroke.

Wilberforce finished removing his pads. He looked as though he couldn't decide if John's remark was an embarrassment or an affront.

—I'm here. Practicing. Sir. Isn't that what you wanted?

—Practice is all very well, John said, but if you're practicing a poor move, it's worse than no practice at all.

Wilberforce stood still, tolerating him. Or perhaps he was using all of his energy to stop himself from uttering an impertinence.

—It's the follow-through, John continued. It looks as though it hurts.

—It doesn't.

—But?

The boy crossed his arms.

—Sometimes you think it's going to?

A blush answered the question. John took up Wilberforce's bat and mimicked his stance. He tried to imitate Wilberforce's stroke, slowing down to magnify the hesitation in the follow-through.

—You've got to stop thinking about your shoulder. Instead of wondering whether it will hurt, imagine that the bat has a will of its own. Imagine it is pulling itself up, like this—

John demonstrated.

—and your arm is only along for the ride.

—You mean some kind of mental mumbo jumbo, Wilberforce retorted.

John handed him the bat. Wilberforce took it with a glare and practiced his drive. John stood behind him, and when the bat crossed his body, John called out:

—Up! You hesitated again. Concentrate. The bat's will.

The second feint was better. John fetched a ball and bowled it gently to him. A quiet but firmly seated *thwack* announced success.

—That . . . that worked, sir!

—Right, John replied, same again fifty thousand times. Carry on, Wilberforce.

✦

In Chemistry, Morgan's shoulder was tired and stiff. Grieves had lurked like some dark agent, intruded into his batting, and then had the nerve to offer advice that actually improved his drive. This after treating him in the most abominable manner over the godforsaken lines. As far as the lines were concerned, Morgan hoped his composition on the Industrial Revolution would provide ample revenge. At any rate, he had amused himself writing it, and with the current state of affairs, if he could amuse himself now and again, he was doing better than average.

The new timetable was another objectionable development. Very little free time appeared in it. Even Prep, which had long been de facto free time for the Upper School, had been curtailed on several evenings in the interests of cricket. Morgan liked cricket, but to have to spend an hour and a half after tea playing it or watching others play it when he might be absconding to the Keys simply turned a good thing into a burden. Besides which, having to retrain his stroke by overcoming instinct fifty thousand times (according to Grieves's arithmetic) promised no joy whatsoever. On top of that, to have to endure Alex's not-very-subtle schemes running bets and extorting cash from his brother and who knew how many others, not to mention the fags' blatant conceit and everyone else's unspoken but obvious sense of tragedy about matters that were nothing to do with them—his father had been mistaken, utterly mistaken, to send him back to the Academy.

As REN droned on about acids and bases and various words Morgan couldn't spell, Morgan's mind slipped back to the Hermes Balcony, to its promise and its miraculous reprieve, to its green-and-brown—to—to

London, its foggy air and foggier parties, its crush of people, its brash independence . . .

He couldn't have said when they appeared to him exactly, but at some point, there the two boys were. At his right elbow, a suave-seeming, knowledgeable boy. Frequenter perhaps of sensational London parties, the kind Morgan had found so taxing. This boy seemed the type to get effortlessly on with bright people. He could flirt without thinking and see everything in its correct proportion. The little man wittering at the front of the room ought to be pitied, the boy told him, not resented. Even more dismal was the earnest character who had sued for Morgan's attention on the cricket pitch just now. That person had relinquished self-respect and had, inexplicably but wretchedly, chained himself to a cabal of old men whose sad lives were devoid of novelty, dynamism, and zing.

Morgan was bigger than this, declared the boy on his right, toying with his exercise book by folding its pages into cunning little figures. He'd be much the better off when he could face reality face on—in the face. Romantic instincts were all very diverting, but only reality was real. And reality was this: He, Morgan Wilberforce, was no longer a boy. His mother was gone. Childhood home, gone. Other frail attachments had likewise passed away. He was a man. He stood six feet tall and was still growing. He possessed comfortable accommodation in a glittering metropolis and was under no compulsion to waste his time in this prison. Whatever he imagined he would miss by leaving the Academy, in reality he would not miss it. The world was far more entrancing.

Morgan could think of no objections. Indeed, he longed to stand up, now, in the middle of REN's lesson, to leave the room, walk out the gates of the Academy, and board a train to London.

He did not move. Perhaps this boy, smooth and attractive in modern-cut suit, was not endowed with power beyond the mental realm. Or perhaps it was the other phantom, the second boy, who had sat silently through the first's manifesto. Morgan could not see the second boy quite as clearly since he took care to remain near the edge of Morgan's vision, but he could tell the boy wore school uniform. He was younger than the first, Morgan thought, younger than he was himself. Yet, this wasn't a past version of himself. This seemed another boy entirely, old enough to attend St. Stephen's Academy and to grasp what it was about. This boy ignored REN's lecture as thoroughly as the boy on Morgan's right, but not out of derision; he ignored it because something more important commanded his attention, something to do with Morgan.

REN pulled down a squeaking blackboard and instructed them to copy the revealed pane into their exercise books. The boy on Morgan's right unfurled an amused lip. They both of them knew—Right and Morgan—that REN's command was nothing more than menial labor for villeins to undertake whilst REN contemplated his newspaper. There were a thousand and one ways to pass an April afternoon without wearing out their hands, or indeed their shoulders, with futile exercise. Right put his feet on the table and began to speak to Morgan of Polly.

Polly, Right said, was looking extraordinarily fine. Morgan could not disagree, but he recalled her new chilliness and her refusal to meet his eye. Right lowered his head as if he might expire with disappointment. Surely Morgan had understood the *thrust* of her behavior? Morgan had assumed that she was tired of him. Right sighed with the pain of a martyred saint and resumed his handicraft with Morgan's copy paper, fashioning crane, toad, vase, tarantula. Morgan really had to learn to use the brain he was born with, Right complained. It was perfectly obvious that Polly fancied the trousers off him. Why else would a girl avoid his eye? Why else, Right argued, would she dress so fetchingly to work the pumps at her father's public house? This theory sounded dubious to Morgan. What, he wondered, made Right so sure Polly wasn't besotted with Nathan or with Laurie? Right begged him not to be funny. Nathan was attractive (as they both knew), but his inveterate puritanism and dour conduct could hold no interest for a girl such as Polly, who yearned for someone scintillating to brighten her horizons. As for Laurie, he had many charms, but he was still a boy, interested in little besides the foul (and delicious) texts his Uncle Anton sent him. Oh, had Morgan not realized that had continued? What did Morgan imagine Laurie was reading so intently just now (yes, across the aisle under REN's nose) if not the latest installment of Etoniensis or Lady Pokingham? If Morgan doubted Right, he could just consult Lydon's trousers (not intimately, external ocular inspection would suffice, young wag) and tell Right if he was mistaken. Morgan could not, after consultation, tell him any such thing.

So, Right concluded, Polly fancied him. She was surely expecting him to return to the Keys on his own as soon as possible. In all likelihood she had plunged into dejection as a result of Morgan's nonappearance this afternoon. Morgan asked hotly what Right expected him to do about it with Grieves badgering him in the most boring fashion imaginable. Right refused to respond, the answer beneath his dignity.

The second boy had listened silently to the conversation. Morgan asked him what he was about. The day was difficult enough without having to endure two phantoms in one lesson. The second boy swallowed and rubbed one of his palms, which was raw in a way that indicated vigorous cricket.

Morgan was hard and his mouth watered. He almost fancied he could smell something—was it leaves strewn across the cloisters? the bite of floor polish? the deepness of the chapel?—something earlier, something previous to the Academy, previous even to the life he could remember, almost like a whiff of life as it had been when S-K founded the Academy and built it up, with the aid of men such as Clement, Burton-Lee, and the heroic, doomed Gallowhill.

REN's classroom adjoined the cloisters, and his windows, high on the wall, revealed a limited but bright square of sky. The late-afternoon sun had turned the tiles of Burton-Lee's House a fiery hue, and in the moment Morgan gazed at it, the light intensified, as if someone had turned on another bulb, or as if a cloud had passed away from the source, allowing this brighter, redder sun to burn across the roof, emblazoning it like the banner of St. George, the sign of diverging paths.

The second boy was looking where Morgan was looking but still said nothing. Morgan felt himself losing patience with this mute apparition. Who was he to sit there stirring sentimental quasi-yearnings?

Indeed, Right rejoined. And honestly, how long did Morgan intend to fester in this moldy den, gazing at rooftops? The next thing they knew, Morgan would be attributing portents to the designs of sunbeams, followed shortly by the contemplation of horoscopes and entrails.

The clock above REN's head promised only five more minutes of limbo. Morgan slouched across the table and assured Right that a fleeting moment of aesthetic appreciation did not equate to taking leave of reason. Right was glad to hear it but cautioned Morgan not to put too high a value on the aesthetic. It was deceiving. Morgan did not disagree. For example, Right replied, if Morgan insisted upon gazing at x's out the window, just what did he intend to do at this crossroads? Would he seize his reason, discard his prehistoric mind and his feeble inhibition before the crusty carapaces of authority, and proceed into an amusing and *stimulating* future? Morgan thought that sounded desirable. Well, then? Right demanded. Well, Morgan replied, he would do just that. He would, for starters, eschew

Prep and proceed to the Keys after tea to turn his energies towards the seduction of Polly. Polly was more than fetching. The past had passed, along with juvenile hopes. Now was the age of men.

Right nodded cautiously, but, Right wanted to know, what about the other one? That relic, the child at Morgan's elbow? Oh, him, Morgan replied. He wasn't worth bothering about. On the contrary, Right rejoined. That other one, that sickly soi-disant spiritualist, he would not simply vanish when Morgan stood up at the end of the lesson. Wouldn't he? Morgan replied. Not a bit! Was Morgan deaf or simply stupid? What had Right been speaking of the whole time? What did Morgan imagine this crossroads was, a crossroads literally broadcast from the rooftops? Morgan assured Right that he comprehended the options before him and had already taken a decision: Right was right, no more need be said.

The bell jolted Morgan in the pit of his stomach as the room burst into commotion. Right vanished, and the other boy was no longer there when Morgan looked.

◆

After tea they adjourned, per the Flea's new timetable, to yet more cricket. At eight o'clock, the sun only just dipping behind the woods, they dismissed to Prep. Nathan hurried to the study, eager to catch the last of the London programs on the wireless, and Laurie paid his customary visit to the library. Without consulting either one, Morgan made for the woods, and the Keys.

Polly was behind the bar wearing another alluring frock, this time in pale green. She nipped into the kitchen as he approached, so he was forced to give his order to her father. Pa (as Polly called him and as Morgan always thought of him) pulled Morgan's pint but did not banter with him as he did with other men. Perhaps Pa did not consider Morgan a man. If that was the case, then Pa did not know Morgan. And if that was the case, it would serve the brute right if Morgan did seduce his daughter then and there! Not that he was the kind of man to deflower a girl to spite her father (not, if he was honest, that he was the kind of man to deflower a girl, full stop), but the evening had a charge about it, a charge Morgan recognized, one that always accompanied great events. The last time he had felt such a charge was the day he and Spaulding— *What* was the point of cultivating sanity if it flew out the window at the most haphazard junctures?

Polly returned from the kitchen carrying a tray of pies, which she delivered to a group of men clad in rural fashions. Morgan flagged her as she passed. She hesitated only briefly before approaching his table.

—Evening, Polly.

—Evening.

They exchanged pleasantries in call-and-answer fashion. Morgan inched his stool closer to her, and when she dropped her napkin, he fetched it. When she asked if he'd like anything to eat, he asked her to choose something for him. More flustered than ever, she returned to the kitchen.

He wasn't going to get anywhere toying with the poor girl, Right said. Had Morgan learned nothing since Rosemary? Morgan froze, disconcerted by Right's refusal to remain a lesson-time daydream, and embarrassed by the allusion to his failure with girls. Right helped himself to Morgan's pint and suggested Morgan refer to him in continental style as Droit. Morgan liked the sound of it. Did that make the other one Gauche? he wondered. Droit exhorted Morgan to concentrate on the matter at hand, namely Polly (the scrumptious piece) and not childish figures or his missteps with Rosemary.

Morgan cringed at his own ineptitude, though in his defense, he'd been a boy then, only fourteen, and incapacitated by a broken arm, a concussed skull, and six cracked—

Droit declared his medical history monotonous and his memory inflated. But Morgan remembered Rosemary perfectly! Everything about her, especially her strawberry lips and her devastating tennis game. There had been tennis all holiday at Longmere that spring. Eventually he'd recovered enough to return her balls, almost, and then—

Yes, yes, she was a nymph with a fatal serve, but what Morgan most needed to remember—what Droit urged him to recall—was that while Rosemary had allowed him to kiss her (once) and to fall instantly in love with her, she had never let him any further than the outside of her blouse or the vestibule of her mouth. Morgan felt it was unfair to expect him to have conquered a sixteen-year-old siren when he was still in the Third Form, not even entirely out of Silk's—

Droit implored Morgan to make an effort with linear thought. If he *would* insist on summoning the past, he'd forever remain its captive. The point of it all was that Rosemary had marred his record, but now if Morgan would simply concentrate, everything would come right. Now, here, tonight, if Morgan would take himself in hand, ho-*ho*, he could and would enter the invigorating reality he had just that afternoon envisioned.

Morgan threw back the rest of his pint, strode nonchalantly to the bar, and asked Pa for a whiskey. Pa pulled a second pint. Morgan took it with a smile, as if he'd only been joking about the whiskey. He drank half of it at the bar and then set it at his table and went down the back of the pub. He glanced at himself in the glass of the hunting sketch. He looked irresistible. He cut out the back, but instead of proceeding down the garden to the toilets, he leaned against the heavy door of the kitchen.

Polly was there. Her face flushed over a gargantuan stove as she dished something out to a plate. When she saw him, she gave a little gasp. Morgan flashed her a fifty-watt smile:

—Hallo, gorgeous.

She failed to mask an embarrassed grin and fumbled the spoon she was holding.

—That for me? Morgan asked, sidling up to her.

She nodded.

—You haven't spoken to me at all, Poll. Why's that?

She looked away. He leaned over the table and retrieved the spoon for her.

—Whatever I did, can't you forgive me, Poll?

—It weren't nothing you did, she protested.

—Weren't it?

—No!

He proffered the spoon, and when she took it, he grasped her hand.

—I'll be in an awful mess if they find out I'm here tonight, he said.

Concern flooded her face.

—Oh, no, pet. What was you thinking?

Morgan mirrored her expression:

—Only of you, Poll.

—Me?

The flush now flooded down her neck and across the bit of her chest that escaped the clutches of her spinster-aunt frock.

—You know they sacked me from school, didn't you, Poll?

—Oh, no, pet! Whyever for?

—Something happened, Poll, something bad. And they think it was to do with me, but it weren't.

—Sommat in paper?

Morgan wasn't sure he approved of this glimmer of shrewdness.

—The point, Polly, is that I'm back now, and if I can tell you a very great secret . . . ?

—Aye.

He inhaled, as if preparing to leap off a cliff.

—I haven't been able to stop thinking about you.

A grave expression came over her. She asked him what he meant.

He didn't need shoving. He'd had enough of being a boy, enough wafting about, a bystander in other people's stories. She gasped as their lips touched, but then she was melting against him, or perhaps he was the one melting. Her lips parted and he didn't know what to do with his hands, but again he could only think, *I want it*—*it* her mouth, *it* her waist, *it* her frock and what lay beneath—her chest, her legs, her . . .

Her tongue reached for his, and his cock was hard, which didn't distress her as it had Rosemary—linear thought, *linear thought*—but his mind suddenly fixed on the problem of what to call it, that place between her legs where boys were supposed to go. The authors of *The Pearl* called it several things, but Morgan was having trouble thinking those words towards Polly. Polly was not Lady Pokingham. Neither was she one of those first-name-only victims of male lust, fit only to flog, deflower, and sell into white slavery. Polly was wholesome. Polly's mouth tasted of ale, and her hair smelt of the mouthwatering scents in that kitchen.

They paused to breathe and he wondered what to say, but she set upon him again, running her hands through his hair in a way that gave him shivers. Then she was running her hands down his back and touching the back of his trousers.

He gasped. He was meant to be running his hands over *her*. She took his lower lip between her teeth and bit it. He yelped, his mouth in hers, and she gave a kind of laugh. Was he succeeding with her? She took hold of his hand and guided it to the buttons on the front of her dress, which she hastily unfastened, continuing with his hand past the edge of her frock, beneath it, beneath yet more fabric, her chemise probably (what did girls call their inexplicable bits of wardrobe?), to the indescribable part inside. It was soft, malleable, warm, like . . . thinking had no place! This was the time for feeling. Her hands fumbled with his flies, and he pressed his hand farther into her chemise as she conquered his buttons and released him. A moment of panic ensued as he wondered whether Polly would admire his cock quite as much as some boys seemed to, but whether she admired it or not, she took it in her hands.

She didn't handle him as he handled himself, and her touch quickly pushed him to the point of—

—Wait, he begged.

—Polly?

Pa's voice from without—she froze.

—Where's that pie?

She hesitated.

—Coming.

And as she pulled away, her sleeve caught his buttons. Morgan tried to help but only succeeded in banging his head against hers. When she finally pulled free, he could see her pulse beating in her throat.

—You're gorgeous, he said.

—Go on.

He did up his trousers. Blood coursed across his face and down the back of his neck. He ached.

—When can I see you again? he asked.

Polly hauled two pies out of the oven and clattered them onto a tray. Winking, she hoisted the tray to her shoulder and disappeared with it through the door to the bar. Morgan, too dazed to think, stumbled into the back garden, through the gate, and into the street. The town clock informed him Prep had just ended. He forced himself to jog to the woods, where he slipped into its darkness and broke into a run.

✦

As Prefect of Hall, Kilby demanded to know where Morgan had been. Morgan opined that it scarcely seemed any of Kilby's affair as Morgan was in the Upper School and had therefore been trusted to do his prep independently all year. This weak-chinned item refused to accept Morgan's rational defense and pressed for details. It appeared Morgan's studymates had not been able to enlighten the flunky, and he claimed Morgan's whereabouts had become his business when Morgan had failed to turn up for prayers. Morgan suggested that Kilby have his eyes checked, for Morgan had indeed attended evening chapel, but due to having been detained in consultation with Mr. Grieves—perhaps the bobby-in-training would like to question their illustrious history master? Oh, had Mr. Grieves departed? How inconvenient—due to their protracted conference on the subject of cotton mills, Morgan had been forced to sit apart from his companions. Kilby considered this alleged state of affairs implausible seeing that he was rigorous with chapel attendance, always making sure to check boys on exit as well as entrance. Morgan confessed this difficult to believe as he had on several occasions noticed Kilby's esteemed eminence conferring with his counterparts in other Houses on the matter of wagers. Perhaps he had been similarly engaged this evening when Morgan had passed into and out of the chapel amidst the Academy's two hundred and twelve other denizens? Kilby lost his patience at this point, and unfortunately, Nathan and Laurie chose that moment to emerge from the washrooms and utter sounds, albeit brief, which betrayed their surprise. Morgan was therefore invited to visit the JCR at his earliest convenience upon changing for bed and performing his evening ablutions.

—Thanks a lot! Morgan said when Kilby had left.

—Where on earth were you? Nathan demanded.

Morgan glared at them both and began to undress. Laurie sprawled across the bench:

—I thought you said you weren't going to the Keys alone anymore.

—It was spur-of-the-moment.

—A promise is a promise, Nathan insisted.

—It was a solo expedition.

Nathan and Laurie took great exception to this claim. They followed Morgan into the washroom, which was emptying as Lower School lights-out was called.

—Whatever you call it, Laurie said, I hope it was worth it. Kilby looked incandescent.

—Sod Kilby, Morgan said. It was worth ten JCR whackings.

They drew near, curiosity fired. Morgan wet his toothbrush and dipped it in powder:

—Polly.

—What!

Nathan looked as though he'd forgotten how to breathe.

—Did you . . . ?

Morgan began to clean his teeth.

—Don't imagine you're stopping there!

◆

Something was seriously the matter with his balls. They'd ached count-less times before, but this was another order of magnitude. Having to see the JCR was a massive impediment to the release his body so urgently required. He sauntered downstairs but his lungs failed to pump with con-viction. It had been a long time since he'd had the cane and even longer since he'd had it in pajamas. He cared nothing in principle for the JCR's fatuous displays, but he had not been prepared to suffer them today.

JCR be hanged, it was worth it for Polly. Her lips, their heat, their strength, the fullness of her tongue, the aggression of her teeth, and—God!—the agility of her fingers and the unspeakable flesh beneath her buttons. Even thinking of her was returning him to—

—Wilberforce, what the hell are you doing?

Morgan pressed against the window and composed his face before his Captain of Games.

—Pondering the ecstasies of cricket, Barlow.

—Don't you think you're in enough hot water? Move, so we can be done with this wretched day.

As Barlow hauled him down the stairs, Morgan tightened the cord of his dressing gown and hoped his cock would get itself under control. It wasn't the worst thing to feel that kind of hunger before being whacked. The worst thing, Silk taught him, was to spunk first. Everything hurt worse after spunking. Still, it wouldn't do to be obvious with the JCR, that med-dling, self-important trio of morons.

—Right, Rabbet began, are you going to tell us where you've been?

—I've already told Kilby, but he don't like facts.

—That's because they aren't facts, Kilby snapped.

—Do you fancy yourself Sherlock Holmes, Kilby? Can you read the history of my evening on my trouser flies?

—You need taking down a peg, Barlow told him.

—Do I, Barlow? Do you reckon that with the same cunning intellect that's led our great House to ruin twice this week?

Barlow stepped forward:

—You don't even belong here, Wilberforce.

—I'm glad we agree. Good night.

Morgan turned on his heel, but Kilby blocked the door.

—Things have changed, you impertinent little pip.

—The Academy is under new leadership, said Rabbet.

—Read that on a notice board, have you? Funny, but as you three are still here, efficient as ever, you'll excuse me if I can't believe everything I'm told.

—Look! Barlow exclaimed. We aren't going to gas around with you all night!

—That is a relief. Can I go?

Rabbet roused himself from his chair and took up the cane, which had been lying across the table.

—Leave off the bravado and touch your toes, Wilberforce. Unless you'd rather speak with Burton-Lee.

Courage draining, Morgan summoned a final bluster:

—I do wish you'd quit flapping like hens and get it over with.

He stepped forward and touched the toes of his slippers.

—Dressing gown off, Rabbet said.

Morgan stood, sighed contemptuously, and removed his dressing gown. Rabbet passed the cane to Kilby.

—Bend over, Kilby said sonorously.

Morgan did, feeling a chill.

—Let's start with six and see how we get on.

✦

John dropped his satchel at the foot of his staircase, collected his post, and retreated to the Keys. The room was more crowded than usual, and Polly informed him that they were out of pies. Tea at the Academy had been inedible, and John felt frantic. Would peas and chips do? Polly asked. They would, John replied gratefully, they would indeed. He collapsed into his usual seat and massaged the base of his skull.

The day was over. He'd marked three sets of books during Prep. Only agreeable things remained.

Polly brought him his tea, and he ran his penknife under the flap of an envelope addressed in his goddaughter's hand. Enclosed was a sketch: two figures ("you & me!") fishing for . . . stars? ("a fishey picknick in boats"). His eyes stung. Things were getting better, and not just generally. The afternoon had delivered his first affirmative encounter with Wilberforce since last term. The boy had taken John's batting advice and appeared buoyed by the results. He would likely be stiff and sore after the day's practice, but tomorrow John would present a regime of exercises and stretching.

The hubbub in the room was growing louder as debate about the looming strike turned to quarrel. John knew he should be concerned about the plight of the miners, and he was of course—of *course*—but Wilberforce had listened to him! John had managed to say the right things and in the right tone. Rehabilitation had begun. For once John felt neither restive nor grim, but only rather pleasantly drained, as he had felt at Marlborough in the good season, when the younger boys had looked to him for direction and he had given it with the kind of warmth and rigor the Bishop had shown him.

It didn't necessarily follow that he'd abandoned every single thing. Maybe some things, the good things, were such a part of his fabric that they couldn't be discarded.

It was a thought.

 Waking up in the morning ought to be banned. It was getting light at all kinds of indecent hours, and even before first bell it was bright enough to make one's head hurt. Morgan hauled himself from bed and went to the toilets.

Everything hurt, more than it had a right to for one of his experience. As the bell rang, he braced himself for the tasks of the morning: washing, dressing, sitting through lessons. They hadn't stopped at six, not that he'd seriously expected it. At least they'd refrained from jawing afterwards. Rabbet had passed him his dressing gown without a word, an atmosphere of unease settling upon them rather than the catharsis corporal punishment usually provided. Morgan left without looking at any of them, his heart beating everywhere at once, his mind focused on regaining control. He knew he'd gone too far with the backchat, but the results had been more than he'd bargained for. From the awed silence amongst the JCR, he wondered whether Kilby's performance had been more than they'd bargained for, too.

As he'd returned to the dorm afterwards, alone in the half-lit corridor, he'd sensed someone beside him. He saw nothing, but he could feel a warm arm bumping against his. The second boy was with him, not to gloat or to criticize but rather it seemed in fellowship, matching Morgan's gait as if he were returning from the same disastrous ordeal. He offered no comment, but Morgan felt this one knew his distress—provoked in equal measure by the despicable JCR and by his own foolish self.

But that was all rubbish that belonged to the previous evening. Now he had to face the ruthlessness of day. On the way to the chapel, he had to pass Kilby; at prayers he had to listen to Barlow's announcements about changes to the afternoon's cricket matches; in Primus he had to face the Eagle's viva on prosody, for which he was unprepared. Droit appeared at this point and cursed the Eagle for his intemperate demands and Barlow for meddling with the cricket timetable. Droit said nothing of the JCR's crimes the night before, but he let Morgan know that they would not be thwarted. Morgan wanted to put his head in his hands. The bench was hard and close to the front of the room. If ever he deserved a bit of anonymity in the back, it was today. Droit told him to quit whingeing and focus on essential matters, namely Polly and her cunning fingers. Thanks to Barlow, the afternoon was impossible, but this evening, being Saturday, afforded ample time. What Morgan had to do, Droit explained, was recruit Nathan and Laurie. He need not visit the Cross Keys alone to canoodle with Polly. If his friends were there, they might usefully engage Polly's father in conversation whilst Morgan and Polly got on with things in the kitchen.

Morgan wondered whether he ought to bring Polly a present. What did one bring a girl when courting her? Flowers? Droit was in his element now. First, he explained, flowers were bulky and thus out of the question. Second, they were not courting Polly, they were seducing her. Nevertheless, it wouldn't hurt to bring an offering. Sweets from the tuckshop? A bit ordinary perhaps, but Droit explained it was all in the presentation. Polly would be delighted if Morgan made up his mind to delight her.

—Apostrophe, the Eagle said. Wilberforce?

—Sir?

—Stand up, boy. And try to wake up while you're at it.

He stood by degrees, cursing Kilby and every JCR in existence. The Eagle repeated the word he wanted defined. Morgan glanced around, but no help arrived.

—Apostrophes show possession, sir, or missing letters.

—Very witty, the Eagle rejoined. And where is the apostrophe in, say, *Batter My Heart Three-person'd God?*

He was on weak sand.

—Before the *d* in *person'd*, sir?

The Eagle marked his ledger:

—Another minus. At this rate, the entire form is headed for extra-tu.

A clamor of protest erupted. Extra-tu wasn't possible, sir. They had cricket. Some of them were in the first match, others in the second, and yet more in the third. The rest had been recruited to referee or keep score. Surely Mr. Lockett-Egan had heard the Head say that attendance was compulsory at all matches. They simply had no time!

And anyway, it wasn't fair, sir. They'd only just returned from the hols. It wasn't fair for the Eagle to expect them to remember so much from the Fourth. That was two years ago, sir! The Eagle reminded them that there had been prosody on their Remove last summer, but they protested it was still too long ago. And anyway, sir, how could they be expected to keep words straight when they had more than one meaning?

—Wilberforce wasn't wrong about *apostrophe*, sir, Laurie argued. And if you'd given him another chance, I'm sure he would have said what you meant him to say, that the apostrophe is the speaker addressing God, which is more or less what he did say.

The Eagle was at the end of his tether, which Laurie muttered must be rather a short tether since it was not yet nine o'clock of a Saturday morning. The Eagle showered them with invective and then commanded them to copy out, again, pages four through seven of their poetry primers, to be passed in Monday morning, no exceptions, on pain of visit to his study, which, he assured them, would deprive no one of cricket as he didn't approve of caning across the hand.

Morgan spent the remainder of the period uncomfortable in his seat but diverted, at least, by Droit's double entendres as Morgan copied definitions for *metonymy* and *synecdoche*, *apostrophe*, *anaphora*, *antonomasia*, and any number of nonsense terms.

✦

—Wilberforce, Mr. Grieves said, a word.

It was barely half past nine; Morgan needed a cup of tea more than life itself, and here was bloody Grieves calling him out of his own lesson before it had even begun, no doubt to bollock him in the corridor like some oversize tyro. If Grieves thought he would get a reaction, he was bloody well mistaken.

The man closed the door and crossed his arms:

—I would appreciate it, Wilberforce, if you would leave me out of your egregious deceptions in future.

Morgan squinted.

—I don't enjoy being accosted by Prefects of Hall first thing in the morning and asked why I saw fit to extend my nonexistent conference with you into evening prayers.

Morgan examined the brickwork.

—Take your hands out of your pockets and do me the decency of speaking to me when I ask you a question, Mr. Grieves snapped.

—What was the question, sir?

—You are on the thinnest ice, Wilberforce!

—Already, sir?

Mr. Grieves flinched, but then, rather than explode, he wrenched open the classroom door and stormed inside.

✦

Something was the matter with his digestion. Everything that John put in his mouth—and that wasn't much—soured his stomach, yet fasting left him light-headed and fractious. What's more, it seemed his colleagues were laboring under similarly strained nerves. John felt that the departure of the Board's accountants would offer some relief, but the Eagle demurred.

—It's a classic scapegoating, he told John at break. The books are a disaster, and since the Board will never admit lack of oversight, they'll fasten onto Burton and wring him till the pips squeak, as the saying goes.

John thought there might be something the matter with the cream in his coffee.

—Germany hasn't proved a very productive lemon under Allied squeezing, he said, so I can't imagine why they think Burton will pull missing funds out of a hat.

—Exactly, the Eagle concluded.

John thought it prudent not to reveal that he was once again failing to follow matters of accountancy and politics. He understood the undercurrents of the Board vs. Burton about as much as he understood the complexities of the TUC vs. Whitehall (or was it the Miners vs. the Mine Owners, or the Proletariat vs. the Capitalists?); that was to say, not much.

John wondered if it was his imagination or whether the world really was growing more irrational and more perilous with each passing month. A better man than he would be teaching at the slum school in London, serving those poor wretches whose fathers, in all likelihood, would soon take violently to the streets protesting wages and conditions down the mines. As it was, John's most pressing responsibilities were his last two lessons of the day and his unofficial maneuvering on the sidelines of the cricket, both enough to turn his stomach. What had ever happened to standing against the world, resolute before white feathers, zealous and bold?

John left his coffee and went to splash cold water on his face. The sooner someone put him out of his misery the better.

✦

The Headmaster pro tem upset their luncheon with a scandalous announcement: Saturday evenings would run differently henceforth. Tonight after tea, the school would repair to the gymnasium. There call-over would occur, and there, the Headmaster pro tem was pleased to announce, they would enjoy a moving picture. Burton perhaps misinterpreted the murmurs of consternation, for he smiled and assured them that the wonders of cinema had indeed arrived at St. Stephen's Academy. Tonight, in common with city cinema—

—Proper cinema, Laurie mumbled.

—they would be shown a newsreel, after which they would have the very considerable pleasure of viewing—

—I'd rather be viewing the backs of my eyes, Morgan groaned.

The Headmaster pro tem informed them that REN had gone to considerable trouble to procure the equipment and reels; he asked them to join him in offering Mr. Eton-Knowles their hearty thanks.

Morgan cursed at length but decided the Flea's announcement need not prove a disaster. They had not been deterred by Barlow's fiddling with the Games timetable, and they wouldn't be undone by the Flea's cinematic ambitions. Morgan needed to relax before he did something drastic.

That afternoon Droit appeared on the sidelines wearing spotless flannels and smoking a French cigarette. Interspersed among droll remarks about the SCR and criticism of the batting, bowling, and fielding of both sides, Droit revealed his Cunning Solution. With Nathan and Laurie they would attend call-over and then slip out once the lights had gone off. The gym would be a sardine box, and none of them would be missed. Morgan declared that he was in no mood for another dose from the JCR, but Droit instructed him to buck up. If Morgan would merely keep his eye on the ball, figuratively and, yes, literally, now as a matter of fact, minding his head—

Morgan recoiled and flailed the bat before his face. A thwack and a clatter. He spun around to see the off stump toppled to the ground.

He had dragged the ball on. His chest clenched. A ripple of applause for the bowler, and Nathan appeared, bat in hand:

—That was close. He almost nobbed you. Who knew Bux had a bouncer?

Morgan's lungs strained.

—What's the matter? Nathan asked.

Morgan staggered from the pitch. The air was too thick. He needed to sit down out of the sun.

Inside the mildewed pavilion, he collapsed on a bench and put his head in his hands. The ball had nearly hit him, and then it had gone right past. For the first time in his life, he'd been out for a duck, and a golden one at that. Bux wasn't even a bowler of note; he'd never been anything but Spaulding's lieutenant, but just now he'd bowled as if . . . It made no sense. He couldn't bear to think about it.

Only a child would complain about Bux. Only a child would expect justice from the world. Certainly it had been wrong for Spaulding to die, but did that mean it was right for other people to do it? Criminals, perhaps, but others? The Old Boys in Long Passage were said to have made a great sacrifice, but from the way everyone behaved, especially those who'd known them, their so-called sacrifice seemed like a monstrosity. If it was wrong for his mother to have died at the age of forty-four, did that mean it was right for Nathan's grandfather to have died at eighty-nine? Justice, plainly, had nothing to do with death.

He could sometimes feel his mother very near, and he could recall, somewhere not in his mind, her lips on his forehead, her whistling of hymns as she moved through the house, the way she would come and sit on the edge of his bed when he called in the night, listening to his dreams and then recasting them, whimsical or heroic. Was she really not waiting at home, having merely been delayed, hungry for everything Morgan could tell her?

The world was ill to the core.

He pressed the heels of his hands against his eye sockets. His chest still stabbed, but he was managing to breathe. His father, too, was breathing, and his sisters, not to mention Spaulding's lieutenants and his Captain of Games. They were all of them breathing: Veronica, Emily, Flora, Bux, Ledge, Andrewes, Morgan himself. This carrying on was nothing short of perversion.

Applause filtered through the cracked window. Nathan had either scored or been bowled out. It was hot. Perhaps he had heatstroke. Perhaps he was unfit, on some level, for living.

The bench teetered as weight settled at the other end. Morgan didn't turn, but he could feel him, an arm's length away, the other boy.

—I don't know who you are, Morgan said aloud, and I don't know what you want.

He pressed thumbs against his eyebrows and the icy pain there. The other boy said nothing, as usual.

—You've got bad manners at any rate, Morgan muttered.

If he was going to start cracking up, he might as well do it properly.

The bench didn't wobble, but the boy moved near and rested elbows on knees. A lock of dark hair escaped his cap. This boy wasn't gauche, not really, but he wasn't Droit, not shrewd, not witty or worldly. Morgan didn't know what to call him; he was simply . . . the other one.

With dusty hands, the boy removed his cap, a Lower School cap in Morgan's House colors. His arm did not touch Morgan's, but Morgan could feel its heat through the fabric of his sleeve, just as he could feel the pressure of this boy's leg against his own. Out of the corner of his eye he glimpsed the boy's palm, bruised from play, and the name tag inside his cap. Written in ink neither blue nor black but a smeary red, the letters *I*, *A*, *M* . . . that was all he could read.

Some days John wasn't sure whether he was employed by a public school or by a training camp for young cricketers. They'd spent more hours playing cricket that term than they'd spent aggregate on any game since 1919.

All right, but if he couldn't indulge in a little hyperbole, what could he do? Nothing worthwhile was happening in the classrooms, but at least conduct hadn't deteriorated further. Burton had been relentless in his Arnoldian pursuit of Games, and the ceaseless cricket had been joined by cross-country, fives, and even badminton. At first the boys ridiculed the badminton, but Burton directed the DCs to work up ladders and offer prizes. Observing the success of prizes with the badminton, Burton introduced them for running and for achievements in cricket. Rewards took the form of points, which could be used as credit in the tuckshop. The Upper School regarded the prizes with thick irony, but the Lower School began to compete for them. John knew that no amount of busy athleticism could ameliorate grief, much less eliminate unsavory practices, but since all this compelled vigorous exercise daily, it went a long way towards draining their energies.

And it happened that the cricket was improving. John couldn't deny that it would make a good impression come Patron's Day in June, nor could he deny feeling a certain vindication watching the game work upon their characters. Jamie had always been philistine about cricket. *There's nothing to it,* he'd declare. *Their men lob cork at your men, repeat until ten wickets fall or your side wins.* People were always scandalized, but that, John supposed, had been the point.

John himself was no cricket sage, but given St. Stephen's aging SCR, he could do more on the pitch than most. If he were the genuine article, he would be coaching them not merely to hit a cork, but to understand the delicate art of building a partnership, two batsmen coming together, watching each other down the pitch, taking their runs and jointly building a fine total, their change of ends after each over bringing the side one step closer to a famous win. And then he would throw in the technical aspects—the off stump of your wicket is the most important of the three, the most difficult and critical to defend—except his remarks would ring beyond the cricket pitch, echoing into the battles they were all of them fighting without even realizing it.

It seemed a great injustice that no competent authority existed to educate St. Stephen's boys physically, intellectually, or morally. When he was at school, they had ridiculed every master for one foible or another, but he had always regarded his masters as reliable on the most basic level. They possessed a mastery of their magisteria beyond reproach. The ways of those men may frequently have been incomprehensible, but there had been reason and experience behind them. The two times John remembered being punished unfairly by a master (once at prep and once at Marlborough) happened because the master in question had been unaware of his circumstances or motives. Boy justice, by contrast, was often unfair, and often an instrument of vendetta. Men were above this. They knew what they were about and had something to impart.

Now that John was a man himself—at least he knew he had to consider himself one; he'd turned thirty in January—he felt he'd somehow fallen into perpetrating a magnificent fraud. Some amongst his colleagues knew their subject matters deeply—Burton-Lee, the Eagle, and Clement—and some possessed a talent for imparting that knowledge—Burton-Lee, the Eagle . . . actually, just those two. He didn't condemn his colleagues whole cloth; he observed each of them doing something of value daily (or at least weekly?). The trouble was, he didn't think any of them had anything authoritative to convey. They were busking. Circumstance demanded he act the role of master, yet he was painfully aware of how poor a specimen he was.

✦

Polly had let him do almost everything except the thing boys aimed to do with a girl. Little else occupied his mind but the sight, touch, and taste of those parts of her body she kept concealed beneath her clothing. She was coy on the topic of actual . . . what to call it? Nathan called it *making love*, which struck Morgan as abstract. Morgan wasn't sure if he loved Polly enough to marry her, but she was very pretty, and he was very fond of her. Laurie referred to the act as *coitus*, a term surely too academic for such a girl. *The Pearl* employed a plethora of verbs, all of them unthinkable vis-à-vis Polly.

Surely the point, Droit mused as they watched the First XI play Pocklington, was not what to call the act, but how to achieve it. And if Morgan was still clinging to the hope that Polly would raise the subject, then it was high time he stopped dreaming. No decent girl would ever suggest *l'amour complet* unprompted. *L'amour complet!* Morgan liked the term. It had continental flair. Furthermore, it made clear that while lesser acts might spring from *l'amour*, it was necessary to penetrate the final barrier to achieve romantic completion. How, though, to raise the subject without coming off a cad?

Droit did not reply, but in Morgan's experience, Droit operated best in the fray. He excelled at appearing just when needed to provide the crucial insight. Morgan decided to leave entirely to Droit the achievement of *l'amour complet*.

Once imagined, however, it was difficult to evict from his mind. Would he at last succeed in acquiring the experience so many of his school-fellows had long since possessed? More important, when could his thirst be quenched? At first it had been enough to see her two or three times a week, drinking in her mouth, exploring, being explored in return, but once he'd experienced release at her hands, it became agonizing to leave her presence without that solace. Now it seemed impossible to endure an-other day without the full feast of *l'amour complet*. Surely she would not deny him if he could propose it in a way that made it seem delightful?

More immediately, he needed to raise money. To succeed even so far as he had with Polly, it had been necessary for him, Nathan, and Laurie to expand their visits to the Keys, and since the visits were mostly for Morgan's benefit, he bought the lion's share of the rounds. It had grown expensive keeping Nathan in pints—his thirst grew in response to the drain that Alex had become—and Morgan had nearly exhausted his whole term's pocket money. He'd had already written to each of his sisters and had used up the funds they'd sent. He could borrow from Colin, who ran a bank alongside his distillery, but the interest was steep. His final hope was his grandmother in Devon; he'd never asked her for money before, and he needed a story that would convince her to open her purse to him without informing his father.

What he needed to do, Droit informed him, was find a service no one else was providing and provide it.

Well, obviously that was what he needed to do, Morgan retorted, and if Droit had any suggestions, Morgan implored him not to be shy.

If Morgan was going to get sarcastic, Droit had other business.

Morgan assured Droit that the sarcasm was unintentional.

Droit lit a cigarette and observed that Polly's father was forever arrang-ing wagers for his customers on the outcomes of various bouts and matches; he seemed to keep his customers happy whilst earning a tidy sum for himself.

Morgan reminded Droit that the Headmaster pro tem had come down heavily when he'd discovered betting in the badminton ladders.

Droit implored Morgan to try a more creative angle. Obviously, wagers within the Academy were not only vulnerable to general enthusiasm, rendering them too visible and too common, but they were also amply supplied by Colin and by Alex. (Yes, of course, Alex had resumed after the badminton. Was Morgan willfully blind?) But, Droit continued, no one at the Academy was offering proper wagers, wagers with proper men on cricket matches played in the outside world. If Morgan could interest a few of those with cash to spare, then he could act as go-between, placing wagers for them at the Keys, returning them real winnings from the real world, and earning himself a fair commission. He might even advise his clients on reasonable bets and give them a taste of winning from the start. Morgan sat speechless as Pocklington's bowler took Andrewes's wicket and Droit exchanged his cigarette for a glass of Pimm's.

 Rain was forecast for Patron's Day, but John had hopes it might not materialize. Since Burton had taken pains to ensure the ranks of Old Boys included the able-bodied, John also had hopes that the match would for once not prove embarrassing. Ever since the War, masters had been drafted to fill out the Old Boy side, but this year Burton assured the SCR that their services would not be required, with the exception of John, whom the Old Boys expected as their captain. John was disturbed to read amongst the replies the odious names of Bradley, Fletcher, and Frick major. Frick had come every year, as his brother Colin was still at the school, but this would be Bradley's first appearance. Until today, John had allowed himself to imagine that Bradley had disintegrated like a bad dream. He was not looking forward to playing cricket with the creature.

The First XI were beginning to look respectable, particularly the House Captains (Andrewes, Radcliffe, and Barlow—though Ward continued to disappoint). They hadn't yet won any matches against other schools, but they'd easily defeat the Old Boys. It wasn't unreasonable to hope that, buoyed by that success, the XI would acquit themselves well against St. Peter's the following week and perhaps even win that match.

Burton, predictably, was in a flap about the day. In addition to parents and a hefty turnout of Old Boys (some of whom, John suspected, had returned to see for themselves what had become of the Academy in its tragedies), several of the Board were expected. For a time, it was rumored that S-K himself might come, but Burton informed the SCR on the morning that the Headmaster had sent his regrets, or rather, someone had sent regrets for him. Burton affected disappointment, but John could see he was relieved. S-K's presence would have been impossibly confusing. It was going to be hard enough for Burton to convince everyone—Old Boys, Board, the school itself—that his government was at last under control and moving the Academy in a profitable direction, that the Second Age was under way. What's more, Burton surely realized that Patron's Day would be his final audition for the post of Headmaster. This would be the Board's first visit since the distasteful swooping of its accountants at the start of term. Apparently, the visiting Board members would stay the night and spend the following day closeted with the Headmaster (pro tem) to review the conclusions of the auditors and presumably the future of the school. It was no wonder Burton's nerves were frayed, but (as John would have informed him if asked) his snappiness was making it difficult for his staff to be congenial.

—They're here! Burton announced at the door of the SCR. Chop-chop!

John drained his coffee and went down to greet the first cab.

✦

It was going to be a historic Patron's Day. Hermes willing, Eros willing, his carefully laid plans would at last come to fruition. The Headmaster pro tem had announced that he would continue S-K's tradition of a nature walk in the evening, and he had asked REN to join them and provide scientific commentary. Morgan resented the Flea for every one of his novel intrusions into their time, but Morgan's curses ceased at this revelation. From seven o'clock until quarter to ten, the school would be occupied on a loosely patrolled nature walk, or back at the Academy under the eyes of somnolent prefects. Meantime, Polly had connived to have the evening free by fabricating an invitation to the home of a willing friend in Thixendale. She had not protested Morgan's suggestion of *l'amour complet*; in fact, she'd agreed more quickly than Morgan had dared hope. Her conditions had been simply that the event must take place off premises of the Keys and at a time of her choosing.

The only remaining obstacle had been the location.

Having watched Morgan concoct and reject any number of ideas, Droit finally revealed the obvious solution. Morgan had protested vehemently at first. Under no circumstances did he, Morgan Wilberforce, intend to return to McKay's barn. For one, it was hazardous and possibly collapsed by now. For two, Polly had once expressed disapproval of the business there. And for three, it was . . . what could he call it? A graveyard?

Droit appeared to think Morgan feeble.

Morgan was anything but feeble, but he was not prepared to complete his conquest of Polly on the selfsame ground where—did he really have to spell it out in words?

Droit was the last who required things spelled out in words, images, or insinuations, but that did not change the fact that Morgan's fears were the only thing standing between him and l'amour complet.

They'd exchanged testy words on the topic before Morgan had agreed to return to the godforsaken barn during a half holiday just to prove to Droit that he wasn't afraid.

During the reconnoiter, his stomach and limbs may have imitated those of a silly girl, but Morgan insisted that it was impossible by the laws of natural science for the past and the present to occupy the same place. Having glimpsed the fallen rafter inside the otherwise enduring structure, he determined not to dwell on the unpleasant.

And as it happened, the barn had a second enclosure, one accessible by a smaller door he'd never noticed before. It would be possible to tidy the smaller area, to make it hospitable, to lay it with rugs, to enter it with Polly (to enter Polly within it, ho-ho—yes, thank you!), and to enjoy her company there all without glimpsing or trespassing upon the other side of the barn.

As much as Droit objected to words like trespassing—superstitious and subservient—he nevertheless praised Morgan's plan for its practicality. And anyhow, Droit reasoned, wouldn't it be the ultimate triumph to achieve l'amour complet on that site, transforming defeat into victory and expunging the unpleasantness for all time?

Morgan could not argue with Droit's logic even though he knew what the other one would think. That boy never needed to speak. He worked on Morgan's nerves with glances and every sinister trick there was. Even bloody Grieves had never troweled on the sadness and regret that boy perpetrated regularly. Morgan had informed the twerp that his conjurer's trick of inducing irrational emotion had quite lost its power. He had outstayed his welcome, and if he wanted to look at Morgan and suggest that having Polly in the barn would never be an act of redemption for—Morgan refused to entertain such thoughts. The whole affair was getting baroque, and the only answer was to do as Grieves commanded them and concentrate on facts.

Patron's Day had arrived. Cabs were crunching across the gravel, and soon the glorious day would begin. Excellent food would be accompanied by diverting cricket. His father was unable to come this year—Morgan was too relieved to ask why—which left him delightfully free of responsibility. After a lavish luncheon and an excellent tea, he would rendezvous with Polly in their nutting bower. There, on the longest evening of the year, he and Polly would abandon themselves to every pleasurable thing, *l'amour complet* would be achieved, and life would change its course for good. Those, in short, were the facts.

Downstairs, the morning post had arrived in the pigeonholes, bringing him an envelope addressed in unfamiliar hand. Its thickness encouraged him to open it immediately.

And already the day was superlative! For here was his grandmother writing him from the wilds of Dartmoor on a day that wasn't his birthday. Here she was extolling his frankness (his failure of imagination) in asking simply for money when he needed it. Here she was replying warmly, confidentially, and materially with a banknote worth more than the pocket money he would receive for the rest of term. The fact that his wagering service was doing nicely did nothing to lessen her unmerited generosity. He was flush! He could now afford to give Polly something special that evening. He would be able to keep Nathan in pints for the rest of the term. Things were turning to good in every sphere. He could even afford to place a second wager in the book Colin had made on the Old Boys match. Nathan had voiced dire warnings about betting within the gates, but Morgan had explained that (a) Patron's Day was an exception, (b) the risk was mainly Colin's, and (c) if they didn't have anything riding on the match, they'd die of boredom watching it. At least half the school agreed, so Morgan had leaned on Nathan to analyze Colin's line. Morgan had originally put a crown on the First XI despite heavy odds on, but now that he had cash to spare, he decided to place a long bet on the Old Boys. He caught Nathan coming down from the dorm and suggested as much. Rather than balk, Nathan lowered his voice:

—You heard Barlow, then?

—What about him?

—Shooting cats half the night, and it didn't sound like nerves.

—Hell's Piss?

Colin's reserve brew was indeed the likely culprit, in Nathan's expert opinion. Morgan grimaced at the memory of the one time he had indulged; punishment had followed crime more swiftly than any JCR justice.

—At any rate, Nathan concluded, Barlow's stuck in the Tower for the next twenty-four hours, so there goes the best bat on the First XI.

Despite his contempt for Barlow's House captaincy, Morgan couldn't deny that without him, the First XI would be compromised, which made a bet on the opposition rather less long.

—It's a bit much for Colin to fix a match he's booking himself, Morgan said.

—He didn't.

—Are you trying to tell me Barlow half killed himself with Hell's Piss and Colin didn't give it to him?

—Correct.

Nathan terminated the conversation by stalking off down the corridor. Morgan could only conclude that Alex was responsible—for this and any other dog tricks at the Academy—in a way he'd grown tired of contemplating. This meant Alex had real money on the Old Boys, and this, combined with Barlow's affliction, meant that the Old Boys had an actual chance of winning.

Morgan caught up with Nathan:

—Let's put ten bob on the Old Boys before Colin moves the line.

—Leave me out of it, Nathan said. And anyway, you're skint.

Morgan handed over the morning's missive, whose contents cheered Nathan considerably.

—Your grandmother is the most brilliant old pet! What's this?

Nathan extracted a second page from the envelope, which Morgan had forgotten in his excitement over the money and the wager. On one side was his grandmother's hand: *I found this in the drawer with the photograph album. I believe your father wrote it when you started school? In any case, it belongs with you.*

Morgan had no memory of his father's having written him anything when he started prep school. Clearly his grandmother was confused. Or his father had never sent it.

Boyo, you asked me to write down the rules of cricket "in a good way and leaving nothing out." I'm sure your masters will teach you the bylaws, but here are a few things you won't find in books.

Always play for your side and not for yourself.

Never dispute an umpire's decision. When the umpire raises his finger, you are out.

Never risk your wicket with a flashy stroke. Remember that running four or six singles is just as valuable as hitting a boundary.

Never blame bad luck. Be a man and admit it was a bad stroke.

He tried to put it away, but Nathan protested:

—My father never wrote me anything like this.

—Count yourself lucky.

Morgan buried the letter in his pocket, tracked down Colin, and, in a flush of enthusiasm, put a guinea on the Old Boys.

✦

John felt like a whirligig and it wasn't even nine o'clock. He'd already greeted a score of Old Boys and could remember none of their names, unless he'd taught them. Amongst those, he'd seen Frick major, Fletcher, and Bradley, all as unsavory as ever, though they professed themselves ready and willing to play for the Old Boys. By the end of breakfast, John had confirmed twenty-seven for the OB side. Tradition dictated that all Old Boys who could physically hold a bat or catch a ball would alternate. The tradition of filling out the side with masters had not come about because of insufficient numbers but because it was bad for morale when the Old Boys lost catastrophically. John had hoped he might avoid actually playing, but the absence of a strong bowler meant he would likely have to lend an arm at some point. He prayed that the day might pass quickly.

On the way into chapel, he was accosted by Andrewes, Burton's Captain of Games and Captain of the First XI.

—Sir, a word. Urgently?

John surrendered:

—What is it, Andrewes?

—It's Barlow, sir. He's retching up his guts in the Tower.

John's heart gladdened at the prospect of a diminished First XI.

—Here to concede the match? he asked with what he hoped was joviality.

—I've got to send someone in for him, Andrewes said, but I don't know who. It should be from Hazlehurst's, but . . .

—Yes? John prompted.

—Barlow's good, sir. We need the best possible substitute.

—And you want my opinion?

—The Head said I was to ask you and choose whomever you recommend, sir.

John realized that he was feeling what would commonly be called a conflict of interest, though evidently Burton did not see it that way. Evidently, Burton thought him capable of recommending a substitution even if it meant his own side would suffer. John cursed the Headmaster (pro tem) for his insight and reviewed the roster of Hazlehurst's Upper School.

—There's Wilberforce.

—He's in the Fifth, sir. We need someone special.

—Wilberforce is special.

—I've never noticed him.

—You will after today. Everyone will.

—How, sir? If you don't mind my asking.

—Can't explain, John replied. Must run. You asked my advice, and there it is. Otherwise, good luck to you and may the better side win.

He dashed off for chapel, leaving Andrewes looking as though he'd swallowed something he had expected to taste much sweeter.

✦

Morgan didn't believe it was true until he saw it with his own eyes: Silk Bradley, alive in the quad.

He was dressed fashionably, but he seemed less elegant than before. His hair was longer, his face wider. He was shorter. Morgan recoiled into the House.

—No, you don't, Laurie said. Don't give him the satisfaction.

His elbow imprisoned by Laurie, Morgan was marched across the quad to where Bradley stood smoking.

Ghosts might walk, but they could not reach inside his chest and interfere with his heart. His heart belonged to him, and although it might stutter, it would not stop pumping his blood. It had no choice. Its nature was to seize and release until the end. Silk Bradley had not stopped it before, and this avatar could not stop it now.

The avatar noticed him at once.

—You still here? it said.

Morgan's tongue lay heavy in his mouth. Laurie brazenly produced two cigarettes, lit them in broad daylight, and passed one to Morgan. A grin broke across Bradley's jaw.

—I heard they turfed you out, Dicky.

That name, on that lip, burned sharper than the first draw of Laurie's roll-your-own, almost as sharp as that first time. *You've never smoked before, have you?* Was it possible to burn to death in the courtyard of an English school?

Bradley stared at him. *Don't suck too deep.*

Simply not possible for anything to continue.

But Bradley continued to stare. Morgan continued to smoke. *Take it easy. Do you want to be sick?* The impossible continued.

—You three playing this afternoon? Laurie asked.

Abruptly Morgan became aware of Bradley's companions, whom he recognized as Frick major and Fletcher. Fletcher sneered in the old way:

—Seeing as you boys put bets on the XI, we've no choice but to take your money.

—Think you can lead the Old Boys to their first victory? Laurie taunted.

Fletcher consulted Frick major:

—Who did you say was on the XI? Andrewes minor, Radcliffe minor, Barking Barlow, who else?

Colin's brother waved his cigarette dismissively:

—Some other little boys.

—Are you playing? Laurie asked Bradley.

Bradley stubbed out his cigarette but didn't answer.

—Wilberforce put a guinea on the OBs, Laurie told them.

The grin returned to Bradley's face and brightened his eyes like—

—If you thrash the XI, Laurie said, he'll be a rich man.

Bradley caught his gaze and held it as he used to. Under his skin, blood.

—Wilberforce!

A call from across the quad. Laurie snatched the cigarette from Morgan's hand and trampled it underfoot with his own. Fletcher and Frick major pulled Bradley away.

—Behave yourselves, boys, Fletcher sneered.

Morgan instructed his lungs to pump, stabs or no, heat or no.

—Wilberforce! the voice called again.

—It's Andrewes, Laurie hissed.

Breathless, dumb, Morgan floated through the crowd, propelled by Laurie to the threshold of the cloisters.

✦

Chapel having convened, John stopped writing down the names of Old Boys who'd greeted him and announced their intention to play for the side. Belatedly he realized it didn't matter. Those who wished to play would turn up at the pavilion, and he would arrange them as he could. Patron's Day always produced an atmosphere of chaos, but he reminded himself that captaining the Old Boys offered a certain protection from it. While his colleagues had to greet parents, charm patrons, organize tours, and give chats on sundry topics, he was freed to the simple demands of cricket. His only tasks were to develop a camaraderie with the men on his side, to choose a position for each man that did not tax his abilities, to flatter their play, and to bowl as savagely as possible to limit the damage the First XI would inflict on age and wisdom. He knew he'd get the best play from his side in the hour and a half before luncheon. The wine carafe would diminish the OBs just as the meal would revive the First XI. After lunch, he knew, his right arm would be the only thing standing between the Old Boys and humiliation.

Why did this match always come down to him? And why had Burton found it necessary to corner him on the way into chapel and tell him in ponderous tones that it was essential everything proceed smoothly today and that "everything" hung in the balance?

The chapel was fuller than John remembered seeing it. Some boys had been sent upstairs to the gallery. John wondered how Burton had drawn such a crowd. Had he sent personal invitations? Or had parents and Old Boys merely flocked to Yorkshire to see what had become of the school S-K had abandoned, the institution so floridly savaged in the *Mail* that Easter, a place now led by a man who until late April had spent his career teaching Latin and Greek? John's eyes couldn't penetrate the crowds, and his head couldn't stand the strain. He tried to think of soothing things.

Morgan's stomach hurt after chapel. The pang that had seized him in the quad had grown, not lessened, at Andrewes's lunatic command.

Nathan's parents had already arrived, and Laurie's grandmother was due momentarily, so Morgan trudged down to the changing room alone. In minutes, the day had turned sinister. Not only had a specter appeared without warning inside the very fabric of the present, but it had looked at him, spoken to him, and shown that it knew him as it used to.

He didn't care what Bradley thought of him. Bradley hadn't set eyes on him in three years and hadn't spoken since the last night of his reign.

That night, Bradley had offered him a drink. Morgan had refused. They sat opposite one another in that study, a room so charged that Morgan had wondered whether he'd be able to keep breathing. Silk had looked at him in a way Morgan had not understood and still didn't understand. He had been preparing a curse when Silk produced a book, red leather, worn.

—Here, Silk said.

—I don't want anything from you.

—Do what you like with it, then.

Silk had dropped the book on the table and gone to gaze out the window into the humid night. Without even checking to see if Morgan was listening, Silk had begun telling him the story of the poacher's tunnel: how in the first generation of the school, there had been a boy called Hermes, who had pioneered every prank there was; how one great night, Hermes had penetrated the heart of Grindalythe Woods and there found its keeper, a creature who put Goliath to shame; how Hermes had won from him the secret of the poacher's tunnel and secured perpetual safe conduct through the woods for himself and his heirs; how Hermes had passed the secret to his fag, inaugurating generation after generation of custodians for the tunnel, each inducted by his fagmaster, each sworn to silence and sworn to exact an oath of secrecy from any he brought through the tunnel, each bound to pass the secret on to his own fag when he left the school. No exceptions had ever been made, Silk told him. No one had ever passed the duty to a friend. Silk was the seventh guardian, and Morgan would shortly become the eighth.

Silk had sliced his own palm with a penknife and then passed the blade to Morgan with blood still on it. In that moment, they became equals; whatever permissions Morgan had or hadn't given for the many acts of that brutally long year, in that moment his compliance became assent. He took Silk's knife and cut himself, releasing his own blood and touching his palm to Silk's, absorbing Silk's responsibility into himself. Silk's blood had not been shed for the whole world or even for any good purpose, but it flowed freely. There had been no vow, no cant or repetition. Silk had only held their wet hands together, as if with pressure he could change blood with Morgan. He'd looked into Morgan's eyes, and Morgan had not looked away.

When Morgan recollected the scene, he imagined any number of things he might have said or done. But the living truth had included none of them. In the real study on the real night, Morgan had accepted Silk's knife and touched it to the fleshy mound of his palm. He flinched even now to remember the slash, deeper than necessary. Later, Silk had wrapped Morgan's hand with a handkerchief tight enough to hurt. This accomplished, Silk had cast a final look across the study. Silk did not touch him again; he merely sighed with the sorrow of seven guardians and said:

—Goodbye, Dicky. Goodbye and . . .

Morgan had stared out the window. Silk opened the door. Floorboards creaked, the door closed. He never finished his sentence. He'd left Morgan alone in the study, hand bleeding and the mantle of Hermes uneasy upon him.

The changing room was empty—except for the other one, who straddled the bench in front of Morgan's pegs, dressed untidily for play. Droit did not deign to appear. Droit was surely disgusted by Morgan's failure to refuse Andrewes, failure of nerve, will, wherewithal.

—I suppose you think it's a beastly honor, Morgan told the boy, but I stand to make a significant sum—significant!—if the Old Boys win.

His companion passed him Barlow's blazer. Morgan began to undress:

—And now, through no fault of my own, I've been press-ganged to play against them. It's rank.

—The only thing rank is your garbling, Droit said.

He stood in the doorway and struck a match against his heel.

—My objections are entirely monetary, Morgan told him.

—I'll bet.

Droit lit a cigarette. Morgan bent to untie his shoes.

—Don't get worked up, Droit said. It's easy enough to avoid the old adder.

—I don't need—

—Just prove yourself incapable of fielding, and Andrewes will put you so far down the order that you'll never have to bat.

Morgan stepped out of his trousers:

—If I do that, the XI will tear me limb from limb—

—Mm, yes, please.

—The Flea will have me on the rack before the day is through—

—Better and better.

—And then they'll turf me out for good.

—Ha *ha*.

Droit took one of Barlow's shoes for an ashtray:

—If you don't want to dodge out of it, just say so, and all the better. That bastard Bradley needs staring down. Thinks he can swan in here, get his buggy eyes round you, rattle you—

Morgan pulled his cricket shirt over his head, muffling the sound for a moment.

—Only reason he's here, Droit continued, is for the consummate thrill of it, the old poof.

—He isn't.

Morgan did up his flannels and put his tie around his waist. The other one fetched him Barlow's cap. Droit looked from one to the other.

—I've had it with this milksop attitude, Droit spat. When it comes to the wall, you always defend him.

—I don't!

—Like that time over the basins, when he came down on you three days in a row. He knew it wasn't your fault, but still it was *touch your toes*, three the first day—

—I know—

—Three the next—

—I *know*—

—And then—

—I remember!

The other one stood by the partition, looking as Morgan had felt after the last harrowing eight, shaking, hardly breathing, then Bradley's hand on the back of his neck, fingers reaching into his hairline, consoling and

231

forgiving him, almost—*if it happens again, expect the same*—goading him to sort out whoever had sabotaged the basins he was supposed to have—

—Don't be *daft*, Droit implored. He knew Fletcher was behind it—

—He didn't—

—He *knew*, but he fancied making you suffer, and now he's here to do it again.

Morgan felt queasy.

—You can't give in, Droit insisted. There's only one response, and that is to stand under his nose and show you don't care.

He offered a hip flask:

—Or you could tell the lot of them to morris off, and go elope with Polly.

The other one offered him a comb. Morgan kicked the bench out of his way:

—Just shut up, both of you.

✦

The sun was darting in and out of the clouds. The Old Boys had been at bat nearly two hours, but Hermes willing, they'd be dismissed shortly. Morgan had spent the time in distant fielding positions, reminding himself about Polly. This evening, this very evening, in a few short hours, love would conquer all. Nothing, not Andrewes, not apparitions, *nothing* would interfere. He would not funk it.

He'd caught out one Old Boy, a codger who'd scored three runs through charity. Andrewes had done the lion's share of bowling and had managed an elegant game, allowing the OBs enough runs to keep their morale up, but not so many that the XI would have to work very hard after lunch. As it happened, Morgan had no chance to prove himself one way or another. He might have dropped the catch, but that would scarcely have made a difference since at that point the man was spent; for all Morgan knew, he'd saved him from a heart attack. As for batting, Andrewes had revealed the order, and Morgan would bat at number nine. The best batsmen, going in first, would score the bulk of the runs while the OBs were recovering from lunch. By the time they got to the middle of the order, the match would be decided.

Now the last OB was coming in, and Andrewes was moving them to a defensive field, with Morgan at long off. Nothing would disturb him there at the edge of the south ditch, not even the last two batsmen, viz, Fletcher and the one who didn't deserve thinking about. Not that Morgan was afraid to think about him. In fact, it was a pleasure to think of Bradley and to recall that he had been a mediocre batsman in his day.

—Do those stretches while you've got the time.

Morgan stirred but no one was there. He concluded that it had been a trick of sound, like the whispering gallery in St. Paul's, making some far-away utterance sound as though it had come from the ditch at his back. He glanced around, but the ditch was empty.

Except now someone was climbing out of it—the other one, *again* at a pointless moment, his hands and shoes muddy, his flannels hopelessly grass stained.

—Talking now, are we? Morgan said tartly.

The boy did not reply. Morgan decided to ignore the intruder and concentrate on the pitch, where Bradley was scoring. Bradley—he was still not afraid to name him—had in his day been wicketkeeper for Hazlehurst's XI. He'd been adept at catching balls, but his prowess as batsman had waxed and waned with the moon. Today it looked as though the moon was . . . whatever it had to be for Bradley to bat well.

The Old Boys had ninety-one. The XI would easily do better than that. There was simply no way he would have to bat, so it was no use—

—Grievesy's got a stinging right arm, the other one said.

Morgan turned on him:

—You'd love to see that, wouldn't you?

Grieves bowling fast, Bradley keeping wicket, Morgan trapped between them.

The boy nodded at a ball headed their way. Morgan moved for it, but it sailed over his head and beyond the ditch, a boundary. Smatters of distant applause reached him. He scrambled down the ditch to fetch the ball, but once he'd thrown it back and negotiated the ditch again, his shoes and flannels were a disaster. He would have to change before lunch.

Morgan's companion took hold of his left arm and helped him stretch it behind his back:

—Grievesy's hounded you all term about your form. He made you do those exercises—

—He didn't make me do anything.

—He found you the rubber tubing so you could do them properly. And he was terrifically withering about your badminton.

—As I said, he loathes me.

—But after he frumped off your badminton, you and Pearl went back to playing Tower Fives, and look what that's done for your stroke.

Morgan pulled away, but the other one refused to let go, tugging his arm until the joint felt it would crack—

—What's the idea—

And did.

—Ow!

—Better, said the brat.

Morgan rubbed his shoulder but found that it rotated freely. The boy smiled. Morgan tightened his jaw, and his fists:

—I am *this* close to going off you.

A cascade of applause drew his attention back to the pitch. Andrewes stood jubilant, his arms in the air; Bradley was walking away, his wicket demolished.

 *Always turn out clean in mind and body.*

Never forget that while you face the ball alone, it takes both striker and nonstriker to make a run.

Always trust your partner. Whether he calls on you to come or to wait, accept his judgment of the ball as you would have him trust you.

Never let a mistake worry you unduly.

Always remember that your character is reflected in your game.

Whatever you do, do it with all your might.

All my love, Father.

He was in the dormitory changing his flannels. Nathan and Laurie were with their people, leaving him to an uneasy solitude. His father's unsent letter, dated the month Morgan started prep school, lay across his blanket, its script regular and familiar. Morgan had no memory of asking his father *to explain the rules of cricket and tell it in a good way*, but such a demand didn't strike him as uncharacteristic. He'd gone through a mad cricket phase, and he remembered having the impression that school would be something like a training academy. He'd been dismally disappointed by his prep school's diet of Latin, spelling, arithmetic, and penmanship.

Nathan thought playing for the XI was a brilliant shot at glory. Laurie said that it was high time the Old Boys match got interesting. Colin offered to take over Morgan's bookmaking at the Keys should he not survive the ordeal. On the First XI itself, those who had spoken to him expressed the hope that he would refrain from mucking things up; Andrewes exhorted him to do as he was told and to keep his eye on the ball. There was no way to tell whether he'd get off with doing nothing or whether he'd be called to prove himself before an audience hostile in more ways than one.

Outside the pavilion just now, Fletcher had brushed hard against him, as if he might, like that night in the changing room, press Morgan to the wall, arm across his throat.

—What did you do to him? Fletcher had demanded that winter evening. He's in a funk.

Fletcher had pressed harder, crushing his windpipe:

—Hasn't been like that since—

—Since Gallowhill?

A ringing cuff.

—Leave him be.

—What's it to you?

—It's to me to see that men like Silk aren't put out by tarts like you.

A heavy shove.

—Little sod.

Fletcher's arm had dropped, and his own fist rose, swinging into Fletcher's cheek, fleshy, hard, sore. Fletcher gasped:

—They only hit when it's true.

He needed food. He needed to focus. He needed to seize this actual day: lunch, cricket, tea, *Polly*. The sun would not set for another ten hours. There wasn't a moment to lose.

✦

The innings had gone a good deal better than John had hoped. The Old Boys had managed a hundred and three, unprecedented in John's time at the Academy. Bradley and Fletcher had done particularly well as the last two in. In consequence, lunch was late and everyone ravenous, not least John. He chose carefully from the buffet, taking not so much that he would become soporific, but enough to fortify him for what was sure to be a long afternoon bowling. Burton would have to be pleased with his management of the Old Boys. As long as nothing tragic happened in the field, the day would have to be classed a success.

John joined his men at what was normally REN's junior table. Burton sat at the masters' table with various personages John did not know. The man looked, for all the success of the day, uncomfortably hot. Perhaps some political concern had exploded in his hands. Irrationalities like that made John certain he would never be a Housemaster, a Headmaster, or any master of visible importance. Give him his lessons, his games, his little demesne. Leave the sticky maneuvers to men who cared for such things.

—You came after Gallowhill, did you? one of the Old Boys was asking him.

—Yes, John replied.

—So you never knew him?

—Alas.

—He and I were boys here together, the man said.

—Were you indeed?

John tried to handle the man gently, but he was seized by irritation at the sentimentality that overcame everyone when Gallowhill was mentioned. Why should Gallowhill deserve such grief?

Meg always spoke of dying as a release from suffering. She quoted exclusively from the milk-and-honey parts of Scripture. This world was a shadow, she claimed. In the next, they would put on glory.

John longed to be comforted by her sentiments, but it was all too abstract. He knew only this life, this concrete, body-bound life, this meanwhile ruled by their inadequacies and yearnings. He reminded himself not to confuse the nostalgia that surrounded him with a philosophical frame of mind.

The man who had been at the Academy with Gallowhill had within his middle-aged face the anxious eyes of a Third Former casting about for the friend who was no longer there, adrift in the crowd without this essential ally. John wondered how he himself would behave were he ever forced to return to the scene of his own schooldays. But this was a topic both unsavory and inapt. The facts were simply that some men never forgot school; they defined themselves perpetually by those old relationships, by that ancient status or lack thereof, and by the boys they had been when everything had pressed together so hard they felt they couldn't endure the intensity of living.

John grimaced at the Old Boy and loaded a fork with cold ham and cheese. Burton was winding his way through the throng. John put his fork into his mouth and ate. As Burton advanced through the room, groups congealed and dispersed around him. John made a mental note to speak with REN about images under a microscope and their similarity to groups in crowded rooms.

His body registered the event long before his brain caught up. First, his limbs froze. A hot tingling spread across the surface of his skin, beginning in his scalp and creeping down the back of his neck. Voluntary motion ceased. His heart and lungs, powered by a reptilian sector of his brain, continued to sustain life. He wished they wouldn't. The rest of his brain sat listless in his skull, like a dumb and captive beast. Eventually it stirred, but only to lecture him on the impossibility of the coming moment. He was mistaken, it told him, about the identity of the person following Burton through the crowds. He was tired and imagining things. The man might look like a person he had once known, but as he hadn't laid eyes on that person since the time he made it a cast-iron rule never to contemplate, how could he hope to recognize that person even if reality broke with its bonds and magicked him to the St. Stephen's refectory? Fact: people changed beyond all recognition between the ages of seventeen and twenty-whatever; therefore fact: this person could not be that person; therefore fact: he had to keep his head and avoid letting insanity run away with him.

The person was surrounded by men John did not know, and the globule was bearing down on his table. He could flee. He should flee. Why wasn't he fleeing? He was not fleeing for the simple reason that the entire affair was a mistake, a hallucination, and a disgusting display of lost nerve. There was simply not the remotest possibility that the person he had left in the place his cast-iron rules forbade him to recall had discovered him here in the most obscure corner of Yorkshire.

—Here he is, Burton said to a graying man in the group. Grieves, our young history master and able Captain of the Old Boys.

The gray man extended a hand, which John's elbow forced him to meet.

—Capital innings, the gray man said.

John swallowed the saliva in his mouth and allowed the man to pump his arm up and down.

—Grieves, this is Overall, Chairman of our Board.

John managed to mumble a greeting. Overall released his hand and introduced him to two or three more gray men, also members of the Board.

They seemed not displeased, yet not as cheerful as they might after satisfactory cricket and satisfactory luncheon. John was conscious of the underside of his rib cage tingling like his face and scalp, and then reality as he knew it perished. The person whom he could not hope to recognize, the person who did not belong in Yorkshire, the person from that outlawed time and place stood before him. This person stopped talking to the gray men and brought his full attention to the precise spot where John stood, lining up their gazes with a recognition that took John's brain and split it.

—Grieves, Sebastian. Visiting us from Marlborough. But you know one another already, I'm told.

A hand was gripping his, though he scarcely felt it.

—Hello, John.

Catastrophic smile.

But Burton was filling the air with explanations great and small, introducing Overall and his men to the Old Boys at John's table. The person continued to grip his hand:

—You look well.

The sooner this moment passed, the sooner he would be able to breathe. Not that breath was strictly necessary. Only his mind existed. Through every disaster, every destruction, it preserved him, the essential him. He could survive without the Academy, without teaching, without anything. Any moment now his hand would be free and he could escape. Before anyone had a chance to look for him, he'd be on a train to Scotland or the Channel Isles or even the Continent if necessary. He could work with his hands, digging ditches, allowing his skin to brown and harden in the Mediterranean sun.

—Bang-up spread, one of the gray men was saying.

The others were concurring. The intruder was smiling, at him. He released John's hand only to come stand at John's side.

—Fearful hock, he murmured in John's ear. And an even worse claret.

John flinched. The person chuckled.

—There I go putting my foot in it again, the person said. It's obvious I haven't changed.

His sleeve brushed John's. John took a step backwards and reached for his orange squash.

—Clever choice, the person said. Then, you've always been clever.

John slammed the glass down on the table. This was the moment to unleash a telling off the likes of which would make the Fifth Form quake. This person was committing a monstrous impertinence murmuring things into his ear. This person had no right to stand near him, no right even to exist. John opened his mouth to say all this.

—We must leave our Captain to his team, Burton announced. Now let me . . .

He conducted the gray men away. They drew the intruder along with them, but not before he could inflict another harrowing smile:

—I shall enjoy this, he said. Immensely.

✦

Nathan's parents welcomed Morgan warmly and insisted he sit with them. Nathan's mother declared that he had grown; Nathan's father congratulated him on his promotion to the First XI. When Morgan tried to explain that it was only for the day, Nathan listed all the boys who had been passed over for the honor. Alex sat beside Mrs. Pearl and impishly stole bites of her Victoria sponge. She pretended to scold him, but his cheekiness amused her. Towards the end of the meal, Alex darted over to the table where Colin sat with his parents. Money changed hands. Alex returned, and while his father chided him, he had the nerve to aim a smirk at Morgan.

—Why do you look like the cat who ate the bird? Morgan demanded.

Alex mimed cleaning his whiskers and licking his paws. He was the most unsavory specimen.

If ever a day demanded a drink, this one did. But having a drink would only give that person a satisfaction he didn't deserve. John did not have time to sift through details of the surreal encounter. He had no time to analyze what the person meant by *I shall enjoy this. This*, what? But, again, there was no time. John had to inspect the pitch. He had to rouse his players from postprandial stupor. He had to make final decisions about fielding positions. Bradley, he conceded, would have to keep wicket. No one else with plausible wicketkeeping experience had presented himself, and the Old Boys had to make a show of trying to stop the First XI.

One of the older men had volunteered to bowl; John decided to let him start. Fletcher had offered to bowl as well, but after the claret John had watched him down at lunch, John didn't trust him hurling hard objects. He would have to bowl himself, as usual, but with any luck the older man, whatever his name was, would provide periodic relief.

John had been watching the First XI for a month. He knew its strengths and weaknesses at bat, and he instructed his bowler (Old Boy circa 1890) to spin the ball as hard as possible and bowl a full length. After eight singles and a boundary, the man bowled a googly and took the wicket. John felt his energy surge. One out, only nine to go.

✦

Droit spent the afternoon in a deck chair, peering through field glasses at visiting females and speculating about their biographies, carnal or otherwise. Morgan sat beside him sipping orange squash. The Old Boys had begun the innings hopelessly, and the XI had scored sixty-two runs in the first hour. Eventually, some codgers rotated on and others off, Grieves came in to bowl, and the Old Boys began to sober up. Bradley had been keeping wicket all afternoon and was getting better by the over.

When Buxton came in, the eighth man, Morgan went to get his pads and to warm up. Evidently, he would bat after all.

He began his stretches; the familiar routine did not calm him.

Never forget that there are ten others with you; if they fail, it is up to you to see the side through. A ridiculous maxim since he was not batting last. The truth was, if he failed, Andrewes and Radcliffe would see the side through and he would be humiliated in front of hundreds of people, including Grieves and Bradley.

Grieves bowled only one ball to Bux before asking for time-out and going to consult with a codger on the veranda. After a brief exchange, Grieves retired to the pavilion and the codger went to the crease. His flabby bowling delighted the XI, and two boundaries later, they had moved within thirteen runs of victory. A glance around the sidelines revealed a number of empty seats. Evidently, Grieves had conceded the match. Morgan would not be needed after all.

A mass lifted from his chest. He never got let off anything, but he was going to be let off this. He wasn't going to have to bat, wasn't going to have

240

to stand near Bradley, and nothing was going to wreck the original point of the day, which was Polly. If the other one had been at his elbow, he would have been wondering whether Morgan was more relieved to be spared Bradley or Grieves himself, but the brat was *not* there, so he could just take his gauche ideas and . . . direct them at the pitch where the spectators had found something to gasp about. Morgan stepped around the veranda. The batsman, dumbfounded, was looking around for explanation. Bradley lay on the grass, holding the ball aloft in triumph. The umpire raised the finger. Morgan's stomach lurched.

—Hang on, Wilberforce, Andrewes said jogging over to him. I'm putting Radcliffe in.

Morgan flushed. After ruining his day, Andrewes now proposed to let Radcliffe go in? He slammed his bat to the ground.

Always obey your captain without question.

Andrewes stood beside him, arms crossed, as the match trudged towards its inevitable conclusion. Radcliffe, in now with Buxton, was hitting the ball, some lazy codger was shuffling after it, Rad and Bux were taking a run, and Bradley was shouting at the codger to move it. Only when they'd taken three did the codger manage to get the ball to Bradley, who did not bother to conceal his frustration and disgust.

—Am I next? Morgan asked Andrewes.

—I'll go, Andrewes replied. You come in last.

No jilting ever felt like this. Andrewes broke a crooked smile:

—It'll be up to us to finish them off.

Morgan tore off his pads. With only ten runs to win and three more wickets to fall, he would never bat. He found himself glancing to the left, looking for the one who fed on his humiliations like a vampire. This, surely, was the time for him to appear with his doleful eyes, eyes Morgan longed to punch until they dimmed black and sank. But instead of glimpsing that boy, Morgan saw that Alex had drifted over to the pavilion and was chatting to one of the XI. Alex met his gaze. His mouth soured.

—Oi, Andrewes said, what's this?

The XI leapt to their feet, and an energetic burst of applause announced that the spectators had not after all abandoned the match. Bux's wicket had fallen, and worse, Grieves had emerged from the pavilion. Alex elbowed closer as Grieves strode across the lawn rolling down his sleeve, his shirt damp at the shoulder. Morgan sat down in disgust.

A flinty conversation ensued between the umpire, Grieves, and Andrewes. Finally, Grieves relieved the bowler and Andrewes trotted back to the pavilion.

—Enough mucking about, he announced severely. Sort yourself out, Wilberforce. If you have to come in, for God's sake keep your eye on the ball, and don't you dare funk it no matter how fast he bowls.

—Right.

Andrewes hauled him to his feet:

—I am dead serious, Wilberforce. If you let that ball past, I will personally thrash you until you bawl.

Morgan couldn't decide whether to be insulted or flattered. He didn't doubt that Andrewes meant it, but he didn't need threats to rouse him. The promise of humiliation was enough.

✦

He was sick to death of being treated like a pawn. He might be a lowly undermaster, but he was still a freeborn Englishman with all the rights due him. Those rights included not being saddled with noxious Old Boys; not being issued directives (*sort out the cricket*) without why or wherefore; not having to bowl unaided for hours while an inebriated side fielded like a flock of mental defectives; and it included the right not to have pestilence from the past thrust up his nose at lunch sans explanation of any kind. Last, finally, and paramount, he, John Grieves, had the right as Captain and as a human being to spend ten minutes in the pavilion applying a cold compress to his shoulder without being harassed by the Headmaster pro tem and asked what exactly he was playing at.

—I'm playing at cricket, thank you very much, and if you expect me to give the XI even a shred of difficulty during the last half hour, I advise you to return to your guests and leave me in peace.

Burton had turned a color that usually preceded volcanic talkings-to, but by some grace he left before saying anything at all. Out of principle, John had remained in the pavilion five more minutes until he felt a chill coming on. Only then had he emerged to do battle with whichever batsmen still remained to the XI.

He made a point of not looking where he knew Burton and the person were sitting. There was simply no energy to spare them beyond cursing their astronomical impertinence. What he needed to contend with was

Bradley, a person John knew to have practiced a level of turpitude that even now made his stomach turn. A better man than he would stop the match and denounce Bradley before the assembly. John wanted to do that. He knew he ought to do that. But he didn't do it. To make matters worse, Bradley had proved an efficient wicketkeeper, and bowling to him made John feel like a conspirator. A call had been made early in the innings for an alternate wicketkeeper, but after seeing John bowl, no one but Bradley had the nerve to stand in the firing line and catch what John was sending down. Now, as John took the ball, Bradley came forward to confer.

—Thank Christ you're back, Bradley muttered.

An instinct to grin competed with the desire to excoriate Bradley for blasphemy.

—Radcliffe's batting hair-trigger. Andrewes coming in now. Watch for the pull shot.

—Yes, I know, John said testily.

—Last is Wilberforce, if it comes to that.

—Oh, it will, John declared.

Bradley gawked at him, struck pleasantly speechless. John waved him back to the wicket and shook out his arm as Andrewes approached the pitch.

✦

Grieves was bowling like a demon. Obviously he'd been sacrificing babies in the pavilion because he was throwing faster than Morgan had ever seen. Andrewes and Radcliffe got a couple of runs off him, but then Grieves hurled the ball so fast they barely saw it. The next moment, Radcliffe's wicket lay shattered on the pitch, and Radcliffe himself lay crumpled before it.

—Blood-y hell! cried Alex. Grieves hit Radcliffe!

Indeed it seemed that Grieves's ball had clipped Radcliffe's foot before taking the wicket. The XI rumbled mutinously, but eventually Radcliffe limped off the field under his own steam. Morgan checked his pads. Alex handed him the bat:

—Good luck.

Morgan walked away from Alex and took his place in front of the one person he wanted never to see.

243

—Well, Bradley murmured, look who it is.

Morgan refused to look at him. He looked at the crowd. He looked down the pitch at Grieves, dusty with the soil of play. He looked at Andrewes, bat in hand, ready to run, training his attention on Morgan as if sheer willpower could make him hit the ball. Morgan squared his shoulders.

—You and Andrewes last, eh? Think you can score eight before Grievesy breaks another foot?

Always smile in all circumstances.

—My money, Bradley continued, says the Old Boys are about to win for the first time this century.

—Shut up, Morgan hissed.

Bradley laughed, and then Grieves thundered forward, the ball whizzed towards Morgan, and the bat flew from his hands.

Technically he'd hit the ball, but it didn't go far, and he wasn't able to run. His hands tingled like the time he had stuck a finger in one of Uncle Charles's electrical sockets. He shook out his arm, picked up the bat, and fixed his eye on Grieves. That Bradley stood so close he could smell his aftershave had no bearing on the moment. His murmurs and his looks were even less pertinent.

Never forget that the wicketkeeper is just as capable of getting you out as the bowler.

Morgan pressed his shoulder down and visualized his left arm swinging up. Grieves jogged forward.

Always face the fast stuff with courage and be happy in the thought that you have not funked it.

Again a brutal impact, but this time he kept his grip. A deep thwack, more bone-tickling vibrations, and the ball sailed over Grieves's head into a gap. Morgan bolted away from Bradley, towards Grieves, bat to crease—then back, coming home, Bradley's face in that almost-smile that could make him—bat to crease—

—Oh, Dicky.

—Come! Andrewes called.

He ran away, back to Grieves—bat to crease—

—Wait!

Stumbling to a stop, he panted. The ball returned to Grieves.

Morgan had taken three runs, and now Andrewes was at the striker's end. Bradley, no longer hidden behind his back, openly regarded him across the pitch. His elbow still thwanged. Rallying what remained of his sanity, Morgan cleaved his attention from Bradley and thrust it onto Grieves.

Thorn and enigma—in the classroom Grieves possessed a freakish concentration, and on the field, his face wore a permanent scowl. He polished the ball, positioned the seam, and practiced his wrist movement without even appearing to think, his gaze trained on Andrewes and the wicket he guarded.

Silk once claimed that all the good men were dead. He'd always behaved as if nothing truly mattered. But here was a man for whom things mattered, a man who had interfered with Morgan's time and his cricket, a man who was playing with the Old Boys as if the good of the world hung in the balance, a man who bowled as if he were capable of murder. Grieves thundered past, and for one delusionary moment Morgan yearned to stand in his way, to feel that resolve compelling Morgan past everything that kept him in shackles.

A cry from the crowd, and Andrewes was barreling his way. Morgan ran towards Andrewes and past him, into the arms of—

—Wait, Silk said.

Not the arms! Not even as a figure of—

—Wait! Andrewes called.

Morgan turned to Silk and gulped for breath. Knowing and known, still and yet—a face that knew the malice of life, a person who had himself found a head draining blood, who might be the only person in the world to understand, when life leaked out and he watched it, helpless before the shadow that took every good thing—

—Look alive, Dicky!

Silk raised his gloves, and Morgan turned to see Grieves hurling a missile. He wasn't ready, and all he could do was put his bat—

It connected. He followed through with the stroke, such as it was, but then—a muddle—the bat was in his hands and also on the ground with the ball. The shock rang in his elbows, high-pitched and nauseating. Andrewes began to run but stopped.

Morgan was mistaken about the bat. The wicket, not the bat, lay at his feet. The game was over and Morgan had lost it. Helpless, crushed, hubbub around him. The umpire was speaking, and Silk was stepping forward to pick up the stumps.

—Blimey, he said. Can't believe you stopped that.

Bux trotted over from the pavilion. Grieves jogged down the pitch.

—Are you all right, Wilberforce? Grieves asked.

—Of course, I am.

How dare Grieves treat him like a girl who'd burst into tears at defeat? Evidently, it was the treatment he deserved, he who let the Old Boys win for the first time this century.

—You pulverized it, sir! Bux exclaimed taking the stumps from Silk.

Only they weren't the stumps. They were the pieces of what had been Morgan's bat, the bat whose handle was still in his hands. He looked to the umpire.

—Am I out?

—Don't be stupid, Bux said, handing Morgan another bat.

Then Bux was jogging away, and everyone was switching ends for the next over. Silk shouldered past him:

—Well stuck, Dicky.

The spectators began talking loudly.

He wasn't out. He hadn't lost the match. But Silk's words lingered, stinging his eyes, the intolerable heat of praise he no longer craved, no longer ate. That age was as dead as the War, that cloister where the night and the study door hid them from the world, when Silk behaved with him as he behaved with no one else.

Sanity! Sanity! Battalions to posts! He was with Grieves now, at his end, his rule. Here Grieves ran, flinging the ball like a catapult. And here Morgan returned after Andrewes took two more runs. This was his end, this prickly domain, governed by a man who might care for Morgan as little as he cared for anyone, but a man now sauntering past him, polishing the ball and looking at him curiously.

—I'm letting Andrewes off easy, Grieves was saying, but don't imagine I'll give up the match without making you work for it.

And something crossed his face—gone before it registered. Grieves waited a moment before breaking his gaze, long enough to let Morgan know the truth: that his resolve had all along been trained upon Morgan, ordaining him to do the things he secretly wanted to do.

Grieves turned away and gestured to his field to pull it back. Then he bowled Andrewes a slow long-hop down the leg side. Andrewes, impatient for the win, struck. They ran, but as soon as Morgan's bat touched the crease, Silk took the ball from the air.

They drew themselves up. Silk threw him the stabbing smile.

—So, Dicky, it's come to this.

Morgan's heart pounded, his arms empty. Silk returned the ball to Grieves.

—Game tied, Silk murmured. Yours to decide.

Trapped again and still! At his left elbow, Grieves lined up to hurl the hardest ball he'd ever bowled; at his right, Silk Bradley waited to drag him under. Morgan turned to Silk and looked him in the eye, two hundred forty volts current direct:

—Why are you here, Bradley? Why did you come?

Silk's face slackened, as if they were alone, no one's eyes upon them, as if he were the person he'd shown to Morgan and Morgan alone.

—Do you have to ask, Dicky?

But Droit was behind him, breathing in his ear:

—*A breathless hush in the close tonight. One to make and the last man in*—

—Shut up.

Grieves was starting his run-up.

—*A bumping pitch and a blinding*—

—Shut up!

—*His Captain's hand on his shoulder smote*—

The ball was coming at him—

—*Play up*—

Beside him a different voice:

—Look.

Whispered but audible:

—Right!

The ball was swinging right. He whacked for all he was worth.

He never wanted to bowl another cricket ball again. His shoulder was throbbing in a way that it shouldn't. Thankfully, SCR duties spared him fraternizing with the Old Boys after the match. A shower (cruelly short), ten minutes with cold compress, then he bundled himself into warmer things and repaired to the SCR. Something was afoot, but amidst buzzing about the match, John couldn't discern what it was. Perhaps it was simply the undercurrent of gossip, which grew into rough surf whenever visitors descended. The Eagle and Clem congratulated him, REN offered condolences for losing, and Hazlehurst uttered some unsober witticism.

The last and only difficulty of the day lay ahead in having to bid farewell to the intruder. It was possible the intruder had departed already, but John doubted he would get off that easily. And indeed, there was the person across the quad. John spoke firmly to himself: This would pass. The person would presently depart. If forced to shake the person's hand, he could allow his hand to be shaken. The person could say what he wished, but John need not respond. He need not, strictly, be present. His body was required, but not his essential self. That could adjourn into the evening sky, which the wind had scraped bare of clouds, making space for the sun to beat down.

Old Boys were shaking his hand. Bradley was nodding in lieu of handshake, one mercy amidst it all. Boys were introducing him to their parents. He relied on his standard line: *A great pleasure to meet you, sir (or madam). It's plain where (insert boy's name) gets it from.* Only rarely was he asked to clarify what he meant by *it*. In the hubbub of the quad, he held his bowling wrist in the other hand to take the pressure off his shoulder, which ached, keenly.

Thank the Lord for trains, which departed at firm and infrequent times, enforcing departures and curtailing nostalgia. Presently the quad thinned. The few who'd come in motorcars drifted out to the parking area, gunned their engines, and roared into the bright evening.

All in all a satisfactory day. He hadn't had to touch the person again after all. Burton couldn't accuse him of mucking up the cricket. There had been no disasters that John knew of, the rain had held off, attendance had been strong. Everyone would have noticed the school's improvement under Burton, and presumably they could look forward shortly to his installation as Headmaster proper. John reminded himself that he and Burton were antagonists and that his rule-by-excessive-games was time-consuming and pedagogically suspect. Still, the Academy could not continue in its pro tem state.

The Eagle joined him beneath the arches:

—Come by if you need a place to change.

John asked his colleague what he meant.

—You *have* had a day. Supper? With the Board after the Ramble? Don't look at me like a half-wit. You saw the notice in the SCR.

—I did not.

—Don't tell me you've nothing to wear?

John didn't think his present attire was anything to be ashamed of.

—Don't be absurd, the Eagle said. You'll have to pop home. I'll cover for you.

John cursed everyone he could think of, Burton first and foremost, and went to collect his bicycle.

✦

Everyone's attention was suddenly upon him, which posed a threat to his otherwise flawless plans. He'd taken rugs to the barn the day before. He'd double-triple confirmed with Polly details of the rendezvous. Nathan would tell everyone on the Ramble that Morgan was back at the Academy, and Laurie would assure everyone who stayed behind that Morgan was on the Ramble. What he hadn't planned for was throngs of people wanting his company.

The other problem, besides losing his guinea, was Nathan and Laurie, whom Morgan found in fierce conversation as tea was beginning. They paused for grace, but each looked to be preparing his next salvo.

—Amen.

—It was none of your business! Nathan hissed.

—It jolly well is my business when people mess my friends about. He's run amok with it all term, but this was just criminal.

—*What* happened? Morgan injected.

They both told him to shut up and nose out.

—How you would feel if I went to your grandmother and peached on you?

—First, Laurie said, I didn't peach. Second, there's nothing to tell her.

—Sure about that, Anton O'Masia?

Laurie flushed:

—You don't know what you're talking about.

—I think I do, Nathan said. And that's how it felt when m'pater took on Alex, only six hundred times worse.

—You two can either tell me what this is about, Morgan interrupted, or take your bollixing somewhere else.

Laurie turned to him with awful stillness:

—Will you keep your ruddy great boots out of this, for once?

—Who made you prefect? Nathan added. Or is that part and parcel of playing for the XI?

Morgan reminded himself that he needed their help. He addressed his bread and butter. Nathan addressed Laurie:

—After you buttonholed him, he went to Hazlehurst and asked if he could have a room to speak to us in private.

—Crikey.

—Twiggy gave his actual study, so there we were, stood on the carpet, except it was Pater. He had Mater wait outside, then he . . . well, I can't bear to think how he was.

Laurie's ears turned red.

—Sorry, JP.

—It's a bit late now, Nathan said.

—I mean sorry you had to take that. I'm not sorry I told him.

—He took every penny off Alex.

—But that's brilliant! Laurie said.

—And, you bastard, he stopped my pocket money as well.

—Why? Morgan exclaimed.

—Because, Nathan replied through gritted teeth, if we can't manage our pocket money like gentlemen and brothers, then we can go without.

—Harsh, Laurie said.

—Stopped it how long?

—Rest of term, first month of the hols.

Morgan gave a low whistle.

—It's shrewd, though, Laurie remarked. If you're skint, beastly Alex can't blackmail you.

Nathan looked as though he was exercising every ounce of self-control not to set upon Laurie with fists.

—So, Laurie summarized, all said a positive outcome.

—That was the least of it! Nathan cried.

—What's worse than losing all your money?

—Having him *talk* to you that way. Alex blubbed. I almost blubbed.

Morgan found it difficult to imagine Alex weeping genuinely. More likely, he'd treated his father to one of his performances.

—That's *it*? Laurie said. You're exercised because your pater took away your pocket money, stopped your brother blackmailing you, and *told you off*? Take a pull, JP!

—No, you take a pull, you ignorant vigilante. Do you have any idea why I put up with this nonsense from Alex all term?

Laurie glanced to Morgan for support.

—Not, you rag, because I'm a coward. I gave him my money because it stopped him doing worse. And now that you've so valiantly put an end to that, he's going to make my life a living hell.

—It's a point, Morgan said.

—But that's *my* point, Laurie persisted. Your brother, your *little* brother, stands over you like the worst kind of bully. It isn't right.

Nathan sighed:

—I don't see what's suddenly made you a moralist.

—Listen, JP, breaking rules is all very well when it doesn't hurt anyone. But when someone blackmails my friend all term, and then decides to sabotage my other friend's match just to win a bet, and then when that someone puts the screws to my friend and to me to recoup his losses—well, there's a limit to everything and that was it.

—Sabotage? Morgan said. How? Does Andrewes know?

—No, Nathan snapped, and he isn't going to.

—But—

—Alex tampered with one of the bats. Obviously.

Laurie lowered his voice:

—Bats don't break from fast balls, even Grievesy's.

—But . . . how can you . . . ?

—Alex admitted it, little beast. Best villains always do. Can't resist boasting.

—But . . .

—Best not to dwell, Laurie counseled. As it happened, you didn't let the ball through, and thanks to you, the XI won. And since Alex had put—what was it, JP? A guinea?

—Two pounds.

—on the Old Boys, he was incandescent at the outcome.

—But how did he tamper with the bats? Morgan demanded.

—He did, that's all, and then he put the screws to us for the loss. He'd have squeezed you, too, if someone hadn't stopped him.

Nathan was holding his head in his hands as if it ached. They stopped talking and finished eating. Morgan, with no inch of nerve left for Alex, was slipping into the jittery state that always preceded a visit with Polly. Then glasses were clinking and REN was making announcements: The

Ramble would depart in ten minutes from the front gates. Any boys opting to stay behind would report to Radcliffe and Kilby. In a slight change of program, REN and Lockett-Egan would conduct the Ramble. Their illustrious Headmaster would bid them good-night later.

—Concentrate on Polly, Laurie whispered. Me and JP will sort out the rest.

✦

The Eagle had promised to cover for him, and since his shoulder was killing him, John went into the Keys to beg some ice and a steak and kidney pie. He'd had to skip tea to ride home and change his clothes, and on achieving Fridaythorpe, he'd realized that he would not survive the evening accident-free unless he ate something substantial. The pie would delay his return, but he'd get back before the Ramble; hopefully no one would miss him.

John scarcely dared to review the day. In the positive column: cricket. The match had come off without tragedy or embarrassment, and as a bonus, his protégé had performed better than expected. John had bowled harder against Wilberforce than against any of the others, and the boy had even survived a broken bat, a phenomenon John had never witnessed, without losing his wicket. John had enjoyed bowling to him. If only there were more such bombastic contests in school life.

He didn't want to dwell on the minus column, but the bald truth was that it required dwelling or he'd never get any peace. Perhaps he was overstating the matter. Nothing calamitous had happened. Nothing even compromising had occurred. The only twist in the day had been the unexpected (and outrageous!) encounter with a person he had known *many* years in the past, before the War, before he was the person he was now. The person had made it plain that they knew one another, but (plus column) the person had said nothing publically about the nature of their acquaintance. He had to stop fretting. Scores of people encountered schoolmates in odd contexts. Marlborough was not a small school, and he had to expect to meet Old Marlburians from time to time. He had known OMs at Cambridge and in the War. The current encounter was no different. The person had leveled no accusations at John and had seemed not to hold a grudge at all. In all likelihood—and this was exactly why it was sometimes productive to dwell on the unpalatable—the person had shellacked his memory with a coat of nostalgia. That was the only explanation for his light and essentially amiable demeanor. Conclusion: nothing compromising had been communicated because the person had nothing unpleasant to convey. The jarring encounter was over and need occupy no more of his mind, heart, or digestion. The pie was coming to him now. He removed the ice from his shoulder, put on his jacket, and took up his fork.

✦

Finally, the Ramble departed and so could he. Morgan checked his appearance in the washroom. Hair slick; face, ears, and fingernails clean; teeth brushed; clothing neat. He made his way to the tunnel and plunged into the woods. His body felt exhausted, suddenly, as if he had walked twenty miles with a heavy rucksack.

—Snap out of it, Droit commanded. I'm not having you drop off just when you need to perk up.

Droit was dressed as for a party. He fell into pace beside Morgan and reminded him that the most important hour of the day was about to unfold. Strike that. The most important hour of his *life*. At last, Morgan was going to take his place amongst men and penetrate that much-desired country. *L'amour complet*. Polly might even swoon.

Morgan didn't think he would like Polly losing consciousness. How would he know she was not suffering some injury at his hands, or his . . . et cetera? Droit glanced severely at him and asked if Morgan was quite sure what it was he was about to achieve. Morgan was more than certain. But was he, Droit pursued, quite clear how he was to achieve it, anatomically? Morgan replied that he most certainly was clear. It was all rather like mucking about with boys, except that you put your cock in that place between her thighs that his fingers had already probed with her guidance. There was no need to be vulgar, Droit retorted, and there was no reason to get touchy. Droit had only Morgan's interests at heart, and to be perfectly honest, girls' bits were a good deal more intricate than boys', and just because she had taken his finger once didn't mean it would be so easy to find again.

Morgan informed Droit that he did not wish to continue the conversation. Polly was more than willing, and they had a good deal of time, privacy, and comfort. Things would take their course naturally, else how did the human race perpetuate itself?

—Certainly not by the bumblings of schoolboys, Droit replied.

Morgan stalked through the woods and ignored his companion, but Droit was not so easily dismissed. It wasn't that he doubted Morgan's amorous instincts. What concerned Droit was Polly.

—You leave her alone! Morgan warned.

But Droit had no personal designs on Polly, though she was certainly a delicious morsel. Droit was only thinking of the inconstancy of girls. Morgan demanded that he explain what he meant. Droit implored him to stop flying off the handle. What Droit meant had been the subject of plaintive literature since bards began barding, viz, the tendency of girls to promise every sort of thing when trying to capture boys. Having hooked their prey, however, girls invariably procrastinated. *I promise* quickly became *I would. Tomorrow* faded to *soon. I adore you* gave way to feeling poorly, and so on, the eternal swindle of the female of the species.

Morgan was fairly confident that Polly would not renege on her promise. Fairly confident was the same thing as doubtful, Droit informed him.

But Droit was not there to undermine his nerve. He only desired to warn Morgan of the pitfalls and with that warning enable him to develop a backup plan.

Morgan lengthened his stride and told Droit that he was sure Polly would wish to do what she had promised to do, but if at the last moment she changed her mind, he would do everything possible to reassure and convince her.

—And if that doesn't work?

Morgan thought that it ought to work, especially as luck had been with him so very much that day.

Droit spat in disgust. If Morgan was going to cling to luck, then he was a child. Men did not believe in luck. Men arranged affairs to their liking, and if impediments presented themselves, men swept them away.

Morgan stopped at the fork that led to McKay's barn. Was Droit suggesting Morgan force himself on Polly if she proved unwilling?

Droit would never suggest such a crude thing—Morgan was glad to hear it!—but Droit was suggesting that girls sometimes found the appearance of overpowering attractive. It was a fact that girls were created in a way that was fundamentally flawed, that caused them to resist what was most natural and right. Therefore, it was Morgan's obligation and his burden as a man to press forward when Polly expressed reluctance. She hoped for it, longed for it, indeed required it from him. If he failed, she would never forgive him. Of course, he needn't behave like a cad, but he must remember that an initial *no* was not an outright refusal, and that if certain sensations were not precisely pleasurable at first, they would shortly become so if she could only be convinced to give them a chance. Morgan himself surely remembered having misgivings about certain sensations that turned out to be very agreeable indeed. So it would be for Polly.

They'd arrived at the wall. Morgan gazed down the slope at the barn. The midsummer sun drenched the scene, nothing like the place Morgan had surveyed with Spaulding that day in the other life when he had brushed against Spaulding for the last living time and recalled the interval in the balcony, hoping for its completion and fulfillment.

Droit hoped Morgan wasn't going to contaminate the evening with unsavory recollections. The time had come to keep his aims in mind, his nature in mind, and to carry on, steadfast, until the final threshold had been crossed. Morgan hopped over the wall, ran down the slope, and crawled through the hatch to the smaller chamber.

Polly was not there, but someone else was.

—Just what the hell do you think you're doing? Morgan cried.

Alex raised his head momentarily, but then lay back and continued smoking.

—Get the bloody hell off those rugs!

Alex tapped his cigarette conspicuously onto the blankets:

—Yours are they?

Morgan crashed over, took hold of the blanket, and rolled Alex onto the hay.

—Listen to me, Pearl. This is about the farthest thing from a joke your puny mind can imagine.

Morgan hauled him to his feet:

—I know what you've been up to, you . . .

—Fragment of festering foreskin? Droit murmured.

—you little horror.

—Think that up all on your own, did you? Alex snapped.

Morgan shoved him against the wall.

—I am not pissing about, Alex. Leave.

A languorous expression came across Alex's face:

—I don't think I will.

—*What?* Why?

—I'm much too keen to see this tart of yours.

—She's no tart!

—None of them are.

Morgan slammed the palm of his hand against the wall in lieu of Alex.

—Just what do you want?

Alex glanced at the ceiling:

—Oh, where to begin?

Morgan took hold of him. Alex appeared to calculate.

—No, Alex concluded, there's too much to discuss right now, but let's start with the money you owe me.

—For winning the match despite the bat you buggered?

—I know nothing of buggery, but you owe me six guineas—

—Six—are you *insane?* How much did you bet?

—The problem isn't the bet I placed, Alex replied. It's the bets I ran.

—*Ran?*

—Thanks to you and that vicious piece of work you call a friend, I'm stuck with a bad book and no way to pay out.

—But . . . I thought Colin was running the book.

—His book was a joke, Alex scoffed. Mine had the best line, until you interfered.

Morgan felt unsteady.

—If you think you can blackmail me, you're mistaken.

—Am I? Alex retorted. Shall I go back to the Cad and suggest someone peruse your love bower? Or how about your poacher's tunnel?

Morgan's heart raced.

—You'll be killed if you do something that low. If not by me, then by every boy in the school.

Alex narrowed his eyes:

—Do you think I care?

They regarded one another. Alex relaxed in his grip, and Morgan realized he'd seen this before, the gaze of someone with nothing to lose.

—All right, Morgan said, I'll get you the money.

Alex tilted his head:

—Hang on a tick. Is that your tart calling?

Shower of dread. It was Polly, calling Morgan's name just outside the hatch. He dropped Alex and crawled outside.

She was more beautiful than he remembered her ever looking. She wore a frock in dusty rose, and behind her ear she'd tucked a red flower. He could scarcely breathe. She reached up and kissed him, her mouth warm, soft, tasting of ale. She pulled away after only a moment and presented her basket. He looked under the cloth and saw four bottles and some pies.

—My aunt, Polly, you are the *most* astounding girl.

She peered over his shoulder to the hatch door. He snapped around, but Alex was not there.

—Do you mind waiting just a moment? Morgan asked. I'm only . . .

He had never been good with words.

—Take your time, pet.

She tugged his ear affectionately and plopped down on the grass. He slipped back through the hatch. Inside, no Alex. A strand of hope.

—Don't be an idiot! Droit exclaimed. He isn't gone, and he won't be until you get rid of him properly.

—But—

—This isn't a nursery. Do you want to go outside and tell Polly it's off?

Morgan did not. Droit unleashed a string of curses and then showed Morgan the panel through which Alex had passed, into the main part of the barn.

—Go on! Droit urged. Or are you still afraid?

—I am not!

—Then get your feeble girl of a carcass in there and teach the little snake a lesson about trespassing on sacred ground.

Morgan squeezed through the panel and found Alex climbing the ladder to the loft.

—Is this where it all happened? Alex asked.

—Pearl, I am warning you. Get out *right now.*

—I'll take that as a yes.

Alex gestured to the fallen beam, a scrap of rope tangled around it.

—Is that the fateful cross? Did Rees rope himself to the same exact thing that killed Spaulding?

A terrible fire froze him.

—You've got to be joking, Alex scoffed. It's too hilarious! And here's you gunning for Tess of the D'Urbervilles on the very spot where that dolt crashed his head open.

Droit wasn't speaking; he was acting. Together they were bounding across the barn and hauling Pearl from the ladder. Crash in the hay, fists falling, gasps. Knees, arms, each blow releasing something jarring and sweet, like a monumental, back-cracking—

—Pax. Pax—

Noise beneath, nonsense.

—Pax—

Arm back, but there—with Pearl, not beside him or upon him but amidst him—the other one, looking and seeing and knowing. Fist falling to the middle of that face, knocking it out.

Pulled to his feet. Dragged to the door and through it. Shoved towards the road. Given a kick and sent on his way.

✦

John had a soft spot for Polly, the publican's daughter. When he first came to the Academy, seven years before, she had made a pet of him. She considered him her particular friend and would climb onto his lap and lisp her lessons to him. They didn't ask much of her at the village school, just her letters, arithmetic, her Bible, a little geography. John used to quiz her on her multiplication tables and her recitations. He had made her stretch her tongue out of its lisp with a gentle, humorous method that did not shame her. Now, at the threshold of fifteen, she no longer asked for his help with lessons, but she still kissed him on the forehead in a way she kissed no one else. His goddaughter had a special kiss for him, too; her practice was to kiss each of his palms and then press them to his lips, transferring her kisses thus. His goddaughter was now the age Polly had been when he'd met her, though far more precocious and demanding in her curiosities about the world.

Presumably Polly would begin to walk out with boys in a year or so. He hoped fervently that no boy would ever do anything to mar the perfect girl Polly had become. Her education had been basic, and her prospects as the only child of a rural publican were nothing grand, yet her simplicity testified to a heart unhindered. Polly loved now as a child; in time she would love as a woman; and then she would love as a mother. She and her husband would eventually take on the pub, providing sustenance and fellowship to an uncomplicated rural society. She knew God, and he knew her. If any misfortune ever befell her, if any boy wounded her or insulted her honor, John would leap to her defense. His pacifist vows notwithstanding, John felt he would be prepared to thrash any boy who did her wrong.

Not that they need worry about that for several years, thank the Lord. Tonight she left the Keys looking as only a fourteen-year-old girl can look before she is aware of her beauty and the power it wields over men. A friend had invited her to a midsummer party. Ribbons flowed through her hair, her cheeks showed a slight and becoming sunburn, and a pulsing, girlish excitement coursed through her conversation and her mien. She would spend the longest evening eating strawberries and trifle in a Yorkshire garden. Polly and her girlfriend would likely braid flowers into each other's hair, make fairy lanterns, and dance and laugh and play whatever games girls played when they imagined the men they would marry. When as a boy John had gone to the Rectory for the summer holidays, Jamie's sisters used to stay up long into the night playing all sorts of unfathomable things—half sorcery, half whimsy—hoping to glimpse their future princes. He remembered once they had constructed a fortune-telling device out of ribbon, an alphabet puzzle, and their late mother's wedding ring. They'd allowed him and Jamie to play it with them, and by candlelight the ribbon and the ring had moved by themselves around the alphabet spelling out the names of the girls they would love. John, the ring said, would marry Eleanor, and Jamie would wed Mary. It had been goosepimply and eye-wateringly frightening, which had egged Jamie on to more audacious questions such as how they would die. When the Bishop had discovered them, John had almost wept with relief, though of course they'd all wept by the time the Bishop had finished with them. Apparently the ribbon and the ring were a sacrilege and a desecration of their mother's memory; furthermore, the apparatus was a classic tool of witchcraft. The Bishop took an exceedingly dim view.

But John's firm habit was never to think of the Rectory, most especially on a day as outrageous as this. Time moved in one direction only, and while history might be enthralling, no good ever came of dwelling on matters that had expired. The errors of his youth had been thoroughly renounced.

✦

She said she wanted to. She said she loved him and consented fully to the thing they had come there to do. She had lain willingly on the blankets he provided. She had herself removed his jacket, his shirt, his trousers, his pants. She had met his cock before, but now unencumbered, it induced a certain awe. Warmth and confidence flooded through him.

—Are you sure? he asked as the tip touched that softest spot.

She was sure. She told him so. He pressed through a warm wetness he had never conceived. Everything he'd read told him to be quick. It would hurt for a moment, but as soon as that threshold had been passed, she would discover a pleasure she couldn't yet imagine. He was pressing against something now. She tightened, there and everywhere.

—Stop.

✦

The evening had turned so beautiful and benign, it was all John could do to force himself to leave the Keys and return to the Academy. But return he must, and soon, before Burton realized John had shirked his evening duties, whatever they were supposed to have been. The sky looked as though someone had daubed it with blushing powder. Roses drooped across the garden walls of Fridaythorpe, and the air was thick with a vibrant aroma that stirred every fertile potential.

John dug his dinner jacket out of the wardrobe and brushed it. He dressed in the languid manner his exhaustion permitted and then did what he could with his hair. After clipping his trouser legs carefully, he mounted his steed and rode off into the exquisite, fairy-filled evening.

✦

He held her as tightly as he dared and kissed the tears from her face. He told her how perfectly beautiful she was. He whispered how much he worshipped her. And it was true. He was not one of those callous boys who decided afterwards that the girl was not as beautiful as she had seemed. Polly had in fact exploded into a beauty he had never recognized before, one softened and deepened by her pain, which he regretted even as he grew stiff again thinking of it. Her red nose and eyes, together with the unfathomable force of her emotions, made him want only to be inside her again. Obviously he would not batter his way a second time, but he would touch her in every way he could think of to convince her of his adoration.

And it was working. Her tears ceased, and she nearly smiled at a witty word. Once he was sure she was not angry, he would fetch the basket and offer her something to drink and eat. Perhaps after some refreshment, she could even be persuaded to try it again. If fifty thousand cricket balls were the key to mastery at the crease, what excellence might unfold from fifty thousand times giving himself to . . . the thing they had just done?

✦

John squeezed the hand brakes too hard and felt himself hurtling forward. By some miracle, he managed to tip the bike onto a grassy slope, saving himself a somersault and a fractured wrist.

The motorcar that provoked his tumble had not come as close as he feared. John caught his breath, and the car pulled over in response to his preposterous acrobatics.

—Sir, are you all right?

John untangled himself from the bicycle and saw Kilby, Hazlehurst's Prefect of Hall. He assured Kilby that he was uninjured, but as he got to his feet, he discovered that his dress trousers were filthy and would require serious attention with a clothes brush before he could present himself at Burton's supper.

The engine choked off, and Fardley got out from behind the wheel. From the backseat emerged Pearl minor, looking as though he'd been run over by a lorry.

—Pearl, what on earth happened? John gasped. Just what's going on here?

Fardley was driving them to the surgery, obviously.

—We're looking for Wilberforce, Kilby announced. You haven't seen him, have you, sir?

—Wilberforce? Why should I have seen him?

—The Head's asked to see him right away, Kilby said. I couldn't find him at the Academy, and he isn't on the list for the Ramble.

Fardley began to examine John's bicycle.

—What's this to do with Pearl minor? John asked.

—Pearl says he knows where we can find Wilberforce, Kilby said. That's where we're headed now.

—And where might that be?

Dread in his chest.

—McKay's barn, sir.

John breathed to gather his wits. Did Kilby mean to say that they were not headed to the surgery but were rather en route to McKay's barn with the embattled Pearl minor as guide? That was more or less what Kilby did mean to say, but he assured Mr. Grieves that if he had any choice in the matter, he would be doing neither. John reminded both boys that McKay's barn was out-of-bounds for irrefutable reasons, both practical and ethical. Kilby was well aware of the fact, but what could he do when the Headmaster demanded Kilby bring him, posthaste, a boy who required fetching from that very locale?

—What would Wilberforce be doing at McKay's barn? John demanded.

—That's what I want to know, Kilby said, but this one won't say a word.

—But, John struggled, you still haven't said what's happened to you, Pearl.

Pearl minor looked fixedly at the ground with an expression somewhere between disgust and rage:

—I had an accident.

—I should say you did, John retorted. In any case it's patently clear that you've come from McKay's barn yourself, so you may stay with the motorcar now.

—But—

—And help Mr. Fardley fit my bicycle into the boot. Kilby, with me.

Wearing his good shoes, his best trousers, his silk dress socks, and his dinner jacket, John led the way up the track to the godforsaken barn.

He thought as he climbed the slope that there was something altogether too dramatic about his visits to Farmer McKay's dilapidated property. His first time three months ago he had already relegated to a different age, and indeed it was. Under no circumstances, including these, did he intend to review that March afternoon, and yet it was hard to imagine that the current evening could end in anything but awkwardness, if not outright disaster. Could someone else have died? More to the point, why in the name of St. Stephen the Martyr did Morgan Wilberforce have to involve himself in every dire happening in the East Riding of Yorkshire? Even more to the point, why had the fates conspired to intersect his bicycle with the search party and thus entrap him in this unpleasant ordeal?

But—and the idea cheered John instantly—given Pearl minor's character, it was possible that Wilberforce was nowhere near the barn. John couldn't fathom Pearl's tactic, but the salient point, which Kilby seemed not to have considered, was that something violent had befallen Pearl minor, and his priorities must lie in revenge. Unquestionably, Pearl was not aiding Kilby out of altruism, not when his injuries appeared largely untreated. The boy belonged in the Tower.

John's heart quickened at the realization that Pearl minor had likely injured himself at McKay's barn. The barn was structurally unsound, a literal death trap. Obviously that was what had happened, and Pearl refused to admit it because he knew that Burton-Lee would break multiple blood vessels just contemplating his crime. Whatever happened, John would secure Pearl an interview with the Headmaster as soon as possible. Burton was equal to the challenge, and when it came to McKay's barn, he would not release his prey until he had learned everything there was to know.

—Why did Burton-Lee want Wilberforce? John asked Kilby.

—He didn't say, sir.

—Congratulations?

Kilby shrugged:

—Won't be congratulations when we're through if Wilberforce really is at the barn.

—Do you think Pearl minor could be telling the truth?

—Anything's possible, sir, but why make it up? Oh, and he says we'll find Wilberforce in some inner chamber.

—I beg your pardon?

—I don't know, sir. Here we are.

The barn stood solitary and exhausted at the top of the slope, as if one thorough wind might blow it down. John sent up a silent prayer—for the soul of the departed, for the sight of an utterly empty barn.

Kilby dragged the door open. Light bled through the slats in the walls, stirring motes and dust, like something suffused with the Holy Ghost. The large beam lay where it had fallen three months before. No other signs of disaster remained. They heard nothing.

—Wilberforce? Kilby called.

No answer. John scanned the area for something akin to Pearl minor's inner chamber. It was a leg-pull, clearly. A colossal waste of time, purpose yet to be—

—There, sir.

Kilby pointed to some panels in the wall, one askew.

—Wilberforce?

—Just a minute, a voice said.

Something rustled behind the panel. John held on to the door for support.

He ought to think of something to say. He ought to secure the site tactically, issue preemptive commands that would assist the unfolding of . . . whatever was about to unfold. The panel shifted. A blond head poked through, dragging behind it the gangly frame of Morgan Wilberforce. His shirt was unbuttoned, his braces hung down to his knees, he carried a jacket in his hand. Seeing John, he froze.

Kilby was making noise. Wilberforce said nothing. John said nothing.

—Who else is in there? Kilby demanded.

Wilberforce jolted to action, blocking the panel. Kilby told him to move.

—Just a minute, Wilberforce said.

—Is there another way out of there?

An involuntary glance from Wilberforce answered the question.

—Kilby, John said, go and wait outside the other entrance. Whoever it is can finish dressing. We'll wait.

Wilberforce cast his gaze to the floor, his face and ears scarlet. John tried to think of what to say. The dust tickled his throat. He coughed.

—Sir . . .

Wilberforce still stared at the ground, his voice nearly a whisper:

—Please, sir . . .

—Get dressed, John said.

He ought to say more than that. He ought to unleash a savage telling off. He ought to seize this overgrown boy and shake him until he dissolved into tears. Instead his own eyes stung, and his lungs ached watching Morgan Wilberforce button his shirt and tuck it into his trousers.

—Sir!

Kilby burst back into the barn, hauling the other suspect roughly. John turned to see who it was. He tried to speak but couldn't.

—You let go of her! Wilberforce shouted. Or—

—You'll what?

Wilberforce dashed across the barn and hurled himself at Kilby. Polly burst into tears. John didn't know whether to come to her rescue or to interpose himself between Kilby and Wilberforce. In the end he did neither. Polly recoiled when John came near her; Kilby and Wilberforce separated themselves.

—Right! John heard himself shouting. Back to the motorcar, all of you!

They looked to him as children in the presence of a commanding adult. Taking advantage of their submission, he led the way out of the barn and down the track. Polly strode past him, followed by Wilberforce. John caught him by the elbow:

—Leave her be.

Wilberforce struggled to free himself, but John yanked him aside and told Kilby to go ahead. When Wilberforce continued to resist, John dealt him a cuff to the ear.

—Before we go down there, John said, you are going to tell me exactly what happened.

Wilberforce set his face in an expression of stubborn defiance. John felt his temper rise:

—If you hurt one hair on her head, I'll make sure you are exceedingly sorry.

—I love her! Wilberforce exclaimed.

—Why was she in tears just now?

Wilberforce inhaled with a hiss.

—What d'you expect when that brute Kilby crashed in and manhandled her like some—

—What were the two of you doing?

Again, the defiant jaw.

—You were in a state of undress, John persisted. I assume you'd done the same to her?

—I didn't do anything to her!

—Wilberforce, you are dripping fault from every pore. She's a child. She—

—She wanted it! She said she did. More than once!

—Wilberforce, are you—

—I did everything she said. It isn't my fault if—

—Just what did you do to that girl?

—It's got to hurt at first, but then it doesn't. It isn't as though I—

John's fist was connecting with something hard and soft, a crack, and then blood was splashing out of that nose and onto John's hand. Wilberforce stumbled, his hand flew to his face, and he sat suddenly on the ground. Then John was yanking him up and shoving him down the track. He found a handkerchief in a pocket and thrust it at Wilberforce, who pressed it against his flowing nose. John concentrated on the acid snake that was writhing frantically inside him. He swallowed against it, but as the motorcar came into view, he gave the boy a final shove and then bent over to let the snake out. It came, scalding sour, dragging with it everything John had eaten.

Down at the gate, Polly was tending to Wilberforce. John stormed between them and put Polly in the front seat. Wilberforce tried to get in beside her, but Kilby intervened:

—You, in back.

Wilberforce sneered but stopped short upon seeing the passenger in the backseat. Pearl minor glared malevolently at him. Wilberforce looked as though he'd seen a phantom, his previously flushed face draining of color. John no longer needed to ask questions. Pearl minor had clearly acquired his injuries in Wilberforce's company, if not at his hands. John's head began to ache.

They drove back in silence. John had no second handkerchief to offer Polly, but Kilby had and did. Polly stared stonily out the windscreen. John had told Fardley to take them back to the Academy. He would send Kilby in with Wilberforce and Pearl and then take Polly home. He'd try to explain somehow to her father, though now that he considered it, what would he say to the man? What had Wilberforce confessed? A shooting light radiated across the windscreen, mirroring the pain inside John's head. The car hit a rut, and John's head hit the ceiling. The light continued to pulse at the edges of his vision in time with the stabbing behind his eyes.

—Sir, Kilby said, leaning forward and touching John's shoulder, can you take Wilberforce to Burton-Lee while I see this one to the Tower?

—I don't need the Tower, Pearl minor growled.

—Shut up, Kilby snapped.

—Shut up, yourself.

John raised his voice and told Pearl minor that would do. He told Kilby he would deal with Wilberforce and asked Fardley to see Polly home. He would explain everything to her father later. Tonight perhaps, or tomorrow. He would deliver Wilberforce to the Headmaster and then raid his classroom for headache tablets.

After they had piled, or rather limped, out of the motorcar, John got a better look at the damage. He addressed himself to Kilby:

—Escort Wilberforce to the washroom. Wait, and then bring him to me in the cloisters.

Then, before any of them could comment, he ducked his head back into the motorcar:

—I'll come by later, he told Polly.

A look of horror crossed her face and she started speaking, though not in any way that made sense to him. He told Fardley where to deliver her, and the motorcar roared away. John turned to Pearl minor.

—Good night, sir, Pearl minor began.

John seized him by the collar and dragged him inside the Tower. At the bottom of the stairs, John surveyed him. Bruises were coming up around both eyes. Several cuts on his cheek required attention. The abnormal shape of his nose explained the gore insufficiently wiped from his face.

—If I ask who did this, John said, I don't suppose you'll tell me.

Pearl minor replied with steely silence. John took the boy's head and examined it quickly for lumps and gashes. None, thankfully. The nose, however . . . he steadied Pearl minor's head and positioned his hand against the boy's nose.

—Deep breath.

A snap. The boy yelped. John released him.

—That's better, John said.

Pearl minor was gasping in surprise and pain, but breathing itself seemed a trial. John took his shoulder and probed his rib cage. The boy yelped again.

—Please, sir, can't I go?

—You can go to Matron. That's one broken rib, at least.

The boy's face darkened with frustration and something like resentment. John started to leave, but then turned back and snatched Pearl's wrists. They were bruised, but the boy's hands showed no sign of trauma.

—Why didn't you fight back?

John kept his voice neutral, as if he were only inquiring into a choice of vocabulary for a composition. Pearl stared stubbornly at the floor. John released his wrists but blocked his escape.

—Why would a boy who took a thrashing like this not defend himself? John asked aloud. He might have been too afraid. But then, a boy who had the nerve to lie to S-K about the events I believe they call the Fags' Rebellion—

Pearl minor glanced up despite himself.

—That is not a boy who lacks courage.

He searched Pearl's face, imagining himself in the boy's place.

—Unless he held you down?

The boy replied with a fierce scowl, and John blanched. Whatever would drive Wilberforce to such savagery?

—You interfered with what he had planned, didn't you?

—Wilberforce *told* you?

John crossed his arms.

—Wilberforce didn't tell me. You did, just now.

Pearl minor looked at him with a mixture of horror, humiliation, and utter disorientation. John capitalized:

—Matron, now. Any detours and I'll hear of it. Go.

Miraculously, Pearl went.

The day could not get any worse. His head was still tormenting him, and he wanted more than anything to go rest in his classroom. Instead, he marched himself to the cloisters. A group of boys who'd stayed back from the Ramble were lounging there. Not seeing Wilberforce or Kilby, John barged into the washroom, where Wilberforce was drying his face. The blood had stopped. Aside from the redness on his cheek, no one would guess what had happened outside the barn.

'—Kilby, I'll take over from here, thank you.

—Sir, I think I ought to—

—You've done a capital job, Kilby. Good night.

With that, John strode from the washroom, Wilberforce in tow.

Wilberforce let John drag him to Burton-Lee's House. John realized that he ought to have taken a moment to smarten himself up, but it was too late now. He knew he ought to say something to Wilberforce, something important and morally astringent, but they'd arrived at Burton's door. This was going to be unpleasant.

John reminded himself that since no one was poised to expire, the evening could not actually get worse. It would get worse for Wilberforce, but John and Wilberforce were not the same person, and in the last analysis— the first analysis!—Wilberforce deserved everything headed his way, up to and including expulsion.

He released the boy's arm. Wilberforce straightened his jacket and the tie he had produced whilst in the washroom. His hands shook. John's chest hurt. Would expulsion really be necessary? He knocked.

—Come!

Of course it was necessary. This boy had done appalling things. So appalling, John could not even connect them with the trembling boy beside him. He took a breath. Wilberforce took a breath. No one was dying. Things couldn't get worse. They stepped into the study.

Things got worse.

Burton greeted them jovially:

—Ah, there you are, Wilberforce. The Ramble's returned?

Wilberforce stood like an animal in the headlamps of an oncoming motorcar. Burton gave John one of his smiles designed to convey the maximum courtesy with the minimum warmth.

—Here you are, Grieves.

His tone made it clear John was intruding. Several of the gray gentlemen from the Board were still with him.

—I was delivering Wilberforce to you, John said.

Burton smiled again, puzzled, polite.

—Thank you.

He turned warmly to Wilberforce:

—And here is the hero of our XI. One or two people have been asking to make your acquaintance, young man.

As Burton drew an unwilling Wilberforce into the room, John saw that not only had things got worse, they had got much worse than he could have imagined. *Bad* and *worse* were mere words, but standing before the window, glass in hand, smiling curiously across the room was the person, the one John refused to think of, the dyed-in-the-wool catastrophe that now engulfed him.

—Stinging right arm you've got, said a gray man.

John struggled to recall which one he was. Chairman of the Board, or had that been another? They'd been introduced, so John couldn't possibly ask for a name now. Was it something to do with coveralls?

—Are you as much of a sergeant major in the form room as on the pitch? the man continued.

The other men chuckled. John sensed there had been a misunderstanding. An ice pick was boring into his skull.

—If that's everything, John said to Burton, I'll leave you.

—Don't be silly. What will you drink?

He could feel himself starting to panic. The room was hot and he couldn't breathe. Burton drew him aside.

—Are you quite all right?

—No. I mean of course, but not exactly. Something's happened.

—What?

John thought his throat might be closing up.

—It's Wilberforce. It's complicated.

—What? Burton demanded.

—It's awkward. I'll come back later once you're quite alone.

Burton drew him farther from the group.

—I sent for the pair of you. The Board wanted to meet the two who so impressed them this afternoon.

—You sent for me?

Burton was making no sense at all.

—What's he doing here? John blurted.

Burton didn't ask whom he meant. He drew the kind of breath that meant he was struggling to keep his temper.

—Awkward, Burton replied. But pull yourself together. I need you.

He led John back to the gray men, who were questioning a flustered Wilberforce. Then the person broke into their midst to hand Wilberforce a glass of lemonade.

—Scotch, Grieves? the person asked.

Was there no way he could escape, even for a moment to use the toilet? Burton turned the brooking-no-refusal look on him. John decided to ignore the person and instead address Wilberforce.

—Did you say good evening to these gentlemen?

This prompted a flurry of introductions. John listened carefully as the gray man gave his name. Overall! He'd been close. He was the Chairman, then. Burton had the grace to slip around to the sideboard and pour John a lemonade. That disposed of the person. How dare that person offer John scotch, as if he knew John's drink, as if John were the same person he had been when he did drink scotch?

John took the lemonade and pretended to sip it. As the men quizzed Wilberforce on his batting, his father, and his people, John concentrated on his breathing, remembering to do it, regularly, and to an appropriate depth. He glued his gaze to the faces of the gray men, avoiding Wilberforce, avoiding the person. He simply couldn't fathom what the person was doing there, and without that knowledge, he had no way of guessing when the person might depart. Was it possible the person was included in Burton's supper party? Clearly it was possible. The last trains had gone.

Conversation stopped. They all looked at him. The person laughed:

—You haven't changed a bit, John. Not a single bit.

—I've changed immeasurably.

The person laughed again. They all laughed.

—Sebastian tells us you were at Marlborough together, Overall said.

—Grieves was a year above me in the House.

—And did he bowl like that when you were boys?

—He's improved.

Burton refilled their glasses.

—And are you Housemaster of that House? Burton asked the person.

John's teeth twinged to their roots. Surely everyone could hear the acid in Burton's question? Instead of ruffled feathers, however, another laugh and obsequious echo.

—That would take some getting used to, the person replied. No, I'm at—

He named another House at their former school. Overall carried on in this vein, quizzing the person about his post as if for the purpose of enlightening John. Burton was nodding as if he had heard it all before, his jaw set so tight that John wondered how the enamel on his teeth was faring. Evidently the person was a Housemaster at Marlborough. He was the youngest Housemaster since someone in the past century, whose name John promptly forgot. His reputation, Overall informed them, preceded him. Before Marlborough he'd been at Trinity. It was all so exceedingly satisfactory that John wondered why Burton was acting as if it were taking every ounce of his strength not to hurl his glass at someone's head.

—So, Overall said, what do you think of our humble Academy, Sebastian?

—It's delightful.

Revived by lemonade, Wilberforce joined the conversation, demonstrating full command of the names in the room:

—Mr. Overall, is Dr. Sebastian joining the Board?

Sebastian laughed again, as did his minions.

—This simply makes no sense, John blurted. Whatever you're playing at, I've had enough.

Burton looked aghast, but John realized that he was indeed tired of being knocked about by other people's whims. He'd done everything asked of him in managing the wretched Old Boys. He'd bowled one of the best games of his life, not that they'd any notion, and probably given himself arthritis doing it. He'd been dragged against his will into the second-most-sordid debacle in the history of the Academy and still faced the ordeal of unfolding it to Burton, if only he could extricate the man from the demonic Board. Now to be forced to stand about Burton's study drinking lemonade beside Morgan Wilberforce—the most compromised boy in the county, at least!—beside a cluster of tedious old men, and beside Jamie Sebastian, who had no business there whatsoever and who appeared to be part of an elaborate, unhumorous cod—it was more than anyone could or should endure.

—May I have a word? Burton asked Overall.

The chairman of the Board stepped with Burton into a quiet corner. The other two gray men began speaking at once, addressing themselves to Wilberforce and probing his opinion of Hobbs and his centuries. Wilberforce's discomfort seemed to dissolve once asked to comment on cricket. John squinted at the intruder, as if glowering would provoke an explanation. Sebastian dropped the light, easy manner and replaced it with something more tentative. He sidled near to John and spoke in an undertone:

—I was most terribly sorry to hear about your father.

John flushed to the core.

—I beg your pardon!

—I would have come to the funeral, but we were told it was family only, so . . .

John choked on air. For Sebastian to speak of matters that had been so thoroughly banned! How could he even respond? And what was this subterfuge growing within him: the temptation to speak of it with someone who had known his father, someone who had in fact seen his father alive more recently than John had himself, someone who'd known his father before everything went wrong.

—We didn't know what had become of you, Jamie continued outrageously.

It wasn't clear whether the first-person plural stood for Jamie alone, or if it signified himself and the Bishop, or perhaps himself, his sisters, and the Bishop.

—I'm alive and well, you'll be chagrined to learn, John said bitterly.

Jamie smiled slightly, an expression full of sadness, regret, and an unendurable pity.

—Overall says you came here after the War?

John nodded mutely.

—Until I read your father's obit, I wondered if you hadn't perhaps died in it.

Jamie hesitated, realizing his gaffe, for if he had not known whether John was alive or dead, then John's father must never have spoken of him after he became a conscientious objector. John knew from the maiden aunts that his father had retained ties with the Bishop after severing them with John. Jamie tried to recover:

—So you see it was a great surprise when I arrived today and learned that the Common Room included you of all people. It's made deliberations easier.

—What deliberations?

Jamie looked abashed again, having apparently stepped into another quagmire.

—Look, John said severely, this has been a most appalling day. I don't like being toyed with. It's inhumane.

Jamie winced, nearly:

—I'll have to leave explanation to our esteemed Chairman.

Overall and Burton were returning, Burton looking yet again as if he would explode like an overblown balloon. He detached Wilberforce from the group and dismissed him for the evening.

—No, John interrupted, wait—there's—can I speak to you, please, for a moment?

Burton sighed heavily and allowed John to buttonhole him.

—Can you send this lot off to look at the chapel? John asked. Wilberforce needs a quarter of an hour of your undivided attention.

—No, I cannot send them off—

—Do you have any idea where I found him, and with whom?

Burton's face drained of color:

—Is there any way this can wait until the morning?

—Absolutely not, John insisted. If you let him walk out that door, I can't vouch for what might happen. For one thing, Pearl minor might come down from the Tower, and if they met—

—What has Pearl minor to do with this mess?

—Plenty.

—You aren't making sense.

—I'm making every kind of sense. It's this cursed, infernal day that

273

isn't making sense, and Wilberforce's catastrophic judgment in every single matter that doesn't involve a cricket ball!

—What's so appalling about young Wilberforce? Jamie interrupted.

Burton visibly prevented himself from barking at Jamie.

—Nothing at all, he said. But if you'll excuse me one moment.

Burton tried to look as though he were merely drifting to the door, but John knew he wanted to thrash about as he normally did. Why wasn't he, in fact? Burton never had qualms about taking a pair of verbal steak knives to whomever he chose. Why should he tolerate a young visitor intruding in a private, sotto voce conversation between himself and his staff? Burton's only word on the gathering had been *awkward*, and he had said he needed John's help. Of course, he hadn't said how, which was typical. He expected John to know everything without being told, like some kind of medium.

—Gentlemen, Burton said, if I might press upon your patience briefly, there is something that requires my attention for a few minutes. Clarke here—

He indicated a boy he'd conscripted from the corridor.

—has volunteered to give you a tour of the House.

Overall and his lieutenants found the invitation agreeable and followed the boy into the corridor, Jamie bringing up the rear. When the door at last closed behind them, Burton turned on John:

—Just what is this about?

John looked to Wilberforce, who blushed and looked at the floor. Burton stormed to the sideboard, poured himself a fresh drink, and downed it furiously.

—We are exceedingly short on time, and this is an exceedingly bad moment. Grieves, kindly get to the point. And Wilberforce—

Burton turned a severe expression on the boy.

—whatever this is about, I expect to hear the truth from you. All of it. Understood?

Wilberforce swallowed as if he might be sick. Burton leapt forward, seized him by the arm, and shoved him onto the settee. Burton then dragged over a straight-backed chair and sat in it.

—Well?

As Burton had not offered John a seat, he remained standing.

—Wilberforce was not on the Ramble this evening, John began.

—Then what took so long when I sent for you?

They both looked to Wilberforce. He swallowed again. John wanted to clip him round the ear. Instead he crammed his fists into the pockets of his dinner jacket:

—Are you going to tell him or am I?

Wilberforce licked his lips. If he could explain for himself, John decided he would revise his excremental opinion of the boy.

—It's difficult to say, Wilberforce began.

—Speak up, Burton snapped. Is there anything about the past twelve hours that you cannot recall?

—No, sir.

—Then stop trying my very short patience and present a brief, audible chronology.

—It's difficult to say, Wilberforce whispered, because . . .

—Yes?

Burton pitched his voice equally low, as if to draw out the words that choked the boy. Wilberforce blinked. John wondered if he would cry. Wilberforce had not cried last term over Spaulding, not when John snapped his dislocated arm back into its socket, never under punishment. Now, though, his face had turned so red that John thought tears might roll down it as they had at his table in the middle of that night, another age ago.

The boy scratched at the mud on the leg of his trousers and spoke in a whisper:

—Because I'm so ashamed of it.

Burton took a quiet breath. The man clearly longed to release his frustration in a gush of verbal abuse, but every aspect of Burton's behavior remained under his express control. John had never understood how Burton had acquired his reputation for extracting confessions, but now he realized he was witnessing the technique.

—We've all done things we're ashamed of, Burton said evenly. *I am come not to call the righteous, but sinners to repentance.*

Wilberforce glanced up and searched Burton's face.

—Go on, Burton told him gently. Show your mettle.

Wilberforce resumed cleaning his trouser leg:

—I was with someone out-of-bounds.

Burton made no sound. Wilberforce cleared his throat.

—I've been seeing her all term. Usually in the kitchen. She's . . . We love each other.

John picked up his glass and wiped away the ring it had left on the table. Burton continued not to speak. Wilberforce continued his confession, omitting details John considered relevant (for instance, that the kitchen in question had to have been at the Cross Keys), but details which, John realized, must have seemed irrelevant to Wilberforce. He stumbled along, admitting to liaisons, outlining his growing devotion to this girl (carefully avoiding naming Polly), and finally his decision, their joint decision, to meet this evening for the purposes of *l'amour complet*. John had never heard the expression; it turned his stomach.

A knock at the door, though Wilberforce and Burton seemed not to notice.

—Sorry, Jamie said quietly.

Burton put up a hand to demand silence but did not break Wilberforce's gaze. John set his lemonade back down before he dropped it. Either he had gone over the edge and begun hallucinating, or there was something revolutionary afoot that he had entirely failed to grasp. He scarcely knew where to focus, on Wilberforce, now narrating his plan to seduce Polly in "the barn," or on Jamie, slinking against the door and watching the scene with fascination. Whatever Jamie had to say to him, it was ludicrous that he intrude upon a most sensitive interview, and what's more, having intruded, that he fail to say it, instead lounging around as though Wilberforce's moral nadir had something to do with him. If not for John's respect for Burton's technique, he would have told Jamie then and there what he thought of his manners. As it was, he inched towards the door.

—The trouble was, when I arrived, someone else was there. Mr. Grieves already said it, so I'm not telling tales, am I?

—No.

It was the first word Burton had uttered. With that gentle encouragement to Wilberforce, he thrust an impatient arm towards John, using his actual finger to direct John back to the spot where he had been standing. John obeyed.

Jamie's hand was resting on the edge of the table beside the door, his fingers, long and slender, running back and forth along the table edge. Jamie, like Burton, seemed mesmerized by Wilberforce, though perhaps Jamie was also mesmerized by Burton's control of the confession. John had never seen anything like it, never seen a boy speak his misdeeds as Wilberforce was doing, never seen Burton sit so silent and still.

Wilberforce confessed to losing his temper at Pearl minor and setting upon the younger boy. He claimed to have come quickly to his senses and sent the boy away. John wondered if this was the truth. It was possible. Wilberforce could have landed the blows to the ribs first, knocking Pearl minor to the ground. He could then have delivered head shots, breaking the nose, blacking his eyes, and cutting open his cheek. If the punches had been accurate, hard, and unexpected, Wilberforce might have done the damage in ten seconds or less. It occurred to John that the Academy ought to revive boxing.

Wilberforce was struggling as he came to the act of *l'amour complet*. He assured them that the girl had consented, not only consented, but had helped plan the tryst. He reiterated the point three times. John felt a sliver of relief, in contrast to how he'd felt when Wilberforce was spewing nonsense outside the barn, the moment when John had wavered in his self-command. But there was no point in dwelling on that. Wilberforce had emerged from the washroom without a glimmer of accusation, as if he'd cleaned the memory as well as the blood from his face. He'd suffer no lasting harm, and anyway, in comparison to what Wilberforce had done to Polly and to Pearl minor, John's momentary lapse was—

—And that's when Kilby and Mr. Grieves arrived.

Wilberforce exhaled heavily, as if that concluded his testimony. Burton sat back in his chair, clasped his hands, unclasped them. He looked to John and purposely did not look at Jamie. And why should he look at Jamie? It was no affair of Burton's if Jamie had appalling manners and insisted on earwigging interviews that were nothing to do with him. Ignoring him was precisely what he deserved.

Burton spoke again in the soothing voice:

—Well done.

Wilberforce glanced up at him, a flood of ridiculous gratitude on his face.

—Is there anything he's neglected to mention, Grieves?

Burton still wasn't looking at him. It was embarrassing to be treated as a valet, and in front of Jamie.

—Oh, John replied icily, only a few minor details.

Burton's attention flashed to him.

—The girl is the daughter of Wakes, the landlord of the Cross Keys. Pearl minor came away with two black eyes, a broken nose, and at least one broken rib. And the barn in question—

Burton leapt to his feet, but John spoke:

—McKay's.

Burton's glance to the door, to Jamie, carried something more than mortification.

—So you see, John concluded, Wilberforce's adventures are all rather economical.

Burton was at a loss. Wilberforce put his head in his hands.

—McKay's barn? Jamie asked. Is that where—

Burton held up a hand to—

—Yes, John replied chirpily.

Jamie let go of the table and approached Burton's desk, piercing the perimeter of their conference.

—Who else knows about this? he asked.

—Kilby, Fardley, and Pearl minor, John said. Otherwise, no one.

—Let's keep it that way, Jamie replied.

A wave of relief crossed Burton's face.

—I'm glad you see it that way, Burton said. I'll deal with it. You can be sure—

—How will you deal with it? Jamie asked.

—Excuse me, John said. I know I'm insignificant, so obviously it isn't worth the trouble to explain anything to me, but I still fail to see what one syllable of this has to do with you!

He finished with a savage glare to Jamie. Burton began to burble. Jamie began to laugh.

—I do apologize, John. How this must look from your perspective I can't begin to imagine.

—Can't you?

—I must seem the most appalling meddler.

Jamie turned casually to Burton, as if they'd known each other for years:

—Do you want to?

Burton waved him on:

—Be my guest.

Jamie appeared not to notice the bitter chill in Burton's politeness. He opened his mouth to make his pronouncement but then hesitated. His teeth scraped his lower lip. He clasped his hands behind his back.

—It's as odd for me as it is for you, Jamie began, and nearly as much of a shock.

—Yes? John prompted impatiently.

—Please believe me when I say I didn't know you were here. I would never have imagined—

—Why couldn't you imagine it? John retorted. Can't believe anyone would employ a Red conchie like me?

—What? No! Nothing like that!

John was struggling to stop himself from throwing a punch at Jamie's head. Jamie sighed at the realization that John did not follow.

—And when we met today at lunch, it wasn't by any means certain.

Burton made a noise that could have been a clearing of the throat but that sounded more like a scoff.

—It wasn't certain in my mind, Jamie said in response. I can't speak for Overall. His tactics are opaque.

—They're nothing of the kind, Burton declared.

—I can't expect you to believe me, Jamie told Burton, but it is true.

—Wait a minute!

They all three looked to the settee. Wilberforce had spoken and was leaping to his feet.

—Sit down and be quiet! Burton snapped.

—But, Wilberforce stuttered, Dr. Sebastian's going to join the SCR, isn't he?

—Wilberforce! Burton barked. You are out of order.

—It's all right, Jamie rejoined. That's correct. I am.

—Why? John exclaimed.

Jamie inhaled.

—Didn't someone just say you were at Marlborough? Good for you. Why, in the name of God, the King, and the Marylebone Cricket Club, come here?

Burton, enjoying Jamie's discomfiture, refilled his drink and neglected to offer either John or Jamie another. A look of comprehension crossed Wilberforce's face, followed swiftly by unease.

—Exactly what are you looking so pained about? John demanded.

Wilberforce spoke to John's knees:

—It's Dr. Sebastian, sir.

—Well?

—He's been here all along. It isn't exactly the way one hopes to meet one's new Headmaster, sir.

John's mind had a string of petulant remarks queued for delivery, but he spoke none. Burton swirled his tumbler, clinking ice against crystal.

John wondered whether he might leave the room now. Wilberforce had been delivered and the essential details conveyed. John needed to go to his desk and retrieve the headache tablets from the lower right-hand drawer. There were at least three left, and if he took them all, he might be able to see straight by the time the supper began. He needed to repair to Lockett-Egan's and borrow his washroom, clothes brush, comb, and possibly his shoe polish. And as for what Burton would serve at supper, John hoped it would not involve cream. There had been a good deal too much cream touching nearly every dish at luncheon, and John did not get on well with cream. It made him feel congested and left his stomach heavy. Besides that, he was allergic to strawberries. Even touching them made his skin erupt. It was appalling the way English cooks depended so slavishly on strawberries in the summer. Could they not vary their ingredients to include more plums, greengages, grapes, or even other berries? But that, obviously, was asking too much. Strawberries grew everywhere in England, so strawberries they would have, morning, noon, afternoon, night, until they all turned fleshy, red, and rotten.

—The last thing I want is to create awkwardness, Jamie was saying, but I wouldn't be doing anyone any favors if I simply left the room to survey the stained glass.

—You'd be doing me a favor, Burton said.

—Not in the long run.

—You aren't Headmaster yet, Burton bristled.

Jamie adopted a strained, patient smile John recognized, only the last time he'd seen that expression had been on the face of Jamie's father.

—I am, actually. Acting from ten July, but technically, as of . . . an hour ago . . .

John watched the two in appalled fascination. Burton's complexion had turned what people called purple. John wanted to advise him to breathe before he broke blood vessels. Jamie, too, was blushing, across his cheekbones as he always had. It had the unfortunate effect of making him more attractive. Here was Burton, undergoing an epic humiliation, and not only that, but undergoing it before an audience of a junior colleague and a pupil who had embarrassed, disappointed, and outraged him in equal measure. He was enduring the extermination of what must have been a long-standing dream.

And Jamie, standing so diffidently, the world his, as it had always been. John could see him calculating how to minimize Burton's humiliation and prepare the ground for alliance. He could see that Jamie was embarrassed for Burton and for the way the scene had unfolded, yet he could see that Jamie did not intend to cede ground. He looked no more accustomed to being thwarted than he had been in childhood. John couldn't see the justice in it, in people such as Jamie who had everything handed to them without trying, or in the maneuvers of a high-handed Board that had double-crossed a loyal man in the name of—what? Why *had* they engaged Jamie? He was a year younger than John, had only been teaching two years (was it?), and knew nothing of St. Stephen's and its unspeakably intricate affairs. John could only conclude that the Board had been dazzled by Jamie's fraudulent charisma, as everyone had been his whole life long.

—Perhaps we ought to speak privately, Jamie suggested.

Burton snapped out of his paralyzed fury.

—Wilberforce! he barked. Go and stand in the corridor.

—Yes, sir.

—You're not to speak with anyone. Is that clear, or do you need to stand in a corner somewhere?

—It's clear, sir.

—Get out.

Wilberforce fled.

—Thank you, Grieves, we'll take it from here, Burton said.

Jamie stepped across his path:

—Please stay. We need you.

—That's quite all right, John stammered, I've got to—

—It wasn't a request, Jamie said.

John felt as though he'd been punched in the solar plexus.

—Drink? Jamie asked.

—No.

—You need one.

Jamie poured two measures from Burton's decanter.

—Our Grieves is an abstainer, Burton told him.

The knot in John's chest eased. For the first time, he felt comforted and protected by Burton's proprietary manner. Jamie let his surprise show, but then he combined the drinks into one glass and took it for himself:

—Shall we?

He gestured for them to sit. Burton took the straight-backed chair. Jamie drew the wooden armchair closer. John was left to occupy the settee Wilberforce had just abandoned.

—This is all very awkward, Jamie began, so let's try to sort things out as quickly as possible.

He looked to them, but they did not reply.

—What's to be done with this boy Wilberforce?

Burton sighed uncomfortably, as if he were suffering indigestion.

—Unless I missed something, Jamie continued, he has just confessed to fornicating with a village girl on the site of that appalling tragedy the *Mail* squawked about. That and beating another boy to something like a pulp. Is there any question of keeping him on?

—Yes, Burton replied.

—You're joking?

—I'm dead serious.

—He's a jolly good bat, but we can't let athletic heroes get away with bullying and fornication.

—One fight is hardly bullying, John protested.

—How old is this other boy . . . what's his name?

—Pearl minor, Burton said. Fourteen.

Jamie looked shocked.

—*That* boy is a menace, John argued. He's been responsible for . . . a good deal more than is generally known!

—Enlighten me.

—Grieves, Burton warned.

—John, you know I'll find out eventually, Jamie said. Can't you save the song and dance and simply tell me?

John looked to Burton, who waved his fingers in a resigned fashion. And so John told Jamie about Pearl minor and the Fags' Rebellion, at least as Wilberforce had narrated it to him in his unhinged condition after Spaulding.

—What a very resourceful community you have.

Jamie was going for wry humor, but Burton took it as sarcasm. John plunged forward with his narrative before Burton could further poison his relationship with his future—current—employer. He gave a précis of the McKay's barn debacle and followed it up with his analysis of Wilberforce's character, venturing before he realized into an account of Wilberforce's night ramble last term, his visit to John's digs, and their unorthodox interview. Not seeing how to extricate himself, John continued until he ran out of words.

Burton looked stunned. Jamie looked as though he'd opened a pie and discovered unsavory ingredients. John wondered where he'd set his lemonade. There it was, across the room.

—Quite a portrait, Jamie said drily. But how do you reconcile your obvious enthusiasm for the boy with the revolting confession he's just offered?

John was suddenly parched.

—Not to mention his egregious habit of disobedience.

—It isn't as though that doesn't go on all the time! John protested.

Burton sucked in his breath; Jamie's brow leapt.

—I don't mean—that is, the school's not—not all the time, I only meant that Wilberforce—

—I understand exactly what you meant, Jamie said. And I think I'm beginning to understand what it is I've been dropped into.

—I beg your pardon? Burton protested.

—May I speak plainly?

—Have you not been?

—And in strict confidence?

Burton threatened thunder but nodded.

—With a few exceptions, Jamie proceeded, present company included amongst them, I have been singularly unimpressed with the SCR. In due course, I intend to make changes. Burton Lee, despite the innate antagonism between us, I wish you to know that I have the greatest respect for what you've done here.

—Is that so?

—Yes, Jamie continued, it is. Having perused Overall's audit, having read the *Mail*, and having endured the Board's blatant and frankly desperate propaganda, I had assumed the school I was about to visit would be a dissipated Dotheboys Hall, fit for little besides shutting up as quickly as possible.

—I refuse to sit here and—

—But plainly my expectations were mistaken, and I credit you with the discrepancy.

Burton fluffed and hemmed. John felt amusement and, towards Jamie, awe.

—I'm sure we are going to disagree about a good many things, Jamie said, but I've absolute confidence that we are batting for the same side when it comes to this school.

—Well, Burton said, trying to recover, cricket metaphors are rather tired, but point taken.

—And John, Jamie said turning that magnetic stare on him, I've no idea what you're doing mucking about in the village here, but it's got to stop.

—What do you mean *mucking about*? If you're suggesting—

—I'm going to need you as a Housemaster, that's all.

John uttered something, but it could hardly be classed as language. Jamie turned to Burton.

—Don't you agree?

Burton frowned:

—I suppose anyone would make a better fist of it than Hazlehurst.

—Good, Jamie said, that's settled.

—Just a minute!

John's wits were returning. He adjusted himself on the settee, but it failed to give him a more commanding position.

—I am not taking on a House. I'm not taking on anything. I was going to resign at the end of term, but since you've put yourself in authority, I'll do it right here and right now!

Burton sighed in exasperation:

—I thought we'd been through all this at Easter.

—That was before—

John was spluttering but he didn't care.

—Just what was the nature of your relationship at Marlborough? Burton asked.

—Nothing! We knew one another. We—he—the House—that is—

—We were friends, Jamie said.

—And you want to resign? Burton asked.

—I do resign!

—I don't accept your resignation, Jamie replied coolly.

—Damn you! What do you mean?

—What I say.

John got up from the settee:

—You can't make me stay here if I refuse. I'm a free man!

—If you don't stay, I'll not only see that this Wilberforce is expelled, but I'll make sure no decent school will ever take him.

The room tilted.

—You wouldn't.

—You know me better than that.

No longer smiling, Jamie's face had the strength of granite. Burton got to his feet and assumed command of the conversation:

—I've no idea who you think you are, Sebastian, but I won't watch my colleague be bullied. If you blackmail Grieves like that—and it is blackmail, as we're speaking plainly—then I will resign, and you can do what you like with Wilberforce and the rest of the staff you admire so very much.

Jamie's gaze fluttered, but only for a moment.

—Unfortunately, he said, my acceptance of this post was dependent on your staying.

—I beg your pardon? Burton floundered.

—Ask Overall. If you leave, I won't take the post, and I don't mind how put out Overall is. He can look somewhere else for a man willing to take on this Academy of yours. Or perhaps he could talk dear old Clement into taking the helm.

The scene acquired a sheen of the surreal. John had faced off against other men, but never two at once as they also battled each other. Now Jamie had outmaneuvered them both. A flare crossed John's vision, and a searing pain his temples. He reached for support, but his hands found nothing.

—Mind yourself.

Burton was at his side, taking his elbow, pushing a chair against the back of his knees, pressing a handkerchief into his hand. John panted against the pain and held the handkerchief against his closed eyes and clammy brow.

—What's the matter?

Jamie's voice was anxious. Burton put a cool glass into John's hand.

—Drink, he said quietly.

John obeyed. The water stayed down. He recovered his breath and then his vision. His eyes felt red and swollen. Burton was sitting beside him, leaning forward, elbows on knees. Jamie, too, had sat back down, though his chair remained several feet away. Burton cast his gaze over Jamie:

—This conversation has been most unedifying.

—I agree, Jamie said. I suggest we take a moment and collect ourselves.

John blew his nose. Perspiration ran down his back, dampening his shirt and trousers.

—Father, Jamie said, let your Holy Spirit direct our words and open our hearts. Help us recognize your will, and give us the strength to stand behind it. In particular, Father, we ask that you help us deal courageously with one another and justly with those in our care. We ask this in Christ's name.

John and Burton sat flabbergasted. S-K had placed regular emphasis on prayer, but he'd never prayed extempore. And neither, so far as John knew, had Jamie.

—I suggest that we consider rationally the question of young Wilberforce, Burton said.

—Agreed, Jamie replied.

—Permit me to summarize. Wilberforce has conducted himself appallingly this term and last. He is an exceptional sportsman, an indifferent scholar, a charismatic personality, and a catastrophically unguided young man.

—And that's my fault, I suppose? John bristled. It isn't enough to issue your diktats unless you give people the authority to execute them.

—What is he on about? Jamie asked Burton.

—All you said was *sort him out*! John continued. How was I meant to do that? I remediated his stroke, stopped him cutting away to the pub during Games, persuaded Andrewes to take him this afternoon—

—And tried him by fire with that right arm of yours, Jamie said.

That voice was stabbing John's chest.

—You did exactly what I expected, Burton said quietly. I've never seen a boy bat like that.

—Neither have I, said Jamie.

Neither had John. Morgan Wilberforce had departed breakfast a wreck of a Fifth Former and arrived at tea a sensation with a cricket bat. Perhaps John had forced the advent, but what had he actually driven into being? A boy who could brave his bowling and win a match, but a boy who could . . .

His pulse quickened. He was not responsible for Morgan Wilberforce, not for his talent and not for his iniquity.

—What makes you think I believe Wilberforce ought to stay? John said to Burton. He's behaved unforgivably towards Polly, and if her father reacts as I would, Wilberforce will be lucky to escape charges.

Jamie's face darkened.

—Not to mention the barbaric assault on Pearl minor and the whatever-it-was that made Wilberforce choose McKay's barn for everything.

—I thought you liked him, Burton protested.

—Are you saying he should be expelled? Jamie asked.

—He certainly should!

Jamie hesitated only a moment before gesturing to the door:

—Tell the boy to come back in.

—Wait! John said. What are you—are you going to—

—You *don't* want me to sack him?

—I, well, not just like that.

Jamie turned to Burton, who shocked John by laughing.

—You, Burton said to Jamie, are arrogant, devious, and far too big for your boots.

Jamie had the grace to blush.

—S-K tried to sack Wilberforce last term, you know.

—I did not know, Jamie said.

—And the two of us tried to dissuade him just as we've tried with you.

—I am not trying to dissuade—

—Of course you are, Grieves. We should be thankful this one's prepared to listen to reason.

—But, John stammered, he doesn't   he never—

—He's listening to *you*.

Burton looked at John. Jamie looked at him, with that look John had vowed never again to endure, the look that showed Jamie knew him, that he remembered what it was to know him, that he realized he'd missed it, tremendously.

—Something does have to be done with the boy, however, Burton said. He'll have to be rusticated at least. Someone ought to give him a monumental thrashing, but I haven't the heart for it, to be honest.

Jamie turned to John.

—Don't look at me! John snapped.

Jamie sighed.

—Can you reach his parents? he asked Burton. Can they fetch him tomorrow?

—The mother's dead, John said. The father's in London, and sending him home will do no good at all.

Jamie grimaced. The tower bell began to toll, and John felt a sudden panic at his inability to explain. If Jamie had been there the night Wilberforce ran away, he would have understood.

—You can't send him home, John said.

How could he untangle what beset this boy, a boy so potent and so fragile?

—He can't stay here, Burton said.

—I know that! I meant—

Could John mean what he meant? It would kill him: to recall the middle chapter, Jamie and the Bishop; and to stay at the Academy, for better or for worse. But the memory of the boy entirely undone pressed on John's chest until he thought it would break.

Jamie stepped towards him.

—John, he said.

John stood where he was. He breathed in and he breathed out again. Sometimes suffering was guaranteed; thrashing about only made things worse.

John looked at Jamie:

—Morgan Wilberforce needs sorting out.

Jamie caught his breath. *We've got to suffer our suffering. There is no shortcut.* Some fatal hand had brought Jamie to the Academy, and that same hand now held Wilberforce. One word from John—

—What do you mean?

Jamie searched his face. John let him search it:

—What do you think?

Jamie, nonplussed, did not look away. Slowly, he set down his drink.

—May I use your telephone? he asked.

Burton, bemused, waved him to it. Jamie picked up the handset and asked for a Wiltshire number. John's mouth tasted hard, sour, metallic.

—Satisfactory, Jamie was saying.

He spoke staccato, uttering one word for every ten from his interlocutor.

—Yes . . . Yes, actually. A case . . . Urgent . . . No, sir. I'm catching the first, at . . .

Jamie looked up.

—Seven oh three, Burton supplied.

—Seven oh three, so teatime?

Jamie listened, holding the receiver as if it might do something unexpected.

—Thank you, he said. Thank you, sir.

He replaced the handset and took a breath. John's forehead throbbed.
—Well? Burton asked.
Jamie went to refill his drink. John put a hand on the decanter:
—What did he say?
His hand trembled. Jamie trembled. Everything dead lived and stabbed.
—Oh, John, what do you think?

PART THREE

Trains were supposed to be soothing. They hurled one across the countryside yet gave the impression of leisure. Trolleys came through at intervals, offering tea and food. Nothing was required except that one sit back and allow oneself to be conveyed. Frequently, the lulling motion induced sleep.

Morgan wanted to sleep. His head was heavy but he could not sleep, or possibly he dared not. Whenever he closed his eyes, fragments of the previous day assaulted him.

—Sir, Morgan said, there's a telephone at the premises of my father's firm. I learnt the exchange by heart. We could place a call at King's Cross.

—Oh, yes? replied Dr. Sebastian, lowering his newspaper an inch.

—I'm sure he'll send a cab for me.

—Are you?

Morgan hesitated.

—Have you spoken with him already, sir?

Dr. Sebastian pressed his lips together.

—It's only that I don't see why you ought to be inconvenienced any more than you already have been.

—Wilberforce, Dr. Sebastian said coolly, I suggest you read that book and abstain from conversation.

—But—

—I think we really must be ruthless and scotch this soothing notion that I am merely here to assist with logistical hiccups. I am sitting in this railway carriage this morning because it is my express desire.

Dr. Sebastian let that sink in.

—This isn't something you can think your way out of, Wilberforce.

The train clattered down the valley. Dr. Sebastian folded his paper and gazed out the window. The tea trolley limped through, and Dr. Sebastian purchased a cup of tea, sweet. He used the first person plural, so the woman did not ask whether Morgan wanted anything. Morgan felt he couldn't put anything in his mouth, but once the woman had toddled away, leaving Dr. Sebastian holding a cup and Morgan empty-handed, he felt bereft.

Yesterday had delivered a ruthless string of crises. Today, he was sitting exhausted, thirsty, and curiously small in a second-class railway carriage with a man he had only just met, a man who had lost no time exerting a penetrating authority over him. No man treated him with such casual command, not since he was a child and his father had been a different person. There had been moments, perhaps, with Mr. Grieves, but Morgan couldn't bear to think of him, or of the wrath Grieves had shown him last night. His stomach fell remembering the fear in Grieves's eyes outside the barn, just before he hit him. The blow itself had thrilled almost as much as it shocked, like the cricket balls thrown without restraint. Then there was the man's unexplained apparition in the cell where Burton had consigned Morgan for the night. Morgan had been lying across the bed in his clothing, head throbbing, mind adrift, when he had become aware of a presence: Grieves lurking at the door. Morgan couldn't remember exactly what Grieves had said—it had happened so fast, he'd been half-asleep, and then Grieves had disappeared and locked the door behind him—but there was something about messes and waiting until one understood, and something about fathers and consigning spirits into their—if he never saw Grieves again, it would be too soon. And as it happened, he had quit that realm. Every crank of the wheels hauled him farther south, away from the classroom and the cricket pitch and the barn and—

He opened the book Dr. Sebastian had given him, a small volume, *The Strange Case of Dr. Jekyll and Mr. Hyde*. He knew the story generally. Veronica used to tell it to him. Doctor drinks potion, turns werewolf. Was

294

it connected with Jack the Ripper? He thought in at least one of Veronica's enactments it had been. Once, she had shown him a greenish liquid she claimed to have prepared according to Jekyll's recipe. If she swallowed it, she said, she would transform under the light of the moon into a long-toothed, ravenous beast; she would scour the garden for squirrels, tear off their heads, and eat them raw; he must pray the squirrels satisfied, for if her hunger was not assuaged, she in her monster form would prowl through the house in search of young meat, and what would tempt her more than the unspoiled flesh of a six-year-old boy?

Why should Dr. Sebastian wish him to read such a ghastly book? Ought he not be subjected to some dreary moral tome?

He began to read. The first page developed a portrait of a lawyer. There was no mention of monsters. Perhaps this was a different Jekyll and Hyde. He read the fourth paragraph twice without comprehending it. The carriage was stultifying. He shut the book and unbuttoned his jacket. He wondered whether Dr. Sebastian would allow him to remove it.

As if in response, the man snatched the book away, handed Morgan his half-finished cup of tea, and wrenched open a window. A fresh wind pounded them. Morgan made to pass back the cup.

—You drink that, Dr. Sebastian said.

Gratitude flooded him. He took hold of himself:

—Thank you, sir, but I don't care for sweet tea.

A flash of—he didn't know what—passed across the man's face but was gone before he could examine it.

—Do as you're told.

The cooler air was helping, but surely the tea would make him retch? He raised the cup to his lips and blew across it.

—Stop playing, Dr. Sebastian said severely. Drink it.

He drank, and with the first mouthful his thirst returned, whipping his tongue to drink the rest.

—That's better, Dr. Sebastian said when he'd finished. A bit less green around the gills. And I think we might remove our jackets, so long as no ladies join the carriage.

Morgan followed Dr. Sebastian's example and hung his jacket on the hook behind him. The minor act left him curiously exposed, as if he had removed his jacket as prelude to a formal thrashing.

—I don't suppose you're going to make me touch my toes, sir?

Dr. Sebastian looked at him oddly. Morgan realized the joke had failed.

—When and if I do, the man said quietly, you'll be a good deal less flippant and a good deal more chastened.

Morgan flushed again and took refuge behind the book.

The Rectory was like many buildings of its time, he supposed, and objectively no more impressive than Uncle Charles's place at Longmere. A cab had delivered them from the station, passing beyond the town and into the green, canal-ridden country. They were in Wiltshire, he learned. The house stood tall, pink-bricked and slate-roofed, atop expansive grounds. The air teemed with insects and small birds. Morgan's school trunk stood on the threshold of the house, a brash reminder of the place he had fled. Dr. Sebastian by contrast carried only a small case. The man wore what he'd worn yesterday, but his shirt and collar were fresh; he removed his hat and wiped his brow.

—Right, he said, brace yourself.

He pulled the bell. It sounded far away, deep in the house. Above the bell rope, a lion in bronze guarded the door. Dr. Sebastian had told him only the name of the place, the Rectory, conjuring an ecclesiastical prison. But perhaps the name bore no relation to the establishment. Perhaps the Rectory was home to some tutor, like the man produced over Easter as an alternative to St. Stephen's. Or had they arrived at a crammer for errant boys, last chance before locking up in Borstal? It was probably seductive to look at but sinister on the inside. Why else would Dr. Sebastian have told him to brace himself?

The lion regarded him, neither hostile nor tame, but conjuring—if it could—something like fear, like sadness, and faintly like love.

A round woman opened the door and greeted Dr. Sebastian by kissing both of his cheeks and chattering away in a stream of questions and remarks.

—Mrs. Hallows, Dr. Sebastian inserted, this is Morgan Wilberforce.

Morgan bid her good evening, but she only looked him up and down. Calling for William to come see to the cases, she ushered Dr. Sebastian inside and took his hat. Morgan removed his school cap, but as she didn't offer to take it, he folded it into his pocket.

—He's in the garden, she said to Dr. Sebastian, but perhaps you'll want the cloakroom?

Dr. Sebastian disappeared behind a panel, and the woman departed, leaving Morgan alone in the corridor. A tall clock ticked, its face revealing the sun chased by Death with a scythe, and the moon followed by a dove with a twig in its mouth. The polished parquet floors, the spotless paneling, the well-dusted rails of the banister, all testified to scrupulous house-keeping. A table displayed several envelopes addressed and ready for posting. As Morgan's eyes adjusted to the indoors, he discerned a wooden cross hanging above the table. Simple, roughly hewn, substantial, it spoke more loudly than anything about the atmosphere he had just entered. It didn't flaunt itself, golden or finely wrought; it simply occupied the wall, an uncompromising announcement. Of what, though?

Was it lavender he smelled, like his mother grew beneath the kitchen window?

A panel opened, and Dr. Sebastian emerged.

—Go on, he said impatiently, mustn't keep him waiting.

Morgan used the toilet, washed his hands, and despite a strong aversion to the looking glass, splashed water on his face. Dr. Sebastian opened the door and told him to stop dawdling. He scrutinized Morgan's appearance, adjusted Morgan's tie, and used the hand towel to clean something off Morgan's ear. The feeling of being treated as a child only continued when Dr. Sebastian ordered him out of the cloakroom, dusted one of his trouser legs, and told him to stand up straight. Without further comment, Dr. Sebastian led him smartly down the corridor and out to a bricked patio.

An older man in a straw hat trimmed roses in an archway. He addressed them without turning around:

—You've had no tea, I suppose.

—No, sir, Dr. Sebastian replied.

—I've waited.

—That wasn't necessary, sir.

The man clipped a yellow rose and turned to them:

—Nevertheless.

He didn't smile in greeting, but something like pleasure tugged at the corners of his eyes.

—Well, he asked, how does it feel?

Dr. Sebastian cleared his throat:

—I can't say yet, but this is . . . what I told you about.

The man acted as though he had only that moment glimpsed Morgan.

—Is that so?

—May I present Morgan Wilberforce. Wilberforce, the Bishop of—

—Yes, yes, the man said impatiently.

—Good evening, sir, Morgan said.

—Your Grace, Dr. Sebastian prompted.

—Your Grace.

The Bishop's mouth twitched.

—You didn't say you were bringing *this*.

The Bishop looked to Dr. Sebastian for explanation, but the younger man seemed lost for words. Morgan was that appalling, then. Worse than the warder of this prison had been led to believe and too disgraceful to explain.

The Bishop beckoned Morgan to the archway.

—What do you know of roses? he asked.

—Nothing, sir.

He handed Morgan the shears.

—Finish pruning this. Any spent blooms, deadhead them.

He demonstrated clipping off the drooping blossom just below the petals.

—This much, no more, the Bishop said. Waste in there—

He pointed to a basket.

—Don't leave it strewn all over the grass. Clear?

—Yes, sir.

The Bishop stalked back to the house, Dr. Sebastian in tow. Morgan stood beneath the buttery roses and quaked.

Morgan found himself silently regarded by the other men. They had left him for ages in the garden before calling him inside. Tea was being served in a room the housekeeper called the conservatory. It looked onto the garden and provided seating for four around a small table. A pool containing lilies and a glimmer of goldfish gurgled in the center of the room. Morgan wondered gloomily whether he'd be expected to rehearse last night's ghastliness, though it seemed long enough ago to have been another term, if not life.

The woman produced cold poached salmon, some dressed greens, and a bowl of blackberries. Despite his uneasiness, Morgan was famished. He scanned quantities and wondered how much he'd be allowed.

The Bishop said grace and made the sign of the cross, a gesture Dr. Sebastian mirrored. Morgan had never done such a popish thing and, despite feeling impolite, couldn't bring himself to do it now. The Bishop dispensed the food and tea in distressingly small portions.

Morgan watched Dr. Sebastian for a cue as to how fast he might eat. It seemed Dr. Sebastian was ravenous as well, for he finished his plate quickly. No one had spoken since grace, but when Dr. Sebastian sat for a minute or more gazing hungrily at the serving platter, the Bishop waved impatiently.

—Go on, he said, I don't suppose you've eaten properly on your journey.

—No, sir, Dr. Sebastian said, reaching for the fish, only a couple of sandwiches.

—And you expect that boy to get along on *a couple of sandwiches?* No wonder he scarcely knows how to speak.

When the food had been cleared away, the Bishop pronounced a second grace and then crossed his legs and fixed his gaze upon Morgan.

—You are a pupil at St. Stephen's?

—Yes, sir.

—*Your Grace,* Dr. Sebastian said.

—Your—

—How old are you?

Morgan told him. The interview progressed factually, how long he'd been at the Academy, who his people were, where his father lived and what he was. He enjoyed cricket? And what had he been reading?

Morgan stumbled over the last query. He couldn't remember having read anything lately, unless *The Pearl* counted, and he knew perfectly well that it did not.

—You do read, don't you?

—Yes, Your Grace.

—Well, what have you read recently?

—Nothing special. I mean, only the ordinary things. We were doing Wordsworth, sir.

—What do you read on your own? A man's character is reflected in what he chooses to read.

Lady Pokingham? Life Among the She-Noodles?

—I see, the Bishop said.

Had he spoken aloud? He shouldn't have eaten. He wanted to eat more. When, oh, when, would they dispense with the sinister preliminaries and bring on whatever torture they intended?

—Jamie, the Bishop scolded, the boy's fainting away. He's got eyes like a panda and he's pale as death. Just what have you been doing with him?

—Nothing, Father!

Morgan choked. Dr. Sebastian poured him some more tea. When he recovered, the Bishop was staring at him, the corners of his mouth turned slightly up:

—I see my son hasn't told you everything.

—He hasn't told me anything! Morgan spluttered.

—Hasn't he indeed?

The Bishop burst into a laugh and rang the bell.

—We'll continue this conversation in the morning, he said to Morgan. Ah, Mrs. Hallows, could you please see young Wilberforce to bed?

Morgan stood, his balance suddenly precarious.

—Good night, Dr. Sebastian. Good night, Your Grace. I'm very sorry, I—

—In the morning, the Bishop rejoined. Just you concentrate on getting a good night's sleep.

Morgan turned to follow Mrs. Hallows. Behind, he heard the Bishop speaking:

—As for you, we need to have a chat about frightening little boys half to death.

—Chop-chop, Mrs. Hallows said.

Morgan tripped after her.

The pleasures which I made haste to seek in my disguise were, as I have said, undignified; I would scarce use a harder term. But in the hands of Edward Hyde, they soon began to turn toward the monstrous. When I would come back from these excursions, I was often plunged into a kind of wonder at my vicarious depravity. This familiar that I called out of my own soul, and sent forth alone to do his good pleasure, was a being inherently malign and villainous; his every act and thought centered on self; drinking pleasure with bestial avidity from any degree of torture to another . . . The women writhed and twined themselves about the floor, fucking, screaming and shouting in

ecstasy—Shut up—*my loving mistress partook of the universal excitement with the rest*—Shut up!—*placing herself in the most lascivious positions, throwing up her legs*—SHUT—*outstretching her arms, she would invite me, in the most licentious terms, to enter the amorous lists*—WAKE UP!—*how tight did her cunt clasp my prick*—DREAMING, YOU'RE DREAMING—*as my piston-rod shoved in*—WAKE—*and out*—MUM—*I had gone to bed Henry Jekyll, I had awakened Edward Hyde*—MUMMY!

—Wilberforce!

Light. Blinding. Woman above.

—Like waking the dead, she declared.

His heart pounded. His cock pounded. Sweat trickled down his—

—Bath's drawn, just there.

The woman indicated a door by the window, which admitted a painful light.

—Breakfast, half an hour.

Where was he? When?

—Speak so I know you're awake.

—Half an hour. M—Mrs.—Matron?

—Mrs. Hallows.

—Mrs. Hallows.

He washed the sweat, the night, and the last two days from his body. The tepid water regulated his temperature. He drank liberally from the tap. The blue tiles reflected the morning light like the sea, not that he had ever been under the sea, but he imagined it as something like this, a half-remembered softness.

That man, the Bishop, had said *in the morning.* Morgan sometimes knew when disasters were coming. He'd known it with Spaulding, and he recognized in this morning the unquestionable taint of calamity. Could he not simply slip beneath this sea and . . .

—Listen, you, it's time to buck up.

Droit stood before the looking glass, slicking his hair back with brilliantine.

—Leave me alone, Morgan said.

Droit looked at him with a wounded expression and demanded to know why Morgan should treat him thus. Morgan launched into a litany of Droit's unwelcome utterances, not least the rubbish with which he'd

301

been oppressed all night. Droit took offense. Was he the one who had provided the foul story of Jekyll and Hyde? Was he the supplier of Lydon's tasteless morsels?

Morgan had to admit that he wasn't. That was correct, Droit confirmed, he wasn't. If Morgan had retained the most appalling selections from his reading, he could look elsewhere for someone to blame, for he, Droit, insisted on quality in his amusements and had been slaving all term to reform Morgan's taste.

The nauseous atmosphere was dispelling. Morgan wished he could have a cigarette. He did have some in his tuck box, but he wasn't sure he dared smoke them in the bathroom of a Rectory.

Droit parted his hair and bade Morgan finish his bath and listen carefully: Morgan must on no account allow himself to be seduced by the glamour of this house or its inhabitants. That uneasy feeling Morgan had sprang from his rather developed instincts. This was no time for false modesty. They both knew that Morgan often understood things about people that people didn't understand themselves. The point was this place. Morgan mustn't let down his guard. They would attempt to seduce him into every kind of nefarious thing, but Morgan must defend himself.

Morgan got out of the bath and dried off, not at all sure what Droit meant.

—You know precisely what I mean, Droit retorted. Why else would they have brought you to a soothing little house in the country if not to lull you into a false sense of security? And why else should they haul you clear across the country to see a bishop if they didn't hope to succeed where S-K failed?

Morgan's stomach turned at mention of his aborted confirmation. He forced himself to breathe calmly as he put on the clean shirt someone had laid out for him. Did Droit mean to suggest that Burton and Grieves had colluded with Dr. Sebastian to coerce Morgan into the sacrament of confirmation? Wasn't that rather far-fetched?

Droit did not think it far-fetched, actually, but in any case, that was not what he was saying. Droit was simply saying that these men had taken advantage of Morgan when he was weak. They had humiliated him and abducted him. They were on no account to be trusted, not Sebastian, not the Flea, not Grieves, and certainly and above all not this sickening Bishop person. Whatever they had in mind, he was not a child, and he must not permit himself to be maneuvered. That was all.

Mrs. Hallows was waiting at the bottom of the staircase. She adjusted the collar of his jacket, and after informing him that the Bishop took his breakfast in silence, she led him to the dining room.

A large table was set for two. Yesterday the Bishop had expected gardening tasks, today obviously Morgan would serve the silent meal. Was it some pious clerical custom to observe silence before noon? A clock on the sideboard approached nine. Perhaps the Bishop's voice required resting, or perhaps he habitually meditated on obscure matters in the morning. Presumably Dr. Sebastian would also keep silence.

Dimly, the circumstances unveiled themselves. Dr. Sebastian, Burton-Lee, or both of them must have contacted his father. His father had tried everything over Easter to give Morgan another start, and now to be wired by the Academy before the end of the term and informed of—Morgan couldn't bear to think it, not without panicking. His father would be so appalled that he would withdraw from the world even more than before. *Unsuitable conduct*, Droit murmured, that was what they would have said. Unsuitable conduct. His father would accept that. He had lost the habit of inquiry some years before. He never, any longer, wished to know the gruesome details, and there would certainly be no point in it now.

Why did his father not tell them to send Morgan home? He could wait there for other arrangements to be made. Unless they considered his unsuitable conduct too unsuitable for a decent career? Perhaps Dr. Sebastian, out of charity and in appreciation for Morgan's performance on the cricket pitch, had scrounged a position for him in the Bishop's household. The Bishop was Dr. Sebastian's father—had that not been revealed last night? And the Bishop was an elderly Bishop, so presumably he required assistance around his premises. Was Morgan being evaluated as a possible secretary? Something like that, but given his recent conduct, the Bishop would wish to prove him as groundsman or footman before allowing him the run of his correspondence.

—You can shut up, Morgan said to Droit.

—Have I spoken?

—Perhaps you'd quit being clever for a minute and remember what Dr. Sebastian said on the train.

Droit groaned and produced a tin of Altoids.

—This isn't something I can think my way out of.

—He would say that, wouldn't he? Droit retorted. He doesn't want you thinking. If you start thinking, you might out-think him, and then where would he be?

—I'm only saying that whatever they want me to do, it's better than dying of boredom at home.

—You say *boredom*, you mean *shame*. When are you going to get it through your head that shame is something imposed by other people. If you refuse to feel ashamed, then they've no power over you.

Droit offered a mint. Morgan refused.

—I'm not ashamed of anything.

—Liar.

The Bishop strode briskly into the room. He nodded at Morgan and came to the head of the table. Morgan wished suddenly for an appropriate uniform, but he stood at attention by the sideboard, hands behind his back, eyes forward. The door opened again but admitted Mrs. Hallows, not Dr. Sebastian. She carried in the breakfast tray and set out tea, a rack of toast, and four eggs. The clock chimed a pretty little bell, the kind of clock a lady would wind. If Dr. Sebastian was the Bishop's son, where was the Bishop's wife?

After a glance to the Bishop, Mrs. Hallows sighed in exasperation and pointed Morgan to the table. He reached for the teapot to pour, but a smack stopped his hand. She grasped him by both elbows and moved him to the second place setting. The Bishop cleared his throat, pronounced grace, made the embarrassing gesture, and pulled out his chair to sit down. Morgan looked to Mrs. Hallows. She regarded him as one might a half-wit, and then, apparently resigning herself to unpleasantness, she pulled out the chair and shoved him into it. As the Bishop served himself an egg and toast, Mrs. Hallows stalked out of the room, leaving Morgan alone before Dr. Sebastian's place setting.

The Bishop seemed capable of concentrating on only one thing at a time. Meticulously, he cut the top off his egg and scooped the white from the cap. He buttered his toast as an artist with a palate knife and then cut it into soldiers. After sprinkling a precise portion of salt on the egg, he broke his fast.

They ate in silence, the Bishop contenting himself with one egg and two pieces of toast. After Morgan had eaten two eggs and two toasts, he glanced to the Bishop, who was still finishing his portion. Was the Bishop gauging the extent of his gluttony? He was still hungry. The eggs were perfectly done, and the last wouldn't be good once it had cooled. The Bishop met his gaze with the expression of a reluctantly indulgent father. Morgan extended his hand towards the egg dish, casually enough that he could pretend to be reaching for the tea if the Bishop frowned. He did not frown. Morgan took the egg. The Bishop still did not frown. Morgan took another piece of toast and put it on his plate with the egg. The Bishop reached for the teapot and poured himself another cup.

Droit provoked him. Morgan's hunger was almost assuaged by three eggs and three toasts, but one toast remained. Droit dared him to take it. The Bishop would think it gluttonous, Morgan argued, especially given the lack of egg to dip it in. But surely, Droit replied, waste offended more than appetite? If Morgan didn't eat it, who would? Besides, Droit continued, what if the toast constituted a kind of test? Morgan had never heard of such an examination. Of course not, Droit replied, because Morgan had never faced a man as sinister as this one, a man determined to intrude into his character in the most cunning manner. Last night he'd tried the old *What do you read?* Now this. If Morgan did not take the toast, it would not only signal his abject surrender, but it would also substantiate his cowardice.

Morgan didn't see why highbrow language was necessary, and as it happened, he was no longer hungry.

—Coward. Worm.

He snatched the toast. The Bishop sighed and gazed out the window. Morgan slathered it with butter and crunched as he ate.

The other one wasn't there, a relief amidst it all; at least it should have been, except that his pointed absence made Morgan suspect something truly awful waiting in the wings.

—Don't worry, Droit said. I've dealt with it.

—What do you mean *dealt with it?*

—Trust me once, won't you?

Seated across the table at the Bishop's left hand, Droit looked imploringly to Morgan. Perhaps he relied on Morgan's faith and approval more than he revealed. He wasn't so much older than Morgan. Perhaps he wasn't older at all. Perhaps he was one of those boys who looked older, a boy thrust into advanced experiences. What if Droit were an orphan or half orphan? What if he had left school early, against his will, and had been forced to get on in the world alone?

The Bishop stood abruptly, jolting Morgan to his feet.

—*Benedicto, benedicatur.* Amen.

Again the tasteless gesture.

—Follow me, the Bishop said.

The Bishop led him through a series of rooms, bursting into each as if he expected to surprise someone doing what he oughtn't. Finally, they arrived at a door the Bishop opened with a key. He ushered Morgan inside.

Books lined three walls. A heavy desk occupied the space in front of the lead-paned windows, which gave on to the driveway. Islands of papers spotted the surface, as if the Bishop had been interrupted sorting his correspondence. A swivel chair faced the room from behind the desk, a chaise longue skulked by the bookcases, and two spindle chairs stood at right angles to the desk, as if a conversation had taken place against its outer corner. The room smelt thickly of dust, leather bindings, and tobacco.

The Bishop was wearing a clerical collar as he had the night before. Now, he removed his jacket and exchanged it for a black garment, the robe-like thing vicars wore during services. He buttoned it up and fastened a wide black sash around his waist. Then, straightening his sleeves, he came to stand at the window. He indicated one of the spindle chairs:

—Sit.

If they were going to savage you or torment you by inquisition, they always sat and made you stand. The Bishop, then, was taking pains to differentiate this interview from others and to make Morgan feel at ease. A trap, naturally. He'd put on a clerical costume, so the moral suasion was about to begin. Morgan took a deep breath and sat as far back as the spindles allowed. The Bishop fixed his attention fully upon him:

—I've made my decision. It's time for you to make yours.

Having delivered himself of this, the Bishop crossed his arms behind his back and stood entirely still. An unwavering stare, keen as sunlight focused through a glass, deep and throbbing as the inside of a heart.

—Sir . . .

Morgan's voice sounded small once he used it, barely penetrating the room.

—What's happened to Dr. Sebastian?

—Dr. *Sebastian* departed last night.

The Bishop pronounced the name as if he were indulging a preposterous nickname. Morgan felt a pulse of alarm.

—Where did he go?

—My son returned to Marlborough. He didn't tell you?

Morgan swallowed. The Bishop exhaled in annoyance.

—I'm afraid my son can be economical with detail, results as we see before us.

He gestured to Morgan.

—Sir? I mean, Your Grace?

—Either will do, in camera. Stop tying yourself in knots.

Morgan felt a sudden and unexpected relief.

—Yes, sir.

—Well? the Bishop persisted. Have you made your decision?

He was not to be taken in by the glamour of these people. He was not to be seduced by their invitations to speak in camera. He was not to let down his guard because of one critical remark about Dr. Sebastian even if it left him feeling vaguely understood.

—My decision, sir, is the same today as it was three years ago.

The Bishop raised his brow but otherwise remained motionless.

—I reject confirmation. I won't go through with it. It's my right, and no one can make me.

The Bishop waited as if he expected Morgan to say more. Morgan closed his mouth and crossed his arms.

—I see, the Bishop said. You're speaking, I presume, of the sacrament of confirmation?

Morgan nodded curtly.

—And have you a reason for this refusal?

—I don't believe in it.

—You doubt its essence or you find it insupportable?

—The latter, sir.

Rather than anger, the Bishop's voice betrayed fascination.

—Are you able to say which aspects you can't abide? Is it the rite itself? The articles of religion?

—I don't believe they're true, sir. It would have been a lie to say them.

—I see. Well . . .

Here was the assault, the admonition, the barrage of persuasion both blunt and sinuous.

—If that is how you feel, you were entirely right to abstain.

Morgan tried to parse the Bishop's declaration.

—Sir?

—It would have been a sacrilege to receive the laying on of hands if you were dishonest about your beliefs. No, the Bishop continued, I fully support your decision.

Morgan thought he might be mishearing.

—But that was in the past, you say? Three years ago?

—Yes, sir.

—Good. And what about the decision facing you today?

Morgan searched the man's face. The Bishop was probing to see how much he knew of the snare they had planned for him. If he could detect its edges, the punishment would lose some of its wallop. Usually when they tried to get you to make a choice—say between a beating and an imposition, or between one kind of beating now and another kind later—the choice was illusory. Whatever you chose, they made sure you regretted it.

—Wilberforce, the Bishop said.

His voice softened, and the new tone, combined with the use of his name, sent an ache through Morgan's frame.

—Do you know what your options are?

—Don't be absurd! Morgan protested. Your Grace.

A twitch at the Bishop's lips.

—Why don't you start by telling me how you find yourself in my study?

Morgan bristled. He did not intend to subject himself to what they'd subjected him to the other night. Précis. He needed to summarize.

Morgan outlined Patron's Day: Dr. Sebastian's visit, Morgan's summons to the First XI, an interlude he labeled unsuitable conduct, his interview with the Headmaster and with Dr. Sebastian, his exile into the corridor for hours, his incarceration in a spare room of the Flea's House, his abduction before breakfast by Dr. Sebastian, an endless train journey to a destination known only as the Rectory, and now his abandonment to Dr. Sebastian's father, a retired bishop who still, as far as Morgan could see, enjoyed putting on the old getups for the purposes of nostalgia. That, he declared, was his testimony.

The Bishop touched the edge of the desk.

—Getups, you say?

This was why it was never a good idea to speak freely with adults.

The Bishop laughed in a burst:

—If the cassock disconcerts you, I'll remove it.

—It doesn't disconcert me. Sir.

—Do you object to clergy in general, or merely to the sacrament of confirmation?

Morgan was having trouble working out the words to use, and the moves to make.

—I object to religion, sir.

—You do, do you? And your parents?

—They don't—they didn't—I mean my father—

—Forgive me, I meant your father.

—You know about my mother, sir?

—My son tells me she died some years ago.

—Yes, sir.

—May she rest in peace.

The Bishop looked directly at him, as if the words were more than formula. He looked as if he believed people continued to exist after death and could thus rest in peace or otherwise. He didn't grow flustered at the revelation. He didn't offer repulsive consolations, such as the notion that God loved her so much that he simply had to have her with him. Or that her death was his mysterious will. Or that she perched even now on a cloud, watching Morgan benevolently and sprinkling raindrops of affection upon him. Or even that the barbaric thing had made him stronger. The Bishop said none of these things.

—When did she die?

—During my first term at St. Stephen's.

—Yes?

—October thirty-first, 1922.

The Bishop absorbed this and then performed the gesture, speaking under his breath:

—May light perpetual shine upon her . . .

Morgan missed the rest.

—Are you Catholic, sir? Morgan said with more belligerence than he intended.

—I am Anglo-Catholic. And yourself? Or, should I say, your father?

309

—He—he's ordinary—he doesn't do things like that!

An expression played again at the corner of the Bishop's mouth:

—Does it distress you when I make the sign of the cross?

—It doesn't distress me! It's only so very popish, that's all. I suppose you worship saints and blood and the pope and everything as well.

—I revere the saints, respect the Bishop of Rome, and approach the mystery of the cross with as much humility as I can muster. Any other questions?

—Why do you wear that costume?

He was being impertinent, but he didn't care.

—It's a cassock, ordinary clerical attire for performing clerical functions. I was making a distinction between our conversations last night and our interview in this room.

—Careful, Droit breathed at his ear.

—Sir, Morgan said with as much weariness as he could summon, whatever you're going to do to me, please could you get on with it?

A shadow fell across the Bishop's face, as if something ominous had entered the room. He glanced around and then unfastened the sash of his cassock, unbuttoned the garment, and exchanged it for his summer jacket.

—I can see I'm going to have to be direct, the Bishop said.

—I wish someone would!

—Very well. Two nights ago my son telephoned to say he'd accepted the post of Headmaster at your school. He also asked my help with a project, one he termed urgent. I have been of assistance to many people over the years, many of them in difficulties, but this was the first time my son had made such an appeal. My time is somewhat freer at the moment, and given that my son . . . it seemed fitting to agree.

The room was airless. Morgan wondered if he would be ill after all the eggs.

—Your arrival last night, as you may have noticed, caught me on the back foot.

Wasn't expecting someone so appalling.

—I wasn't expecting someone so young. But over the evening, my son took me into his confidence: the project was a boy well regarded by those in authority at St. Stephen's, a boy who had attracted my son's notice for his cricket and for his conversation, but a boy who had committed offenses grievous enough to merit expulsion.

—Why not expel him properly? His father wouldn't have him home, I suppose.

—The point that's eluding you is that my son clung to the view that this boy might not be entirely lost. Perhaps, he thought, something could be salvaged.

Morgan stared at the rug, its rusty patterns worn nearly through:

—I shouldn't think so.

The Bishop stirred in a way that indicated the end of the interview. He breezed by the desk, not even pausing as he grasped Morgan's elbow and pulled him to his feet. He conducted him thus back through the warren of rooms to the entry hall. The woman appeared as if summoned by telepathy.

—Mrs. Hallows, will you kindly see that young Wilberforce locates his games attire in that trunk of his? He's off for a run.

She nodded. Morgan managed to free his elbow from the Bishop's grasp:

—The Bishop is mistaken—

—The Bishop is not mistaken.

The Bishop gripped the back of his neck and led him through the front door to the foot of the drive.

—Down there, right at both forks. Three miles, you'll find the market square. Cathedral's on the right, can't miss it. Go round to the Chapter House and ask for Miss Flynt.

—Sir—

—Your call's booked for half past ten. It is quarter to now. Chop-chop.

—What call, sir?

The Bishop breezed away back to the house:

—When you return, I'll expect your decision. Please tell him that I've made mine. In the affirmative.

They looked at him disdainfully in the Chapter House, and no wonder. Sweat was pouring off him as he stood before them in running kit. Mention of the Bishop and Miss Flynt gained him admittance but did not elicit welcome. He was made to wait in a stony corridor, cooling off too quickly, while someone located Miss Flynt. She burst from a dark-paneled door carrying a pile of paperwork.

She was not an old woman. She was not old at all. She filled her smart little frock with a most appealing figure. Her hem hung modestly low, her décolletage remained concealed, but her lips were full and red as if stung by bees. He longed to put them in his mouth and suck the hurt away.

—Wilberforce? she inquired.

He extended a hand, which she ignored.

—This way.

Without having looked at him long enough to appraise him, she slipped back through the door. He hurried after her, wondering whether she was wearing any scent, and if so, what.

—What's your position here, Miss Flynt? Morgan asked.

She located a piece of paper on one of the desks in the room, rang for the operator, and announced her readiness for the call she had booked. After some moments, she replaced the handset. Clearing a space at the desk, she indicated that he should sit in the chair beside the telephone receiver.

He couldn't stop looking at her. Her accent revealed a decent background. Her position indicated an education. Everything else about her appearance and manner testified to a perfect ripeness. How he would enjoy loosening her hair from its pins, relieving her of her cardigan, and investigating her stockings and the skin just above them. It was one of his favorite parts of the female anatomy, that span of inches above the stockings and below the rest. If he could only be allowed to run his fingers and his lips across it, regularly and at leisure, he felt sure something profound inside him would be soothed.

—Miss Flynt, he tried again, I wonder if you might be able to assist me once this is all done.

He waved at the telephone as if gestures could erase it. She looked at him with a trace of mirth. He decided it was encouraging.

—I'm new to the area, he said, and I know I look a fright, but I was wondering if later this afternoon, when I'm dressed, you might do me the kindness of showing me round the cathedral.

The mirth grew around her lips, those plump, vivid—

—Have you an especial interest in cathedrals?

—Oh, yes, Morgan said. They enthrall me.

The apparatus on the desk interrupted with an offensive blare. She put the receiver to her ear:

—Deanery . . . yes, I'll hold.

—If not this afternoon, perhaps tomorrow, Morgan persisted. When's your day off?

The door opened, revealing a middle-aged man in a cassock. Miss Flynt raised a hand as she spoke into the phone:

—Yes. Hold, please.

The cassock-wearing man spoke urgently:

—Mrs. Flynt, chapter meeting.

—Coming, she snapped.

Morgan gaped at her:

—Mrs.? But, the Bishop said . . .

She pressed her lips in exasperation.

—My father is really very stubborn about my marriage.

She put the receiver in his hand and pushed him into the chair.

—Morgan?

His name from the receiver, crackly connection, but the voice, unmistakable.

—Good morning, Father, Morgan said.

—I've had a call from Burton-Lee. Is it true what he says?

Could he pretend the connection had failed? They had left him alone in the room. If he simply put down the telephone, everyone would assume trouble with the wires.

—Probably not.

—I think you had better explain yourself.

—I'm not sure I can, sir.

—None of that. This is extremely serious.

—They've disposed me again?

—Just you drop that jaded tone and answer my question.

Morgan's hand felt weak as he held the receiver. He could put it down, but now no one would believe the connection was to blame.

—Did you abuse Alex Pearl as I was told?

—We . . . He was . . .

—*Morgan!*

Shock, appall.

—And that girl, did you insult her?

—No!

He tried to steady his voice:

—I never insulted her. I love her. *Nous avons fait l'amour complet.* There's nothing the matter with love!

Silence on the line. (Was the call over?) Then a sigh, or something like it.

—She's not yet fifteen, I'm told.

—Isn't she?

—Do you not even know?

—Why should I?

—For God's sake, boy!

Coarse language on outings was one thing, but Morgan had never heard his father blaspheme. And *boy*? As if Morgan were not his son.

—Does the age of consent mean nothing to you?

—She consented. She said so plenty of times.

His father's voice low, lethal:

—God help me, it's lucky for both of us that I am not in the same room with you.

It wasn't happening. It was all just passing before him, like the blood pouring out of Spaulding's head, like Grieves taking his shoulder and wrenching it into place, like the sounds he had heard behind his father's door that night after the funeral.

—Are you disowning me?

—How dare you put on injured innocence, and to me?

Morgan waited for a petulant reply, but none came to him. His father's voice softened, but he could hear the effort it took.

—I will never disown you, boyo, but I can't lie. I am immeasurably let down.

Morgan forced his voice to find volume.

—I'm sorry, sir.

—Yes, well, I don't think you're anything like sorry. You don't like my being angry with you, but for you to feel remorse, you'd have to grasp just what it is you've done. And plainly you haven't.

Anger was clouding his father's judgment, but this wasn't the time to point it out.

—Shall I join the navy?

Another silence.

—If I didn't know you better, I'd accuse you of flippancy.

—Sir, I'm not—

—As it is, I'll take that suggestion as a sign of your preposterous immaturity.

Like branches across his face, Kitty Deadlock on his palms.

—To be perfectly honest, I don't know what to do with you, but I can't have you home just now.

Too ashamed of him, too ashamed for others to see.

—I'm too angry. If Bishop Sebastian can keep you another day, I'll make arrangements for you to go to . . . someone.

Orphaned, fully this time. He tried to speak, but a rock filled his throat.

—Please tell the Bishop I'll leave word tomorrow at the latest.

—Oh!

Morgan's voice leapt like a child's.

—The Bishop said to tell you he'd taken his decision. In the affirmative.

—I beg your pardon?

Morgan repeated himself.

—Well, his father said, I'm at a loss for words. All I can say is you had better get down on your knees and give thanks properly.

—Father, you know I don't believe—

—Boyo, I'm ringing off now, so I'll just say this: if you want to live, sometimes you have to die, in a manner of speaking.

Silence on the line, and it went dead.

Back at the Rectory, he hung on the lion bell, panting. Mrs. Hallows admitted him instantly, as if she'd been standing on the other side of the door.

—His Grace is waiting.

She turned and clacked down the corridor. His side was stabbing from the second run. When he'd left Mrs. Flynt's office, some weaselly number had informed him that the Bishop was expecting him in less than half an hour. He'd had to take the run at speed, which, following the unspeakable telephone call, had left him limping towards the cloakroom and clutching the basin. Being sick always hurt, and this would be no exception. Bending over the toilet, he felt it all come up—three eggs, four pieces of toast, three cups of tea. His stomach writhed even when empty, a muscle in spasm, a joke that wouldn't quit. Mrs. Hallows found him on his knees.

—What's all this?

He wiped his eyes and got to his feet. She stood in the hallway, holding the door. He pulled the chain on the toilet and rinsed his face with cold water.

—Enough filly-folly! she exclaimed. The Bishop is in the summerhouse.

—But . . .

He could scarcely form words. Surely the Bishop did not wish to see him . . .

—As you are, she said. His Grace's instructions. Don't stand there gawping, young man.

She led the way through the conservatory, where they'd eaten the night before, and onto the patio. The sun blazed, and he longed to plunge into the canal at the foot of the garden. Mrs. Hallows clomped down a trail of flagstones to a gazebo set before two willow trees. The Bishop looked up and marked his place in a book.

—Sir, Morgan began, I'm a sight. If I might just—

The Bishop pointed to a seat, thanked the woman, and filled two glasses from a pitcher. The lemonade was sweet enough to settle Morgan's stomach and sour enough to restore his head. The Bishop nodded again at the seat he wished Morgan to take. It gave way as he sat, swinging backwards.

The Bishop asked no questions, yet his gaze constituted a sort of embrace, as if speaking were unnecessary between them. He didn't ask whether the call had come off. He didn't ask what Morgan's father had said. He looked at Morgan as if he knew all that but awaited something else. He waited not in supplication or pity, but with the intensity of a watchman, bow in hand, arrow notched, waiting on the walls of a city against attackers in the night. The Bishop looked at him with authority, as if the power of his gaze could transport Morgan back to the room with the voice coming through the telephone—*immeasurably let down, preposterous immaturity.* His father had truly said those things. And Morgan had done the things he had done. He felt a flash of relief that his mother was not alive to know.

The Bishop continued to gaze at him, infinite will, unflinching presence (*desperate case, you aren't sorry at all*). The seat swayed again beneath him. What, given liberty, would this man do to him?

—Sir . . .

Morgan's voice scratched.

—What's going to be done with me?

—Done with you? the Bishop repeated. It seems to me events are already doing quite a lot with you.

Morgan searched the man's face.

—Something is knocking at the gates, the Bishop said.

A surge of alarm—had he spoken out loud about the city and the gates?

—It's battering, isn't it? Nearly splitting the timbers.

Morgan found himself nodding, gripped by the Bishop's muscular and uncompromising . . . compassion.

—The question, I think, isn't what's to be done with you, but what you will do.

A cloak of lead slipped from his shoulders as another, searing skin snapped tight around him.

—What *can* I do?

—It seems to me you have two options, the Bishop said. You can continue to fortify the gates and hope that what's knocking will grow discouraged and depart.

—It won't, though, will it?

The Bishop blinked as if something pained him.

—Otherwise, Morgan said, I can open the gates.

—Yes.

—But that's suicide.

—It rather depends on what's knocking.

—You said battering, not knocking. Enemies batter. Who opens the gates to an enemy?

The Bishop took a sip from his glass as if they were in a summerhouse on a June day sharing lemonade after a morning's exertions.

Morgan scanned his memory of the *Iliad*, of classic sieges Mr. Grieves had narrated. Who but a traitor would open the gates to the enemy? He ought to have paid closer attention. When it mattered, he was vague about the things he was supposed to have learnt.

—*Batter my heart*, the Bishop said, reaching for the jug to refill Morgan's glass. *For you as yet but knock, breathe, shine, and seek to mend.*

He knew that! They'd done it with the Eagle, the day something essential happened. But what?

—That I may rise and stand, o'erthrow me.

—Oh, don't make me sick again! Droit cried kicking the swing into motion.

They'd read it the day after Kilby— after Polly—

—Bend your force to break, blow, burn—

Isn't that what had happened in the unspeakable interval this morning? Wasn't he being burnt even now?

—You're not going in for this claptrap, are you? Droit said severely. The whole thing's so ludicrously transparent.

Was it?

—Out you're sent on a stiff run, Droit continued. Then they spring that unforgivably maudlin scene on you. Next, sprint back until you're puffed beyond endurance. Finally, without even allowing you an uninterrupted moment to retch up your guts, they haul you outside so this number can moon at you and quote clerical poems. Wake up, Dicky!

Morgan's arms raced with goose pimples. The Bishop sat forward:

—What?

—Sir?

—What happened just now? Don't lie, I haven't the reserves.

Fire at the all-but-direct accusation that he lied habitually and without qualm.

—It's only . . .

How could he phrase it? He had been told off professionally by a figment of his imagination, a figment that had called him by a most disagreeable name.

—Sometimes I imagine people.

—Here?

Morgan nodded.

—This person, the Bishop asked intently, is he, or she—

—He.

—Is he part of the battering, or is he inside the gates with you?

Droit lounged on the swing, running a damp handkerchief across his brow.

—Inside.

The Bishop received the news somberly. His gaze drifted to the space Droit occupied, not that he could see him. Other people couldn't see figments of your imagination. That was what made them figments. No one could barge their way into your mind unless you let them.

But sometimes he said things he didn't mean to say. Words came off his tongue before he even noticed. Was it possible for Droit to escape his bounds and wander, free, in the world?

—I go where I like, Droit whispered, do what I like.

—But you're mine, Morgan told him.

—You've got your pronouns jumbled, Dicky. Just watch—

—Stop calling me that.

—What have I called you? asked the Bishop.

Never had Morgan been more aware of the surface of his skin. Every minute something contrived to send his blood rushing, superheating his face, his chest, the back of his neck, any place blood could flow.

—Let us not waste time, the Bishop said. Explain, please, how I've addressed you.

—I didn't mean to say that out loud, sir.

—See, Droit hissed.

The Bishop set down his glass.

—Would it help if I were direct again?

Morgan couldn't endure anyone else being direct. But he wasn't a coward. How much worse could it get?

—You asked what was to be done with you, and while I quibble with your phraseology, the question does need answering.

Morgan cast his gaze to the ground, feeling as though he might be on the verge of a soothingly familiar interview. *What's to be done with you, Wilberforce? I don't know, sir. Of course you do, touch your toes.*

—But before we can answer it, the Bishop continued, you are going to have to stop behaving like a sullen schoolboy who exerts no agency and yet submits to no authority but his own.

The remark stung like a slap.

—Which do you want me to do? Morgan replied. Take action or submit to someone's authority? Because I'm not exactly clear how I'm to do both.

—That is the sullenness I was speaking of, the Bishop said, and I've had enough of it, thank you. It's doing nothing to diminish the danger of your situation.

Danger?

—And the impertinence isn't attractive. You're better than that.

—I shouldn't think so, sir.

—Self-pity is even less attractive.

The Bishop spoke mildly as if discussing the design of his garden, but his very lightness gave his remarks the snap of the sharpest cane.

—When are you going to tell this number what he can do with his disapproval? Droit murmured. Perhaps if he plunged that ancient cock of his somewhere nice, he'd stop fixating on schoolboys he'd never met before yesterday.

—I don't want to be this way.

—No, the Bishop said.

Morgan waited for clarification, but it didn't come.

—My father's going to arrange for me to go somewhere.

—And then?

—I don't know. I suppose I'll be sent to one of my uncles. I suppose they'll find something for me to do. I suggested the navy but . . .

He couldn't bring himself to repeat his father's response or even to summarize it. If not the navy, then perhaps the army, or the shipyards. He'd never given any thought to his future as it had all been so fixed: school, university, the firm, marriage, children, carrying on until . . . he couldn't think that far into the future. Now, though, the itinerary was canceled.

A clarity dawned. He was being banished. This shame would continue until it ran its course, one year, five, ten. His punishment would be to endure it and to absent himself from society until everything wore off. They hadn't even expelled him to his face. S-K had at least summoned him repeatedly after Spaulding, berating him, bullying him, and generally letting off steam by shouting at him. They, by contrast, had treated him as a pariah. Burton had disarmed him, extracted the hideous confession, and then exiled him to the corridor. Grieves had stood as far from him as possible, looking as though something precious inside had been shattered. Dr. Sebastian for his part had treated him, he now realized, as a prisoner under transport. If Dr. Sebastian had explained nothing, it was because criminals forfeited the right to explanation. Morgan had been so consumed by vexation that he hadn't until this moment recognized the ignominy of his position, but here it was: His father and the Academy were disposing of him. He would endure the exile alone, without father or mother, without Nathan or Laurie, without Grieves, without any of the irksome citizens of the Academy, without anyone at all.

—Not quite, Droit smiled.

Morgan inhaled sharply.

—You're undergoing an ordeal, the Bishop said. You've been undergoing it for some time, I think.

Words like a puff of air from the shade.

—You aren't entirely alone, though.

—Oh, don't worry, sir, Morgan said bitterly. I've got company enough.

—I wasn't referring to him, the Bishop said.

—He had better not speak of me that way, seditious old—

—I was referring to myself.

Morgan couldn't speak.

—You needn't face this ordeal alone, the Bishop said. I could stand with you. If you wish.

—I do wish.

He'd spoken before thinking, and now Droit was closing his fingers around Morgan's wrist to stifle his pulse. The Bishop sat forward and looked at him, his gaze a dog spike, his will driving it into the sleeper, as if with mere eye contact he could secure Morgan's entire being.

—Mr. Rollins, Your Grace.

Mrs. Hallows had materialized beneath the gazebo, a man at her side.

—Yes, very well, the Bishop replied.

—What's to be done with this one? Mrs. Hallows asked.

Morgan tried to stand, but the Bishop snatched his wrist, the very wrist Droit had been strangling.

—Your Grace! Mrs. Hallows protested. Doctor . . .

His wrist shackled, Morgan looked to the Bishop, who had turned pale. The doctor told Morgan to step aside, but the Bishop kept hold of him.

—Mrs. Hallows, said the Bishop with effort, please see that young Wilberforce has a bath and some lunch.

—Of course, Your Grace, but—

—He may have run of the library, and please find him some writing materials.

He was still holding fast.

—*Batter My Heart*, he said to Morgan, copy it out six times, three copies with each hand.

The Bishop's voice was gravelly. The doctor stepped forward and loosened his grip on Morgan's wrist. As the doctor eased the Bishop into his chair, Mrs. Hallows swatted Morgan back to the house.

37 She led him testily upstairs and began to draw a bath. Sunlight streamed in the bathroom, and from the window Morgan watched the two figures in the gazebo.

—Mrs. Hallows, he asked, is something wrong with the Bishop?

—There is nothing wrong with His Grace. Only the last thing he needs is to be disturbed by helter-skelter visits from Master Jamie and ill-mannered boys who are nothing to do with him.

Her surliness was not mere unsociability, then. His behavior offended her. His behavior offended even himself. She mumbled something about His Grace not exerting himself.

—Has His Grace been unwell?

—His Grace last month suffered a heart attack, she declared. He's only home from hospital a fortnight.

—Crikey! I mean, I'd no idea. Dr. Sebastian didn't—

—He wouldn't. And neither would His Grace. Impossible, the pair of them.

She got him down a towel.

—Doctors tried to send him to Wight to recuperate, but His Grace wouldn't have it. The Dean took a strong line, but best they could get was His Grace's blessing to take on more curates and his promise to rest at home until Michaelmas. Of course, he's still buzzing over his archdeacons like heaven-knows-what, but Miss Lucy fends them off when she can, and I do my best. Lord knows it's a poor lookout.

Having delivered herself of this, Mrs. Hallows turned off the taps and announced she would leave him in peace. He would find lunch in the conservatory when he was ready. He thanked her, and she left exuding motherliness for the first time.

He lowered himself into the water. She'd made it cool enough for summer, but not so cool as to chill his muscles, which had tightened after two runs. He leaned forward and rubbed his calves.

The Bishop, who had seemed a titan of strength, far more robust than Morgan felt himself, was actually in poor health. He was supposed to be resting, not taking on desperate cases. How then had he managed to grip Morgan's wrist so hard? Hard enough, in fact, that he'd left a mark. (Or had that been Droit?) (Could Droit leave a mark?)

He didn't know what to think, so preposterous was the line of inquiry.

There he was in the bath with Droit again. Of course, physically he was alone in the bath, yet somehow Droit inhabited it, too. Not quite inside him, but perhaps after all . . .

He needed to stop treating fancies as reality. He'd fallen into the habit and it was confusing him. He was not, like Laurie, an artistic character. He did not even hold eccentric attitudes, like Mr. Grieves. All told, he considered himself a realist and an entirely ordinary specimen of English boy—man. Though if he was a man, why had he been abducted from school, and why was he now incarcerated as a child in the Bishop's house? He could feel his mind whizzing down this line of argument. (He wouldn't be treated that way!) (Yet plainly he was.) (He would resist!) (To what end?) (Soon people would come to their senses and he would be allowed to return to ordinary life.) Although he knew all the ways and reasons he should reject what had happened today, most especially what had just happened in the summerhouse (Nothing! Nothing had actually happened!), he kept coming back to the Bishop's holding his gaze as he had held his wrist.

He was exhausted; that was why such thoughts seemed attractive.

But, oh, to be always weak. To have no recourse against that atmosphere, to be free to indulge in it, or compelled to submit to it—was there so much difference between the two? Certainly, he ought not to indulge, even now beneath the bathwater, in the memory of the Bishop's . . . what to call it precisely? Not exactly his gaze or his touch or his words, but some thickness in the air when he turned all three upon Morgan, as if emitting an electrical-magnetical field.

He needed to pull himself together and stop bandying metaphor with a clergyman who was (a) unwell, (b) abrupt, (c) by profession steeped in grand ideas, (d) too quick to form attachments to strangers, and therefore (e) to be avoided. Morgan knew everything he needed to do. If he was to survive all of this intact, he needed to stop being a child and get on with it—*it* meaning what he needed to do!

The layers of muscle refused to flex. The bath cooled. A mantel of bereavement swept across him, scraping against everything he had lost, and everything he had now to renounce. He felt small, eyes full, chin weak. He got out of the bath and dripped on the mat.

Library was something of a misnomer. The room contained books, but not so many as the Bishop's study. Its primary purpose seemed to be leisure, judging by the chairs, settees, fireplace, and end tables positioned throughout. Mrs. Hallows had provided foolscap, pen, and ink at a writing table Morgan considered feminine. Perhaps it had once belonged to the luscious Miss Flynt. He could easily imagine her setting her stack of papers down upon it, slipping herself into the slender chair, and completing her correspondence, perhaps with the very pen he was to use!

Mrs. Hallows decamped before he could ask for clarification of his task. The Bishop had said to copy out that poem of the Eagle's, *Batter my heart* something, six times. (At least he had not offered witticisms re six of the best, ho-ho, thank you very much.) Hadn't he, though, included a peculiar instruction to make three copies with each hand? Did the Bishop suppose him ambidextrous? He'd never written anything with his left hand. How could he copy out a poem of unknown length using a maladroit hand?

It was too hot to stay indoors and write lines for which he lacked a text. He unlatched the window and let himself out to the garden. Soon his shoes and socks had come off, his trouser cuffs been rolled up, and his feet were dangling off the platform into the smooth canal. If he got in, would there be an undercurrent, or snapping turtles? How long could he resist plunging beneath the water?

No one was summoning him. Back at the Academy they'd be—like steel to think of that place; he resolved never to think of it again.

Yet, he mourned it. St. Stephen's Academy had witnessed the greatest and the most dire moments of his life. Once he'd felt that Grindalythe Woods was expecting prodigious things of him. But little boys felt all sorts of things. That didn't make them true.

And what of the wish slips? That, surely, must have been the height of his young lunacy, believing that the balcony he had discovered had belonged to Hermes, and that the dusty box of wish slips therein had belonged to that fabled Old Boy, and further that Morgan's three wishes were indeed heard and received by some power competent to grant them. He couldn't bear to think of what he had wished. Perhaps if he refused to think of it, he would at some point in the future cease to remember.

The Rectory canal bank was not St. Stephen's Academy, and any boy possessing a holiday to himself in summer ought to consider himself king of the world. In all the bunking off Morgan had done over the years, he had never found himself master of such a day. Anyone else would consider it ideal. But no one else had done what he had done and broken what he had broken. No one else occupied such an uncertain position: captive? guest? criminal? orphan?

He withdrew his feet from the water and reclined on the grass in the sun, his head dizzy. He would close his eyes, and open them . . . did it matter when?

A whistling, like arrows over walls. They mustered in the scale formation the Romans copied from the Greeks, but still the arrows pricked. His men fell around him, shrill of shells. Captain Cahill said they made your ears feel like bleeding. His men had fallen on top of him, arrows penetrating the gaps of their armor. He couldn't move his limbs, couldn't stop the shells, coming, coming—

—You alive, or what?

A dark Adonis blotted out the sun. Morgan inhaled, and coughed.

—Are you poorly? the creature asked.

Blood rushed to his cock. He was far from poorly. He sat up and licked his teeth. The creature licked his lips.

—You're awfully far away, Morgan said. Why don't you sit down here?

Dark Adonis puzzled, then spoke:

—Mrs. Hallows wants you.

The creature extended a hand—a firm, marvelous hand.

—Best move before she turns savage.

—She hasn't been savage yet?

The creature laughed. Morgan let himself be hoisted.

—I'm Morgan.

—I know. William.

William led him to the kitchen door and called for Mrs. Hallows, who shortly appeared. The look of fear on her face gave way swiftly to relief, then fury. The next thing Morgan knew, his ears were being boxed and she was unleashing a rebuke equal to one of Matron's. Where had he gone? How dare he disappear without bothering to tell anyone? Did he think they had nothing to do but hunt down wicked boys? The cuffs continued.

Had she or had she not left him in the library? And where was the work the Bishop expected?

His ears rang, and her words no longer distinguished themselves. Far in a corner of the kitchen, Droit lurked, his hair damp from swimming, wet patches seeping through his soft-collared shirt. He plunged his finger into a bowl cooling by the window, brought it out dripping with custard, and sucked. Morgan burned with shame. Almost gratefully he retreated to the library.

He was thirsty. He was hungry. She'd told him to expect no tea until he'd finished his penance, as she called it. He would have called it prep. The Bishop had said nothing to make him believe it was an imposition, certainly not anything as popish as penance. Whatever you called it, he needed the verse.

The books mocked him with their calfskin secrets. He concentrated his scant mental powers on remembering enough to generate a lead. They'd read it with the Eagle, so it was likely to have been one of Wordsworth's bits of bunkum. Laurie had made rude comments about the pastoral poems. In them the landscape typically represented a woman, didn't it? A woman ripe for conquest. But the Bishop wouldn't have asked him to copy a thinly veiled erotic lyric, would he?

He performed a systematic skimming of shelves until he came upon a volume of Romantic poetry. It contained many boring verses by wordy Wordsworth, but none about battering hearts. On quick glance, "Nutting" did seem risqué. It reminded him of—nothing that he ought to be contemplating if he wished to stay sane. Could the battering-heart poem be a more obscure work of the dreary poet? He didn't know as much as he supposed he ought about Wordsworth; he knew that the man went stiff over daffodils and the French Revolution, and that he otherwise spent his time mooning over fey, abstract subjects with other opium-eating characters such as Shelley (a girl if ever there was one), Byron (a crackbrain and a rake), and Keats (also a girl, and a hypochondriac to boot). Perhaps one of Wordsworth's nancy friends had written the Bishop's poem? The index of first lines disclosed nothing about battering by any Romantic poet. If only he had paid more attention!

He had to think. The day they'd read it with the Eagle, the point had been something to do with the punctuation, but they hadn't discussed punctuation when trawling through Wordsworth's treacly ejaculations. Wait! They'd read it briefly *because* of its punctuation, and then the Eagle had ordered them to copy scads of useless definitions out of their poetry primers. If that had been the context—and he was now certain it was—then the fluttering-heart poem had come from the poetry primer!

Which meant it could be anything, from Lord Randall My Son to brownnose Browning.

He was standing at the garden window watching William clip hedges when Mrs. Hallows intruded and demanded to know what he was about. If he thought such obnoxious disobedience was a clever sign of a modern mind, then she failed to see why the Bishop was bothering with him. Morgan considered defending himself, but he couldn't find a place to begin. Mrs. Hallows continued her assessment: The youth of today were a monstrous invention. They'd never suffered life's travails. They kicked up everything in their path, considered the world their plaything, felt it owed them every luxury their small minds could imagine, scorned what others had made—

—Didn't fight in the War either, Morgan interrupted hotly. And they died for us, all those brilliant, heroic men. We're parasites. We know!

She stared at him, stunned.

—I'm quite sure I'm guilty of everything you say, Morgan continued, but I'll tell you something I am not, and that's a telepathist. Which is why I'm incapable of guessing what book contains whichever poem the Bishop babbled at me. Call me what you will, but I'm not a magician!

They faced one another, breathing more heavily than physical stasis demanded.

—What poem? she demanded.

—I haven't the first idea.

—How does it go?

He sighed loudly and told her: battering hearts, blowing and burning. That was all he had.

In a few moments, she had a volume in her hands. She slammed it on the writing table and, after running her finger down an index, turned to a certain page. Throwing him another glare, she stalked away, muttering (*lazy, ignorant, godless*).

He could not remember detesting a woman more than this one.

The poem wasn't what he remembered. It was something to do with a woman kidnapped by an enemy and betrothed to him. But it seemed that her rescuer was even more savage than the unwanted husband. The woman did not sound well in the head. Was she asking to be ravished? Were her requests to be battered, burned, and conquered sarcastic, or was she warped?

That I may rise and stand, o'erthrow me. Droit had made a jest about that, but if Morgan was honest—and wasn't he supposed to be, at least to himself?—if he was honest, he could imagine a situation in which being overthrown might, done properly, indeed make him rise and stand in Droit's sense of the words.

Sometimes Silk knew how to make him hard merely with words. Other times, Silk seemed to know the secret: that Morgan's cock liked it when Silk conquered him. How many times had Silk compelled him against his will? Had he ever? Even recalling it, he felt the heavy flow of blood and hungered for Silk's touch. Spaulding had overpowered him in the Hermes Balcony, an overpowering entirely welcome and delicious. Thinking of Spaulding wasn't allowed, yet thought of him was more real and more recent than memory of Silk. And since by outrageous phenomenon he had seen Silk again in the flesh only . . . *two days ago?* . . . could Spaulding not exist as well? There was no reason in the world that he couldn't return from where he'd gone, resume his place in the Flea's House, and find Morgan one lazy afternoon to carry on where they had left off. The notion felt so entirely plausible and palpable that, beside it, reality seemed a twisted dream from which he would shortly awake.

Reason, your viceroy in me, me should defend.

He hoped that his reason would indeed defend him from everything threatening his sanity, yet in the poem, was reason not weak, captive, untrue?

He had to stop depending on figments of his imagination or he would shortly go round the bend. He had to think clearly about them and sort out once and for all what they meant. Figures of the imagination: Who else had them? Macbeth imagined a bloody dagger. That was a figment. But he was cracking up and had scorpions in his brain. (Literally? Perhaps not.) Hamlet saw his father's ghost, but that couldn't have been a figment because other people saw it, too. So, if other people could see your figment, then it wasn't a figment, but a ghost. But other people didn't see Droit. Droit was something rather like the imaginary friend Flora once had. The only difference was that Flora's friend remained entirely under Flora's control, whereas Droit . . . He wasn't sure he liked Droit as much as he once had.

But Droit was suave, Droit was witty, Droit did not allow anyone to take advantage. He knew much more about other people and the world than Morgan knew, much more than that childish specimen, the other one, the creature who showed himself only when Morgan was at his worst, who never fought back, who had looked at him as he—perhaps the fight with Alex hadn't really occurred that way. Perhaps they had struggled longer, more desperately. Perhaps the cracks he had felt under his fist were his own knuckles.

Why did the Bishop insist he copy out the poem six times, three with each hand? He'd already done the three with his right (*avec la droite, Dieu et mon droit!*), but he could barely form letters with his left. What's more, his hand was smearing the ink. If he was meant to write with his left hand (*avec la gauche*, and how very gauche it was!), then why not go all the way and write like Hebrews, from right to left? He was having to turn the page and draw the nib along it as if sketching hieroglyphics, not the sensible code of English. This was going to take forever, and he was fainting from hunger. The Bishop wouldn't even be able to read the left-handed copies. The pen was doing everything except what he wanted it to do. The room was stultifying. HE ABHORRED THIS POEM AND THESE LINES. IT WAS THE WORST IMPOSITION HE HAD EVER BEEN GIVEN!

✦

Fourteen times six. Eighty-four lines. Short ones. It could be classed with the mildest of punishments. If not for the unsavory subject matter (*nor ever chaste, except you ravish me*) and the eccentric ambidextrous requirement, it would have been nothing more than a few minutes' labor, the most perfunctory of smacks. But the fourteen lines (so it was a sonnet, then, only ten beats per line) written *à gauche* brought him to the verge of frustrated tears. He finished the last, broke the nib, and only just restrained himself from hurling the open inkpot across the room. Instead he screwed the thing closed and stomped off to the kitchen.

A ruddy girl labored over onions with a knife. When Morgan asked where Mrs. Hallows was, the girl shrugged and continued her teary chopping. Why was everyone in Wiltshire chronically incapable of supplying information? He needed food immediately. He scanned the kitchen but saw nothing but onions.

—Did Mrs. Hallows say anything about me? Morgan demanded.

She grunted. The entire household was bent on galling him! He asked after William, but apparently William had Gone Out.

—Is there anything to eat? Morgan asked.

—Dinner at eight, she told him.

The clock on the wall declared it half past five. He was dizzy with desperation. What would Droit do? (And where was Droit when he needed him?)

—I'm frightfully sorry, he said, taking a step towards her. I'm afraid I've forgotten my manners, Miss . . . ?

She stopped chopping and blinked the tears from her eyes.

—Maryanne, she whispered.

He gave a little bow.

—Morgan Wilberforce at your service. And what an attractive frock that is, if I may say so.

She blushed. He was relieved that she did not think him as preposterous as he sounded to himself. The remark about her frock thawed the atmosphere, however, and she began to chat back to him. What was for dinner? A relatively large menu involving meat, a tart, various vegetables, a soup, and a trifle. Was the Bishop expecting company? Not company, only Miss Agnes and Mr. Goss. Possibly Miss Lucy, and if the children were feeling better, then also Miss Elizabeth, but if not, then only Mr. Fairclough. Morgan could make no sense of her speech, but he paid her another compliment, this time about her hair, and then confessed that he was faint from hunger.

Why had he not said so? He was pale as a sheet. Mrs. Hallows had left no instructions (Hadn't she, the spiteful hag?), but Maryanne knew better than to let people faint away. She wiped her hands and fetched a plate of scones from the pantry. Morgan fell on them.

He was devouring his third when Mrs. Hallows breezed into the kitchen. He froze midbite. Maryanne punctuated the silence with chopping. Mrs. Hallows took in the scene.

—Finished, have you?

He nodded. She consulted the clock.

—Upstairs, change for dinner. Bishop's study in half an hour.

He fled before she could examine the situation more closely.

39

No one had told him what to wear to dinner, of course, and he'd only the clothes in his hateful trunk. Given Maryanne's testimony that there would be no formal company, he decided that his Sunday uniform would be too much. Instead, he chose the cleaner of his trousers and the rest of his summer uniform. He decided he had better polish his shoes, and he gave himself a going over with a flannel. Thus attired, he took the embarrassing lines and went downstairs. He wasn't at all sure of the route to the Bishop's study, but if he could find it without having to encounter Mrs. Horrors, he might have a chance of maintaining his composure.

He thought he had the wrong place when he knocked, but then a key turned. After a silent interval, he let himself in.

The Bishop was gazing out the window and gripping the swivel chair as if his balance depended on it.

When people behaved awkwardly, or when one felt awkward oneself, it frequently helped to behave as if one belonged there. Morgan sauntered over to the Bishop and peered out the window at the empty drive. Time passed.

—Why do you suppose she uses that particular floss? the Bishop asked.

As he said it, a bird came into focus before them, a small, brown thing jutting about a nest in the corner of the hedgerow.

—Perhaps it was all she could find, Morgan suggested.

—I've laid out five types at the foot of the hedgerow, but that blue floss is all she will touch.

—Perhaps it's the color of her mate.

The Bishop seemed not to have considered this. They watched until the bird hopped away. The Bishop sighed.

Morgan had determined not to make the first move, but now he found himself submitting to it:

—I did the lines, sir.

—So you have, the Bishop said, stirring from reverie. And here I thought we were going to have to put the screws to you the first day.

Morgan felt his face reacting as it always did, but he kept his arms at his sides and his feet still. The Bishop sat down at the desk to examine the lines, as if they contained a signed statement and not six inept manuscript copies of a poem. Having scanned each page, the Bishop selected one and instructed Morgan to read it out.

At least there weren't any tricky words. He glanced down and was horrified to see the Bishop had chosen one of the gauche copies, produced by an inmate of an asylum, plainly. He looked up in protest, but the man waved him on.

He read. The Bishop did not interrupt. Morgan thought he might have mistaken one or two words, but he didn't stumble. The Bishop folded his hands pensively, fingers touching as in that game Morgan's mother used to play: *here is the church, here is the steeple, open the doors and see all the—*

—Well, the Bishop said, who is knocking at the gates?

Morgan's mind deserted him.

—I don't know, sir.

—Don't you?

—And it was battering, not knocking.

—*For you as yet but knock, breathe, shine, and seek to mend?*

Were they talking about the poem now or the metaphor (was it metaphor?) about the walls of Morgan's city, which referred to . . . he wasn't sure what, but something real nonetheless?

—I thought we were speaking of both, the Bishop rejoined.

Had he spoken again without meaning to? He had to pay attention so he wouldn't say anything blasphemous, or worse.

—Who is knocking? the Bishop repeated.

—No one's knocking, Morgan replied petulantly. That's the problem. The woman wants someone to knock and come and get her, but they aren't.

—Ah! How do you know?

—She gets desperate, doesn't she? She's probably going to faint as soon as the sonnet's done.

He was pleased to have got in the word *sonnet*. At least the Bishop would know he had some education.

—She starts out begging this chap to batter her and knock her down. Then it's divorce me, untie me, and the next thing you know it's imprison and ravish me. She's like someone out of a story by Lord Crim-Con—or—

It was happening again. He was saying things he didn't want to say. The Bishop was looking at him keenly. He needed to extract himself.

—Or Etoniensis or some such. She's wrong in the head, that's all.

—I see.

The Bishop narrowed his eyes as Morgan's father used to when he suspected Morgan of failing to level with him. If the Bishop pressed him about Lord Crim-Con, he might pass the name off as a mispronunciation of an ordinary name. He would say he had no particular story in mind, merely something his sisters used to read to him when he was small, and so perhaps he had misremembered it. Etoniensis could be a mishearing of some Latin personage. The Romans were always getting up to questionable activities. Perhaps the misheard Etoniensis passage was about a slave auction. Plausible!

—You see the speaker as a woman? the Bishop asked.

Morgan nodded. The Bishop wondered to whom she was speaking. Who was this rescuer she addressed? Address—that was the punctuation part!

—It's apostrophe, sir, isn't it? And she's speaking to some three-headed deity, like the Hindus have. But did people like this Donne chap know about Hindus, sir? Or did they have some three-headed Druid god back then?

—Wilberforce, please read the first line again.

The Bishop gave his command with strained patience.

—I've never been good with poems, sir.

—Read.

—*Batter my heart three-person'd God—*

—Now stop being willfully thick and identify *three-person'd God* without recourse to paganism.

—Is she meant to be speaking to God, sir?

—You tell me.

—I don't follow *three-person'd*.

—No, the Bishop said tartly, and you don't follow when I make the gesture that distresses you.

He put his hand to his forehead, his chest, his heart. Morgan froze. He'd made a colossal—had he actually said that about Hindus? Could he pass it off as a joke?

—Oh, Morgan stuttered, if that's all you mean. I was thinking symbolic, underneath it, a kind of allusion—

—Stop backpedaling and read from the beginning, all the way through.

He hadn't been willfully thick, but he couldn't imagine why he had so entirely failed to grasp the meaning of a poem that turned out quite transparent. They read it several more times, taking it in turns. When the

Bishop read, chills raced across Morgan's scalp. The Bishop catechized him more thoroughly than the Eagle ever had on any poem, and when he got stuck on a phrase, the Bishop, rather than explaining, would simply read it over with different emphases until it unfolded. The poem was not about a girl who was wrong in the head. It was about . . .

—You want me to say it's about me, don't you?

—Is it?

—No, sir! I mean, there's the business with the city, but I don't want God to do anything with me, certainly not imprison or ravish me.

The Bishop merely looked at him.

—And anyway, I don't believe in things like that.

—You're an atheist?

—Not exactly.

—Vaguely?

—No, but—stop trying to pin me!

—I apologize. Perhaps it's time to change the subject.

—I really think we should, sir, no disrespect to your profession. I just don't think it's worth discussing. It isn't practical. God isn't a magician. That's just superstition.

—I agree.

—I don't know what happens after we die, but the point is that's then and we've got to be now, so, all right, we've got to try to treat other people decently, but otherwise—may I be entirely honest, sir?

—I expect nothing less.

—Oh. Well . . . as far as I can see, religion and the Bible are just a waste of time. God has nothing to do with real life.

—Again, I apologize. I can see I've adopted entirely the wrong tactic with you.

Morgan wasn't sure what to think of the Bishop's employing tactics with him.

—Let us forget about Donne.

The Bishop emphasized his suggestion by dumping the six sheets of foolscap into a wastepaper basket.

—Let us return to the conversation we were having earlier today, and to the metaphor we both employed to describe your state of mind. Something is battering at the gates, you said?

It sounded fey now.

—I think, sir, that I must have been . . .

—Disturbed? I concur. You'd been whisked away from school, thrust into a strange household, and then subjected to two bouts of stiff exercise and an unpleasant telephone conversation. I should say you were disturbed.

Morgan wished the Bishop wouldn't mention telephone conversations, but at least he grasped the essential facts. On second thought, he summarized as if . . .

—Sir, did you plan all that?

The Bishop's eyes flickered.

—Sir, Morgan demanded, how long am I to stay here, and what exactly do you require of me?

—Perhaps you'd do better, the Bishop said, to forget about what I require of you and work out what you require of me.

With this, the man abandoned his seat behind the desk to come and stand beside Morgan, focusing his gaze again on him in the magnetic fashion he had employed in the summerhouse.

Morgan didn't know if he had any energy left for dueling. He'd been feinting the whole time, trying to avoid traps, trying to hedge against his own errors. Only now he wasn't sure that the Bishop was playing the same game.

—When you were a boy, the Bishop said, breaking the silence, how did your father deal with you?

The mention of his father dealing with him stirred that childhood yearning even now.

—He'd listen until the truth came out.

The Bishop nodded.

—And even when the truth was horrible, Morgan continued, he stayed with you. Even when he was punishing you, he never left, and then afterwards you'd be with him and away from the horrible thing, and you'd know there was nothing too horrible for him to deal with.

The Bishop leaned against the edge of the desk.

—That's what you need now, isn't it?

Morgan's arm wrapped around his face as if to scratch the back of his head. The fabric of his blazer scraped across his cheek, sunburnt and raw. A little bell began to chime, and far away, a deeper one. A hand gripped his forearm and pulled it gently from his face.

—You aren't a little boy any longer. It's up to you to choose whose hands you put yourself into.

Morgan's throat hurt:

—I don't want to put myself in anyone's hands! That's what it means to be grown-up, to be only in your own hands.

The Bishop relaxed his grip:

—We are always in each other's hands, but often we've no idea into whose grasp we've fallen.

He froze. The Bishop froze. Someone knocked at the door.

—Yes? the Bishop called.

—In the drawing room, Your Grace.

—Thank you.

Morgan felt urgent. The Bishop released a fragment of a smile.

—I mustn't ask you to make important decisions before dinner, he said. We wouldn't want you to feel pinned.

—Sir, I didn't mean—

—Let's take that as read. We'll continue tomorrow after breakfast. Now our dinner guests have arrived.

The sense of menace was dispelling.

—Who are the dinner guests, sir?

—I couldn't say with certainty.

The Bishop unlocked the door with a key. Morgan followed him from the room.

—Oh, and Wilberforce? the Bishop said as they descended.

—Sir?

—I'm afraid I must ask you to refrain from flirting.

—*Sir?*

—With my staff and with my family.

They broke through the corridor and into a red chamber.

—You know what I mean, and I would consider it a personal favor if you would spare me the song and dance of pretending that you don't. Elizabeth, darling, how are the children?

The Bishop broke habit and introduced all of his guests to Morgan, presumably so Morgan would understand in no uncertain terms with whom he ought not to flirt. Three of the Bishop's daughters had come that evening to attend him. Elizabeth, his eldest, was married to Mr. Fairclough and had four children at home with the croup (thankfully on the mend).

Agnes turned up shortly after Elizabeth, and her husband, Mr. Goss, arrived sometime later, delayed by trains, curse them. Last to drop anchor was Lucy, who turned out to be Miss Flynt. Her husband did not make an appearance, and no one seemed to expect him. All of the Bishop's daughters were as attractive as Miss Flynt, though only Miss Flynt was young enough to give Morgan any consideration. Not that she was considering him—she was married—but if she weren't married, he suspected that he could convince her to consider him very seriously indeed.

—You've met all of us save Flora, Agnes said with a heart-stopping smile.

—Our other sister, Elizabeth explained.

She's the beautiful one, Agnes told him, but she wastes it grubbing away for trade unionists.

—Surely no one could be more beautiful than the three of you, Morgan said.

The Bishop cleared his throat.

—They aren't trade unionists, Lucy corrected. Our sister is working to establish a school and hospital for poor children in Bristol.

—Their parents are trade unionists, Agnes said.

—Some of them.

Agnes winked at him:

—Trade unionists or Red communists.

—Everyone who works with his hands isn't a trade unionist or a communist! Lucy replied hotly.

—All the young men of Flora's acquaintance are Bolsheviks, Agnes insisted.

The way she said *Bolsheviks* made his trousers tighten.

—So, she continued, apart from Flora, you've met the whole family? Father, did you say he's met Jamie?

—Stop being mischievous, Agnes. You know perfectly well he has.

Agnes sipped her sherry. The others sipped their sherries. Morgan sipped his lemonade.

—My sister's name is Flora, too, he said.

The conversation revived as they interviewed him about his sisters, delighted that he, too, was a youngest and only son like their brother. Did he give his father half as much trouble as their brother did? When they found out about his mother, they surrounded him in a chorus of pity—their mother had died, too!—allowing their sensational hands to touch his jacket, his hair, his cheeks. It was as much as he could do to keep his trousers presentable in the midst of them and their intoxicating scents.

—Father, did you hear that? Agnes demanded. This poor boy is half an orphan.

The Bishop pursed his lips. He seemed to treat Agnes rather as Morgan's father had treated Emily when she was going through her Difficult Stage, with a certain firmness underpinned by indulgence.

Morgan tried to imagine how it must have been for Dr. Sebastian to grow up amongst them, with the addition of beautiful, bolshie Flora. They spoke of Dr. Sebastian as if he were still an incorrigible boy. The picture corresponded in no way with the man who had brought Morgan down on the train. He couldn't help feeling that something about the portrait was untoward. The whole evening was ludicrous, but then so much had been ludicrous lately that he saw no reason to resist this.

When they went in to dinner, the Bishop sat Morgan beside him and filled his glass halfway with hock. At Morgan's other side sat Mr. Fairclough, and across from them, Lucy. He was grateful the table was wide or he might not have been able to stop himself reaching for her with his foot.

Conversation during the meal tiptoed around the Bishop's health, a subject that irritated him and occupied his daughters in equal measure. Dimly Morgan became aware that they had come to dinner en masse to check up on their father. Lucy emphasized repeatedly that life at the cathedral was under control. The archdeacons were managing splendidly (*Sowing their oats*, the Bishop muttered), and the two new curates actually had to be stopped from taking on too much in their zeal. Today's chapter meeting had adopted several resolutions concerning the east gutters (*Resolutions are not actions!*) and concerning recruitment for the choir school.

—What I can't understand, Agnes said, is why Jamie thinks he ought to leave Marlborough and move house hundreds of miles away to go and work at a dreary little school no one's heard of.

—Let us leave your brother out of this, the Bishop said.

—Agnes has a point, Elizabeth rejoined. The choir school will be up and running next year. Why go somewhere else in the meantime? It's unsettled.

—Has he got himself into a mess at Marlborough? Agnes asked with ill-concealed hunger.

—No, he hasn't! the Bishop said with raised voice. When your brother gave his notice this morning, they were devastated. The fact is St. Stephen's is exceedingly fortunate to have him.

—St. Stephen's? Elizabeth asked. I've never heard of it. Have you?

She turned to her husband, but he had not heard of the Academy, and neither had Mr. Goss.

—I've heard of it, Lucy said.

Morgan set down his fork.

—St. Stephen's Academy in Yorkshire, Lucy continued. It was in the papers at Easter.

—Lucy, the Bishop warned.

—We all know what you think of the *Mail*, Father, but that doesn't mean they were wrong.

—Not that place where the boy was killed? Elizabeth asked aghast.

Lucy nodded with satisfaction. Morgan clamped tongue between teeth.

—But that's dreadful! Agnes cried. What in God's good earth is Jamie doing at a place like that?

—Turning it around, I should think, the Bishop retorted.

—But, Father, you can't let him! Agnes insisted. He's throwing everything away! And think of what it will do to the choir school once it opens.

Morgan's heart began to pound.

—And, yes, Agnes continued, I know you and he—but seriously, Father, what kind of Headmaster will he be to this place, St. Swithin's—

—St. Stephen's.

Agnes waved impatiently at Lucy.

—If there's even a shred of truth in the *Mail*, the place is dreadful and ought to be closed at once. What good will it do for Jamie to hack up there, practically fresh out of school himself—

—Agnes, that will do.

—and *fiddle* with the place for a year before leaving it in the lurch when he comes home for the choir school. It's madly irresponsible.

Morgan wondered if he might be sick at the table. All three of the Bishop's exquisite daughters and two of his well-cut sons-in-law agreed that St. Stephen's was a sewer that would ruin anyone who came near it, most especially their brother, who was in any case a callow youth unqualified to be Headmaster of anything.

The Bishop set down his cutlery, daubed his mouth with a napkin, and rang the bell. Everyone looked to him, for his decision on the fate of their brother and the fate of his own choir school. The Bishop smiled in a way that made Morgan suspect a knife.

—Wilberforce, he said mildly, you've been exceptionally quiet. What have you to say about all this?

His mouth tasted of steel. He wondered if he could have some more hock.

—Is Dr. Sebastian really only going to the Academy for one year?

—I don't believe it's been settled, the Bishop said.

—But, Father, Lucy protested, you've wanted the choir school for ages. It took all that time to get it approved, and even longer to get the Bishop's palace fitted out, and now it's almost ready. Who else can run it but Jamie?

—Everyone always said he'd run it.

—But that doesn't mean he must, the Bishop replied, or that he will.

Morgan felt the urge to swear. He concentrated on what he was saying:

—If Dr. Sebastian is going to St. Stephen's pro tem, do they know that?

—They ought to know it! Lucy declared.

The table looked to the Bishop.

—I don't believe that was the understanding.

An explosion of disbelief. The Bishop turned placidly to Morgan. Morgan struggled to think straight.

—Is it very impertinent to ask how old Dr. Sebastian is, sir?

—Quite impertinent.

—He's twenty-eight, said Lucy.

Morgan swallowed, as much to give the impression of thought as to pull himself together. Twenty-eight wasn't as young as the girls made it sound. (And did that mean they were all over thirty? Even luscious Lucy?) Twenty-eight wasn't barely out of school. Twenty-eight was old.

—Sir, Morgan asked, do you think Dr. Sebastian can save St. Stephen's?

The Bishop held Morgan's gaze as he had in the study, even as the girls fluttered amongst themselves.

—If St. Stephen's can be saved, James can do it.

A fullness settled in Morgan's stomach, like eating a large dessert. The alarm of the day lifted for a moment, and he felt a relief like the arrival of a summer thunderstorm to drive away the heat and bring them air they could breathe.

The girls were gabbling, reiterating points, harping now on their brother's chronic insubordination, his penchant for unwise heroics, and his selfishness in proposing to leave the Academy after only a year.

The cooling air turned quickly cold. Dr. Sebastian could save the Academy and rescue it from everything wrong. The unexplained authority he had exerted in the railway carriage he would exert over the school, over people such as Colin, Laurie, perhaps even over Alex. But if Dr. Sebastian remade the place into the kind of school it could be (the kind of school it had once whispered to Morgan about wanting to be), then a garroting loomed. They would grow fond of him. They would trust him, depend on him, require him. And then he would leave.

It wasn't right to make people trust you and then abandon them. It was worse than failing to help in the first place. It was almost as bad as exiling them in their hour of need.

—Wilberforce, Agnes said, slicing through the chatter, did you come down with our brother?

They stopped talking and turned again to him.

—Yes.

This seemed to settle some question.

—And what did you read?

He hesitated, confused.

—Dr. Jekyll and Mr. Hyde for the most part.

A moment of silence, then Agnes laughed:

—I suppose theology is exactly like that at times, isn't it?

Morgan nodded mutely. They fired questions at him, but he couldn't answer. He wasn't clever enough for girls like these. They kept speaking of doctrines and of orders and the ways in which those topics intersected with the works of people such as Dr. Floyd—a name that vexed their father—and Dr. Young. The Bishop objected most strenuously, and Lucy quickly took his side against Agnes, who was enjoying herself enormously. Good and evil were not the same as the conscious and the unconscious, the Bishop insisted, and Agnes was glib to suggest it. Everyone looked to Morgan as if he were on Agnes's side. She winked at him again.

—I suppose, Father, that it's Wilberforce's Jekyll and Hyde ideology you've determined to reform.

Lucy threw Agnes a savage glare. Even Elizabeth's face revealed horror. The Bishop lowered his voice:

—Agnes, dear, that really will do.

Agnes plunged forward, but her darting gaze made it clear she knew she'd committed a blunder and was trying to cover it up.

—You'll forgive me, won't you, dear? she asked Morgan.

He would forgive her anything if she would use that velvety tone towards him again.

—The last thing I would dream of doing is intrude. You know that, don't you?

—Of course.

If only she would intrude regularly, deeply, and personally.

—Splendid, she replied with a smile. Why don't you tell us everything.

Some hot thing blocked him from speaking. The Bishop cleared his throat and refilled Morgan's glass. Morgan looked to him for a clue as to what he was doing wrong, but the Bishop was looking across the table.

—Here's the trifle, he announced.

Arrival of the dessert diverted them, but to Morgan's chagrin, Agnes resumed as soon as they'd been served.

—Don't imagine you're getting off that easily, she said. Tell us every juicy detail about our brother.

He abandoned thoughts of stuffing his mouth with trifle.

—He's very impressive.

Lucy snorted.

—Oh, yes, Elizabeth deadpanned, enormously impressive.

—He . . .

What else was there to say about the man?

—I believe he made quite an impression on the Board. The chairman clearly thought the world of him. And he made an impressive start. He isn't a man to be afraid of anything, or to hesitate. He even impressed Burton-Lee—he's the Headmaster pro tem—even if things were awkward between them. The only person he didn't impress was Mr. . . .

They were staring at him in . . . disbelief? Horror? He drank the hock.

—It's time you girls stopped tormenting young Wilberforce and let him eat, the Bishop said.

Something in the man's expression provoked in them the opposite behavior.

—You can't possibly stop there, Agnes insisted. Where and when was this? He hasn't told us this story!

When exactly had it been?

—The day before yesterday? Morgan said. At . . .

They hung on his word. The Bishop set down his spoon and looked at him indulgently. He had to think straight. Had there been some sort of confusion in the room?

—At St. Stephen's.

—St. Stephen's? Agnes repeated.

Morgan nodded.

—St. Stephen's from the *Mail*?

Again he could only nod.

—But—I'm not following this—what were you doing at St. Stephen's? Up in Yorkshire?

—Playing cricket.

Agnes looked to her sisters, but they were equally baffled. She turned to her husband:

—Darling, have I got scatterbrain? I'm simply not keeping up.

—It isn't scatterbrain, Elizabeth replied. I'm not pregnant and I'm not following either.

Lucy, mouth full of trifle, let out a muffled squeal. She tapped the table as she swallowed.

—You aren't from Oxford at all, are you? she exclaimed.

—Of course not, Morgan said.

—But . . . ?

—He's from Jamie's new school! Lucy told them.

—But, Agnes wrinkled her brow painfully, you said you came down with our brother.

—I did! Morgan said exasperated. We came down on the train yesterday. If you can call it coming down together. I'd call it more like kidnapping!

He had thought these girls liked him, fancied him even, but now they were pressing him to admit things that didn't belong at a family dinner, and furthermore acting as though Dr. Sebastian's economy with information was a widespread family trait.

—Just a minute, Lucy said. How old are you?

Morgan blushed.

—I'm twenty-two.

—Oh, yes? the Bishop said.

A chair scraped at Morgan's right. Mr. Fairclough stood and placed his hand on Morgan's shoulder:

—I say, old chap, could I borrow you for a moment? There's something I need to . . .

He gestured to the door and gave Morgan a bashful, desperate expression. The girls had stopped speaking again. Morgan looked to the Bishop, who nodded, imperfectly hiding his amusement. Morgan wiped his mouth, folded his napkin, and followed Elizabeth's husband from the room.

At the bottom of the drive, Mr. Fairclough produced a case:

—Smoke?

—Thanks.

The cigarette was smooth, expensive, well kept.

—Sorry for all that, Mr. Fairclough said. They don't mean to be cruel. They always carry on when they get together. And I think the Bishop was being a bit naughty with them.

—I'm afraid I've no idea what you're talking about, Morgan said.

—Yes, you do, Mr. Fairclough replied. This family thrives on incomplete truths. All we knew was that an acquaintance of James was the Bishop's new project. No one said it was anything to do with the new post.

—Oh.

—Or that the young man was still at school.

—I—

—You aren't twenty-two, plainly.

A pinch as something bit the back of his neck.

—Sixteen?

—Seventeen . . . I don't know why I said that.

Mr. Fairclough gazed at the field.

—I've said worse. They push you to it. You should see what it's like when Flora's there.

They finished their cigarettes in a comforting silence. Morgan's neck itched. Mr. Fairclough slapped his own cheek.

—They're eating us raw. Come on.

They went back to the house. Mr. Fairclough paused outside the dining room but then turned instead in to the library, where Morgan had suffered the hideous lines earlier that day. That ceaseless, purgatorial day.

The sun had not set, but Mr. Fairclough lit a lamp and took it to a little piano Morgan had not noticed earlier. He sat, ran his fingers down the keys, and began to play something liquid, like the bath-warm, fish-filled, syrupy sea.

—So, Mr. Fairclough said, what did you do?

Morgan thought to protest, but he didn't want Mr. Fairclough to stop playing.

—A lot of things I shouldn't have.

The music pressed against his rib cage.

—I only wish I could think straight.

—Isn't that why you're here?

Morgan leaned on the piano, head on his arms, feeling the vibrations.

—I can't seem to stop doing things I don't want to do.

The music lightened, as if the mosquito-filled air outside had come into the library with them.

—Of course, I want to *do* them, but I don't want to *have done* them.

The whole summer enveloped them, conjured by Mr. Fairclough, infusing them with its lushness, its ease, its memory of Longmere and the woods where Emily would run away and be found, be brought home again.

—I didn't think I would turn out like this, you see.

Mr. Fairclough applied the soft pedal.

—How dreary, he said, to have everything turn out as expected.

His right hand slipped, but just as it struck an off note, it crossed over the left and fell into a ravine of off notes, until they combined into a new atmosphere, like the ferny floor of the forest after tea, where one might encounter any type of thing, anything one had imagined or failed to imagine.

—But when things don't turn out, it's a failure, Morgan said.

—Too much of the unexpected is chaos, Mr. Fairclough said. But you've got to leave a little space, I think.

—For what?

—For breath.

As if in illustration, he lifted his hands from the keys, inhaled, and then plunged back, following the notes somewhere new, like a wind blowing a schooner west across the sea, turning the world, disturbing and disordering everything, and as Mr. Fairclough's fingers rippled the keys, the sound pulsed through Morgan like the thrill of Polly's kiss, like Spaulding grabbing him from behind, like Grieves hurling cricket balls. The music tickled, pounded, shook him entirely apart and sewed him back with sharpest needle, drawing new thread through him, savaging him as nature savaged caterpillars in their chrysalis. He'd been altered before, and he was being altered again, into what, he didn't know.

The piano fell silent. Mr. Fairclough massaged his palms. Morgan felt he ought to stand up.

—What's that called?

—Oh, Mr. Fairclough said vaguely, how about *After Dinner with the Bishop's Daughters?*

Voices in the corridor. Mr. Fairclough got up from the piano.

—Come on, he said, before the girls descend.

They repaired to the conservatory, where Mr. Goss stood before open doors, lighting a cigar. Mr. Fairclough again offered his cigarette case to Morgan. The tobacco opened his veins.

The trouble, he realized, was that he couldn't work out whether he was in the middle of a disaster or not. Sometimes it seemed as though all was well, and all would be well, that he was merely spending an unconventional interval with people who wished him no harm. But in turns he had a powerful sensation of catastrophe—one of his own making, one immanent, or both.

Mr. Goss puffed his cigar:

—What's your specialty, then?

Morgan wondered if he was being addressed.

—At cricket.

—Oh, Morgan said, drawing strength from the cigarette, I haven't got one.

—You did something to impress my brother-in-law, Mr. Goss said.

—I got lucky. The bowling was savage.

Mr. Goss laughed:

—You survived, you mean?

They all laughed, and Morgan fell into describing the end of the match. Mr. Goss, it emerged, was a keen cricketer.

—But you say this master who nearly killed you had also directed your rehabilitation from the shoulder injury?

Morgan couldn't think of another way to put it.

—A great favorite, is he?

—Rather the opposite.

They found this preposterous. Morgan was unable to explain Grieves in a way that made sense.

—He's a pacifist.

—Not much of a pacifist if he's crippling Sixth Formers, Mr. Goss said. Sounds to me as if no one has the measure of this man.

—You can never get a handle on him, Morgan complained. He's moody. He persecutes. He misunderstands.

—Sounds like every schoolmaster I've ever known, Mr. Fairclough said.

—But he isn't like any schoolmaster. He's . . .

Morgan thought of sitting at Mr. Grieves's table that night. He thought of Grieves throwing a punch that made his nose bleed.

—Is he your Housemaster? Mr. Goss inquired.

—No!

—Pity.

—He isn't anyone's Housemaster. He's got rooms in Fridaythorpe.

—How very peculiar, Mr. Goss said. This school of yours really does sound the most thumbs-backward establishment.

Mr. Fairclough laughed again:

—Whatever it is, it's the perfect garment for James.

—Oh, yes, tailor-made! Mr. Goss replied.

—No wonder he took your case, Mr. Fairclough said.

—Old boy's got to be over the moon James would—

Mr. Fairclough cleared his throat. Morgan stubbed out his cigarette and decided he would accept nothing else from either of them.

—The girls have gone through, said the Bishop from the corridor.

—Right, said Mr. Fairclough, grinding out his cigarette, ready for this?

Having conjured the coliseum, he took Morgan's shoulder and led him from the conservatory:

—This, too, shall pass.

In the library, the Bishop was sitting on one of the settees. Lucy was handing him a glass. Elizabeth and Agnes had taken positions on either side of him. Mr. Fairclough made for the sideboard, while Mr. Goss retreated to Agnes's side as if his batteries had discharged dangerously in her absence. The girls glanced at Morgan while trying to appear as if they were ignoring him. Lucy was recounting some bit of cathedral business. Mr. Fairclough poured two glasses and brought one to Morgan.

—Go on, he murmured. You look as though you could use it.

The Bishop's port was sweet, deep, ancient. It tasted less like drink and more like the blood of civilization. Morgan felt he could live on it.

The girls continued to eye him as Lucy's tale gave way to Elizabeth's report on the children's croup. Eventually Mr. Fairclough and Morgan drifted back to the sideboard, where Mr. Fairclough refilled their glasses. The clock in the corridor chimed ten.

—Father, Lucy said, isn't it time this boy was in bed?

The Bishop looked about as if he'd just remembered Morgan.

—Staying awake, Wilberforce?

—Yes, sir, Morgan said firmly.

—Be serious, Father, there are things we mean to discuss with you.

—Oh, yes?

—It isn't right to discuss them in front of this child.

—I'm not a child!

He looked to Agnes for support, but she avoided his gaze.

—You'd no trouble discussing any number of things in front of him earlier, the Bishop said.

—Oh, very well! Lucy snapped. On your head be it!

—The point, Agnes said, is that you're meant to be resting, not doing spiritual direction, and certainly not cleaning up messes for Jamie—

—Messes he didn't even make! Lucy added.

—Mr. Rollins was most distressed this afternoon to find you—

—Rollins is a ninny.

—Father! Elizabeth pleaded. You promised . . . you . . .

The Bishop relaxed his fighting stance and took her hands in his.

—Darling, I've no intention of breaking my word. But you can't expect me to sit here all summer clipping roses.

—That's exactly what you said you would do! Agnes retorted.

—There are many ways to recuperate, the Bishop said quietly.

He looked to each of his daughters, giving them the gaze Morgan impulsively labeled The Magnetron. It seemed to soothe them, with the exception of Agnes, who burst into tears. Her husband patted her hand.

—It's the baby, he explained.

Morgan filled his glass and Mr. Fairclough's a third time.

—All right then, Lucy said, what about Jamie?

—What more could there possibly be to discuss? the Bishop asked.

Lucy looked to Elizabeth, who looked to Mr. Fairclough.

—Father! Agnes exclaimed through her tears. Be serious for once!

—I'm perfectly serious.

—If Jamie's on the point of moving house up to Westmorland—

—Yorkshire, Morgan said.

Agnes tensed:

—then it won't be possible to wait and see any longer.

The Bishop frowned. Morgan wished he could bathe in the port, it was that deep.

—I've said they should have an epistolary courtship, Elizabeth added, but you know how Jamie is about letters.

—If my sisters interfered in my private life, Morgan blurted, I'd give 'em beans!

They looked at him as if he'd sprouted appendages.

—Wilberforce has a point, the Bishop said.

—He hasn't a shred of a point! Agnes retorted. He's an impertinent little boy, and this is exactly why he ought to be in bed.

Elizabeth shot her husband a look, and Mr. Fairclough took the glass from Morgan's hand. He felt robbed. There was still good port in it.

—Father, Agnes said firmly, if you won't do something about Jamie, I will.

—It sounds as though your brother is on the brink of ruin all round.

—Don't mock, Agnes cried. It's true!

—And what is his response to your sisterly concerns?

—Father! Agnes cried losing her composure. Oh, I wish I could shake you!

She began to pace, leaving Mr. Goss forlorn beside her empty place.

—You know Jamie listens to nothing and nobody! You *know* what happened the last time we tried to discuss it!

—Please can we not dwell on that? Lucy begged.

—And then, Agnes continued relentlessly, not a fortnight later he's whizzing off heaven-knows-where, on a day, I might add, he was meant to be looking in on you—

—I do not require this continual looking in on! the Bishop said. I'm not an invalid.

The girls contradicted him in one voice.

—And, Agnes said above the fray, next thing we hear, Jamie's accepted a *ludicrous* post at some *cesspool* in the middle of nowhere and is going to resign the most promising position he's ever had.

—Headmaster's a promotion, Morgan snapped. And the Academy is no cesspool!

Agnes turned on him, once his collaborator, now his foe:

—If you don't keep your nose out of our affairs, I shall box your ears.

—You can box away, but it doesn't make you right.

Lucy went to Agnes and put an arm around her waist:

—If this school of yours is so first-rate—

—I never said—

—then how do you explain the boy who killed himself in a barn—

—Lucy, really—

—committed suicide, Father, in a barn, all because of beastliness gone awry!

—You don't know anything! Morgan cried.

The room went silent. He turned to the sideboard. He hadn't been able to stop his mouth from speaking. What would stop his hands from striking? He took the half-empty port glass and drained it. He drained the other one. His blood pounded more slowly. He thought he might face them without committing an assault.

—It wasn't suicide, his mouth was saying. It was a—an accident. A bloody hellish accident.

No one shut him up. He could hear the blood in his ears, like being under the sea.

—And it wasn't beastliness. Spaulding was the best person you could know, and he was trying to save Rees. We both were. Nobody wanted to die. It was the stupid, bloody rafter that fell. And then Spaulding was dead instead of Rees, and it was the biggest swiz that's ever been, and if God cared about anything, instead of buggering off and leaving things to us, then he would have stopped it, but he didn't, and so Spaulding is dead when he shouldn't be, and I'm taking up space for no reason at all.

Still no one spoke. His mouth sticky and sour, he turned again to the sideboard; Mr. Fairclough blocked the decanter, but Morgan won the vessel and filled his glass with a proper measure. People spoke of draining a glass in one drink. A capital time to do just that. He concentrated on swallowing and breathing through his nose—a feat of skill now he attempted it—drawing the redness down his throat, the only thing in the entire world capable of soothing him. Snares and ruin might wait in every inch, but this elixir could fortify him from the inside against speaking when he shouldn't, acting when he shouldn't, thinking what he shouldn't, and most of all against loving when, where, and whom he shouldn't. This blood was already altering him, oral transfusion, depth and wisdom leeched from its oaks, feeding him with everything he longed for and lacked.

He set down the glass. Kerfuffle behind him, someone at his elbow leading him liquidly across the floor. The someone had magical feet of the soft-shoe, the type that whirled his sisters across dance floors and wore clothing that fit and dazzled everyone with smiles. The arm was guiding him now. Soon they would meet cheek against cheek. The waltz, his mother said, was a dance so scandalously intimate that one must dance it only with one's wedded husband. His wedded husband had him by the elbow, and he was swooning.

—Steady on, old boy.

His husband was supporting him, sweeping him away from Spaulding and out to a dance floor more cavernous and fine. Another hand took his other elbow. Suitor? Rival? Oh, ecstasy of a summer night! How many fingers would finger his—

—You listen to me, boy.

Pinching his face.

—I don't care what becomes of you, but you had better be perfectly clear about one thing. Are you following me?

—As bees to the honeypot.

Pinching his ears, stinging, twisting.

—If you cause my father one iota of harm, you will regret it bitterly.

—Mmm.

—Repeat what I said.

—If daddy is baddy, you'll go maddy.

A blow—ringing inside and out all at once. Then Lucy stood before him, lips more red than he could stand.

—I swear I'll give you a smack you'll never forget, she whispered.

Then someone was pulling her away and his husband was leading him by the waist to the upstairs dance floor. It wasn't a dance, though, was it?

—Where have you got him?

—St. Anne's.

People were talking and something was hurting on his face. Had it been Lucy that stung him?

—Come on, said the arm round his waist. Easy.

The arm pulled him up the way Rees had pulled him when he slid down the grass, when his own arm didn't work. But his arms worked now, and he was holding on to the bathroom basin, and the man was pressing a wet flannel against his face, and it was like every kind of reprieve there was to have. Except Spaulding wasn't having a reprieve. His face was still broken open, the blood goring onto the floor. Had they put it back inside when they buried him? It wasn't right for him to be mauled that way. To die was bad enough, but to have his head ripped open, and for nothing except being brave enough to climb all the way up there and cut down the rope to let Rees away from . . . Why couldn't he have caught him? If Spaulding had fallen a foot closer, all that blood would have stayed inside.

He was being leaned over the toilet, and it was all pouring out of his mouth, that precious casketed gold, down the pipes, never to return, and it had been so very good going in. His cheeks stung, his nose full, his throat tight against everything.

—Is he really dead forever?

He couldn't stop it. He couldn't stop anything.

—It would seem.

—But he was so alive! He had everything . . . He was *alive*!

He was being lifted to his feet and supported to the bed. He collapsed across it and clung as it spun, and a weight like a slab of marble fell upon him.

A candle in darkness. A ghost in dressing gown loomed giant above him. He gasped.

—Take this, the ghost said.

A warm hand pressed pellet into one palm, glass into the other.

—A phial. Like Romeo. Will everyone think I'm dead?

He put the pellet on his tongue and sipped from the glass.

—I think perhaps you'll wish you were in the morning.

A ghost of a smile on that face. Could ghosts have ghosts of smiles? Did that make them doubly spectral, or did a ghost of a ghost add up to something alive?

—Lie down.

His limbs obeyed. Was he possessed? The ghost touched him, rubbing his forehead and holding it. What did it want with him?

His forehead warmed beneath the hand, tingling, but not like the slap. And then a kind of cloak was upon him. Sleep was coming, but it held no danger, not beneath this cloak. Here only the benign, the naïve, the . . .

He sat at the Bishop's breakfast table wishing he were dead.

—I'd offer you the hair of the dog, the Bishop said, but somehow I feel that would be irresponsible.

He said grace and poured black coffee into Morgan's cup. Morgan had never tasted coffee, but the smell of it was the only thing in the room that did not make him want to retch. He sipped it tentatively; it did not burn his tongue or turn his stomach. A slice of toast clanged onto his plate.

—Eat that, the Bishop said, with or without the butter.

Definitely without. The very word *butter* sent an oleaginous shiver down his neck. The Bishop scraped marmalade across his own toast with the vigor of one stripping metal. He chewed at a most offensive volume.

—I propose we begin right away, the Bishop said, before you wake up and start thinking again.

—Sir, whatever you're going to do, please could you do it as quickly as possible? I know it's part of the punishment to make you wait, but to be perfectly honest, I can't endure it today. Not without going mad.

The Bishop made a sound like a snort.

—Can't have that. I'm not kitted out for Bedlam. Right, it's settled.

Breakfast seemed to be over, and they'd only just sat down.

—Breakfast, then torture.

—Sit down before you fall down, the Bishop said as they reached the study.

Morgan collapsed into one of the spindle chairs. The Bishop adjusted the curtains, admitting a painful quantity of sunlight, and then sat in the other chair. Morgan braced himself. First the inquisition, hopefully brief. Next the rebuke. Finally, the punishment. He'd no idea how he'd cope in his present state, but waiting would be worse. The Bishop folded his hands and stared at them. Time passed.

—I'm very sorry, sir, Morgan began.

It usually helped if you indicated your intention not to make excuses.

—I've no excuse.

The Bishop looked up from his knees.

—Perhaps you'd like to tell me what you're sorry for?

Had he done other things he'd no memory now of doing? Stumblingly, he forced himself to expand the apology. He was sorry for having behaved so badly at dinner, for having drunk so much, for having spoken in such an ungentlemanly manner to the Bishop's daughters. It was all insult upon injury, he knew, as the Bishop was being so charitable as to keep him a few days until his father could sort out where he was to go.

—Oh, for goodness' sake, Wilberforce! I thought we were past this.

He felt he might blub again, and in the light of morning!

—It isn't safe to leave you on your own, it would appear, even to sleep.

—But I didn't do anything in my sleep! I didn't even—

He blushed.

—No, the Bishop said tartly, I should think you didn't in that condition.

He wished the lid of the tomb that had pressed last night would fall and crush him now. He wished another rafter in the godforsaken barn would fall upon him and obliterate him. Was that what he had been hoping without knowing it when he took Polly there? That somehow the business that had gone wrong before would go right this time and take him where he deserved to go?

—You know perfectly well I'm not keeping you here until your father makes arrangements. Don't you?

He nodded, willing his eyes to clear.

—Then let us hear you say why you are here.

He swallowed.

—I don't know, sir.

—Try.

Refusing to release him, refusing to let him drift or disguise.

—I've gone wrong somewhere.

—Yes?

—And everything's ruined.

—Everything?

—Everything I can see. Except . . .

—Except?

—Except you act as though it isn't entirely.

—Do I?

—Like Dr. Sebastian acted about St. Stephen's . . . Is it really as bad as the girls made it sound?

—I've the impression you don't think St. Stephen's is beyond hope.

—It can't be! There've been some messes, I grant you, but it isn't all rotten. There's plenty of good there!

—James will be relieved to hear it.

—All it needs is someone to sort it out. It wants that!

—When you say *sort it out*, are you using the term as you used it yesterday when speaking of your father?

He felt the toast crawling his throat.

—I suppose so.

The Bishop nodded.

—And what should this sorting out entail?

—I don't know, sir. I'm not Dr. Sebastian!

The Bishop pressed his fingers together and waited for Morgan to continue.

—Well, the first thing he ought to do is sack some people.

—Such as?

Morgan caught himself before falling into the trap.

—If Dr. Sebastian wants a turncoat in the Academy, he can have the nerve to ask the questions himself, and then he can ask someone else because I'm not a sneak and I'm no longer a pupil.

The Bishop tapped his fingers:

—You've made a great number of assumptions. Do you care to find out if any are true?

—Of course, they're true!

—Has anyone told you you're no longer a pupil at St. Stephen's?

Morgan boggled at him.

—Second, if you support James's efforts, how is it turning traitor to aid him?

He continued to boggle.

—Third, I thought I made it clear that what passes between you and me is strictly confidential. The seal of the confessional, if you like.

—You didn't make that clear at all.

—Then I apologize, the Bishop said. Now, I think we ought not divert ourselves any longer. James will sort out St. Stephen's. Who is going to sort out you?

Morgan looked away, his voice suddenly husky:

—I don't think I can be sorted out. And that isn't feeling sorry for myself. It's the truth.

Sometimes when you couldn't look at people, it helped to look just above them. Then they thought you were looking at them, but you didn't actually have to.

—You aren't beyond hope.

The Bishop leaned forward and put a hand on Morgan's wrist. The gesture unleashed all he'd worked to repel, and his eyes surrendered to everything English boys were trained to resist.

—I wish that were true, sir.

—It is true.

—If someone could sort me out, it would be a miracle. But I don't believe in miracles.

—That doesn't mean they never happen, the Bishop said gently.

—If you . . . knew someone . . . who could sort out a person like me . . . It's much worse than I've said. It's a ruin, one disaster on top of another . . . but if you knew someone, perhaps . . .

—I know someone.

Morgan reined in his breath. He stopped looking above the Bishop's head and allowed his gaze to fall to the man's face. Was he misunderstanding this as he misunderstood so much?

—You haven't misunderstood.

—But we only met two days ago. I'm nothing to you. And what about your health?

The Bishop sucked in his cheeks:

—If you understood all my motivations, provided they could be understood, what difference would it make?

What difference *would* it make? Either he suspected the man of cynical designs, or he trusted the man to deal rightly with him. Everything else was decoration.

—Your daughter said you were a commander.

—Besides a bishop, you mean?

—It's what she called your work.

—Spiritual direction? That doesn't involve commanding. If anything, it involves standing beside people and helping them work out how the Holy Spirit is directing them. But you needn't worry about that.

The Bishop stood as if to signal the end of the interview.

—I've no intention of trapping you or otherwise inflicting religious notions you find so distressing.

—They don't distress me—

—You've asked two things of me, nothing more. Yesterday you asked me to stand with you. Have I managed that?

He thought of yesterday, of the Bishop standing by while he behaved . . . however he had behaved . . . not losing his temper, not granting the girls' requests to send him to bed; he thought of the figure in dressing gown bringing him water and aspirin; he thought of the Bishop this morning, shepherding him from breakfast to the study, standing now with him in the light that slammed through the windows.

—Yes, sir.

—And today you've asked me to help sort you out. Is that right?

Morgan breathed in, and out.

—Will you put yourself in my hands?

Was he not already in those hands?

—Entirely in my hands.

Could he? The Bishop opened his palms, wide and creased.

—You don't know these hands, but then you didn't always know your father's hands. Did you?

Morgan shook his head.

—Yes, sir. I mean, I'll do it.

The Bishop struck a gaze deep into him. He extended his right hand to Morgan. Feeling it might transmit electricity, Morgan took it.

It was warm and dry. It clasped his, like a tutor who proposed to work him past his current abilities, like a father who knew him better than he knew himself and would not stand for inferior performance.

—This isn't a performance, the Bishop said.

Had he spoken aloud again?

—It will go much easier if you can keep this moment in that head of yours and remember that you have put yourself in my hands, voluntarily and with no coercion. Remember that this is your project, not mine. You're free to leave whenever you wish.

Morgan felt himself grinning.

—I suppose I do get confused rather quickly.

—Only when you start behaving like the sullen schoolboy we saw so much of yesterday.

Morgan took back his hand. This was going to be unpleasant.

—Right, the Bishop said, tapping the desk, if we are to go on together, you'd best be called by your Christian name.

A surge of alarm.

—Does that distress you?

—No, sir. And I really wish you'd stop—

—It's Morgan, isn't it?

He could only nod. The only man besides his father to call him that had been . . . Mr. Grieves. And how long ago?

—I must now obey my physician for an interval. In the meantime, you may take as much exercise as you can stand, without diverting my staff please, and then you may sit in the library and begin your written account.

—Of what, sir?

—Of everything that needs sorting out.

—Oh, sir! I couldn't possibly write it down in words.

—Is your hand deformed?

With that the Bishop unlocked the study door and held it. Feeling suddenly dejected, Morgan dragged himself from the room.

—Courage, the Bishop said. The port will have finished punishing you by lunchtime, I should think.

He felt a flush of shame at the word *punishing*, as if he were a small boy shy of the subject. They reached the corridor, where Mrs. Hallows stood, apparently awaiting the Bishop.

—And, Morgan, the man said, only your right hand today. These eyes need gentle treatment.

The Bishop scanned the page Morgan had painfully produced and then turned it over. Finding the reverse blank, he collapsed into the chair behind his desk.

—Morgan, he said.

Morgan winced at the alien sound of his own name, and spoken with such disappointment. The Bishop pursed his lips and allowed his gaze to return to the document.

—Unsuitable conduct? Whom did you allow to write this? The sullen schoolboy?

He disliked the appellation. In point of fact, it was a civilized and legible accounting. It had seemed decent when he read it over. He didn't recall anything sullen about it.

The Bishop set the paper wearily on the blotter.

—If you insist, I suppose we must take you as we find you. For the moment.

He poked in a drawer, produced a pair of reading glasses, apparently alien, and placed them on his nose.

—Item one: unsuitable conduct last night. Item two: unsuitable conduct on Patron's Day. Item three: general disobedience. Item four: failing to honor one's father.

The Bishop peered over the glasses:

—*One's*, Morgan?

—What's wrong with that?

—Can you not write *my father*?

Morgan had nothing to say. The Bishop resumed his recitation.

—Item five: sloth. Item six: luxuria. Item seven: failing always to tell the truth. Item eight: miscellaneous unsuitable conduct. You've quite a flair for generalization, haven't you, boy?

And he was back with Burton-Lee, facing him as he'd faced him the final term of his first year, the term Burton interposed himself between Morgan and Silk, the term Burton oppressed Morgan with the tacit goal of shielding him from a more perilous oppression in Study No. 4.

—Not much of a sorting out, is it? the Bishop continued. Disobedience, disrespect, laziness, lying, lust, and behaving in an incorrect manner at an incorrect time. How very pedestrian!

Was the Bishop mocking him, or was he disappointed in Morgan's misdeeds? Perhaps he was accustomed to dealing with criminals.

—It isn't murder, I grant you.

—Would that it were! the Bishop retorted. At least then *one* could grapple with it. Instead you've provided a most insidious accounting. When was the last time you told the unvarnished truth?

—I haven't lied! I don't lie. Unless . . .

—Let us see if you can tell the truth about the first item, the Bishop said. Let's move beyond this delightful euphemism of yours and hear exactly what was unsuitable in your conduct last night.

Morgan shifted in the chair. The spindles were hitting his back in an awkward place. How had he got himself trapped in a verbal confession, before a bishop, in a locked study? He tried to summon the little courage at his command. The Bishop was still sitting there, as if he had nothing to do the entire afternoon except wait for Morgan to explain matters to his liking.

—I drank far too much, Morgan said. And then I began to say things I didn't mean.

—Didn't you?

—Of course not!

—Truth, Morgan.

—I . . .

—What do you remember saying?

—I poked my nose into the conversation about your family. It was none of my business.

—Perhaps not, the Bishop said, but I don't recall your issuing advice. I seem to recall your saying you wouldn't like it if your own sisters interfered in your private life the way that my daughters were interfering with their brother's.

—It wasn't for me to say.

—Why not? the Bishop replied. They were carrying on appallingly. It did them good to hear the impression they were giving.

Stunned, Morgan looked for traps.

—Your remarks were certainly unwelcome, but they weren't untrue, and as far as I can see they were heartfelt. Same for your spirited defense of St. Stephen's.

—It was so awkward, sir. I couldn't bear to hear them talk that way about it, or about . . .

—Go on.

The Magnetron held him in its heating, hurting beam.

—I lost my temper. I shouldn't have said all that about what happened.

—You were there when that boy died?

Morgan nodded.

What did you say his name was?

—Spaulding.

It wasn't right to say the name out loud.

—Spaulding, the Bishop repeated. Did you know his Christian name?

—Charles.

—Charles Spaulding, may he rest in peace.

He was speaking of someone else, not the Spaulding Morgan knew, the person he'd tackled across the football pitch, the person who'd held him so deliciously in the Hermes Balcony, the person whose head—

—So, the Bishop said quietly, you were close enough to know his Christian name. You saw him die. Had you ever seen anyone die before?

This wasn't what they were meant to be talking about.

—It's exactly what we're meant to be talking about, the Bishop said.

—No, Morgan replied bitterly, I hadn't seen anyone die. And I'm not going to talk about it. The point is—was—the girls were talking rubbish, and I lost my temper about it, and it was wrong. That's it!

—What's wrong with telling someone off when they're talking rubbish about someone you knew well who is no longer alive to defend himself?

There was a giant pit somewhere, if only he could sense its edges.

—As far as I can see, the Bishop continued mildly, you behaved with admirable restraint. You were forced to listen to an overly intimate discussion of your future Headmaster, a man for whom you feel some degree of respect, unless I'm very much mistaken.

Morgan did not contradict him.

—Then you had to endure some unkind gossip about your school and about boys of your acquaintance. Finally, you had to put up with humiliating snubs from my daughters. It's little wonder you took advantage of the decanter.

—I knew it wasn't allowed, sir.

—Had I forbidden you to drink my port?

He thought.

—No, sir.

—Had I told you to stop what you were doing?

361

—No, sir.

—Yet, you thought you were doing the forbidden and you did it anyway. That was one way of putting it.

—You were angry?

—No, sir.

—Try again.

Sod it.

—I was furious. Everyone was being perfectly horrible, and so I thought sod them, and sod this, so that's why I acted so . . . unsuitably.

The Bishop stood up and turned to the window.

—You certainly lost control of yourself with the port, which led to the general loss of control, but I'm afraid I can't agree with your verdict. Your behavior was entirely suitable. If apologies are owed, I'd expect them from my daughters. Alas, we may wait some time for those. So—

The Bishop turned back to the room.

—the best we can add to your account is a charge of rudeness under provocation, and in defense of a place and a person who meant a good deal to you.

He was surrounded by snares, no inch of floor safe, but all invisible, shifting.

—It isn't very impressive, is it? the Bishop asked. What do you imagine the punishment ought to be?

Again, Morgan childishly blushed at the word.

—The JCR would take a dim view, he said. Drinking, six. To excess, extras. Rudeness, getting above oneself, another six.

—At once?

Morgan chuckled grimly.

—Well, the Bishop said, fortunately for you, or perhaps unfortunately, the JCR do not sit in judgment of your behavior last night. I do. And it's my view that the circumstances were extenuating and that the port has punished you sufficiently.

He didn't like the way the Bishop used that verb with the object *you*. It sounded personal.

—The interesting thing about last night, the Bishop mused, was what became of the sullen schoolboy.

Apparently he was going to have to put up with that distasteful label.

—He turned spiteful?

—He wasn't there. Early on we had Casanova—and I'm quite interested in that instinct of yours to flirt your way out of uncomfortable
situations—and later we had—

—The drunk.

—The impassioned defender. You see, I thought that when the subject
of St. Stephen's arose, the sullen schoolboy would treat it with scorn. But
the alarm you plainly experienced at the suggestion that your new Headmaster might abandon the school after a year, that is not the response of
a boy who cares for nothing.

Morgan's voice sounded too small for the room:

—It isn't done to care, not since the War. They were the ones who
mattered, and they're dead.

—What about those of us left alive?

Morgan shrugged.

—Yes, well, I see we've strayed to St. Stephen's again when we're here
to talk about you. However, I've a feeling you've had about as much conversation as you're accustomed to having in a year of Sundays strung
together.

The Bishop consulted a pocket watch.

—And I see it's nearly four. Fairclough will be here shortly. It's time
you got changed.

—For what, sir?

—A run and a bathe. My son-in-law is a keen cross-country man. You
look distressed. Still feeling the port?

—Sir, I'm not distressed. It's only that I can't think what I'll say to
Mr. Fairclough after how I acted.

—If it discomfits you, consider it part of your punishment.

He couldn't decide which he disliked more: suggestions of his distress
or references to his punishment. The Bishop unlocked the door and
shooed him out of it.

—We'll speak again after tea.

Morgan tripped down the stairs.

—And Morgan? the Bishop called.

—Sir?

The parting shot was becoming a signature move.

—I shall be most curious to hear where you've acquired copies of *The
Pearl*, and who procured them for you.

363

The Bishop was right about Mr. Fairclough: he delighted in the cross-country run. After a trying quarter of an hour, the port released its hold on Morgan, freeing him to enjoy the exercise. Mr. Fairclough led him on a varied but essentially pleasurable trot through field and woodland, returning periodically to a stretch of towpath along the canal, or was it several canals? To Morgan's relief, Mr. Fairclough did not mention the night before. He rarely spoke, except to deliver scenic commentary. Morgan couldn't decide if he was being trained up by a keen master, minded by a masculine nanny, or taken out for exercise like some borrowed hound. The run slowed along a deserted stretch of canal, and Mr. Fairclough mounted a footbridge. After surveying the horizon, he announced it safe to bathe. They stripped off and plunged into the water, cold and muddy underfoot. Mr. Fairclough suggested they swim to the next bridge and back, so they proceeded, pacing one another.

As disagreeable as it had been to sit trapped in the Bishop's study being forced to give an accounting of himself, he felt with each stroke through the water that something in the outside world was changing. The Bishop had judged him less harshly than he had judged himself, yet in another sense the interview had been harrowing. The Bishop had bored into . . . into more than his character—into the inmost tree ring of his self! And then just as Morgan had escaped the room, the Bishop had made that most objectionable remark. The man who had defended his defense of Spaulding would not defend his reading material. So the allegiance Morgan had sensed was only an illusion designed to make him lower his guard. If the Bishop thought he would admit to anything, he had another think coming!

His arms were shaking, unaccustomed to the breaststroke. He switched to crawl and plunged his face into the murky canal. This was his project. He could leave whenever he wished. He had put himself into the Bishop's hands and asked to be sorted out. That had all sounded captivating under the weight of an arduous swollen head, but how did he imagine things would progress now? Did the Bishop propose to cross-question him each morning, noon, and night until he'd excavated Morgan's crimes? The rest of his offenses would not shrivel under the Bishop's judgment. Breath by breath the Bishop would trap him into confessing himself; next he would remonstrate, voicing disapproval Morgan could have cited himself months ago, and then? Perhaps the Bishop possessed some clerical sleight of hand that would detach Morgan from his failings and send him home to his father a well-scrubbed, purged specimen. In sum, predictable and vacant.

He knew very well what people like the Bishop, like his father, like Grieves, would think if they really knew him, but even though he sensed he'd gone wrong, he didn't believe in his inmost tree ring that his deeds were as consequential as they thought. There was no war on, and even if there were, who'd fight over such a gas-filled, wire-tangled yard of no-man's-land?

But he'd taken a wrong breath and was now standing ankle deep in silt, coughing the canal from his lungs. Mr. Fairclough stood by, ready to beat him across the shoulders if necessary. It did not prove necessary. When he recovered, Fairclough proposed a race to the bridge a few hundred yards away. Morgan leapt forward and kicked with all his might, turning his head only every sixth stroke for a sip of air. At last, his hand scraped masonry, but Fairclough was already leaning under the footbridge, gazing up at the bricks.

He could win at nothing. This wasn't something he could think his way out of.

He caught his breath and stretched under the water, his head against the canal bank. Fairclough floated beside him, eyes closed.

—Do you trust the Bishop? Morgan asked.

—Oh, his companion replied, it rather depends on the circumstances, doesn't it? I wouldn't trust him to oversee the ledger of a tuckshop, let alone interpret accrual accounting, but in anything that doesn't involve arithmetic, I trust him.

—How far do you trust him?

—How far do you need to trust him? Fairclough asked.

Morgan allowed his body to float, his front breaking the surface.

—A long way, possibly.

Fairclough made a sound like understanding.

—Would you trust him to keep a confidence?

—Implicitly.

—Even from his son?

—If the Bishop gives his assurance, you can trust it.

—But, Morgan persisted, it's a bit more complicated than that.

—Is it?

—What if he asks about something that goes beyond what I've done?

—Should you peach on your friends, you mean?

Morgan was relieved not to have to say it. Fairclough seemed to ponder the matter. He was still pondering when he began paddling back to the footbridge that sheltered their clothes.

—You aren't at school here, are you? Fairclough said.

Morgan conceded that he wasn't. Certainly not given the way the Bishop had responded to his drunkenness.

—Perhaps you ought to take advantage of that.

Morgan kept pace beside the man as the bank where they'd left their things came into view.

—He's the most peculiar clergyman I've ever met! Morgan blurted.

Fairclough laughed loudly and switched to backstroke:

—He's certainly a character, but for all that he's thoroughly orthodox.

Morgan felt his thoughts being swirled around like the mud beneath them.

—Sir, you aren't one of those people he . . . sorted out, are you?

Fairclough laughed again.

—Oh, I think having one's father-in-law hear one's confession would be taking things a bit far, don't you?

They regained their clothes, pulled them on over wet skin, and took off at a light trot down towpath. When they reached the Bishop's garden, Fairclough made his farewell.

—You aren't coming to tea? Morgan said, feeling suddenly anxious.

—Not like this. And I'm expected home.

A flood of questions filled Morgan's mind: where the Faircloughs lived, how Mr. Fairclough made his living, how long he had been part of the Bishop's family, how old his children were, along with countless others he could have asked at any point in the afternoon had he not been so thoroughly occupied with himself.

—Are you comfortable? Fairclough asked.

Morgan replied that he was. It had been an excellent outing. Belatedly he thanked the man for taking the time and trouble to—

—I mean in your room, Fairclough said.

Was he, comfortable?

—It's a fine room.

—St. Anne's always leaves me feeling a bit adrift.

Someone had said something about St. Anne last night, hadn't they?

—Where does St. Anne come into it, sir?

Mr. Fairclough released his right leg and began to stretch his left.

—The name of the room, surely you've noticed? They've all got names. I've slept a few nights in St. Anne's, but it always feels rather loose somehow, as if someone else might be knocking around in there with you.

Morgan shivered.

—If it gets on your nerves, ask Mrs. Hallows if you can move to St. Mark's.

—What's that like?

—Compact, like the gospel.

Morgan approached his room with a trepidation that annoyed him. It had just gone six o'clock. There was nothing to make a person uneasy in a sun-soaked bedroom overlooking a garden.

What kind of someone else had Mr. Fairclough meant, knocking around with him? Morgan reminded himself that he didn't believe in ghosts, certainly not in the warm light of summer.

He rinsed under the bath taps and toweled dry. When he returned to the bedroom, Droit was lounging across the counterpane trimming his nails with a penknife. Morgan's scalp prickled.

—Now listen, you, Droit said.

—Don't start.

—Get dressed, Droit told him. And for sod-all sake look smart. Enough of this scrapping about.

Shame descended. Had he been looking scrappy? Last night had they thought him callow, or lacking taste?

—I'd think a bit less about what those harpies thought of you, Droit said, and a bit more about how you're going to survive the next interval. And if you're still nursing those feeble notions of yours, you can jolly well un-nurse them.

—Why can't I simply tell him the truth?

Droit looked as if he had suggested taking up prostitution. Morgan rallied a defense, but Droit folded his knife and propped himself up on an elbow:

—Since I can see you've had a time of it, I'll keep things simple. Just what do you imagine is the point of this cozy exercise with your Bishop person?

Morgan couldn't think of a way to explain it without sounding wet.

—You can't, can you? Because not only *is* it wet, but it lacks purpose. Or rather it lacks a purpose for you. For him, the old dodger, he gets to be a hero to Jamsieboy, he gets to relieve the boredom of having to recuperate his silly health, and he gets to enliven his dry old years with spicy accounts.

—He isn't like that.

—Oh, no? What does a withered old widower know of *The Pearl*? This item just fancies locking himself away with you, rattling you, and making you tell him things he has no business knowing.

He'd bathed, but a film clung to him. Some foul measure of canal sludge still fermented in his stomach.

—He's nothing to be afraid of, Dicky. He can't do anything to you, unless you let him.

—What would he do to me?

Droit got up from the bed and brushed off his clothes:

—Calm down. I'm only saying you hold the cards here, so there's no reason to pander to his ploys. Don't sulk. And don't wear that tie.

Morgan set his House tie back on the hanger. Droit had a point. He'd left last night behind, so he shouldn't appear in the same ensemble again. Besides, it made him feel he were going to Prep, or for an evening in the Flea's study. He was no longer the little boy who secretly looked forward to Burton's extra-tu, and he had nothing to do with the creature who, while there, wondered what Silk was doing and whether he thought at all of Morgan.

He was seventeen years old and no longer at school. He selected the tie he wore on exeat. He combed his hair. It was the best he could do.

 In the summerhouse they sat knee to knee, just as REN supposedly sat with boys he intended to purge. Morgan drew the swing back. The Bishop could corner him all he wanted. He could grab his wrist. He could breathe all over him. Morgan had made up his mind: he was sticking to his story about *The Pearl*, and no stare from the Bishop could force him to renege.

Except the Bishop was moving his own chair backwards. He now sat several arm's lengths away.

The man had ended tea abruptly, suggesting they adjourn to the summerhouse and lance the boil before Morgan worked himself into a state of indigestion. Now the man was staring at his hands and waiting for Morgan to sally out to exposed ground. Well, he wasn't born yesterday. He dispatched a skirmisher:

—Sir, who was St. Anne?

The Bishop looked up in surprise.

—The mother of Our Lady.

—Why are the rooms named after saints?

The Bishop blinked.

—It was my wife's innovation.

—Why did you never remarry, sir, if it isn't too impertinent a question?

—It is exceedingly impertinent.

The Bishop crossed his legs.

—Was her name Anne? Morgan pursued.

The Bishop's eyes narrowed. Were clergy allowed to glare?

—It was Clara, he said.

—I'm sorry she died. Why did you put me in St. Anne's?

Firing questions was almost entertaining. Why had he not taken command sooner?

—It's bright, the Bishop replied, and it has an adjoining bathroom and a soothing outlook. Are you uncomfortable there?

—No, sir.

The Bishop did not look confident of his reply.

—Remember, the Bishop said quietly, this is your project, not mine. You can leave whenever you wish.

He could! He was in the driver's seat and had been from the beginning.

—You can catch a train to London tonight. I can have a taxi here in half an hour.

That wasn't what he meant exactly. He only meant he didn't have to sit and endure twisted conversations. The Bishop gazed at the wisteria covering the summerhouse:

—You and I both know what you were referring to when you alluded to Lord Crim-Con—

Morgan flushed to his eyeballs.

—and the good Etoniensis. Perhaps you're wondering how a bishop should know anything about Victorian pornography, but when I was your age, I wasn't a bishop. And Queen Victoria was still on the throne.

Morgan's balance wavered. The Bishop twisted his cuff links idly:

—I didn't realize there were still copies of the old rag floating about, but apparently it's like Count Dracula.

—Bloodthirsty?

—Undead.

Morgan wished the swing were lower so he could keep his heels on the planks of the gazebo.

—I'm sure it's dreadfully immoral, he said, but I don't see what harm it does. It's only words.

—Many a man has made the pen his sword.

Morgan leaned forward and planted his feet:

—It's just a rude magazine. We don't pass it around. We only read it for a laugh.

—Surely for something more than a laugh.

—Well, if you really want me to say it, we read it for a wank.

The Bishop listened with maddening serenity.

—And I know it's the sin of Onan and all that, but can you really say it's that wicked? Think of the alternatives.

—Fornication, you mean?

What a word for a bishop to use!

—I—you said it. So given that, is a bit of a wank such a terrible thing?

—Are you asking me or telling me?

—I'm telling you!

The Bishop nodded.

—All right, I'm asking.

—Very well, the Bishop said, if you're asking. Is *a bit of a wank* such a terrible thing?

Morgan squared his jaw. If the Bishop thought he would embarrass him into dropping it, he was mistaken.

—I would say, the Bishop began, it may not be *such* a terrible thing so long as it doesn't encourage mental corruption or become a substitute for congress with one's wife.

—I haven't got a wife.

—Which is why I say it may not be the worst of options before you. Onanism is not quite the same as masturbation, by the way.

He felt he would start bleeding from his ears!

—I've no idea what you mean.

—Onan's sin was coitus interruptus, the Bishop replied outrageously, spilling his seed, which the Hebrews thought contained an entire human life, on barren ground, something akin to murder.

—That's bunk, Morgan declared. It takes two to make a baby.

—Indeed.

—So the sin makes no sense!

—But of course, the real problem with Onan was his disobedience and selfishness.

The Bishop looked at him as if that answered everything. Morgan set his jaw:

—You can't stop there and expect me to understand. I'm no clergyman.

—No, the Bishop replied wryly. But you might recall that Onan's brother had died.

—*So?*

—So Onan was expected to impregnate—

—Sir!

—his sister-in-law Tamar to ensure the continuation of his brother's line. Onan enjoyed coitus with her, but then betrayed her by withdrawing prematurely, on more than one occasion.

Whoever would, or *could* . . . ?

—So in disobeying strict custom, he not only killed the family line of Tamar and his brother, but he took grave advantage of his sister-in-law, a young widow helpless but for the support of her husband's family.

Cad.

—The same cannot be said, the Bishop continued, of seventeen-year-old boys releasing their frustrations with *a bit of a wank.*

—Then why do grown-ups make such a commotion about it? Morgan retorted.

—Do they? Were you punished for it as a child?

—No! I never—no.

He held the cards. He could determine the moves.

—At school, then?

—No, sir.

—In that case, I fail to see the commotion, the Bishop said. But we were speaking of the exceedingly blue compositions by men calling themselves Lord Crim-Con and Etoniensis. The latter was Swinburne, by the way.

Morgan had never heard so many appalling things in his life. The Bishop took out a handkerchief and used it on the back of his neck:

—The problem with Lord Crim-Con is not that boys find it arousing, or even that someone has written explicitly about what we normally reserve for our private relationships. The problem is what exposure to such very degrading material does to the reader, in particular the young reader.

—What's so degrading about it? Those people are having a jolly good time.

—Are they? the Bishop pursued, unabashed. I recall it as frightfully mechanical and repetitive, this part into that one, ad nauseam.

—I suppose it's meant to be all procreational, your wife closing her eyes and thinking of England.

—Of all the—if you'd even the *slightest* idea, I can't believe you'd speak that way.

The Bishop got up and stepped to the edge of the gazebo. Blood rushed across Morgan's skin.

—Forgive me, the Bishop said to the canal. I'm afraid I was insufficiently prepared for a discussion of marital intimacies.

—I suppose you planned to tell me off and leave it at that.

The Bishop turned and looked at him with . . . pity.

—If only you knew how much I understand.

Morgan wanted to punch someone. If the Bishop weren't old and unwell—

—Sexual union is a gift from God. Perhaps when you've spent some more time with Mr. Donne, or the Song of Solomon, you'll begin to appreciate it for yourself.

—You can be awfully patronizing, Morgan retorted. I'm not a child.

—Aren't you?

—No, I bloody well am not! I've made *l'amour complet*, and it was the best thing I've ever done.

—*L'amour complet?* Ah. Yes, I was wondering when we'd come to that.

Morgan opened his mouth to reply, but nothing came out. The leaves had given way beneath him and he was plunging headlong into the pit.

Mrs. Hallows brought a jug, tumblers, and a candle covered with a hurricane glass. Darkness had fallen, leaving the fireflies, the candle, and thin bleedings from the house their only illumination. She went away, and the Bishop set a tumbler before him. Morgan ignored it.

—Whatever you've got to say, Morgan began, I won't tolerate anyone rubbishing her.

The Bishop sipped from his glass.

—She's a lovely girl, and before you say it, she isn't fast or loose or anything else.

Crickets punctuated the darkness. The candle flickered across the Bishop's figure.

—And the other thing you've got to understand is that she consented, more than once. She said she wanted to. She even said when we should so she wouldn't get a baby.

—What went wrong?

—Nothing went wrong.

—I'm sorry, the Bishop said, I was under the impression that shortly afterwards you found yourself in your Headmaster's study forced to give a most awkward explanation.

—That was nothing to do with Polly!

—My mistake.

—We love each other!

—I'm delighted to hear it.

Morgan couldn't see the Bishop's face clearly enough to judge his tone.

—May I ask how she took the news of your departure from St. Stephen's?

—She . . . I told you it was all terrifically sudden. No one even told me what—

—Yes, forgive me. How do you imagine she will take it when she receives your letter?

—What letter?

—The one you wrote her, naturally.

—I haven't written any letters!

—How very callous.

They sat in silence. Morgan willed his temper to subside. Sweat trickled down his neck. He decided to loosen his tie and let the Bishop be scandalized.

—This girl is in love with you, the Bishop resumed quietly. She trusted you with the most intimate part of herself. She bestowed on you the singular honor of being the first to know her thus, even before her husband, and you disappear without a word to her, not even a sentence on a postcard?

He wanted it to stop. He willed it to stop. He would wake up shortly and find himself . . . *himself* again, not this creature the Bishop described with voice as mild as cordial. He drew his knees to his chest.

—You must have been discountenanced indeed not to think of it, the Bishop said. It must be painful for you to be separated from her, loving her as you do.

If he could murder the creature with thought alone, he would.

—Morgan?

That name like broken glass under his eyelids.

—Please don't call me . . .

He could hear the Bishop standing, but he couldn't raise his face.

—It isn't Morgan Wilberforce we speak of?

Knuckles to rainbows against his eyes.

—Has he got a name, this fellow?

If only he did. Droit may have been with him, but he couldn't pin it on Droit. He couldn't pin it on anyone.

—It must be a measure of the crisis this boy was undergoing that it made him forget the girl he loved.

—He's a cad, Morgan said bitterly. He wouldn't know love if it punched him in the face.

—He exaggerated his feelings in the excitement of the act, perhaps? Many a boy has. Sexual congress is strong drink. He may not have the maturity to handle it.

—Obviously not.

—But there's no reason he couldn't write to the young lady now and attempt to make amends for leaving so abruptly.

—It'd take more than an apology, after everything.

—Everything?

The wool of his blazer oppressed him, to look at and to feel.

—It was bad enough how it ended, with that beast Kilby barging in.

A voice not his own thinly narrated: Kilby and the master bursting into the barn, demolishing the atmosphere he'd struggled to establish; how he'd labored to soothe her, to reassure her, to make her see what they'd done as the wonderful thing he knew it was, and just as he'd managed it, in they barged like Roman soldiers, clomping over everything with their hideous boots, dragging them down the hill like criminals—which he no doubt deserved, but not her, never her!—sending her home alone. To think of Polly abandoned—

Something was cutting him from the inside. He punched at his skull until it rang with pain. A dry hand surrounded his wrists, stopping the blows.

—Why was she crying?

The voice softer than the hands, deft enough to slice out his heart.

—Because . . .

He tugged at his hair until his neck seized:

—Because it wasn't just as they'd planned, not in the instant. It almost was.

She said yes, but then she didn't, and just as he . . .

—He couldn't stop.

—Couldn't? Or wouldn't?

—Didn't.

Fingernails into wrist. But the dry hands had him, only this time they held with authority.

—Stop that, the voice said.

—I deserve it, and worse!

In his head a single word, silent but breaking his throat: *Help*. The hands fell to his shoulders—*Help*—pulling him out of the ball—*Help!*—forcing him to sit upright.

—I've got you.

Hauled to his feet, dragged stumbling into the thick, dark garden.

—Breathe in and out.

His lungs like pierced balloons. The garden tilted, ground rose up.

—Oh, no, you don't.

An almighty whack across his shoulders, and his lungs filled with air.

—That's better. Come on, in and out.

His lungs obeyed that voice. In and out, out and in, bringing the garden inside him, exchanging things with the minuscule branches of the tree in his chest, inflating him like a bellows, excoriating him back to life.

Those hands guided him through the garden, knowing the way. They removed his jacket, tie, collar, discarded who-knew-where. They compelled his lungs to do their work. The sweat stopped coursing. Pungent things surrounded them, consoling them and insulating them from whatever lurked outside the garden, lying in wait.

Later, the hands made him drink, cool and sweet, flushing the panic from his mouth. They sat on a bench beside the canal. The dark water cooled the air and drew a wind, smelling of earth. It was about to rain. A hand reached out to calm him. He oughtn't to need it, but he didn't draw away.

—Just you concentrate on breathing. I'll do the rest.

What a notion, to cede everything but breath to the hands, all thought, all defense.

—You aren't out of it yet, but hopefully you're far enough from the fire that you can feel the air.

Heavy globs fell on them. The sky flickered.

—I'm standing beside you.

He didn't understand what the Bishop was saying, but it took everything to stop himself collapsing onto the man's knee. The wind swept a curtain of water across the field, across the canal, across them. The hands lifted him again.

—Come on. You might be grateful of a downpour, but if Mrs. Hallows finds me out here, I'll never hear the end of it.

The Bishop led him inside to the red room, where he'd first met the Bishop's daughters. Rain whipped against the windows. Morgan's shirt had splotches across it like wet hives. He shivered.

—Oh, bother, the Bishop said, we've left your things outside.

He peered out the window much in the way of a boy trying to decide if he risked sneaking out.

—Will you be all right if I leave you for a moment?

Morgan felt a wave of fear.

—No, the Bishop said, you're right. Follow me.

It seemed a great effort, but he followed. In the corridor, the Bishop opened a cupboard and extracted a jacket, which he held up to Morgan. Back into the cupboard it went, and after some muttering, the Bishop produced an Aran pullover. Morgan put it on, the cream wool smelling of some piece of Sebastian family history. He turned down the sleeves. The Bishop, having closed the cupboard, looked twice at Morgan and shook his head.

Back in the red room, the Bishop rattled at a cabinet. Morgan stood next to the lamp burning on the table, the room's only illumination. He wanted to stand closer to the Bishop. He felt as if he ought to be wearing dressing gown and slippers, being told to take his fingers out of his mouth.

The Bishop returned to him bearing an old-fashioned glass.

—You've had a shock. Drink that.

Morgan smelled the amber liquid.

—Don't look so scandalized. That's all I'm giving you.

Morgan drank it, fire down his throat, strong and comforting. The Bishop took the glass away as if Morgan had obediently swallowed medicine, then steered him to a chair near the window, miles from the little lamp. The chair had no arms, the kind of thing he imagined a princess sitting in to have her slippers changed. A wing chair, higher, was beside him. The Bishop sat in it. Morgan looked longingly to the lamp across the room.

—Do you think, the Bishop asked, you can manage a bit more?

He didn't think he could manage anything, but the . . . thing . . . still waited. He could feel it, in the dimness of the room. More than anything, he did not want the Bishop to send him to bed.

—Before we can close the cover on this, the Bishop said, we really must make an effort, I think, with the route you took to this particular error.

His chest eased. He liked the word *error*. It sounded correctable.

—I assume you've known this girl for some time?

Morgan nodded, but the Bishop had had enough of his mute passivity. Firmly, the Bishop elicited an outline of the Polly episode, how he'd known her since his Fourth Form year but had only that term come to see her in a romantic light.

—Erotic, I think you mean.

His teeth twinged to hear such a word on the Bishop's lips, but he couldn't deny it. Not when their recent acquaintance had occupied itself so heavily with those types of activities.

—Kissing?

—At first.

The Bishop sat back in the wing chair and put his fingertips into his jacket pocket.

—Go on.

—Do you really want me to describe everything?

—I think we've had enough of that with Lord Crim-Con, but am I to assume a wide range of activities more than osculation but less than *vera copula*?

377

The hardness was returning to the Bishop's voice. Morgan's heart had begun to beat again in his stomach.

—What was that extraordinary phrase you used? *L'amour complet?*

A flare, burning everything he had swallowed.

—Where did you hear that? the Bishop asked.

—Nowhere.

Droit had said it, hadn't he?

—It puts quite a gloss on the act.

The Bishop resumed, pulling the story from him as if from nests of carded wool, the delicious intervals in the kitchen of the Keys, and the notion, perfect in its conception, of taking advantage of Patron's Day to plan their tryst, in the green and mossy bower, their dear nook—

—Let us leave Wordsworth out of this, the Bishop said severely. Your persistent impulse to romanticize fornication neither deceives nor impresses me.

—It wasn't wicked, Morgan protested feebly. She enjoyed it just as much as I did.

—And you know this how?

—She made all the maneuvers, most of them anyhow. She laughed. She said it felt lovely.

The Bishop seemed to accept this, but Morgan felt sure he was saving his attack for another moment as he guided Morgan through the rest of the story, their burgeoning romance, his suggestion of *l'amour complet*, her ready agreement.

—You were in love, were you?

—*Yes*, sir.

—She must be a delightful young lady. Polly, you say she's called?

—Yes, sir.

—Polly what?

—Just . . . Polly. Her father owns the Cross Keys.

The Bishop found each detail more fascinating than the last. Did Polly's mother assist in operating the pub? Morgan thought that . . . well, actually he had the impression that Polly and her father were on their own. The Bishop evinced sympathy; he could well understand how she and Morgan had consoled one another on this point. Well, actually, the subject had never come up, but just because he didn't possess an accurate family tree for Polly did not mean he loved her any less.

The Bishop did not mean to suggest it. There were many ways to fall in love. Their conversation must have been occupied with other matters, Polly's plans for the future, perhaps? Her taste in music? Reading? Politics? Where had she stood on the Strike, for instance?

They hadn't discussed politics, Morgan informed him, because politics were colossally boring, and everyone knew girls didn't care for them. And before the Bishop continued making his point, Morgan could tell him that he quite got the thrust of it, but Morgan's point was that his affection for Polly was intangible and not caused by casual conversation.

—Very well, the Bishop conceded. I suppose you have sufficient intellectual stimulation at school. The last thing you need is to discuss philosophy with a charming young girl of—remind me how old she is?

He prepared to say something hot in return, but his brain had got disorganized.

—My age.

—She is seventeen?

—More or less.

—Which? More? Or less?

—She may not be seventeen this year, but we're essentially the same age.

—Morgan, the Bishop said, removing his fingers from his pockets, stop equivocating.

—I never asked her directly! It's rude to ask ladies their age. My wretched father was on about this same thing.

—Morgan.

—What! he yelled.

It felt better. He sat up straight. Yelling let the fire out. Let it burn the Bishop to a crisp.

—I don't know her date of birth! Happy?

—No.

—Neither am I! he shouted. You can say what you like about . . . about what happened later, but everything else was nice. She knew what she was about, and it was the nicest thing that's happened to me in donkey's years. It's only dirty old men who fixate on the precise age of girls.

—The law happens also to concern itself with the age of consent.

—Oh, that!

—Yes, said the Bishop, that. Let me be sure I have this straight. Your acquaintance with Polly this term took on a new dimension, one pursued mutually. You felt affection towards her, as well as a powerful sensual attraction, which you typically labeled as romantic love.

—It was love!

—Love that did not trouble itself to find out anything about Polly, her interests, her family, her hopes, her prospects. Or even whether fornicating with her constituted unlawful carnal knowledge.

—It wasn't like that!

The Bishop got to his feet and stood, eleven feet tall.

—Yes, Morgan, it was.

The fire poured down, searing every inch of skin.

—I do believe it didn't occur to you, but the fact is—the truth is—that Polly is not yet even fifteen, at least according to my son's sources.

Which had to be . . . Grieves. Morgan's lungs walked out on strike again.

—And, as you confessed earlier, in the moment of penetration—

If he never breathed again, this would stop.

—You proceeded . . . Morgan?

He glowered at the man.

—Breathe in and out! the Bishop commanded.

No longer consoling, the man handled him without pity.

—I won't have you dodging out of this with self-induced hysteria.

The Bishop towered above him. Would he not momentarily break?

—Please, sir, he gasped. I can't bear it.

He couldn't bear it, and yet he did. There was no retreat. No hiding from everything his heart dressed up. No reason not to hurl upon the flame the last, sheltered pieces of the wreck called Morgan Wilberforce.

—There's something more, said the tongue in his mouth.

—Go on.

And so he began to tell the Bishop about Alex.

The telling kept the panic at bay. He named the things he'd done, the knocking, kicking, twisting, hang-the-rabbiting, kitty-deadlocking, sorcerer's-apprenticing, so many times they blurred together, and then in the barn, how he'd—how given full rein—how easy, how ardent—how vital it had seemed to make Alex behave (to make himself behave?).

—Behave yourself, how?

A tickle in his throat. He coughed.

—To stop from—

Another cough.

—He really is the most infuriating—

The tickle wouldn't stop and neither could he, cough upon cough. The Bishop got to his feet without urgency. He drifted to the door, where he rang a bell. The spasm spread to Morgan's entire windpipe. The Bishop, unalarmed, waited for Mrs. Hallows to arrive and then held a half-tone conference. She disappeared, and the Bishop stood languidly against the frame, arms crossed:

—Enjoying yourself?

—If you think—I'm—doing this on—on purpose—

—Save your breath. You're going to need it.

He continued coughing, eyes streaming, breath in knots. The Bishop stood aside for Mrs. Hallows, who brought in a water jug and deposited it unceremoniously on the table beside their empty whiskey glasses. She murmured something to the Bishop about the hour and then clomped away. The Bishop filled the glasses and handed one to Morgan.

When, at length, Morgan had calmed the tickle enough to speak, the Bishop opened a window. The rain had stopped driving but still fell steadily.

—Now, the Bishop said, what was it you had to stop yourself doing to Alex?

Morgan poured himself another glass of water and drank it. Then he started to tell the Bishop about Silk.

Had we but world enough, and time,
This coyness, Dicky, were no crime.

Peter Fanshawe Bradley, protégé of the doomed Gordon Gallowhill; Silk Bradley, who had shown him what his cock was for, who had with Baker's Dozen pressed from him the tears that built like meltwater behind an insufficient weir.

Accounting, both parts: payments first at the edge of a cane. Then—*let us sport us while we may*—lessons—*like am'rous birds of prey*—lessons in a different register, from a different Bradley, the one he showed only to Morgan, then and only then. Lessons played in every key but acted quite in concert. *Let us roll all our strength, and all our sweetness* (had there ever been a time he protested and meant it?) *and tear our pleasures with rough strife through the iron gates of life.*

The one night he boycotted Accounting, Silk had not come to the dorm to fetch him. Eventually Morgan had grown afraid, afraid that something had happened to Silk, something like the shadow, only he hadn't known it then. He'd gone to the study and found Silk at the window huddled under a rug, empty bottle in hand. Morgan had brought him another, but rather than take it, Silk had asked Morgan what he wanted. When Morgan reminded him about Accounting, Silk had said, *Accounting is canceled.* The emptying out happened in a moment, instant as bereavement, only who was he to compare—*the grave's a fine and private place, but none, I think, do there—*

Colleywest and crooked, that's what it was, and then after The Fall, Silk had scarcely spoken to him, which was a relief—wasn't it?—because . . .

He felt so terribly confused regarding it from this distance.

The Bishop asked no questions. Had he been talking for minutes or hours? At some point Mrs. Hallows had brought a tray with tea and biscuits. Their cups stood empty now, his voice rasped raw. Still the Bishop didn't speak but merely reclined by the window.

He stopped talking. One of their silences developed. His head spun as if fighting sleep.

—You cared for him, the Bishop said quietly, very much, I think.

Morgan stretched his neck. His muscles threatened never to return to their plastic state.

—Perhaps even as much as he cared for you.

—He didn't care for me.

—Even you don't believe that.

He didn't know what to believe. He had said everything there was to say about Bradley, past, present, and to come, and the Bishop was sitting there running his fingertips along the lead in the windowpanes. Morgan had never spoken of Bradley, except diffusely to Grieves, but now he had put words to it in the most concrete manner. To judge by the Bishop's demeanor, Morgan had conveyed nothing at all. Perhaps Bradley had in truth been nothing. Perhaps the disorder had been always in his own mind. Nathan and Laurie never dwelt upon characters from that time. Only he quailed encountering Bradley in the quad. Only he had imagined himself trapped between Grieves and Bradley, a pincer of cricket balls and longings. The Bishop saw nothing out of the ordinary in the tale even though

Morgan had talked of him for longer than he'd talked of anything else. A high tide of shame engulfed him, not the shame from the garden, but the shabby, naked shame of mistakes and mistakefulness.

—I'm sure I've made too much of him, Morgan said.

The Bishop put both feet on the floor:

—I'm sure you haven't.

Relief and weight in one.

—I'm sure, if anything, you haven't made enough.

And the alluring desire to sob, loudly and at length.

—The entanglement you describe was grave, the Bishop said. *Is* grave.

A wash of horror and embarrassment as sustaining as it was caustic.

—You say you saw him recently?

Morgan nodded.

—Three days ago?

Was it?

—But he'd never come before?

—Never.

—Why now?

Why indeed. Bradley had given no answer: *Do you have to ask?* As if Morgan ought to understand Bradley's every motive. Certainly that day he had shown himself partial to Morgan's success even though he'd been playing for the other side. But if Bradley wanted to put things right between them, why had he not come sooner? Why had he come two months after Spaulding, surely knowing that Morgan had seen Spaulding's head spill blood, as Bradley had seen Gallowhill's, when Gallowhill was mighty in his eyes.

—He, too, had seen someone die?

—Yes.

—So he was a person bereaved?

—I suppose.

—Just as he was a person who misused his position.

Morgan nodded.

—And his charisma.

Oh, yes.

—A person capable of cruelty. A person capable of love.

A person capable of both. And a person without anyone to sort him out.

—What was it he said to you, when your bat broke?

—All he said was . . .

In undertone, as they'd switched sides, *Well stuck, Dicky.*

—He was being sarcastic, Morgan said.

Yet Morgan had flushed when he said it, a flood of pleasure from the times Bradley would say that thing.

—Was that a name he used to call you when he was being sarcastic?

Perhaps at first, when Silk had chanced on the nickname, but mostly when he used it . . .

—It's what *he* called me, in private. It isn't right that—

Dark edged in.

—Has someone else been using the name?

—Yes—No. I mean—

And the Bishop was on his feet, no longer static, dragging a footstool to sit directly beside him, their knees at the same level. He smelled of the ineluctable something he'd smelled of all the other times he'd come near—hauling him through the house, whacking him across the shoulders, acting as though his hands could conjure things and make them do his bidding. The Bishop did not touch him. He spoke near a whisper:

—Are you ready to tell me about him?

Morgan froze, a claw at his ribs. The Bishop leaned forward.

—Remember, you're in my hands.

The Bishop could say that. He could sit there with his nearly silent voice and his nearly remembered smell, but nothing gripped his chest.

—I can't.

Bent tighter like bows, like sticks too far.

—But?

Squeezed breath, crushed undersea, life pressed nearly out—but then, like a hook, a minuscule yet potent fishing hook, the Bishop's ring brushed against him.

—What has he told you?

Don't you dare, you bloody peaching girl of a—

—Alex was trespassing.

Worm. Slave.

—On sacred ground!

And it was spilling out, the blackmail, the bets, the unnerving nerve. Had he delivered those punches, or had he only watched as someone else threw them? Had it been his fist that felt bone crack beneath it? And had he really seen the other one in Alex's face? Could he have blacked those eyes—all his heart, all his mind, all his strength—obliterating the face he never wanted to see again?

—Which face did you never want to see?

He sounded like a lunatic. For all he knew, he was a lunatic. Lunatics imagined things that weren't there. Lunatics entertained figments of the imagination, two boys, like something from that painting in Uncle Charles's corridor of the young man—was he a scholar?—with a winged figure on one shoulder, horned on the other.

—Which is which, though? the Bishop asked.

It wasn't as simple as that, Morgan protested. Droit didn't spend all his time tempting him to pleasures of the flesh. Some of his time, perhaps, but to be perfectly honest, Morgan wasn't convinced that sensual pleasure was so awful.

—I don't believe I said it was.

He couldn't keep his place in this debate. He'd never been good at argumentation. That was Nathan's line. If you needed something argued, you sicced him on it. But even though a dreary person might accuse Droit of devilishness, Morgan agreed with what he said most of the time.

—The most dangerous untruths, the Bishop said, are truths moderately distorted.

But if that were the case, then the other one ought to have been prattling away, urging him to turn from wickedness, scolding him for his sloth, his drunkenness, his wrath, his lies; whereas he rarely spoke at all, and what he did say was unmemorable.

—What does he do, then, this other one?

—He turns up when everything's gone wrong, and instead of suggesting anything useful, he just moons at you.

—When was the last time you saw him?

—Not since Alex.

Deserter.

The Bishop rubbed his forehead:

—And that time you say he was mingled with the boy you were beating?

His teeth ached at the words, but he couldn't deny them.

—And the other times he turned up when you were weak?

Whenever circumstances were beneath Droit's dignity. On the way back from the JCR. Alone in the pavilion. Out by the ditch. Things of that nature.

—So, the Bishop summarized, Droit exists to make things jolly and to advise you about people's motives, whereas the other one seems to have no purpose other than to stand with you when nobody else will.

—I wouldn't put it like that.

—Why not?

He wouldn't put it like that because it made the other one sound . . . like someone he ought to view differently.

—Why does this other one distress you so much?

—He doesn't! And please will you stop using that word, sir? It makes one sound hysterical.

—I apologize.

The Bishop didn't say whether he apologized for suggesting that he was hysterical, or for drawing attention to his actually being hysterical.

—I don't like him because he gets on my nerves. And before you ask, he gets on my nerves because he barely speaks.

—Perhaps his task isn't to speak, but to stand beside.

—If that's the case, then a jolly good job he's done of it, buggering off when things turned horrid.

—I thought you said you'd ground him to a bloody pulp. Weren't those the words you used?

Those words might have been used, but Morgan didn't see why the Bishop had to attribute them to him. Still, he supposed it was true anyway. Yet another thing he'd ruined.

—Oh, I'd be surprised if he's gone for good, the Bishop said with bizarre cheeriness.

—But I thought the point was for me to get past these figments and start seeing things clearly.

—They aren't what's standing in the way of seeing clearly.

A draining, then, like when the wireless switched off, when rain stopped. Here it was, the man's true program: to lecture him about sin. This man was not who Morgan had begun to think he was, not the fisherman casting the golden hook, not the possessor of dexterous hands. He was merely a clerical item from the last century, one of S-K's ilk, playing a long game to trap him into a searing moral address. He had been the worst kind of idiot to think otherwise. He slouched in the chair and prepared to put up with it.

—Am I to assume by your posture that the sullen schoolboy has returned?

—Assume what you like.

—I'm not going to lecture you, if that's what you're hoping for.

—If you're going to sashay about sprinkling words like *sin* on everything, the least you can do is say what you mean.

—Do you know what sin is, Morgan?

—It's what boring people call jolly amusing things they're too scared to try themselves.

—What an innovative definition, the Bishop mused. So murder is amusing, you'd say?

—No, but—

—Adultery is jolly?

—I wouldn't know, but—

—Dishonoring your mother, bearing false witness, theft—

—All right! It's a list of things you oughtn't do. And some of them are in the Ten Commandments and are quite nasty, but loads of them don't harm anyone else and are only called sins because they make boring people jealous.

The Bishop, with tremendous effort, got to his feet and pulled Morgan along by the sleeve. Without explanation, save a command to carry the lamp, they slogged across the house to the kitchen. Morgan set the lamp at the table where what's-her-name, that delightful girl, had been slicing onions. The Bishop collapsed into a chair.

—I'd be grateful if you would . . .

He gestured vaguely at the stove. Morgan went to the doorway to look for Mrs. Hallows, but the house was dark. Feeling like an oversize tyro, he lit the hob and then found some milk to heat in a saucepan with Ovaltine powder. The Bishop seemed to be concentrating on his own irritating obsession with breathing in and out. Whatever had come over the man had taken the wind out of the moral lecture, but Morgan didn't think the Bishop's daughters would approve of his sitting up so late. No doubt his physician had commanded him to bed by sunset. Morgan took an apple from a bowl, sliced it, and set it before the Bishop. Once the man had nibbled a wedge and sipped half a mug of Ovaltine, he began to breathe with less effort.

—Thank you.

—Shouldn't you be in bed, sir?

The Bishop's hands fluttered around the mug:

—I think I had better.

Morgan's stomach dropped. They hadn't resolved anything. He had talked himself into the most compromised position he had ever occupied. Now the man proposed to go to bed?

—I'm sorry, the Bishop said, smiling weakly. The spirit is willing, but the flesh . . .

—I've kept you up far too late, Morgan said, clearing the table. Your daughters will never forgive me.

—It's none of their affair, the Bishop growled.

Morgan felt a flicker of pleasure at his vehemence. The Bishop tried unsteadily to stand, but Morgan was at his side, taking his arm. Slowly, they mounted the stairs, Morgan carrying a candle from the kitchen. The Bishop's room lay down the corridor from Morgan's. Morgan helped him inside and lit a lamp there for him. Someone had already drawn the drapes and turned down the bedclothes.

—Sir, do you . . . ?

—I can manage to undress myself, thank you.

—Sorry, sir.

The Bishop softened:

—You're the one due an apology. I'm afraid I haven't done very well under this . . .

He clutched one of the bedposts.

—I'll leave you, Morgan said.

 He held the candle in one hand and the doorknob to St. Anne's in the other. The corridor creaked. He startled at the sound of the hall clock chiming a half hour, but which? Darkness closed in, as if it would ooze its way across him and down his collar.

He was too old to be afraid of the night. He refused to give it satisfaction. He was going to open the door. That was what he was going to do. He was going to open the door, set the candle on the bedside table, strip off, get under the covers, close his eyes, and go instantly to sleep. His teeth could stay uncleaned. Could he wait until morning for the toilet? Perhaps not.

Downstairs, he used the cloakroom without allowing his gaze to fall upon the glass. Veronica always said you couldn't see vampires in a looking glass, so you never knew, when you were surveying the room in one, say brushing your teeth, or, worse, covering your face in soap, whether a vampire was drifting up behind you, ready to sink its fangs—

He was in the cloakroom of a clerical household, on a summer's night in the appallingly advanced year of 1926. If he couldn't pull himself together here, he was a lost cause.

He decided that flushing the toilet would disturb the house (and summon demons from the basin, as Veronica always—enough!). He took the candle up the stairs, along the corridor, and over the threshold of St. Anne's.

Someone had turned back the bedclothes. Droit lounged across them, shoes on feet, cigarette in hand, ashes piled upon the sheets.

Then he was back in the corridor, door closed. Candle wobbled, mind raced: Hiding place? Cloakroom, kitchen, conservatory—

—Come.

He gasped, his heart—but the Bishop stood beside him, taking the candle and leading him away from the door. He tried to protest, but his teeth chattered. Not the golden hook, but an attendant net?

The Bishop had leaned heavily on him earlier, but now the man pulled him with firm assurance. Inside the Bishop's bedroom, the lamp still burned. A worn leather book lay open on the bed.

Words came from his still-chattering teeth: He didn't want to disturb— he didn't—St. Anne's. (What had Fairclough told him to ask for instead?) Saint—he'd—shortly . . .

The Bishop showed him a divan:

—It's lumpy, but you won't be the first to have slept on it.

—Sir . . .

His protest died in the dark.

—Just tonight until we can arrange somewhere else for you.

The Bishop produced a flannel.

—Wash your hands and face. Your teeth will have to wait until morning.

He set the candle next to a basin filled with water. Morgan did as he was told. When he'd finished, the Bishop had placed pillow and blankets on the divan.

—Get undressed, the Bishop told him.

He stripped down to vest and pants and slipped beneath the scratchy blanket. The Bishop sat beside him, as his mother used to when she came to say good-night.

—I'll hear your prayers, the Bishop said.

—I don't . . .

The Bishop folded his hands and began to say the Our Father. He said every word as if he meant it, as if it never got old. *Thy will be done* seemed an indictment of every vanity and willfulness. When he reached the end, to the bit about evil, the room closed around them, dark darker, cold colder. Morgan's eyes pricked.

—*Lighten our darkness, we beseech thee, O Lord.*

Morgan waited for the darkness to obey. The Bishop moved his lips in some other silent words and concluded in the gestural manner Morgan had come to expect.

—Put your head on the pillow.

Then the Bishop's hand was on his forehead, heavy and warm.

—*Defend us from all dangers and mischiefs, and from the fear of them; that we may enjoy such refreshing sleep as may fit us for the duties of the coming day.*

How could he endure another day like this? Wouldn't it be better to die in his sleep?

—*And grant us grace always to live in such a way that we may never be afraid to die; so that, living and dying, we may be thine, through the merits and satisfaction of thy Son Jesus Christ, in whose name we offer up these imperfect prayers.*

His thumb scraped down Morgan's forehead, then horizontally, as if placing a seal upon him. Morgan clenched his jaw.

—I'll be here all night, the Bishop said. I'm a light sleeper. You've only to call.

He adjusted the blankets, snuffed out the candle, and turned the lamp down, though not entirely out. Morgan lay rigid beneath the rug, the divan indeed lumpy beneath him, but beneath both him and the divan, the Bishop's floor stood still, supporting them as weakness drew in and drew him into sleep.

His mother was singing in the kitchen, a song in Irish he didn't understand. She sliced bread fresh from the oven, the kind of bread only she made. He rushed in from the garden, threw his arms around her waist, and buried his face in her apron.

—You've come back!

He wanted nothing but to touch her and to climb into her lap, as he was doing. Nothing mattered anymore, not where she had been or why she had gone away or why she had come back, or even whether she was still angry with him. She was back and he would surrender everything to keep her.

What a transubstantial miracle for her to walk, breathe, bake, and feel warm beneath his arms, to smell like herself, to sound like herself, to be *alive*. It had seemed that the rift could never be mended, but now after so much time, it was.

Mr. Grieves sat on the other side of the table in his cold-water flat.

—They're coming, he said. You'll have to hurry.

But he was wearing only pajamas. How could he escape in bare feet?

—You'll have to go as you are, Mr. Grieves said.

And that boy, Ripping Yarns, met him outside. They were coming down the road even now, he said, and even if Morgan went back for his clothes, all the windows would be locked, every door stopped with wax. They were outlaws, Rip said, but once they got away, they'd have no end of a jolly time.

And he was running back to the garden, stubbing his toe, pounding the door:

—Let me in, let me in! It's a matter of rife and death!

Rip was at his neck like snow and Morgan was screaming until his throat hurt:

—Let me in! I've been a waif for twenty years!

Up stone stairs to the Hermes Balcony. Spaulding was waiting. He wasn't dead after all.

—I never was, Spaulding said with a smile.

And he was touching Spaulding, his chest, his hands. He was warm, firm, alive. How the mistake had happened Morgan couldn't guess, but none of that mattered because Spaulding was here now, and they had all the time in the world. They could finish what they'd begun. Spaulding would play rugby, and when summer came, he'd play cricket, and when it was Patron's Day, he'd win the match instead of Morgan, which might be disappointing, but nothing compared to having Spaulding back. It was like being allowed to take an exam over; they tore up your first paper so you could swot properly and get things right the second time.

Spaulding unbuttoned Morgan's trousers:

—You know what *sui generis* means, don't you?

Morgan did know, but he couldn't think of it just then.

—It means *pine box*, Spaulding said.

Morgan lay rigid on a divan, heart racing, cold to the core. The blanket had fallen away. A light burned dimly.

Spaulding wasn't alive. Not really. But he had seemed so vital. He had been *warm*.

What had he said about *sui generis*?

Morgan tried to reach for the blanket but froze. *Sui generis* didn't mean *pine box*.

Something had been in his dream just now, in his very mind as he slept, and that something was not Spaulding.

Bugger off! Morgan thought in his loudest voice.

The cold sank deeper.

Bugger the hell off!

And the Bishop was at his side. He took the blanket from the floor and placed it over him. Lit the candle, sat down. Morgan shivered and kept shivering. The Bishop placed a hand on Morgan's chest and began to re-cite the Our Father. With each word, heat flowed, through the blanket, rewarming his blood.

When he finished, Morgan was no longer shivering. He felt safe for the first time he could immediately recall. The Bishop tucked the blanket around him, and he felt a sudden and drowning desire to be the Bishop's child, not a visitor, not a case, but his real child, like Dr. Sebastian and Elizabeth and Agnes and Lucy and even beautiful, bolshie Flora.

—Did your children sleep here when they had bad dreams?

The Bishop smiled faintly.

—Some of them did.

—Who else slept here?

—Oh, the Bishop said vaguely, I've slept there many a night when the bed wouldn't do.

Morgan wasn't sure what he meant, but he felt a curious lack of desire to ask questions. If he were indeed the Bishop's child, adopted but real, then he wouldn't need to question every single thing.

The Bishop gazed at him beside the flickering flame, as if he would watch until Morgan fell asleep again. But even if he did, Morgan realized sharply, nothing could defend him inside his dreams.

—Sir?

The word felt formal and twisted, not like the man beside him.

—What is it, Morgan?

—What does *sui generis* mean? I do know, but I can't quite . . .

—*Sui generis*, of its own kind or species?

Morgan thought, but he couldn't see what it had to do with Spaulding, or coffins.

—Where have you been hearing it? the Bishop asked with an infinite delicacy.

And so he tried to relate something of the dreams, but when he tried to describe the aftermath, the phenomenon of delayed terror and recognition, his explanation sounded like one of Veronica's stories.

—It's daft, he concluded. You get confused dreaming. I was probably afraid during the dream, not after.

—I don't believe you're confused at all. You're seeing things more clearly than you have in some time. You didn't believe that *sui generis* meant . . . what was it?

—Pine box.

Saying the words made him cold again.

—You're supposed to be sorting me out, not letting me go off my dot.

—I can understand why you were shivering, the Bishop said, but there's every sign of hope.

—*Hope?*

—You weren't deceived. The attack failed.

A wave of relief, and an undertow—

—Attack?

The Bishop held his gaze.

—That's an awfully dramatic metaphor for some bad dreams.

—It isn't metaphor, the Bishop said.

Something poked his ribs. He sat up:

—And now you're going to tell me a heap of theology, I suppose.

The Bishop said nothing.

—Well, Morgan said, whatever you say about all that teaching and healing and sacrificing, it didn't help Spaulding. He's still dead.

—He is.

—So what has he got to say to that, your spectacular Jesus?

The Bishop sighed, but not a sigh of impatience, more a sigh of pain:

—He suffered.

A ghost of a smile pregnant with compassion:

—And he is still suffering with us.

—Why do you have to make everything so abstract? Morgan snapped. And if you try to tell me she's really alive, larking about like an angel somewhere, I'll . . .

The Bishop caught his gaze, as if he'd left his trunk open and his tuck box unlocked.

—I mean . . .

—Your mother is dead, the Bishop said, as dead as the host in the valley of bones.

He wanted to argue until the Bishop forgot what he'd said. But the Bishop looked as if he'd finally seen the truth; he looked as if he thought Morgan knew what came next.

 He fell asleep after all. He didn't dream again. The Bishop sat beside him that night, and when Morgan woke, the Bishop was dressed, reading a book by the window. Morgan's entire body hurt, as if he were a tyro set upon by the Fourth. His throat stung. His eyes ached.

—You'll want a bath, the Bishop said.

He left the room and returned shortly to report that Mrs. Hallows was drawing one in the upper bathroom.

—Not the one in St. Anne's. Don't worry.

Relief at the news mixed with shame at his fear, which belonged to the night. In the light of morning with the sound of shears outside the window, he had no business on a divan in the Bishop's bedroom. He wasn't the Bishop's child, and it had been wet to wish for it.

—I was thinking an outing today, the Bishop said. Could you manage that?

—I'm not an invalid, he croaked.

—I didn't mean to suggest it. Very well, then, breakfast in half an hour. Chop-chop.

He bathed without incident. Breakfast passed in silence. They ate porridge, which Morgan found singularly satisfying. He had thought the Academy's porridge had ruined the foodstuff for life, but he was mistaken. Perhaps if he could eat bowl upon bowl of it, with the summer honey Mrs. Hallows set out in a dish, it would soothe his throat and fortify the muscles in his eyes, which had so failed him lately.

They had not finished eating when the doorbell rang. Presently, Elizabeth breezed into the dining room, dispelling their silence and everything that had passed between them.

She chattered away to her father, bidding Morgan a simple *Good morning*. She did not like the pallor of her father's cheeks, but she was relieved to hear that Mr. Rollins had promised to come by this morning. She hoped her father would mind his physician and, once the man had left, catch up on his resting.

Morgan's chest sank in disappointment. He'd liked the sound of an outing. If the Bishop was going to rest, what would become of him all the long day?

—Come along, you, Elizabeth said, kissing her father on both cheeks. Yes, you.

Morgan looked up uncertainly.

—You can't expect to monopolize my father. Besides—

Her tone softened:

—there's something I need help with. And I was quite hoping you'd be able to do it.

Elizabeth—Mrs. Fairclough as he forced himself to think of her lest his tongue slip—drove a motorcar. He had never ridden in a motorcar with a woman behind the wheel. Mrs. Fairclough drove competently; at least she kept to the left, maintained a civilized speed, and applied the brakes without violence. The wind blew noisily in the windows, precluding conversation. They'd traveled a few miles when she brought the vehicle to a halt beside a green.

—Here we are.

Morgan decided he would adopt a policy of asking no questions. Demanding explanations merely advertised one's ignorance and emphasized the authority people had over one. When someone wanted him to understand, someone could explain. Until then, he would drift.

Mrs. Fairclough led him across the green to a village school, whose mistress appeared to be Mrs. Fairclough's bosom friend. The woman had charge of a crowd of little boys who spoke with country accents and wore no uniforms. They were in the midst of a spelling lesson, and the air crackled with pent-up boy energy. They seemed cheerful, but Morgan had the sense that fisticuffs could erupt at any moment, if only to relieve the tension.

Mrs. Fairclough was introducing him to the Dame:

—Wilberforce comes from the public school where my brother will be Headmaster next term.

The mention of her brother elicited excitement, as did the words *public school*. Then Mrs. Fairclough was speaking of cricket, and somehow she was giving them the impression that he, Morgan, knew everything there was to know of cricket, and not only knew it, but could and would impart it. Today.

The Dame was overjoyed by the suggestion, as were the boys. She rang the bell to signal their break, and Morgan had to accept the invitation to accompany them outdoors.

One of the older boys introduced himself as Kemp. Kemp proposed to show Morgan their equipment, which consisted of some battered stumps, two cricket bats, three balls, and two sets of pads lacking adequate straps. Some of the boys occupied themselves wrestling to the ground, but a group of five or six hovered near Morgan. He deduced that Kemp was their self-appointed leader. The boy possessed an intangible command, probably thanks to his nerve and his ease with words. Morgan realized that his own presence posed a challenge to Kemp's rule, but having seized upon Morgan as his property, Kemp was attempting to neutralize the threat.

Kemp took charge of the match, sorting boys into sides and assigning the fielders positions and the batsmen an order. He hammered the stumps into the ground with a bat before Morgan could stop him, and then he took a ball and headed to the crease.

His bowling wasn't disastrous. He had the line, and he had the length, but he had the same line and length every time. He'd assigned most of the smaller boys to the batting side, and they showed little flair. It didn't help, Morgan thought, that Kemp berated them with a nearly ceaseless stream of advice. A few hit the ball, and the incompetence of the fielders allowed them twenty-six runs before Kemp bowled the side out.

The Dame had disappeared with Mrs. Fairclough, and Kemp presided over the changing of sides, giving the ball over to the tallest man on the other side, a wan boy who looked as though he needed to start eating breakfast on a regular basis. Kemp maintained his commentary as that boy, called Fetch, bowled. Unlike Kemp, Fetch's bowling was erratic. Morgan feared for the safety of the batsmen, especially given the ill-fitting pads.

A timid boy with wild hair approached the crease and, cajoled by Kemp, faffed about with the pads. The boy did not look at Morgan, but Morgan sensed him wanting to look, as if he possessed a telegram but could not, for fear of interception, transmit it.

—Come on, Twist! Kemp said. Do you think Wilberforce has come all this way to watch you mess about?

Twist left one of the pads behind and took his place before the wicket. Fetch narrowed his eyes and bowled. The ball hit Twist on the unpadded leg; he stifled a yelp, and Kemp unleashed a string of abuse. Was Twist there to watch grass grow or to defend a wicket? He tried out other gems of sarcasm the other boys found witty, but which Morgan considered tedious in the extreme. He'd encountered plenty of domineering boys and bullies, which he had no doubt Kemp could be when he wasn't trying to impress, but this was the first time Morgan had observed the condition in boys so much younger than himself, boys he could in fact influence.

—That'll do, he said.

He approached Twist, affixed the missing pad, and arranged his body into a decent stance.

—Keep your eye on the ball, he said. Use your feet, and follow through there.

He guided the boy's arms. They were small and thin enough to break.

—Good.

Twist blushed at his word. Embarrassed, Morgan left him and approached the bowler.

—Fetch, is it? Would you mind awfully?

The boy glanced to Kemp, but Kemp was busy repeating and mangling Morgan's advice to Twist. Morgan took a gamble.

—Right, you lot! he called.

He jogged over to the batsmen. They gathered around him, eager yet wary, unsure of their allegiance.

—You can't come in without getting ready.

They looked at him uncomprehending.

—A proper batsman never comes in unless he's fully warmed up.

He demonstrated the stretches Mr. Grieves had assigned him. He told them to work on those, well away from the distractions of the crease, and he assigned Kemp to oversee them.

Back at the crease, he relieved Fetch of the ball and nodded to Twist. Then he took a light run-up and bowled the most direct ball he could. It bounced, Twist swung, and his bat connected, sending the ball past another of the little boys, who watched it go.

—Run! Morgan called.

Twist and the lackadaisical fielder ran.

Morgan bowled to the remaining batsmen and observed the fielding of the rest. They were small and untrained, but not entirely without hope. The biggest impediment to their development, Morgan thought, was Kemp's tiresome combination of criticism and interference. Morgan had managed not to alienate Kemp, but it had taken every ounce of restraint, invention, and diplomacy that he possessed. How Grieves coped, particularly with one as obstreperous as himself, Morgan had no idea. It was no wonder he'd bowled hard enough to kill him.

The Dame called them in to their dinners, which the boys had brought from home in tins and cloths. Morgan, ravenous, wondered whether Mrs. Fairclough was going to take him somewhere and feed him, but before she had stopped chatting to the Dame, several of the boys, including Twist, dragged him to their tables and presented him with bits of their dinners. He straddled a bench and devoured sandwich squares, apple slices, biscuits, and pastry corners. They flooded him with questions about cricket, interrupting each other before he could answer. He cut through the hubbub and addressed his first protégé:

—You're Twist, then?

— We only call him Twist.

—It isn't his real name.

—Full of surprises, are you?

—Like Oliver Twist.

—Because he's an orphan.

—Shut up, Brasenose.

—Shut up, Brasenose.

— *Shut up*, Brasenose.

—Well, he is.

—Half orphan.

—He's from the orphan hospital.

—Shut up, Brasenose.

—Shut *up*, Brasenose.

Morgan regretted asking. He looked for Kemp, but Kemp had surrounded himself with a coterie of the older boys, presumably to make it plain that he hadn't wanted to sit with Morgan in the first place. The boys around Morgan were still silencing the one they called Brasenose, and Twist was staring at the ground, his sandwich idle in his hand.

—I'm a half orphan, too, Morgan said.

Twist's eyes remained downcast; his sandwich twitched.

—So am I! said another boy near him. But I don't come from the hospital like he does.

—Shut up! several urged sotto voce.

—Boys, said the Dame, suddenly in their midst, we have spoken more than once, have we not, about that expression and how vulgar it is?

—Yes, miss, they murmured.

—What do we say when we wish someone to stop speaking?

—*Be quiet*, they murmured.

—That's right. Or, if we feel particularly vexed, we might say, *Hold your tongue.*

—Yes, miss.

Morgan wondered idly if any of them knew how to swear.

—Now, I'm afraid that Wilberforce has to leave us for today—

Groans of disappointment erupted through the room.

—but perhaps if you are very lucky, he will agree to come back another day.

—Anytime, Morgan said.

The Dame looked pleasantly surprised.

—Well, she said, if you mean it.

—I always mean what I say.

If only it were true.

—In that case, she said, it would seem that you are the answer to our prayers. Isn't that right, boys?

Apparently, it was right. They all began again to speak at once. Morgan discerned the words *match*, *Croffs*, and *parish day*. The Dame eventually made them speak one at a time, guiding them in sketching for Morgan their circumstances:

There was an important cricket match on a day known as Parish Day, in a fortnight's time. This year, they would be playing against the boys of Croffs School, who were very good indeed. Last year had been the first time they'd played against another school, and the match had gone poorly. With Morgan's help, they might have a chance this year to play with honor. Furthermore, some of them had the idea that important personages might attend Parish Day, and if they acquitted themselves well, they thought it not beyond the realm of possibility that these personages might find it in their hearts to be beneficent.

Then Mrs. Fairclough was extracting him from the schoolroom and promising to bring him again tomorrow at the same time, and Morgan was waving goodbye to the swarm of them. He felt warm in his chest, in an agreeable way, for the first time since he could recall.

 After feeding him at her home with her two eldest children, who had recovered sufficiently from the croup, Mrs. Fairclough drove Morgan back to the Rectory. Mrs. Hallows reported that the doctor had been and gone, and that the Bishop was resting. He would rest the remainder of the afternoon, and he left instructions for Wilberforce to take himself for a run and then to retire to the library for letter writing. Tea would be served in the conservatory at six.

—Thank you, Morgan said to Mrs. Fairclough. For . . .

—Don't mention it. Well done today.

He was immeasurably embarrassed and felt he would prefer her ear-boxing, but Mrs. Hallows rescued him and conducted him upstairs. His things had been relocated, she informed him. She led him to a door at the far end of the passage.

The room was small, containing a single bed, a bedside table, and a straight-backed chair. His trunk occupied the floor by the wardrobe, and a narrow stand held basin and jug.

—You know where to find the bath.

She pointed out the towels hung on a rail behind the door and then left him.

Above the bed hung a cross. Plain, dark wood, like the one downstairs but smaller. The bedside table contained a single book. Above the wash-basin he made out an etching of a man writing and a winged lion curled at his feet like a dog.

He sank down on the bed facing the chair, window on his left, head-board on his left, cross on his left. An inexplicable sense of discipline surrounded him, but not a petty, oppressive regime; rather, something like the containment and longing he had felt in Grieves's rooms that night. The object over his bed—and he already thought of the bed as his—ought to irritate him, but it didn't. It hung there as an unabashed declaration, of what he wasn't sure. As his breath came suddenly jagged, he was seized with a mysterious combination of restriction and safety. Here nothing could get at him. The only authority hung over his bed, silent and allur-ingly austere.

The chamber was cramped and dim, the bed narrow, the decor mo-nastic. It was not by any stretch of the imagination a room for someone like him. The hunger everywhere in his body had never been so keen, or so nearly fed.

✦

—So, the Bishop said after greeting him and pronouncing grace, how are the letters coming along?

He didn't ask about the outing. He didn't ask about the new bedroom. He didn't ask about the run, or anything else in Morgan's day. He asked about the one thing Morgan did not wish to discuss.

—They aren't, he admitted.

The Bishop tsked.

—I tried, Morgan said, but whatever I put sounded wrong.

—To whom did you attempt to write?

He had tried first to write his father, but the experience had been so unbearable that he had turned instead to Laurie and Nathan in an effort to regain his composure. This had proved disastrous since he had been unable even to begin relating what had happened, never mind why, and when it came to explaining Alex to them, Morgan had actually grown short of breath at the recognition of . . . He might as well have gone at their study with a hatchet.

Only one letter had not been consigned to the wastepaper basket, but Morgan knew very well it would shortly go there once the Bishop learned its addressee. The Bishop looked expectantly. Morgan sighed in his best aggrieved fashion and confessed that the letter was for Polly. He removed it from his jacket and surrendered it to the Bishop, who regarded it disinterestedly.

—Do you require a stamp?

Morgan gaped.

—Ah, I see I've disappointed you again, but I'm afraid I can't object to your writing this girl.

—I haven't sealed it, Morgan said, showing him the flap.

—That's unwise.

—But, you'll want to read it.

—Only if you require assistance with spelling.

—At school they always look over your letters.

—This isn't school. As previously discussed.

Strangely defeated, Morgan took back the letter. It wouldn't put anything right with her, but at least it would end his barbarous silence.

The Bishop served a leek pie and then broke his custom and conducted conversation as they ate. He inquired into Morgan's outing and listened attentively to Morgan's descriptions of the boys, their cricket, their sorry equipment, and the subtly fraught relations among them. The Bishop let him witter on, but when Morgan realized he had eaten nothing while the Bishop had finished, he pulled himself together.

—I've talked too much. I'm sorry.

—Nonsense.

Morgan paused long enough to shovel the pie into his mouth, but then at the Bishop's urging embarked on his impressions of the Fairclough household and of the Bishop's granddaughters. Morgan hadn't spent enough time with them to form any firm judgment, but his off-the-cuff descriptions appeared to amuse the Bishop and to vindicate some private theories he seemed to have held.

—Sir, Morgan said at last, what's to become of me?

The Bishop still looked amused:

—I'm sure I've no idea.

Morgan suppressed his irritation at being taken lightly.

—I mean, the woman at that school asked me to come back tomorrow. They've got an important match in a fortnight, and they're in a desperate state.

—Would you like to do that?

—I wouldn't mind. I don't know the first thing about training little boys, but their play is rather dire.

—That takes care of your mornings.

—But what else am I meant to be doing here?

The Bishop looked impassively:

—What do you think?

—Sir, has anyone ever told you you've an infuriating line in sphinxes?

The Bishop unleashed a belly laugh but said nothing.

—Dr. Sebastian brought me here hoping you could sort me out.

—Yes, but that was only the instigation. As I recall, you subsequently put yourself in my hands.

—Exactly. So how will we know when I've been sorted out? What will it involve, and how long will it take?

—You speak as if it's a mechanical procedure, like building a canal boat.

—Why can't you answer a simple question? Morgan snapped. You and your offspring seem to get a perverse delight in hoarding information. It's mean!

The Bishop put his hands on the table. Morgan started to backpedal, but the Bishop held up a finger.

—I'm sorry, he said. You are doubtless correct in your analysis of my family, as you've been correct in your other analyses this evening.

Morgan wondered if the Bishop had just paid him a compliment.

—But, the Bishop continued, I'm afraid I can't be as definitive as you'd like. Before you get angry again, I'll go over things so far, shall I? You said you felt you'd gone wrong in some way. Last night during a long and rather harrowing interview, we began to chart the territory.

403

Morgan was annoyed to find himself blushing again.

—In the course of this expedition, we seem to have disturbed something, which proceeded to pursue you even into your dreams.

The chill returned, goose pimples on his neck.

—Have I covered everything?

Morgan could only nod.

—So, with your consent, I propose to continue until the terrain becomes clear.

—Do you mean I'm going to have to make revolting confessions like that every day?

—Possibly.

—Then I do not consent.

The Bishop sat back in his chair.

—That's your prerogative, of course. Perhaps you've some ideas of your own as to how we might sort you out?

—I've told you everything. Why can't you deal with it and have done?

—And how do you propose I deal with it, presuming we can even agree what *it* is?

—The way people always deal with it! How many kinds of punishment are there?

—A good deal more than you've imagined, the Bishop replied.

—Frightening me won't work. Whatever punishments you've got in mind, I'd be much obliged if we could get on with them.

—I see, the Bishop mused. You think I'm trying to frighten you?

—Of course you are.

—I've not the slightest need to frighten you. You're scared stiff already.

Morgan realized he was going to have to cede ground.

—I was last night, I'll admit, but I'm not a child. I'm not going to quake in my boots at the threat of whacking.

—Corporal punishment doesn't intimidate you?

—It certainly doesn't. Of course it hurts, and I'd just as soon avoid it if possible, but I'm not a coward.

—That's the last insult I'd level at you.

Morgan wondered again if he'd just received a compliment.

—Look, obviously I've done some rotten things, so I don't see what we're waiting for. Punish me and have done with it!

The Bishop poured out the rest of the tea and rang for Mrs. Hallows.

—I'm not impressed, the Bishop replied, with your memory. It seems that whenever you leave my presence, a type of oblivion comes over you, necessitating a tiresome review of what has passed between us. Therefore, I would appreciate it if you made a particular effort to listen to what I'm about to say, to hear, mark, learn, and inwardly digest it.

The Magnetron again.

—First, you have put yourself in my hands, which means I will decide when to punish you, how to punish you, and indeed whether to punish you.

Morgan swallowed, feeling empty and full at the same time, as he had felt in the little bedroom, but more ticklish.

—Second, before anything of that kind can occur, we must complete our excavation so that we have a clear picture of the truth, as much as it can be known. The truth of Morgan Wilberforce.

Was it possible to grow allergic to one's own name?

—Third, I'm forming the impression that you, Morgan, are far too fond of physical punishment. You can take that expression off your face; I don't mean after the manner of your Etoniensis. Oh, you didn't detect that about him?

Morgan, appalled, could not even swallow.

—I mean you've come to rely on it as a cheap settler of accounts, a way to pay your debts without having to undergo repentance. It gives you the satisfaction of having been courageous, but it fails to touch you where it counts.

Morgan was so furious that he was afraid he might start swearing.

—Finally—and I've lost count of what number we're on—I should make it clear that I've no intention of punishing you, physically or otherwise, until you display a rudimentary understanding of what punishment is for.

—I know what punishment is for, Morgan snapped.

—Oh, yes?

—It's to discourage you from doing whatever it was you oughtn't to have done; it's to discourage other people from trying it on; and it's to clear the air. Unless idiots are giving it, in which case it's to advertise their dazzling power over everyone.

—Yes, yes, the Bishop said airily. That's all very well for school, but it's nothing to do with penitential suffering.

Morgan's ears went hot.

—Penitential suffering is precisely what you mean when you talk of being sorted out, by your father, by me. It's a different kind of punishment altogether than the crude sanctions necessary to maintain civil society. It's nothing to do with discouragement and everything to do with atonement.

—I thought that's what *he* was supposed to have done, Morgan scoffed.

—Exactly.

—So what is your *point?*

The Bishop placed his hands, palms up, on the table:

—Follow me.

After a gooseberry fool, Mrs. Hallows cleared, and the Bishop announced his intention to retire, then, at half past seven in the evening.

—You may have a turn around the garden until eight, the Bishop told him, and afterwards, you may spend the evening in your bedroom as you're so keen to be punished.

—But . . .

—Tomorrow we'll make a start on your reading, but for tonight, you may borrow a book from the library if you wish.

Morgan felt unexpectedly ashamed in the face of the Bishop's instructions. He had indeed brusquely demanded the Bishop get on with punishing him, but he didn't expect to be sent to bed hours before dark, like a little boy, and yet benevolently be permitted to read, denied even the edge of outrage.

The Bishop came to stand beside him. As he'd done in the night, he placed his hand on Morgan's head and repeated the words he'd said then. When he removed his hand, his voice was soft:

—You know where to find me. Don't hesitate.

He stalked around the garden in a fury but came indoors at eight o'clock even though no one made him. Taking the book he'd used for the wretched lines, he went up to his dormitory, or his cell as he decided to call it. He removed shoes, jacket, collar, and tie and hurled himself across the bed. It sagged. The evening sunshine streamed in the window. He opened the book and perused its contents.

Had we but world enough, and time . . . He closed the cover. He knew that poem and would never forget it, but seeing it with his eyes might prove ruinous; it might transport him backwards in time, northwards in space, into a person he never wanted to inhabit again. Still, it pressed on him, the nearly irresistible urge to look, as if its lines could deliver the sensations he longed for but abhorred. Reading the verse would not materially conjure Bradley or the secret realm they occupied while obeying the poet's command, yet he could feel with every nerve their closeness and pull . . . *Your quaint honor turn to dust, and into ashes all my lust* . . . His chest ached to breaking. His cock filled and stiffened. He threw the book across the room.

Droit would appear momentarily. He would lounge on the edge of the bed and use phrases from the verse to make scathing remarks about the Bishop. He would work Morgan into a frenzy of embarrassment. A frenzy of longing. A frenzy of grief.

He got up to leave the room but remembered the Bishop had told him to stay there. He'd said it was a punishment (hadn't he?). Morgan was in his hands, and the man had decreed that he spend the evening in his cell.

The object above his bed reached into his cavities as it had earlier, stroking the ache, transforming the craving he felt for Silk into the odd, stiff hunger he had felt earlier for the perfect discipline the room had seemed to offer.

How did the other poem go, again? *Like a usurp'd town* . . . He'd copied the cursed thing out six times, thrice with each hand, but still he couldn't remember. His memory was indeed hopeless. Perhaps he was aging before his time and would shortly fall into the blissful oblivion of the ancient.

He fetched the book from the floor and turned to the page of Donne that had nearly done him in two days before: *take me to you, imprison me, for I, except you enthrall me, never shall be free.* The couplet in sonnets always kicked you in the guts. This one kicked through to the other side. *Nor ever chaste, except you ravish me.*

 The days acquired a routine that began to settle him. Mornings with the boys, afternoons taking exercise and doing whatever tasks the Bishop had set him: reading, letter writing, composition. Sometimes the Bishop joined him for part of the afternoon, enlisting his help in the garden. In the evenings they had tea together, which might develop into an interview or be cut short by an early retirement.

Morgan took to discussing the boys with the Bishop, who referred to them as Morgan's project. The school, it emerged, was a charity for the sons of seamen killed in the War. Most of their fathers had sailed from Southampton and died in the Mediterranean, the Bishop told him, their ships sunk by U-boats. The vicar of the village church and the vicar of a seamen's church in Southampton had had a personal connection. The war had left so many widows that it was impossible to help them all, but through the efforts of these two vicars, the village had organized a subscription to give an improved primary education to these widows' sons. Some families had, in the intervening years, moved closer to the village as employment permitted, but boys whose mothers still lived in Southampton were boarded out with local families during the school term.

Morgan asked about the boy they called Twist and why such a distinction ought to be made about him since they had all lost their fathers. The Bishop did not know the boy, but if, as the others claimed, he came from the orphans' hospital and yet had a mother living, it could only mean she had surrendered him. He would certainly be accommodated during term in a local home. Why, Morgan asked, would he have come to the school and not stuck with whatever provisions the orphans' hospital offered? The Bishop could only conclude that someone had taken a liking to him and raised a subscription for his maintenance. That or he was clever at something.

Morgan wrestled with the project, both technically and tactically. The boys liked his instruction, though they went in for enthusiasm more than discipline. But Morgan found the subterranean battles with Kemp and his lieutenants draining. Each night he relayed Kemp's maneuver of the day and his own response. The Bishop listened, chiming in with a murmur that echoed an important point in Morgan's monologue, or an unnoticed sympathy Morgan might choose to adopt, or a satisfaction with the outcome of a particular matter. When Morgan solicited his advice, the Bishop only occasionally gave it. More often, he opined that Morgan knew what he was about. Morgan did not think he knew what he was about, and the Bishop's confidence struck him as supremely misplaced. Whatever he managed to get right with the boys, he considered luck or else the natural outcome of their efforts.

He had wanted to do something about their deplorable equipment, in particular the pads, which he deemed not fit for purpose, but acquiring new kit proved an ambition beyond the reach of man. In the end, he enlisted Mrs. Fairclough and her needle to fashion improvements to what they had. Furthermore, he judged it terrifically slack, not to mention fatal for morale, that not one of the boys had in his wardrobe a complete set of flannels, shoes, and shirt fit for cricket. He hadn't hoped for caps, but to play in mufti struck Morgan as obscene. Mrs. Fairclough again came to the rescue. She could not produce cricket uniforms for twenty-seven boys, she said, but she could manufacture eleven caps for them to share as they came in and out of play.

When Parish Day arrived, Morgan's boys took the pitch with a pride that exceeded their yellow-and-purple caps. They did not beat Croffs, but they scored respectably and did not allow the other side to wipe the floor with them. Morgan was particularly proud to see Twist hit a boundary, one of only three in the match. A lump formed in his throat as Twist took his six runs and received the uninhibited love of his fellows. When it was over, the vicar tormented Morgan with embarrassing compliments he didn't deserve. It was all Morgan could do to stop himself interrupting the man to read him a lecture on the moral urgency of decent kit.

The boys clung to his person more ardently each day, and in the festive atmosphere after the match, Morgan learned that their term finished at the end of the week. They would be leaving the village and returning to Southampton, or Soton, as they called it. All of them professed despair at the thought of losing Morgan.

—But you'll come back next term, won't you? they asked. You can teach us football.

It was clear they referred to association football, a game dismissed at the Academy as vulgar, but regardless of Morgan's views on soccer, he would not be there in September to teach it to them. They were so distraught when he confessed this that he was forced to backpedal, telling them that he was expected elsewhere, but that if fate was kind, they might see him again before they were very much older. They invited him to their prize-giving fete on the last day of term. The Bishop instructed him to go.

The Dame outdid herself producing a great number of prizes, most of them certificates she had lettered to honor things like Best Orthography, Most Improved Deportment, Most Selfless Citizen, Best Attendance (a three-way tie), as well as many named prizes, each of which carried a sixpence reward, something the boys considered a fortune. Morgan felt a surge of pride when Twist received the Joseph Raulph Ravencliff Butler Prize for Elocution.

—Who's he? Morgan whispered to Mrs. Fairclough.

—The butcher.

Twist had been, according to the blackboard, on the program already, and after receiving the prize, he came to the front to recite his poem, which was by a lady poet and even in its brevity exerted a torque on Morgan's mind. He couldn't remember the words exactly afterwards, but he clung to a phrase: *the truth's superb surprise.* He had received many surprises from the truth in his life, but none he would class superb. Did the poet intend it sarcastically?

After the program, many of the boys approached Morgan to introduce their mothers. Kemp did not, although Morgan saw him with a woman who seemed timid, the type to smile with half a cringe at everything in case it bit her. Twist did not have anybody with him. Morgan went and congratulated him on his reading and his prize.

—You won't be back next term, will you? Twist asked.

Morgan considered repeating his equivocation, but Twist's expression stopped him.

—I'm afraid not.

Twist nodded solemnly and offered his hand:

—Goodbye.

—Goodbye, Twist.

The boy withdrew his hand and turned away, but then, spinning back as if he'd forgotten something, he threw his arms around Morgan's waist.

—Don't go!

Morgan couldn't speak. His hands hung useless in the air.

—It's the best thing I've ever had, Twist cried. Please!

He was sobbing into Morgan's jacket. Morgan looked around for help. His hands fell on the boy's head, which only summoned fiercer tears. Finally, he managed to unwrap himself and, kneeling down, took out a handkerchief to wipe the boy's face. He searched for something to say that would impart courage, but everything sounded hollow before he said it.

—Remember what I taught you.

Twist started to sniffle again. Morgan's skin crawled from the inside. He stood up, clapped Twist on the back, and fled.

—I've spoken with your father, the Bishop told him over tea.

Morgan was finding it difficult to eat, and this announcement made him sharply queasy. The Bishop explained that arrangements had been made for Morgan to go up to London the next morning. His father would expect him in the afternoon.

—But . . . I'm not sorted out yet.

The Bishop's mouth twitched in a way that had become familiar. Their chats had continued regularly but had not repeated the freakish agony of those first days. Morgan had even ceased to think of them as moral interviews. Life with the Bishop had come to seem ordinary, as if Morgan were a young relation spending summer weeks at the Rectory whilst getting on with his project at the village school.

They had spoken several times of Silk, of Spaulding and Alex, Nathan and Laurie, of Grieves, of Morgan's father, and, when he could stand it, his mother. Perhaps the most striking characteristic of the fortnight had been Droit's absence. At first Morgan had expected him, but now, listening to the Bishop tell him he was to return to London, Morgan realized he hadn't thought of Droit in some time.

—These things take time, the Bishop replied cryptically

Would sorting him out take more time than the Bishop was at liberty to give? Or did he mean that Morgan's case was too stubborn to resolve? Or that it had ceased to interest him? Alarm quickly gave way to shame at having taken advantage of the Bishop's hospitality for so long. Who was he to grow comfortable there? The Bishop had already done him more favors than he could ever repay. How dare he feel . . . orphaned?

—I'll organize my things.

—Mrs. Hallows will sort all that, the Bishop said.

They wanted to be rid of him that desperately.

Somehow he managed to carry on a light conversation, relating what details he could bear from the fete. As soon as possible, he pled exhaustion and fled to his room.

Outside the door, his throat clutched. If he went inside, he would lose his composure; what's more, he sensed something sickening awaited him. He dashed into the room only long enough to retrieve a packet of cigarettes from the lining of his tuck box. Avoiding the Bishop, he escaped the house.

Down at the canal, he lit his first cigarette in more than a fortnight and inhaled to the bottom of his lungs. His veins opened. Blood flowed. He struck out down the towpath, raising his heart rate, stockpiling weapons against . . . whatever. By the time he returned to the Rectory, he was older, stronger, more capable.

Perched on the mooring, William smoked a cheroot. Morgan took his last cigarette from the pack.

—Got a light?

William, surprised in thought, felt for his matches. A smile squared his chin in a way that made Morgan feel someone had thrown a lance through his chest. He touched William's hand as the flame touched his cigarette.

They smoked. Morgan deliberately failed to look away. He smoked down to the last sliver, so close it singed his lips. Cut grass clung to William's trouser cuffs.

Morgan smiled. William flicked the end of his cheroot into the canal.

Morgan put his hands in his pockets. William put his hands in his pockets. They walked to the next footbridge. The grass there was overgrown, the Rectory far behind. William led him under the archway. *Mind nettles* was all he said.

His cock was astonishing.

Afterwards they had nothing to smoke. They lay under the footbridge and watched the light play on the water. Morgan's head spun without the aid of drink. The air was warm, birdsong filled it, and the sun acted as though setting could not be rushed one cubit. Superb surprise, and a restoration of how things ought to be: languid, sated, so gorgeous one could weep.

The Bishop was sitting in the summerhouse when he returned.

—I thought you'd gone to bed, the man said.

—I took a walk.

The sun had dipped below the canal. The Bishop got unsteadily to his feet:

—I'll make my goodbyes now. My son will collect you early.

—Dr. Sebastian? But I thought . . .

The Bishop looked as though he were making an effort to drag himself back from somewhere distant.

—I see I've left things out again. Term ended today, and as he's going up to town tomorrow, he offered to accompany you.

—I can go myself.

—Nevertheless.

Gorgeousness had fled, and the sour bars closed again.

—Will you sit, the Bishop asked, and permit me to bless you?

Morgan wished to do no such thing, but he lowered himself into the chair the Bishop had abandoned. Then the Bishop's hand was on his head, transmitting that horrible paternal rope, which had ensnared Morgan since his arrival. It was essential to pull himself together. Momentarily the man would release him. He had not to dwell on what was happening.

—Godspeed, Morgan.

—Thank you, sir.

A monstrously insufficient thing to say, but later when he'd recovered himself, he would write a letter thanking the man properly. Just now, such things were beyond him.

The Bishop went to bed. Morgan went to the drawing room and poured himself a measure of whiskey.

Four fingers later, his composure returned. He didn't fancy the bedroom, but he couldn't sleep downstairs, not with Mrs. Hallows charged with waking him at who-knew-what hour. He filled the glass to the rim and took it along to fortify himself.

Droit fell into step beside him:

—Don't panic. We'll sort it out. Lucky the old scarab has decent whiskey.

—Yes, Morgan said, weaving slightly.

—Just leave it to me.

Morgan wasn't sure what Droit wanted left to him, but it sounded reasonable to leave things to someone else. He threw back the rest of the whiskey, stripped, and dove under the covers, where a spinning oblivion took him.

The morning was so intolerably grim he almost felt grateful to the whiskey for distracting him. His head was like a bell at midday, and his eyes ached as though someone were squeezing them into too-small trousers. It was all he could do to shave, and even that did not proceed without incident. The arrival of Dr. Sebastian, chipper and well groomed, at six o'clock seemed incidental to the military operation required to haul Morgan's body where he had to haul it.

Dr. Sebastian carried a small case and Morgan the string-wrapped box Mrs. Hallows had provided for the journey. They had a carriage to themselves, but by some miracle Dr. Sebastian did not insist on conversation, instead retreating behind his newspaper and leaving Morgan to close his eyes. He woke as they were pulling into Waterloo. His eyes screamed. His stomach lurched. There was no way he'd make it through the day.

Dr. Sebastian led him briskly from the station and into the cacophonous streets. Morgan felt a sliver of gratitude towards his hateful boater for blocking the sun from his eyes. After a harrowing march across bridge and park, they arrived at a facade in Pall Mall. It was a club. Dr. Sebastian's club.

They repaired to the cloakroom, where they found flannels, soft white soap, cologne. After washing his face, combing his hair, and applying a zesty aftershave, Morgan began to feel less inhuman. Dr. Sebastian asked if he was hungry. Morgan was not.

—Good, Dr. Sebastian replied with a roguish smile. Civilization first. Lunch later.

Morgan found it oddly agreeable to follow the man blindly. It was all rather like the secret outings Emily and Captain Cahill organized for him when they'd first come to London.

—Sir, Morgan asked, what about my father?

—He's expecting you at teatime.

Morgan couldn't conceive why they'd left at such an ungodly hour, except that Dr. Sebastian must have things to attend to.

—I won't keep you from your business, Morgan said.

Dr. Sebastian turned the Bishop's lip-pursed expression on him.

—Behave yourself, he said sternly.

✦

At the British Museum, Dr. Sebastian purchased a leaflet for Morgan and then bounded up the stairs to the Egyptian rooms. While Dr. Sebastian fell into a mind-numbing conversation with a docent, Morgan drifted over to a colorful sarcophagus surrounded by a school party in straw hats and pinafores.

The girl sent a jolt through him, head to groin. Was it the shape of her legs in the stockings? Was it the pinafore, announcing schoolgirl yet displaying a woman? Or was it the heart-slaying warmth of the smile she sent his way?

She tittered with a clutch of other girls. Morgan sidled into their midst and pretended to examine the case.

—What did they do with all those beetle thingies? the girl asked.

Her hand fell on his sleeve, warm, light, paralyzing. He pressed the leaflet into the pocket of her blazer. He needed to say something, but where in the great universe to start?

A woman called, and the girls departed in a fit of giggles. He followed at a distance as they descended to the ground floor. In the commotion of the entry hall, the girl looked back over her shoulder—for him?—for him! He snaked through the crowds, following to the rotunda.

His hand was in his pocket, and Droit's was on his pencil:

To the young lady who asked about the scarabs, I apologize. For behaving like a cad, for thrusting my leaflet at you without a word. You were more than attractive. Circumstances were not as they appeared.

Unaccountably, I have come under the authority of my Headmaster, who is flogging me round the museum. There would have been a good deal more flogging if he saw me conferring with a young lady as charming as yourself. You may not have noticed him examining papyri nearby.

I'm no use at dancing, but I did hit a hundred and fifty in an afternoon last month.

If this hasn't appalled you, why not leave word with the librarian in the reading room? Direct your notice to Anton O'Masia. Not my real name, but I promise to make it worth your while.

He amazed himself that he had thought to carry a pocket notebook and pencil with him. It was the habit of a man seizing control of his destiny.

He entered the library and approached the desk. Across the room, the girl and her party consulted with a tweed-suited man.

—Good afternoon, he said to the librarian.

She was a mousy woman. He flashed her the smile of a man seizing control of his destiny.

—Could you very kindly give this to the young lady over there, when it's convenient? I'd be much obliged.

He pointed out which young lady he meant. The mousy woman said she would see to it. Morgan thanked her with another seizing-control smile. She smiled back. He sauntered from the room.

—I'd be very much obliged, Dr. Sebastian said icily when Morgan returned to the gallery, if you wouldn't wander off.

Morgan murmured apologies and inquired into Dr. Sebastian's conversation with the docent.

—Where did you go? Dr. Sebastian replied.

Morgan found the museum rather dizzying, so he couldn't say with certainty where he'd been, but he'd earwigged an interesting conversation about scarabs and had drifted after the group to hear more.

—And what did you ascertain about scarabs?

He wished for his leaflet, but he no longer had it.

—They were plentiful. And sacred. The museum is exceedingly lucky to have them.

Dr. Sebastian narrowed his eyes:

—Wilberforce, we are not going to get on at all if you continue to treat me as I presume you treat the Common Room at St. Stephen's.

—Sir?

—As old, blind, and indifferent.

Before Morgan could protest, Dr. Sebastian led him in peremptory style downstairs to the Roman coins. That tedious examination was followed by an interminable survey of sketches by someone Morgan pretended to have heard of. His head still throbbed from . . . things that didn't matter to a man seizing control, but his stomach had recovered itself enough to growl aggressively. Dr. Sebastian at last emerged from scholarly absorption:

—Oh, dear, we've forgotten about lunch, haven't we?

Morgan had not forgotten about lunch. He would never forget lunch, and he hoped that Dr. Sebastian's amnesia would not mean surrendering the meal. The man consulted his watch:

—We can still make service at the club if we're sharpish.

They wound their way through the growing crowds outside. Morgan froze halfway down the steps.

—One moment, sir. I'll be right—

He did not wait for Dr. Sebastian's reply but dashed back inside, across the entry hall, out to the courtyard, and into the library. His mousy librarian was not at the desk. The tweed-wearing man was.

Droit ran a hand through his hair and straightened his collar. He approached the man with the calm seriousness of one in control of his destiny. He was sorry to disturb the man, but he wondered whether anything had been left for Mr. O'Masia. The tweed item looked over his spectacles as if he recognized him.

—Yes, sir.

He handed Morgan a library slip. Morgan pocketed it and strode in scholarly manner from the room. Outside, Dr. Sebastian looked a thunderstorm. He said nothing the entire march back to the club.

They arrived just in time to catch the end of lunch service. Morgan thought he might faint from hunger, and the aroma of food in the dining room only brought on the crazed panic of a long fast.

They ate without speaking, like the Bishop's household, but more awkwardly in the middle of a club. Dr. Sebastian declined dessert, much to Morgan's dismay; his nerves restored by food, he now felt distinctly uneasy.

—Follow me, Dr. Sebastian said.

They retired to a small, empty room whose purpose Morgan could not guess. Dr. Sebastian closed the door and turned on him:

—Empty your pockets.

—Sir?

—You heard me, Wilberforce.

Morgan laughed from nerves, but Dr. Sebastian held him in a glare like the Bishop's, only more savage. He emptied his jacket pockets onto the table beside him. There was nothing incriminating amongst his few belongings: the notebook and pencil, a clean handkerchief, some coins, a half-empty box of matches, no cigarettes thankfully—because he was a man who had seized control of his destiny!—and an unopened envelope addressed in juvenile hand.

—What is this?

—It's from one of the boys at the village school where I . . .

He had control. The weights of yesterday could bugger themselves. Dr. Sebastian returned the envelope to the pile.

—And the rest.

When one was well and truly trapped, it was best to stop struggling. Ways out might present themselves later, but men in control of their destinies knew better than to make things worse. He turned out his trouser pockets and the library slip. Dr. Sebastian scrutinized his face before picking up the paper and scrutinizing it.

—Who is Anton O'Masia?

—It's a pseudonym.

—Obviously.

—He's the uncle of a friend.

—I very much doubt it.

—Honestly, sir. I only borrowed the name.

Dr. Sebastian turned the excavating gaze on him again. Having decided he was telling the truth, he pocketed the slip.

—And who is Miss Miranda Peacock, and why does she propose to meet in the restaurant of Harrods at half past four this afternoon?

She said she would meet him? *She said she would meet him!* Why had he not read the missive earlier? Half past four was less than an hour away! He had only three shillings on his person. What did things cost in the restaurant at Harrods?

—Wilberforce! I've asked a question.

No diversion drew Dr. Sebastian's gaze. They were standing together in the little room and there was no way out.

He admitted everything. When he said it in words, it sounded cracked. Dr. Sebastian stared at him. Morgan wondered if he was about to get a clip round the ear.

—Wilberforce, Dr. Sebastian said unsteadily, you are the most infuriating boy it has ever been my fate to care for.

—I'm sorry, sir.

—You aren't the least sorry. Don't speak. Sit.

Dr. Sebastian thrust him into a chair.

—I am going to make things exceptionally plain.

At last.

—You are no doubt resigning yourself to a permanent dismissal from St. Stephen's. Perhaps you even engineered this escapade in pursuit of that goal.

He had never tried to get disposed! Dr. Sebastian held up a hand:

—You don't know me, you don't trust me, you aren't comfortable in my presence. I can only say, too bad. I am not dismissing you from St. Stephen's, not today, and not before time. Just you resign yourself to that!

He couldn't mean it. There were so many things he could do to get disposed.

—I do mean it. I've never meant anything more. You are returning to St. Stephen's come hell or high water. You have fallen into my care, and you are going to remain there.

Had his father disowned him?

—However, Dr. Sebastian continued, towering over him now, you ought to know that I see straight through your maneuvers, and I won't stand for them. The more you insist on pursuing your juvenile enterprises, the more painful you will make it for yourself.

Just what could the man mean?

—You know the *disce aut discede*. You've drawn the third option.

—Sir?

—You are going to stay—at St. Stephen's and in my care—and so long as you insist on behaving this way, you are going to be punished. You've no say over the first part, but the second is entirely in your hands.

He felt two inches tall. He wondered whether he might wake up and find everything restored as it ought to be.

—Any questions?

He could not think of a single thing to ask or to say.

—Good. Come with me.

His legs carried him as if through water. Not only was this actually happening, but it was going to continue to happen. There wasn't going to be a way out later. This was going to hurt, and keep on hurting.

They entered the library, a breathtaking room two stories high. Dr. Sebastian had a word with a man behind a desk and returned bearing a reference volume.

—Sit.

Morgan sat. Dr. Sebastian placed the tome before him.

—Turn to the page with words beginning *a-n-t* and read out the entries to me.

They had fallen into an entirely new dimension of the bizarre. Unsteadily his hands leafed to the page.

—*Antoeci. Antonine. Antono* . . .

—Go on, Dr. Sebastian insisted.

—*Antonomasia. Noun. Substitution of an epithet for a proper name. e.g., The Iron Duke for The Duke of Wellington.*

Dr. Sebastian snapped the book shut and returned it. Then, hauling Morgan up by the elbow, he dragged him from the room. They retrieved their hats and departed the club.

—Sir, Morgan stammered as they strode up Pall Mall, I didn't—

—It's plain someone's been having you on. Perhaps you'll see fit to tell me about it sometime.

When they arrived at Harrods, Morgan felt his lunch rising.

—Sir . . .

Dr. Sebastian took his elbow again:

—I said you'd be punished, didn't I? It's starting now.

His feet did not consent, but they carried him through the crowded store and upstairs to the restaurant. Dr. Sebastian did not release his arm. Fate did not release him from its jaws. The girl—Miranda something— was standing by the entrance, holding a satchel and a magazine. Morgan's feet stalled. Dr. Sebastian forced him on.

—Hello, she said.

—Hello.

She giggled and looked curiously at them.

—You're a brick to meet me, Morgan began.

—Shall we go in? she asked.

Morgan smiled. She laughed again. Dr. Sebastian adjusted his grip on Morgan's elbow. He wasn't leaving, St. Stephen's or this man's grasp. He was staying and being punished. This was the beginning.

—I say, this is awkward, but I'm afraid I can't stay, as much as I'd like to.

Her face fell.

—I've made a mess of things. It's rotten of me. I'm most awfully sorry.

She forced a smile:

—It doesn't matter.

—It does. You're spectacular, and I mean it when I say I would rather be meeting you right now than anything else. I can only hope you'll be able to forgive me.

She didn't smile, but she didn't frown, either.

Outside in the street, Dr. Sebastian released him:

—Well stuck. Still breathing in and out?

—Unfortunately, sir.

—Good.

Dr. Sebastian hailed a taxi.

—Prepare yourself for the next dose.

They got in the cab, and Dr. Sebastian gave the address of Morgan's father's house.

◆

His father received him with a combination of wariness and fear Morgan had never before seen, as if Morgan were an ogre and his father captive to it. His sisters were coming to tea. Emily and Captain Cahill, it emerged, were leaving for Spain in the morning.

— On holiday? Where?

—Barcelona, to live.

Morgan spluttered. He'd written Emily two letters from the Bishop's and received one in reply, but no mention of Spain. It was one thing to be hoicked around London by his future Headmaster, but for his own sister to leave England without telling him? What else were they keeping from him?

—Won't you stay? his father was asking Dr. Sebastian.

—I couldn't possibly intrude on a family occasion, but I'm afraid I must take a few moments of your time before I disappear.

His father's shoulders sank; he gave Morgan a look that froze his blood.

—You'd better come through, his father said.

The man overreacted, of course. Morgan tried to explain: he'd been wrong to arrange a rendezvous without asking permission, but she was a perfectly decent girl, and they were only meeting in a restaurant. His father didn't see it that way. He most especially did not see it that way given the telephone call he'd received from the Bishop a short while ago.

His heart was doing the kinetic things it had taken to doing lately.

—Oh, yes? Dr. Sebastian asked. What did he say?

—I cannot—will not contaminate this home with the details, but—

His father turned in Morgan's direction but did not look him in the eye.

—I think you know perfectly well what I'm talking about.

Morgan forced his throat to swallow.

—Not really, sir.

He reeled under the blow, his father's hand to the side of his head.

—How dare you toy with me! And how dare you take liberties with the Bishop's staff?

Where was the pit to swallow him now?

Dr. Sebastian turned:

—Get out.

Morgan fled to the corridor.

He thought he might be sick. He could hear nothing through his father's door. He sank to the bottom of the front-hall stairs and slammed his head into his hands.

He could feel him, a few steps above.

—Bugger off, Morgan said, not lifting his head from his arms.

He heard him slipping down one step at a time, as Morgan used to after he'd been sent to bed. Morgan did not have the strength to address the boy or even to actively ignore him. He was sitting beside Morgan now, wearing the short, gray trousers and knee socks of Morgan's prep school. The hall clock ticked over. The boy rustled in a pocket for something—a yellow ball the size of a marble. Meticulously, he picked the lint off and handed the ball to Morgan.

Softly sweet, a butterscotch like those his mother used to put in their stockings back when Christmas was still good. A warm drop of water fell on Morgan's wrist. The boy kicked him, but not hard. Morgan wiped his face with a sleeve:

—Thanks.

———

—Come, Dr. Sebastian said, emerging from the study.

Morgan staggered to his feet. He was to go with Dr. Sebastian. He was not staying to tea. He was not returning to his father's after all. His father had asked Dr. Sebastian to convey his farewell.

—Farewell? Morgan choked.

—He isn't disowning you. Pull yourself together.

Air returned to his lungs.

—What about Emily? I've got to say goodbye.

—You can write her a letter.

Dr. Sebastian put him on the train and asked the conductor, in Morgan's presence and accompanied by a tip, to ensure he stayed entirely out of trouble.

—Have you got anything to read? Dr. Sebastian asked. No, of course you haven't.

Morgan hoped he wasn't going to foist another appalling novel on him.

—In that case, Dr. Sebastian said, you can sit there and think.

Even more appalling.

—And don't forget what I said, Wilberforce. There's no getting round this, not today, not tomorrow. You're going to learn how to suffer one way or another. There's only one path out of this.

—What's that? a small voice asked.

—Through the fire.

The boy sat beside him all the way home. The Bishop's house wasn't home, of course, but his mind kept using the word. The boy's feet did not touch the ground. They sat together in silence as the countryside slipped away and grew orange, pink, gray, night.

Mr. Fairclough met him in the motorcar. Morgan was glad for the darkness so Mr. Fairclough might not see his face. The car crunched up the drive, and his heart lurched at the sight of a light in the Bishop's study.

—Old boy's sat up, Mr. Fairclough murmured.

Facing the guillotine couldn't actually be worse.

—You must have given him quite a fright.

Morgan's head swirled. He was used to things not making sense, but now they had begun to refuse sense in an entirely more perverse way.

The Bishop met them in the hallway. Mr. Fairclough abandoned Morgan and drove away in his motorcar. Morgan steeled himself to be ordered to the study, but the man lit into him as soon as the front door closed.

—How dare you? How *dare* you?

Morgan wanted to ask how the Bishop had found out about William, but he couldn't summon the nerve.

—Cat got your tongue?

—I . . . I didn't think it through.

—I suppose you didn't think through drinking six inches of my whiskey, either.

Morgan hung his head.

—And what about that outrageous stunt of yours at the museum?

—I wasn't thinking at all, sir.

—You aren't getting off that easily. When, I'd like to know, did Casanova reappear?

Was that antonomasia?

—I saw no sign of him last night, the Bishop said, although it's possible you were a bit off form. Were you?

Morgan shrugged.

—What happened at that prize-giving?

—Nothing, sir.

—You had to say goodbye to those boys, didn't you?

—So what?

—I understand they were very fond of you.

—I thought that was supposed to be a good thing.

—It's a very good thing, until you have to leave them.

—I'm not sentimental, sir.

—I expect one or two of them were.

Morgan shrugged again, wishing they could get back to William or the whiskey.

—So you abandoned those boys—

—It wasn't my fault!

—No one said it was—and returned here where . . . of course. I've been quite slow on the uptake.

Morgan looked daggers.

—You returned here and were upended by the news that you were to travel home the next morning.

—It was a logical time to leave, Morgan said. The term was over. I'd stayed past long enough.

The Bishop uncrossed his arms in astonishment.

—Surely you didn't think I was sending you away?

—You said Mrs. Hallows would sort out my things.

—Oh, for mercy's sake, the Bishop said to the ceiling.

—In any case, it's a good thing you didn't have time to send them on, since I'm back on your hands until my father has got over his monumental loathing for me.

—You thought . . . I can see what you must have thought. Oh, Morgan.

His eyes pricked. He clenched his fists:

—I don't see what was so wrong with William anyway. He's my age. I asked him. It was just two chaps mucking about.

He tossed his hat onto the table and made for the cloakroom. The Bishop blocked his way:

—We aren't finished.

—You can shout all you like! Morgan cried You can quote Bible things at me

He tried to push past, but the Bishop seized his wrist.

—but you can't—

Sharp, crushing—Morgan gasped in pain. The Bishop released him and exhaled with deliberate slowness.

—I've made a mistake, the Bishop said. I've had you in my household three weeks. I've treated you as I treat my own children, but I haven't treated you as my child.

Waves crashing towards the frightened breath in his lungs.

—That will change as of now.

Morgan, panicked, looked for the nearest means of egress.

—Go upstairs, wash your face, clean your teeth, change into your pajamas, and wait for me in your room.

Morgan quaked.

—Go.

✦

The boy was there already. He, at least, wasn't afraid of the little room. He made no comment, but when Morgan returned from the bathroom, he was standing on Morgan's bed, shooting pebbles at the wastepaper basket with the aid of a catapult.

—Don't fight, he said. Hurts more if you fight.

Morgan's chest seized up. He sat down. He felt naked.

✦

The Bishop drew the straight-backed chair to face him. Morgan drew his feet onto the bed.

—Nothing you can say will make me think badly of it, Morgan told him. It was decent. He's decent.

—It's called gross indecency, I think you'll find, and it carries a prison term.

—I thought you were broad-minded.

—Morgan Wilberforce!

The Bishop's face was pale, his voice rough enough to scrape:

—Whether or not I am *broad-minded*, as you call it, has no bearing on the perilousness of your actions yesterday evening.

Morgan set his jaw.

—You are both exceedingly lucky not to be in custody of the police.

His skin, as if swarmed by wasps.

—I don't see how—

—Under a *footbridge*, Morgan?

The whole swarm heavy upon him.

—I would be letting you down, the Bishop said, if I failed to censure your behaving this way. It is exceedingly dangerous.

—I'm not afraid.

—Of course not! the Bishop retorted. But did you ever bother to consider William? What did you imagine would become of a groundsman with little education, few skills, and a family dependent on him for support if he were discovered to have *mucked about*, as you put it, with a member of a bishop's household?

—He . . .

Wasps in his breath.

—You didn't . . .

426

The Bishop's stare, a stream of stings.

—But it wasn't William's fault. He—you can't sack him.

—I've no *choice* but to sack him!

Venom, blood.

—As for fornication, the Bishop continued, you know my views.

Wasps in eyes.

—The abuse of that gift has costs, Morgan, and refusing to believe it will not make the injuries disappear.

Morgan consulted the ceiling.

—But beyond that, beyond your recklessness with regard to the law and your selfishness with regard to William—

Morgan cast his gaze to the floor.

—it's plain you've never given a thought to how your actions affect *me*.

—If you don't like losing your gardener, don't sack him, Morgan muttered.

—Watch your tone. You aren't too old for a slippering, young man.

Morgan had never felt more appalled in his life. He drew his knees to his chest. The Bishop lowered his voice:

—I am a bishop with the care and oversee of a large diocese. I and those I employ, from archdeacons to vergers to gardeners, all must remain beyond reproach. Otherwise I will have failed the flock I've sworn to serve.

The Bishop's voice continued uneven, salt upon sting:

—How do you imagine it felt having to speak to William of this? Having to dismiss without reference a young man I've known, whose family I've known . . .

—Please, sir, it's all my fault!

—Your fault is yours, his faults are his, and mine are my own. We shall all have to answer.

Nothing was too severe for him now. He wished the Bishop had a rack to strap him to, until he changed into a better person.

The Bishop made him kneel and say his prayers.

—I don't care if you consider yourself a Mohammedan, the Bishop said in answer to his expression. No child of mine is going to bed without saying his prayers.

Prayers included not only the Our Father, but also the confession and

427

various intercessions offered by the Bishop. The sting continued, enduring and unendurable. Afterwards, the Bishop waited while he got into bed.

—I am persuaded, he said, that neither death, nor life, nor things present, nor things to come, shall be able to separate us.

With that, the man put out the lamp and left him in darkness.

✦

He was barreling across the pitch, fifty yards no-man's-land, Spaulding in sights, plug in mains—but the ground was falling away and they had him, bound and dragged. Plains, passes, hot, cold, heights, depths: citadel. They stashed him in the moat, cold water to his chest, rising oily—throat, chin, ears. They laughed and shouted words he didn't know, until arrived a young Captain of the Guard, sharp of suit, glint of sword. He lit a cigarette and put it between Morgan's lips.

—Don't worry, he said. No one hates you.

Morgan spat out the cigarette:

—You can't keep me here!

The Captain of the Guard gave a signal and they hoisted him out of the water and lay him dripping on the flagstones.

—But no one's keeping you, he said. You came to us, Dicky.

Gasp, stiff, sore, dark.

When he was too afraid to come to her room, she always answered his call. She would bring him a glass of water and something from her bedside table. When he stopped crying, she would speak of what they would do tomorrow, and the things they had to look forward to.

If he needed her hard enough and called even harder, couldn't she come, just for a moment, here where no one would see? He'd whisper in her ear—*they said I'd come to them*—and when she'd heard, it wouldn't be true anymore; it would be absurd and taste of barley sweets and her cool hands. What was the cry that could make her, *make* her—

56

Mrs. Hallows woke him from dead sleep.

—Up you get, she boomed. Bath's drawn. Prayers in half an hour. St. Luke's.

He rubbed his eyes and tried to make sense of her words.

—Chop-chop.

✦

—Sir, Morgan said upon entering the red room downstairs, there's something I need to say.

No one's keeping you. You came to—

—What I have to say, sir . . .

The Bishop paused in his arrangements. Morgan tried to get his footing.

—Sir, you know how I feel about religion. I'm afraid I can't go in for all this praying.

The Bishop turned to him:

—Do you have prayers at school?

—Yes, sir, but—

—Morning or evening?

—Both, sir, but they aren't—

—And did you stage conscientious objection at St. Stephen's?

—No, sir—

—Then I see no obstacle to your joining Morning Prayer here. Before, when I was proceeding in error, I reasoned that you were in desperate need of sleep and that you required delicate handling. Thus, I did not press the point.

—Thank you, sir.

—But now that I've determined to treat you as my child, I expect your presence at quarter past seven daily, except Sundays, when we shall depart for the cathedral at half past nine sharp.

—But, sir—

The Bishop moved abruptly near:

—It is the way things operate in this family. I can only say how sorry I am it took me so long to cotton on.

The Bishop did not explain what he had cottoned on to. Instead, Mrs. Hallows entered with Maryanne, the Bishop indicated where Morgan ought to sit, and together they began to say Morning Prayer.

Morgan tried to focus on what was being said and read, but all he could think of was William, so glaringly absent, sacked because of Morgan's selfishness. When would the ruthless business end? He'd been careening from one error to the next since . . . at least since he tackled Spaulding. Back in the Tower after knocking himself out, he had sensed a shadow beyond the curtain and knew it wanted to savage everything. Did he not determine to thwart it? And did he not fail absolutely? Had the thing distracted him? Stalled him off? Or had Morgan enlisted it— *refusing to believe won't make it untrue*—was he sunk to his neck in it, deeper than he'd realized, deeper than he could stand to know?

✦

Breakfast, silent, searing. He could scarcely swallow his porridge.

—Sir, I can't bear it.

—I think you can, said the Bishop.

Morgan poked at his bowl.

—And we aren't going anywhere, the Bishop said, until you've finished that.

—I'm not hungry, sir.

—It is a moral duty to maintain one's health and one's strength. I won't have you shirking because a proper sense of remorse is making you uncomfortable.

The word *uncomfortable* didn't cover anything. If this was what the Bishop meant by treating him as his child, Morgan thought he'd prefer the orphanage. He forced down the porridge. The Bishop ate beside him, silent, holding him as if by the scruff of the neck.

Yet, holding him.

✦

—I know you're angry, sir, Morgan said as they reached the study, but—

—I'm troubled, Morgan, and I'm most painfully let down.

Panic rising, neck, chin—

—Please, sir, send me away instead of William.

The Bishop pushed him into the usual chair, and then, rather than sitting himself, the man began to pace.

—I don't see how you can sack him, Morgan continued, and have me back in your house.

Not to mention treat him as . . .

—There was a reason I asked you not to flirt with my staff. It's why you mustn't flirt with anyone's staff.

The Bishop came to stand at the corner of the desk.

—Your position and William's are different, and your actions carry different consequences. You've very little notion of your privileges. I intend to see that you learn to take them seriously.

Dread again—had he no reserves?—stinging eyes, snipping breath.

—But what if I never . . . ? What if I can't?

—You can.

Morgan swallowed.

—I also mean for you to try harder with your studies next term. You've a perfectly good mind, but if you don't make an effort, you're going to grow up muddled and ignorant.

—I'm nowhere near the bottom of the class, sir.

The Bishop raised his eyebrows. Morgan dried up.

—My point is that you ought, if you weren't so accustomed to muddle, to acknowledge that your errors with William turned upon the sin of disobedience.

That?

—Sir, if I'd known why you didn't want me to do it, I wouldn't have!

—But you didn't know, did you? There's a world of things you don't know.

—Obviously!

The Bishop began to pace again.

—Do you trust me, Morgan?

—Yes, sir.

—To what extent?

—To every extent.

—Then why, the Bishop reeled on him, did you not trust me enough to obey me?

He knew nothing, understood less. Every thought cast him back to the cold fear of the moat. He couldn't put things right with William. He couldn't put anything right.

—You ought to whack me from here to Christmas, sir.

His voice without strength.

—I deserve it. I'm vile. If you only knew the truth—

The Bishop turned:

—*There is no health in us.* That is the truth.

The words echoed from before, that voice like the hands in the garden.

—There's a reason we say that prayer every day. It isn't theater.

The man came to sit beside him.

—And it's why we ask forgiveness.

Except he didn't deserve it.

—None of us deserves it, the Bishop said, but we've been commanded to ask for it, and to accept it.

He reached for Morgan's chin.

—Just you concentrate on getting that through your head. Or should I say heart?

His heart rose up in fear—or was it protest?

—As for your punishment, I'm not prepared to consider it when distressed, as I presently am. So you can just be patient.

A flicker.

—But for now, perhaps you'd indulge me?

—*Anything,* sir.

—And tell me about that prize-giving.

He tried not to fight, but the truth was so abysmal.

—Then he started acting like an octopus and saying not to go.

The Bishop continued raking over the horrific afternoon, returning like the worst kind of bully to the moments that most made Morgan want to pull out all his teeth. He spared him nothing, not a single admission of a solitary discomfort. When the Bishop finally allowed a silence to develop, Morgan felt as though he'd been thrown down three flights of stairs.

—Distress is not merely something to suppress or flee from, Morgan. It can also constitute a . . . nudge.

Morgan scowled.

—You liked helping those boys, didn't you? You liked them. You felt wretched having to leave them. Perhaps you even felt you were abandoning them?

432

Something blocked his throat.

—How cruel to have to face Twist, whom I always pegged as a favorite of yours—am I wrong?—to have to face his unfettered grief.

—Don't try to tell me there's any point to grief, sir.

—There is in this case.

—What, a nudge? By whom? For what?

—You do some work for a change.

Morgan wriggled his shoulders.

—All I know is that pottering about with them was the only time I haven't been appallingly unhappy in a long while.

—Good.

—So it isn't fair to have it end.

—And yet it has to end because you have to go back to St. Stephen's, don't you?

—Exactly.

—And yet, you've discovered you're rather good at that type of thing. You rather like it.

—So what!

—So, my *dear* boy, you are very shortly headed back to a school which is in great disarray and which contains many boys in need of rather similar attention. Are you not?

 Being treated as the Bishop's child was every bit the ordeal he feared. Whatever imperiousness the Bishop had once displayed vanished before this new overbearing. Before, Morgan realized in retrospect, the Bishop had taken care to acquire and retain his explicit consent; now, that was swept away before a superior authority. The Bishop did not ask Morgan's consent because he was treating him as a son, with every permission fathers enjoyed. He demanded Morgan's presence at prayers (which Morgan disliked, even as he felt calmed), he instituted a bedtime (hateful, healthful), arranged a program of regular exercise (respite in the day), he assigned reading (discussed each evening), labor (removing tree stumps from the edge of the property), and letter writing (a fixed rotation through his father and sisters). The Bishop dictated Morgan's every activity, even down to which rooms he was to use for his reading and writing. Despite the variety of pursuits, Morgan felt under arrest.

The worst was a practice called examination. Each evening before lights-out, the Bishop would come to Morgan's room, sit on the chair as he had done that night, and take Morgan through a point-by-point examination of the day. The first night it had taken over an hour. When they finished before Morgan's bedtime, the Bishop made him lie down and close his eyes while he read to him. Although Morgan considered this a childish practice, he always fell asleep before the Bishop had finished.

After a week, the Bishop broke routine by summoning Morgan to the study rather than coming to his room. Morgan felt exposed walking across the Rectory in pajamas, dressing gown, and slippers. He passed Mrs. Hallows, who was dressed. The Bishop, too, wore ordinary clothes. Apparently Morgan was a child soon to be sent to bed after a talking-to in his father's study.

Unlike the examinations in Morgan's room, during which they sat knee to knee, this one the Bishop conducted from behind his desk. Morgan stood before him like some boy summoned to his Housemaster, except that his actual Housemaster never summoned anyone anywhere. Something unnerving was afoot.

The Bishop told him to begin, and as Morgan raked over the day, the Bishop pressed harder than usual on Morgan's errors and into the decisions he had not even realized he was making.

—I wasn't thinking about it, sir.

—And that, as previously discussed, was your first error. How long do you intend to squirrel round with this, Morgan, before you start thinking?

—But, sir, you can't go through the day thinking and thinking and thinking!

—I'd settle for one thinking, the Bishop retorted.

They were speaking again of the sin of disobedience. Another regular item on the list was fleeing the truth. The Bishop seemed to think many of Morgan's errors sprang from these seeds.

—Sir, Morgan said, may I ask something directly and not have it be an impertinence?

The Bishop nodded.

—People have been trying to reform me forever and a day, but I keep winding up in the most appalling messes. Last resort, they shipped me down here. You're the biggest expert in England on sorting people out, and I got into just as much trouble with you.

—What is your question?

—How will you know when to give it up?

The Bishop thought. Then he got up from the desk and told Morgan to sit. Morgan fell into his usual chair.

—You're right that you've haven't been behaving as my child.

It hurt.

—My children would have stumbled into a good deal more trouble.

—Sir?

—You heard me. They would have behaved worse and trusted me more.

He had been trusting the man. As much as he knew how.

—But, the Bishop said, taking a seat beside Morgan, perhaps the time has come to stop pad-footing and swallow the toad.

—Sir?

—It's time, I think, to put some screws to you, young Morgan.

Everything previous had not been screws enough?

—We've built up your terrain and got you started down a few good habits; I think you're just about ready to handle some distress.

He was using that word again.

I suppose you're going to make me learn how to suffer, like Dr. Sebastian said.

—He said that, did he?

Morgan had expected the Bishop to treat his remark as impertinence, but now he was looking as though Morgan had cottoned on to his true purpose.

—Exactly what kind of suffering did you have in mind, sir? Morgan asked wryly.

—Every kind.

The Bishop's expression was not wry. Morgan laughed.

—I'll take that as evidence for my hypothesis, the Bishop said.

Morgan tried to look grim, but his mouth kept laughing. The Bishop smiled along with him.

—Hypothesis: a good many of your errors spring from a failure to submit to suffering.

—Sir, I've had more suffering than—

—Been subjected to, not submitted to.

—Only feeble people submit to suffering, Morgan said. Sometimes you have to put up with it, but giving in to it is just . . . wrong.

—Giving in to unnecessary suffering is indeed wrong. I am talking about suffering that's unavoidable.

—Well, if you can't escape it, Morgan said, then you've just got to grit your teeth.

—Did our Lord grit his teeth on the cross, would you say?

Morgan sank back in his chair.

—Sir, please can you stop bringing God into things?

—What are you afraid of?

—I'm not afraid of anything.

—Don't contradict me; trust me. And answer my question.

Rebuked, Morgan glowered at the bookshelf.

—I've no idea if he gritted his teeth, but he certainly didn't seem to be enjoying it.

The Bishop wrenched Morgan's chair around to face him:

—You need to learn how to suffer, Morgan, first of all because life deals suffering—has already dealt it—and the more you thrash about trying to escape it, whether through gritting your teeth or outright flight, the deeper you will fall into the pit.

He wanted to sit there silently until the Bishop dismissed him, satisfied or fed up. But something was reeling him towards the man, like the golden hook, but thicker. This man was saying things he didn't comprehend, things he ought to treat with the choicest scorn a public schoolboy could command. This man was not his father, much less his conscience, and ought to be reminded of the fact. Yet despite the putrid coating, there was something irrationally attractive in what he was saying. Something destructive enough to be the truth.

It had been such a long time since he and the truth had got on.

—We don't have to take what we're dealt, sir. We can fight.

—Some things. Not others.

—Are you saying we should all be pacifists and turn the other cheek?

He wasn't arguing to win; he was arguing to be defeated.

—I am saying, Morgan, that we have to suffer our suffering. There is no shortcut. Of course *he* promises endless shortcuts and has done since . . .

—Genesis three?

A slivered smile at last:

—Who says reading is a waste?

—But if there's no shortcut out of suffering, what does it matter how we take it?

—Perhaps, the Bishop said with the first hint of wryness, once you've taken it properly, you'll be able to answer that for yourself.

A tense chill settled on him, a terrible discomfort he both feared and craved.

—Does this mean you've changed your mind about punishing me, sir?

The Bishop appraised him.

—It means that it's time to start distressing you. Mentally, emotionally, physically.

The Bishop asked him to enumerate encounters that would cause him distress. It took some prodding for Morgan to admit them. Nathan and Alex, obviously. Polly. Silk. Grieves. His father.

—And where do your friends pass the holidays? the Bishop asked.

As far as Morgan knew, Laurie would be with his grandmother in France, and Nathan would be home in Annaside.

—I don't suppose they've a telephone in Annaside?

The question made Morgan uneasy, but in any case, he thought the only telephones were in the public house and the post office.

—Fine, the Bishop replied. I shall write to Mr. Pearl in the morning.

Morgan's arguments accomplished nothing save provoke the Bishop to write the letter immediately, as Morgan watched. At least, Morgan reasoned to himself, it was highly probable that Nathan, Alex, their father, or all three would reject the idea of visiting Morgan.

The Bishop sealed the letter, demanded the address, and rubbed the envelope against the blotter.

—Right, the Bishop said, beyond the Pearls, your father has made arrangements to come to us the last fortnight of the holidays.

Morgan flushed, stunned.

—In the meantime, we'll have to work on your courage.

He probably deserved it, but was he really such a coward?

—We'll ease you into it, shall we, and begin with your forte.

The Bishop stood:

—Take me through it from the beginning. Start as far back as you can recall and keep going until you reach the present.

—Sir, I know I'm thick, but what do you want me to tell you?

—How you've been punished in the past, and by whom.

There wasn't so much to tell. His father, occasionally his mother, his sisters' rough justice if you could call it punishment, masters at school, the JCR. The methods were terrifically uninteresting: deprivation, imposition, seeing-to. The usual.

—A pedestrian topic, I see.

—Sorry to disappoint you, sir, but it isn't worth the candle.

—*It* meaning?

The word inconveniently stuck in his throat:

—Punishment.

—Yet you've importuned me more than once, have you not, to punish you for things you've done wrong.

—I might have wished we could get it over with.

—And by punishing you, I would be releasing you from the discomfort of your remorse?

Morgan thought that sounded abstract.

—In your mind, punishment is a penalty to remit, but it doesn't do you much good, does it?

Didn't people punish you so *they* could feel better and get on with forgetting about it?

—You don't appear to have the faintest notion that your errors come at a personal cost.

—Believe me, sir, you've made the costs more than clear. Which is why I wish you'd let me write to William—

—A personal cost to you, Morgan.

—I got sent down from school, twice, I—

—If you can't appreciate the damage you're doing, at least you can feel it in your physical person.

That sounded ominous.

—You're experienced, aren't you? the Bishop continued. You know the drill. You aren't afraid. You can take whatever your JCR dishes out, can't you?

—Yes, sir.

—In short, the entire subject is an occasion for pride.

—I wouldn't say that.

—I would.

They assessed one another. Morgan felt a heady mixture of combativeness and fear. Was the Bishop criticizing him for his stoicism? Accusing him of false remorse? Preparing to punish him, or refusing ever to do so?

—I am not merely a man of the cloth, the Bishop said. I am also the father of five children, five exceedingly difficult children, and the fact that none of them has yet gone off the rails ought to tell you something.

He unclasped his arms and removed his jacket.

Like all the real things, you could imagine all you wanted, but then suddenly they happened.

Morgan removed his dressing gown and draped it across the back of the chair. It was difficult, more than he'd guessed, to submit before the man, but at least when it was over, he'd know where he stood. The Bishop would see it wasn't pride, but courage. He'd no idea how the Bishop planned to go about it—just what sort of implement he would retain from his career as a father—but whatever the weapon, Morgan would not shirk.

He looked to the Bishop for a cue where to stand, and the sudden gaze struck a spike of excitement, the terrible nerves of the arena.

—Put your dressing gown back on, the man said.

Morgan flushed and, in obeying, felt more exposed, not less. But he needed to put the gaffe behind him. If they were adjourning to another room, he needed his reserves.

The man had once threatened him with the slipper, a humiliating and juvenile implement, though effective enough when wielded by energetic prefects or masters, which the Bishop was not. A wave of fascination and horror washed over as it occurred to him that the Bishop hailed from S-K's generation, when they had all been so enthusiastic about the birch, whether at home, school, prison, or the navy. That ritual had never been enacted during Morgan's time at the Academy, though S-K had threatened him with it, but it was said you had to cut the rods yourself. The Bishop was rummaging in a drawer, searching for a knife? Given everything—everything said, thought, done, and failed to be done—it made sense that the man would choose as solvent such a trial. Only great bloodlettings could restore the Greek world, and only the violence of the nineteenth century could tear him away from those who held him (those he held?).

The Bishop closed the drawer and came to stand beside him.

—Put out your hand.

His ears weren't working. His eyes weren't working. The Bishop was holding a wooden ruler. Nothing made sense.

—Morgan.

—That's for *girls*.

—*Morgan*.

—I'm not one of your daughters!

The Bishop stood his ground.

—Sir!

The Magnetron as never before.

His right hand did as the Bishop told it. The man took his wrist, adjusted its position, straightened his fingers, and told him to hold still.

The wooden thing came down across his palm.

It simply wasn't happening. This creature Morgan had almost trusted had unmasked himself as the worst kind of dope. He had never understood, Morgan or anything. Now he was employing a milksop technique, just as Morgan had been green enough to imagine rescue.

The thing fell again. He trained his attention on the edge of the desk. The less he interfered, the sooner this mortifying scene would end. The third snap established a slow and steady rhythm, transmitting sensations too inadequate to acknowledge.

He'd never been caned across the hand, but he'd watched it happen to Laurie, and after three of the Flea's stingers, Laurie's palm had been swollen and bruised. This nursery accoutrement would accomplish nothing beyond making a little girl squeak.

Should he pretend to wince?

—Don't move.

—Sir, please, it doesn't even sting.

—Be patient, the Bishop replied.

Silk would do it properly. He'd start with Kitty Deadlock, and by the time he'd finished, they'd need iodine and a story about clawing through brambles.

—Switch.

Morgan stared, uncomprehending and appalled.

—Other hand.

Was it cowardice or an iron self-discipline that kept him there, taking the unthinkable insult on the chin, or the . . . it wasn't happening, the left hand offering itself, the right tingling at his side.

—Now, the man said, resuming his tempo, why don't you start by tell-ing me what this is for.

On top of everything he wanted to converse?

—I suppose it's for all the times I acted like a girl and ran away from distress, like you're always on about.

Steady, stubborn, not faster, not slower, now having the gall to prickle.

He'd suffered more in this house than he'd thought possible, but even the worst had eventually passed. This indignity promised to continue all night, and then, when it finished, to keep on humiliating him in perpetual remembrance.

—Sir, how can you—

Sharper, hotter.

—William got sacked, and I'm getting *this?*

The Bishop touched Morgan's arm, supporting it as it began to tremble.

He could kill himself. That's what he could do. He could find some-thing in the kitchen. Then the man would see how wrong he'd been, how comprehensively and revoltingly he had misjudged Morgan. Painted across his kitchen floor, he'd find the only logical outcome.

—Switch.

His hands, rogue agents. But soon he'd—

—Morgan, look at me.

His head refused, but his traitor's eyes snapped to that voice, to that face, to the unnerving sight of his own hand reddening beneath the thing. It fell not by the dispassionate will of gravity, but with intent and force, driven by the Bishop himself. He had an eye, a wrist, timing; Morgan struggled to keep his hand from pulling away. Never had he been made to stand there, fully upright, and watch. He'd never been forced to look his opponent in the eye, unless that opponent was taking satisfaction from it.

The Bishop wasn't taking satisfaction. He proceeded not with appe-tite, nor with a Sunday-school teacher's grim duty, but with resolve, like a surgeon conducting an operation in the field, unruffled but urgent, caring not for the patient's cries because he was saving a life. And between blows, his gaze held, responding to Morgan invisibly but clearly as if he could see to the heart of the battlefield.

—Switch.

Did a battlefield take sides? Did a patient remove his own shrapnel? The Bishop continued steadfast and keen, looking straight inside where Morgan could never see.

—Ah!

—Stay.

A word to his hand, to his heart. The man let go of his arm and trained the weapon on the weakest place, that useless hand that couldn't write, couldn't catch, inept in every sense, no longer telling him to switch but letting the sting rise, at-the-edge, beyond, ringing his nerves like a cold bell, like the days that kept coming and going, where nothing changed until it got worse, and you could try everything but it didn't matter how good you were or how bad you were or how many tears you shed, you still woke up every morning and knew nothing was right.

The Bishop let go of his shoulder. His head rang. His breath . . .

—That will do, the Bishop said, setting the thing on the desk.

His hands fled, pressed beneath his arms. He had won. He'd withstood the barrage without ceding ground.

He looked to the Bishop—saw his face, felt instantly bereft.

—Interesting, the Bishop said.

—What? Morgan balked. What's *interesting*?

The Bishop paused.

—That's all I'm prepared to say at present. But—

He took him by the shoulder and led him to the door.

—Having got that exercise out of the way, I can see we're going to have to pull out the stops with you.

—I'm not an organ. And I'm not your experiment!

The man hesitated.

—I know you aren't.

Morgan pulled away:

—Do you want to know why we'll never agree?

The Bishop stared at him.

—You know what I'm talking about. It's because if he exists, he doesn't care. You say he loves us, but then when people get scythed down, he just stands there and feels nothing and *does nothing*.

The Bishop looked to the floor, and then back to him:

—*Jesus wept.* The shortest verse in the Bible.

Morgan clenched hot fists:

—I suppose that's why you want me to blub.

—When Jesus wept, he didn't *blub*. He wept as a person overwhelmed by sadness and agitated by anger. He wept with the wrath of God in the face of death.

Morgan slammed the bedroom door. He didn't want to think. He wanted to switch off. His head pounded. His hands throbbed and stung. He threw off his dressing gown and put out the light.

Just what did the man mean by whacking him in such a systematic and objectionable fashion after weeks of declaring him unwhackable? And then declaring him, or it, or something else, *interesting* yet refusing to elaborate? Then referring to the most humiliating experience of Morgan's life as *that exercise* and suggesting that it had been a mere prologue, something to be got out of the way before the real artillery could be rolled in.

Was he at a school for suffering, taught by the Bishop? Or was the truth as it had seemed just now, the Bishop ministering to him, and to things unseen?

 The weather was entirely out of tune with the moment. The rain ought to be lashing the windows of the train, wind howling across the fields, driving sheep to shelter. He himself ought to be three days into a February cold, head heavy, throat raw. Or imprisoned in school uniform, shivering in a third-class carriage, having run out of pocket money and desperate for tea.

He was in the peak of health. The sun blazed and the train chugged through a countryside rampant with wildflowers. He was wearing light summer clothing and traveling in a first-class carriage with the Bishop, who ensured a steady supply of tea and sandwiches. The Bishop passed the first leg of the journey reading his prayer book and then moved on to the newspaper, interspersed with naps. Morgan had bought a magazine at the station, but after gorging on the minutiae of cricket, golfing, tennis, and sailing, he had nothing to defend him against the unsettling summer's day.

The Bishop had revealed nothing of their itinerary, but at the change in London, it had been impossible to conceal their destination.

—I don't know what you're hoping to see, Morgan said, but the Academy's empty during the holidays.

The Bishop had given him a look of fifty Christmases.

—And I hardly think your physician will approve of your hacking up to the barn, if that's what you've got in mind.

The Bishop continued to look at him. Morgan took the man's newspaper and read it.

Somewhere in the middle of Lincolnshire, Morgan asked acidly whether the Bishop was amusing himself with the cloak-and-dagger.

—I am not amusing myself. But knowing you, even imperfectly, I'm convinced that discussing matters in advance is an error.

—I thought you wanted me to do more thinking, Morgan snapped.

—During the trial, not beforehand.

—If you're hoping I'll go there and blub over Spaulding, you're in for a disappointment.

The Bishop flagged the tea trolley.

✦

They arrived in York and were met by a man in clerical costume who bundled them into a motorcar and maneuvered timidly through traffic. Morgan hadn't set foot in the place since his father moved to London. It was smaller than it had been. Alien shops had opened. But the rest of it—walls, gates, the turn at the theater that led to their house—bored into his skull and every bony substance. The clerical chauffeur glanced in the mirror.

—You're hungry. Evensong, then tea.

They pulled around the back of the Minster. Morgan was in the peak of health; he felt sick.

Evensong took his every nerve and scraped. He concentrated on breathing in and out; at least, he thought scornfully, the Bishop ought to approve of that. There was nothing visible to fear, yet he felt prey to the dread he'd known in the Tower, when he'd crashed into Spaulding so hard it opened a fissure in the world, permitting the slow, nearly undetectable infusion of the thing.

Now the place crawled with it. The windows of the Minster might admit sunshine through stain, the choir might assault the ears with sounds deep enough to hurt, the clergyman leading the service might read that prayer the Bishop liked to say about the night, but the voice of that clergyman was one Morgan had hoped never to hear again, and the darkness was too potent ever to be deterred by prayer.

—Wilberforce? the clergyman was saying. David's son? Of course.

The Bishop was speaking with the man, the man whose name Morgan had made it a point never to recall.

—You've grown, said the man. You look so much like your mother.

—My sisters look like my mother, Morgan retorted. Except for Veronica. She looks like my father, and so do I.

The clergyman asked after his sisters by name and smiled in a way that made Morgan want to swear.

—I didn't realize you knew one another, the Bishop said.

—We don't, replied Morgan.

—I had the sad duty of conducting Mrs. Wilberforce's funeral.

—You didn't know her!

—Alas, said the man.

It was a hundred degrees in the nave. He was going to be sick in a moment. But rather than conducting them as promised to tea and then the Academy, the clerical chauffeur stood subserviently by as the vile clergyman gestured to the north of the church in the direction of the saint-whatever chapel, the place Morgan had vowed never to return.

A rush of shame, then, like oil from a trapdoor: this wasn't a stop on the way to their destination. He was monstrously stupid not to have realized it at once. He reeled on the Bishop:

—You can *just* forget it. You absolute beast!

—You don't have to go there, the Bishop replied. You have a choice.

—You're bloody well right, I do. I'm not your plaything!

The Minster's wide doors stood open to the summer. A clutch of foreigners peered inside. Dust blew across the threshold. Droit, in summer suit, stood with a girl under the portico, pointing to her guidebook and taking a lick of her ice cream.

He didn't have to do anything. He could leave the whole tomb and go sit in the sun. He could buy ice cream and eat it. It was the kind of summer's evening not seen in Yorkshire, not since Patron's Day, since—

—You're hungry and exhausted from your journey, the clergyman was saying. Why not have a seat in the sun while I pop back and change, and then we'll—

Morgan turned away and strode down the aisle to the chapel.

The other one was there. He sat in the back corner, leaning against the chairs in front of him, head buried in his arms. His suit was dark. His shoulders were shaking. This was why he needed his lights punched out.

Yet, he was there. He wasn't outside in the sun. He was there in the slow-chapped chapel. Four years had passed; other people had got on with things, but this one remembered.

On wet Remembrance Day they were supposed to blub for a lot of men who got in the way of bullets, but nobody wept for women who got in the way of nothing, who enlisted for *nothing* but got scythed down sitting in their beds at night. (Emily had told him eventually, how she'd had a headache, how she'd sat up in bed just after they'd put out the light, and how—) Nobody blubbed for boys who saved people from their own stupidity and then got themselves scythed open so that everything they could and should have been was over. Nobody stood in the rain and remembered them, whose only crime was pitying when they shouldn't. People went on with their pointless lives, imagining it was a summer's evening fit for walking and flirting and enjoying, and no one remembered what the thing had done, no one remembered that it still even now hadn't been repaired, could never be repaired, and even more that the thing still hung around them, smirking its gigantic, unconquerable grimace because it had won, it would always win, and they could do nothing against it.

The Bishop stepped into the chapel and gazed at the carvings up by the place where the box had been before they'd lifted it to take it out and Emily had thrown herself across it and—

The Bishop moved to the chair beside the other one and sat. He, too, leaned forward, crossed his hands, and lowered his head.

—Give rest, O Christ, to thy servants with thy saints, Charles Spaulding, Elizabeth Wilberforce, Clara Stires Sebastian. Where sorrow—

The Bishop's voice broke, the other one sat up, and Morgan fled away from them both, across the room and down the longest, farthest row.

The place between his shoulders strained to snapping. It took such an effort to hold them back when all they wanted was to fall forward and leave the walls unguarded, let the battering win. Every corner of him hurt and still there was more. It hurt in his person, in his mind, and yet also somewhere else, flooding the city and sweeping it away.

Before they took the box away, they'd said those words the Bishop had said. The clergyman sprinkled water on it—*All we go down to the dust*— and the men surrounded it, and the time was ending, except he wanted it to go on and on—*Alleluia, alleluia*—and when Emily made that sound and everyone else started to sob, he heard her voice in his head, not remembered but real, *Take care of my Morgan, take care*—and he had promised, meant to—

Her Morgan wasn't there anymore. He'd grown up. Been kicked up. That boy was dead as she was, the boy she had loved, the boy who had known the truth and got on with it.

An arm fell across him, not the Bishop, not the other one, but somehow warm, alive. The arm knew. It hurt as he was hurting, and it stayed with him even as he fell forward onto the chair, onto that knee which could hold everything: she was never coming back, and it mattered so colossally that it cut him out of ordinary life. Even when he was most physically with people, he wasn't with them, because he hadn't given himself to them, or the truth. But he was giving himself now, surrendering to this pain, pain deserved probably, but where was the forgiveness? He was sorry! So sorry! No one heard him. No one stopped it. No one brought her back where she belonged.

Even so, the arm continued with him, sorrowing with him, having been with him all along, even at his worst, and even now when he was weaker than he'd ever been, now that he was admitting it, how broken and desperate and blind and deaf, and how unanswerably *needy*—he, Morgan, her Morgan, his Morgan, called by name, known by name, always, always known—

A clatter. A crash. Across the chapel, the Bishop was sliding to the floor.

Morgan was on his feet and shouting, shoving chairs and crossing the aisle. This was not an event of the mind. This was an event of the body. He felt for a pulse. For breath. Were you supposed to press on their chest? Their back? The Bishop's face was the wrong kind of pale, but the skin wasn't cold. No blood poured out.

He put a hand on the Bishop's head and another on his heart and tried to remember what to say against the dark.

Breathe.

Shaking.

Breathe!

Silent, still.

Come from the winds and breathe upon these slain!

Dark before, behind, above, below, a heatless, heartless nothing.

That I may rise—

Rattle.

That I may stand—

Footsteps?

—I say . . .

Man, breaking into—

—Your Grace!

Into the time, making it run—fast, far, loud. And with the man, people, noising, pushing Morgan aside.

—Please!

But now, even now, those eyes were fluttering. That mouth was stirring. Bone to bone, flesh to flesh. And they were helping the Bishop to sit upright, breath going in and breath coming out, helping him to a chair. And Morgan's eyes were streaming, but he didn't care because the Bishop was breathing and he knew where he was and when he was and who he was, and he was reaching for Morgan's hand:

—You're stuck with me a bit longer, I'm afraid.

People were bringing water, and other people were rushing back with smelling salts and flannels and more water, and brandy, and before the kerfuffle died down, the Bishop was getting to his feet, accepting the brandy and refusing the hospital, with a force Morgan knew, sending away the people and insisting on being taken where he was expected, where tea and bed awaited.

Morgan and the chauffeur took his arms, but he walked under his own power out of the chapel, out of the Minster, into the sunshine and the motorcar. And the chauffeur was driving them through the streets, out of the city, along the highways, across the cooling evening, passing people on bicycles and farmers with their sheep and two little girls tangled with flowers. The Bishop gazed out the window as if surveying a long-delayed homecoming. His hand held Morgan's wrist, whether to give reassurance or receive it, Morgan couldn't tell.

Then the lanes were familiar, and they were pulling through the gates and into the quad, and the motor choked to a stop, and it was quiet.

The Bishop squinted through the glass:

—This is it, then?

Morgan nodded. The man rolled down his window and perched his elbow on the sill. He smelled the air. He looked to Morgan.

—I see.

The man nodded, then laughed:

—I see!

Morgan laughed, too. He didn't understand, but he laughed.

The chauffeur was getting out of the motorcar then and helping the Bishop, and Dr. Sebastian was hurrying from somewhere and putting his arm around his father's waist. The Bishop was protesting, and Dr. Sebastian was telling him off, for coming up, for disobeying his physician, for doing what he always did: listen to no one and risk life and limb for his own stubborn—

—Just what are you laughing at? Dr. Sebastian demanded of Morgan.

Morgan couldn't answer. He could only lean against the motorcar, ribs shuddering, lungs wheezing with laughter.

They took the Bishop into the little garden behind the Headmaster's house, where there was tea and bread and butter. Sunset poured across the walls, and Dr. Sebastian continued to scold.

—It was warm, the Bishop said. The circumstances were trying, and I momentarily . . . It's very embarrassing. I beg you to change the subject.

—I shan't change the subject, not until you admit—

The Bishop kept his eyes on Morgan, as if what mattered was the two of them and what had passed between them and around them and within them, even now. As if they had come to St. Stephen's not to view his son's project but to understand Morgan's

—You aren't immortal, Father. If you won't hear reason—

—Oh, I'd *much* rather hear about this young history master Wilberforce has told me so much about.

Dr. Sebastian looked to Morgan, a glance of displeasure so sharp that Morgan felt the blade, that he might do to the Academy what the scythe had done to people he loved—

—Sir, Morgan said, please don't change the Academy. I know it isn't the best place in the world, but . . .

How could he say he loved it?

—I've been brought here to make changes, Dr. Sebastian replied.

—It's a good place, Morgan said huskily. I know it doesn't look it, but it has been. It wants to be. If only someone could understand it, it would be good again.

His head pounded. His throat ached.

—Wilberforce, Dr. Sebastian said, sit down, eat those sandwiches—

—Sir—

—And have a little faith.

He ate until he wasn't hungry anymore, and then Dr. Sebastian sent him to bed. The light was fading, and in the little room of the Headmaster's house, the lamp had no bulb. He got under the covers, eyes swollen, bone-weary, unable to rest. He'd gone to bed without examination, without prayers, without anyone's hand on his head. Was he a person who needed such things? Such things, and such and such things . . .

He had gone by his own will, down and more down, and there at the bottom, where the hurt kept hurting, there, down there, someone . . . something was happening.

The dark drew near. He felt it as he breathed—thick, adamant—but in his ears a rumble, like footsteps barreling, him in sights as if nothing else mattered, impact coming, too late to dodge—a thousand rushing—captain—breath—now, now—*now*.

ACKNOWLEDGMENTS

My grateful thanks:

To Jennifer Gibbs, Jennifer Turner Hall, Jean Wagner, Camille Guthrie, Andrea Codrington Lippke, and Penny Ghartey, for encouragement, accountability, and probing reads.

To Cameron Henderson-Begg, for insights sharp and gentle, and for cricket tutelage.

To Nell Mead, for advice medical, historical, and dramatic.

To Joseph Housley, John Collins, and the hive mind of Twitter friends, for help with language, period, law, munitions, sport, and custom.

To Alice Tasman, for warmth, realism, ambition, and vision.

To Jonathan Galassi, for enthusiasm and belief.

To Christopher Richards, for the most excellent, sensitive, and challenging editing I could imagine.

To the Reverend Andrew C. Mead and the Reverend Victor Lee Austin, for inspiration, in every sense of the word, more than they know.